CONTENT WARNING!

The Secrets & Scars Series is a dark MF contemporary MC age gap romance that contains subjects that may be triggering to some readers, including but <u>not limited to</u>:

- Emotionally dark and traumatic.

- Abuse from parents,

- Graphic violence,

- Drugging,

- Non-consensual acts including rape outside the relationship,

- Demeaning acts,

- Suicidal thoughts & self-harm,

- Kidnapping,

- PTSD Trauma,

- Trauma from Religious Extremism,

- Exposure to cultish situations,

- Emotional & physical blackmail,

- Explicitly detailed sex scenes,

- Killing, brutality and gore,

- Backstory includes stillbirth,

- Pregnancy trauma,

- Death of a child.

Beautifully RECKLESS

Secrets & Scars Series
— Book Two —

SARAH JD

Cover by Nat at DAZED Designs
Many thanks to my Alpha & Beta Readers: Gini, Anoesjka, Melissa, Stevie, Tiffany, Cheria, Arriana, Tamarra, and my proofreader Jen.

1

ABBEY

Stumbling backwards as I round the corner, I plaster myself to the wall of the narrow passage just as a set of voluptuous breasts come bouncing my way.

"The crowd is hungry tonight, Angel." Shandi beams, tossing her sweaty bra at me where it smacks me dead in my face. "I bet they'd love a baby mumma shaking her milky tits at them."

My glare is nothing new as I peel the hot pink lace from my face, stacking it on top of the other lingerie I have bundled in my arms.

"Give it a rest, Shandi. Stop trying to get Angel out on the stage." Ariel slaps Shandi's bare arse as she squeezes past, both women giggling as Shandi gives a playful shake of her well endowed butt with a wink over her shoulder.

Sighing, I shake my head, fighting back a grin.

Who would have thought I'd end up in a strip club? No one I know, that's for sure, which is exactly why this is the perfect place for me.

"I go on in five minutes," Ariel smiles playfully, hitching up her breasts so the tops of her nipples peek over her black lace bra. "Make sure you watch from side stage. I'm doing my new trick tonight."

"Sure, I'll try to make it." I roll my eyes, smiling. "As soon as I get this in the wash and clean the vomit from the men's toilets, I'll be sure to watch you squeeze baby cucumbers from your hooha."

Ariel gives my shoulder a playful slap. "Girl, this ain't no hooha. This is grade-A pooosey," she coos, thrusting her pelvis at me.

"Stop it." I giggle, shaking my head before leaving her to limber up in preparation for her set.

My cheeks are red, just as they usually are when conversation turns to anything remotely sexual, so I force myself to think of something else. Anything else as I weave through the maze of passages heading towards the back room, where the washing machine thuds loudly on the spin cycle.

Dropping the pile of lacy undergarments into the basket, I move to the dryer, watching the clothes spin.

My reflection stares back at me in the glass door.

I look like me, but also, I don't.

My hair is a dusty pink now, thanks to Martini and her pink shampoo, allowing me to have a temporary change without really doing any damage to my hair.

A fake nose ring glints in the light, reminding me that this new life I'm living is nothing more than an illusion. A bad attempt at a new identity as I hide away from the police, my family, Daniel and his mates, and the Southern Sadists MC.

The curve hugging clothes Ariel insisted I wear to help me blend into the vibe of this place feel too revealing given how big my twenty-four week baby bump is.

Even so, Abbey Delany, the good little Catholic girl from Fox Pines with her makeup free face and golden blonde hair would stand out like a green grape in a bowl of deep red cherries in this place. Hence the appearance change.

But I'm not her anymore. I can't be if I want to keep my unborn baby safe.

As if the little tacker can hear my thoughts, the sensation I started feeling last week flutters, like a ghost of movement, so light it barely registers. But I know my baby. I know he or she is reminding me that soon enough, I will hold him or her in my arms.

"I'll find somewhere safe for us, little carrot. I promise," I whisper, running my hands over my bump, hoping my baby can hear me and feel the safety I want to provide that I haven't felt in so long.

Even here, at Leather and Lace, I'm not truly safe. It's not the best environment to be living in, but it's better than living on the streets of Melbourne. Better than the shelters where cops lurk and questions are asked.

It's been over three weeks since I fled Ringo. It was by chance that Ariel and Martini found me defeated and crying, sitting on the curb outside Leather and Lace. They took me in. No questions. Just a lumpy couch, a job cleaning, and a little security.

It's more than I had before, and I don't even have to take my clothes off and dance on the stage. You could even say I'm happy.

Kinda.

Sorta.

Okay, maybe that's a lie I keep trying to tell myself to stop myself from thinking about him… Ringo.

A sudden burst of shouting from the club shakes me out of my thoughts, and I frown.

It kind of sounds like a fight has broken out, but it could also just be overexcited patrons watching Ariel squeeze those cucumbers out. She's definitely a crowd favourite.

I should probably hurry side stage to show my support, but since I'm not in the mood for another anatomy lesson, I'm happy to stay tucked away in the back of the club, minding my own business.

The laundry room door suddenly slams open, ricocheting off the wall and nearly taking Ariel out as she stumbles inside, fear stark on her face.

"Ariel?" I ask, stiffening.

"Girl, you gotta go!" Her voice is urgent, her hands waving frantically.

"W-what?" I take a step back as my stomach twists.

"The cops are here. They're looking for you."

My eyes widen as panic grips me, the walls suddenly feeling like they are closing in.

"How?" I whisper. "I don't understand."

"Shit girl, come on." Martini appears behind Ariel, pink glitter shimmering over her bronze skin as her claw-tipped nails wiggle in my direction. "You are Abbey Delany, right? The missing girl plastered all over the news?"

My breath catches.

My name.

They know my real name.

"I told you my name was Angel."

Ariel scoffs. "We knew who you were the second we saw you. Why do you think I insisted on changing your look?"

"To blend in," I whisper.

"Yeah, and so you didn't look so much like that sweet girl on the news." Ariel darts her worried gaze between me and the door. "Come on. You have to go. We don't have time for this."

Snatching my hand, Ariel tugs me through the door while explaining over her shoulder as we rush through the passages. "Freddie is trying to stall them out front, but it's only a matter of time before they come back here."

My heart is practically in my throat as we run, weaving back through the maze of passages until we reach side stage where Shandi is bouncing up and down impatiently waiting for us.

"Hurry! They've started their search."

Shandi shoves my backpack into my hands, and I clutch it to my chest as Daffney rushes up, stuffing a wad of cash inside.

"I can't take that," I protest.

"Girl, we look out for each other," Ariel snaps. "Take the money and run. Come back when things cool down. You'll always have a home here."

Tears prick my eyes. "I'll be back. I promise."

The stage door swings open then. Smoke and neon light spilling over us, as the audience comes into view.

Time slows as my gaze lands on someone I never wanted to see again.

I stiffen as my blood turns to ice.

Daniel.

His venomous glare finds me instantly, and his lips curl as he mouths a single word.

"Gotcha."

"No." The word barely escapes me, fear making my knees weak as I stumble back into my friends.

"Out the back door," Shandi snaps, taking charge, and I don't hesitate.

I run.

The club is a maze, but I know my way through the old building, and I hope like hell my knowledge of it has me at an advantage.

I shuck on the backpack as I run, white knuckling the straps as I hurry down some stairs before bursting into the kitchen. A bowl of wedges flies from Chef Bow's hands as we collide raining potatoes on us both and I cry out an apology while ignoring Bow's curses.

"Sorry!" I leap over the carnage, almost stumbling when a deep bellow echoes from the passage I just escaped from.

"Stop!"

A ripple of fear zaps down my spine, but I don't stop. I keep running.

Risking a glance over my shoulder, I find Daniel bursting into the kitchen, his eyes locking onto me before he slips on the wedges still strewn across the floor.

An "umph" flies from him as he crashes to the tiles, and a satisfied smirk tugs at my lips momentarily.

Bow blocks Daniel's path as he staggers to his feet. "You can't be in here!" Bow snarls, waving his butcher knife at Daniel.

"Get the fuck out of my way, you crazy fucker!" Daniel yells, and as much as I don't want Bow to get hurt, I can't stick around to find out. I have my baby to think of.

Shoving through another door, I rush out into yet another passage that forks off into different directions.

One leads back around to the front part of the club. It's a passage the security guys use. And the other leads to the laneway behind the club.

Taking the one that leads to the back laneway, I hurry down a short flight of stairs and then back up another before rushing out into the last passage that leads to the back door.

I'm so close. It's right there, my eyes zeroing in on the old rusty door as I run, but before I make it two steps, a hard body crashes into me from behind.

"You fucking whore. Did you really think you could run from us?!"

My heart stops as the familiar voice registers.

Donny Allen. Daniel's mate and probably one of the cruellest people I have ever met.

We stumble into the wall, and I turn my body as much as I can to protect the swell of my stomach, the movement disloging the arsehole trying to tackle me.

He trips and falls to his knees, giving me just enough time to shake him off, and I turn to face him.

I'm struck frozen for a beat as I stare at Donny, only now noticing how much he looks like his uncle, the police officer that threatened to harm my sisters last year when I tried to report what Daniel and his friends had done to me.

Donny and his uncle have the same round face. The same dark eyes with lashes too light compared to their dark brows. Even their sneers are the same.

His eyes glint. "What did you think would happen when we found out you were up the duff with my kid?"

My stomach lurches. "It's not yours."

He sneers. "Could be. It could be any of ours. But we both know whose dick was inside you the most."

His sinister eyes fall to my stomach as he points, but I shake my head, not wanting him to ever think he has a claim on me or my child.

I know it could be his. But who the sperm donor was doesn't matter to me. All that matters is that those monsters never get their hands on my little boy or girl.

"You assume I wasn't sleeping with anyone else," I mutter, wanting him to think the baby isn't his or any of theirs. "News-flash, arsehole. This baby was made with love, and the father is a real man that doesn't have to force himself onto women!"

By the time I finish, I'm screaming, my emotions getting the better of me, but the slight moment of uncertainty flickering across Donny's face is totally worth it.

"Nice try, slut," he scoffs, smirking at me like the cat that got the cream. "We both know you didn't have anyone else fucking your muckhole, so yeah, that baby is likely mine, and once it's born, I'll take it and throw you back to Daniel so he can do with you as he pleases."

My chest rises and falls rapidly as my emotions spill over, falling from my eyes in the form of tears.

"I fucking hate you!" I scream, and he snickers before lurching forward.

A squeal flies from me as I spin, making a run for it, but I only make it a few steps before his hand fists in my hair and jerks me back hard.

I flail, scream, hoping someone from the club will hear and come and save me.

Donny spins me to face him, his hand like a brick as it slaps hard across my cheek.

I see stars before my left eye with black rimming my vision as I try to fight back, slapping and scratching while I scream.

Donny curses, and I can tell by the way he's trying to get control of my hands that he's working to avoid really hurting me.

Because let's be honest, if he really wanted to, he'd smash his fist into my face and knock me out, just like he's done three other times before. So the fact he hasn't done that means he doesn't want to hurt me.

Well, he doesn't want to hurt my baby, which means he has to be careful with me.

My nails claw at his face as he tries to grab my wrists, before I lean in and latch my teeth onto his arm.

"Ahhh! Fuck!" He lurches back, giving me more room, and I don't think. I react.

My knee slams between his legs, and he drops, a strangled gasp wheezing from him, as I bolt for the back door.

Yelling echoes down the passage, heavy footsteps pounding the floors as what sounds like a herd of men get closer.

Not waiting another second, I bolt for the old rusty door, my hands outstretched ready to shove it open.

The moment my palms hit the door, it bursts open, and relief washes over me as the taste of freedom becomes within reach.

Stepping out into the cooler night air, it takes me a second to realise that everything is far from okay as hands grab me from both sides.

I scream, the hands tighten, practically lifting my feet off the ground as I'm carried forward towards the open door of a black SUV.

2

ABBEY

"Let go of me!" My scream rips through the alley, bouncing off the tall brick walls that stretch at least ten stories high, swallowed by the shadows of the city night.

"Stop struggling, love. We don't want to hurt you." The deep timbre of the voice is chilling. Lethal. And unfamiliar.

"No! Stop!" I scream as loud as I can, flailing, trying to wrench myself free as my frantic eyes dart from the man that just spoke, then to the other man on my right.

"We need to get you out of here to safety. Hop in." The other voice mutters with annoyance as I land a kick to his shin.

The open door of the SUV looms closer as they drag me, dread clawing at my chest like razor-sharp talons.

No.

I can't let them take me.

I scream "no" over and over as they get me to the open door, the one on my left shifting his hold to guide me while the one on my right maintains a death grip on my arm.

I don't know these men. If I were to guess, I'd say they might be cops or something similar. The type that wear suits and drive cars with blacked out windows. Detectives maybe?

I don't know what they want with me, but there's no way I'm getting in their car.

Even as I continue to struggle, the men bark at each other to be careful of my stomach, and I can't help but wonder if they're more friends of Daniel's and Donny's fathers.

Suddenly, I'm yanked back, and the man guiding me on my left disappears from my side before the man on my right stiffens, turning us both to face someone new.

It takes me a moment to process what I'm seeing, the dark shadows of the alleyway playing tricks on my mind.

"Fuck. Come on now, Hush. Let him go." The man still gripping my arm yanks me closer, and I go without a fight, not because I'm scared of what I'm seeing, but because I'm so confused.

"Dee?" I whisper, certain I'm hallucinating, because there's no way the small mute girl who moved to Fox Pines last year is standing before us with a knife the size of my forearm pressed to the other tall man's throat.

Her big dark eyes flick to mine briefly, giving me a nod, before they lock back onto the man holding me, her expression morphing into a deadly sneer that nearly makes me pee my pants.

What is happening right now?

"You know, Hush, I consider this foreplay." The tall man pinned under her knife's blade dares to chuckle, not looking scared at all. "You sure you can handle the Devil?"

Dee just rolls her eyes, like holding a massive knife to some guy's throat is the most normal thing in the world.

I don't know why they are calling her Hush, or what she is doing here, but I have to admit, it's a relief to see a familiar face. The only problem is that because of me, she might get hurt.

"Dee. What are you doing here?" I ask, trying to take a step forward, but the man at my side tightens his grip, refusing to let me move.

"That's a good question, *Dee*." The man next to me hisses her name, his tone like acid. "Why are you here, holding your fucking ninja blade to Devon's throat? Have you forgotten that you work for *me*?"

"She hasn't forgotten."

That voice.

I know that voice.

Tears sting my eyes, and my lip immediately starts wobbling as a tall figure steps from the shadows, the glint of a gun aimed right at the man holding me.

"For fuck's sake." The other man who referred to himself as the Devil, groans rolling his eyes. "Why the fuck are two of your team here going against you, Griff?"

"Shut the fuck up, Devon. I'm sure it's nothing but a fucking misunderstanding," the man holding me snaps, but I can hardly focus on anything but the newcomer.

Jared.

I grew up with Jared, crushing on him for years, and now he's here, a gun firmly in his grip, looking nothing like the sweet blond-haired, blue-eyed boy who used to shove marbles up his nose just to see how far he could snort them out.

Now, this version of Jared is nothing but pure man, his gaze hard and just as lethal as the two men trying to kidnap me.

"You wanna tell me why the fuck you have a gun pointed at me, Crow?" The one holding me, Griff I think the other man called him, snarls in Jared's direction.

Crow? Why did he call him Crow?

"I should have it pointed at your cousin, since he tried to flirt with what's mine," Jared snaps back, giving Dee a quick wink when their eyes meet. "But since we all know Hush can handle herself, and you have your hands on my friend… well. You're a smart man. You understand."

"Lower your gun now, Crow, and I'll forget this ever happened," Griffin snarls.

Devon, or the Devil, or whatever his name is scoffs. "I won't fucking forget. They aren't part of my crew."

Devon stiffens and sucks in a sharp breath when Dee digs her blade a little deeper, a thin line of blood trickling down his neck.

"*Hush,*" Griff warns, squeezing my arm tighter as he does.

She simply arches a single brow at him.

"Fucking hell, kid. We're doing this for your aunties."

Dee rolls her eyes again, completely unfazed.

"And we're doing this for our friend. Let Abbey go now, Griffin," Jared demands, his voice so cold it almost makes me shiver.

The door I escaped through minutes ago bursts open with a whoosh, and suddenly Griffin releases me, shoving me behind him, a gun already in his hand. Jared, Dee and the other man,

Devon, whip around, weapons raised, their eyes locked onto the new threat.

For a long tense moment, nothing but stunned silence fills the alley as the figure in the doorway remains still.

Shifting to the side to see past Griffin, my eyes land on not one, but two forms in the doorway.

Daniel and Donny.

"Is she there?" a voice yells from inside, and my knees nearly give out at the unmistakable voice of Officer Allen. Donny's uncle.

The moment Donny shouts "Yes!", Devon fires his gun, the bang like a clap of thunder, echoing off the alley walls. Fragments of brick explode, as Daniel and Donny yelp, diving for cover back inside the passage while Devon chuckles darkly.

"Fucking pussies."

"Time to go," Jared snaps, spinning and shoving Griffin aside before he grips my arm, dragging me down the alley.

"Seriously, Crow. You really gonna snatch my mark?" Griffin growls from behind us as Dee falls into step.

"I was, but now I'm helping you keep her safe by taking her, so you two can hold them back."

My eyes widen at his words, and I glance back over my shoulder as we hurry away, just in time to see Officer Allen step out, his gun raised at Devon.

I squeak and duck as gunfire erupts behind us, and the three of us take off running, the other two men in suits covering our retreat.

"Hurry," Jared hisses, passing me off to Dee, who grabs my other arm and pulls me forward faster as Jared shifts behind us and starts firing back.

"Oh my God," I cry out, terrified Jared and Dee are going to get hurt, and dare I say, even a little worried about the men in suits too.

As we near the mouth of the alley, Dee points to the left, and we bolt that way, where she darts forward to yank open the door of a ute parked on the street.

She gestures again, holding it open, and I nod quickly, climbing in before she follows, sliding in next to me on the bench seat.

Gunfire echoes out of the alley as Jared sprints towards us, the driver's door flying open before he leaps in and fires up the engine.

"Everyone okay?" he rushes out, slamming the ute into gear and gunning it out of the parking space.

"Yes," I squeak before a thumb pops up in front of me, and I realise it's Dee's way of letting Jared know she's okay while he frantically bounces his gaze between the road and the rearview mirror.

A ragged breath shudders out of me, and I realise I'm trembling.

Reaching around me, Dee grabs the seatbelt and pulls it across me, clicking it into place.

"T-thank you," I murmur, tears blurring my vision as I try to look at her.

What the hell just happened?

One minute I was doing laundry, and the next I'm being hunted down by too many people to count, nearly kidnapped by suit-clad men in an alley, and then saved by a five-foot-nothing mute girl and a six-foot-something boy I grew up with.

"How? What?" I shake my head, trying to make sense of it all as hot tears track down my cheeks. "I don't understand."

My gaze shifts to Dee.

She's a small, mysterious girl who never speaks and hardly interacts with anyone, but who once approached me at the school swimming carnival, and used her phone to type out messages to find out if I needed help.

She knew.

All my friends knew I wasn't in a good situation. They all wanted to help. Lexi tried, but I begged her not to because every time they tried, Daniel made me pay.

I felt so ashamed of what was happening. I couldn't wrap my head around what my parents were forcing on me, or why having sex with Daniel was such a big deal. All I wanted was to make them happy and for things to go back to the way they were before I ever let Daniel Stone near me.

Now, Lexi's the one that arranged for me to be taken away from my parents and saved me from my fate of being forced to marry a monster. And Jared… Jared's the one saving me from the monsters that destroyed me over and over, making sure they can't do it again.

I don't deserve my friends. But I love them.

Dee reaches up, offering me a tissue, and I take it, her kindness squeezing a sob from me.

"T-thank you."

"I don't think anyone's following," Jared mutters, easing his foot off the accelerator as he relaxes back into his seat. "Fuck, Abs. I wasn't expecting this."

I turn to him, noticing his gaze fixed on the swell of my stomach.

"I wasn't expecting *you* to come and save me. Who were those men?"

Jared's blue eyes meet mine briefly before flicking back to the road as he sighs.

"Well, the guy that had hold of you is Griffin Marx. My boss."

My eyes widen. "Your boss? Where do you work?"

Dee leans forward, catching Jared's attention, and raises her brows at him.

In fascination, I watch them have a silent conversation with just their eyes as I sit between them before Jared speaks again.

"I'm a part of the Marx crew. Griffin's men in the Fox Pines district."

I raise a brow. "And what do you do for him?"

He glances at me warily from the corner of his eye as he drives.

"Whatever he needs me to do."

I roll my eyes. "Look, I get that I probably have no right to pry, Jared, but I can't help but worry because you have a gun. *They* had guns." I jerk my thumb in Dee's direction. "She has a huge bloody knife. I can't help but think your involvement with those men is anything but legal."

Again, Dee's thumb pops up in front of my face, and I glance at her.

"Is that confirming that I'm right?"

She nods.

I blanch.

Jared swerves the ute.

"Fuck!"

Gripping my seatbelt, my wide eyes lock onto the hood of a car speeding alongside us, and I realise it just merged onto the road, nearly clipping the side of Jared's ute.

"Dee, glovebox," Jared snaps, and I frown, watching her quickly pop it open to reveal another gun.

My eyes widen as she takes it out, and Jared curses, swerving the ute again.

"Fuck off!" he yells, and I flinch.

I'm slow to the party, because while Jared and Dee arm themselves with guns, I'm still sitting here wondering what the hell is going on. But then, the car next to us speeds up, and Daniel's menacing glare comes into view.

"Pull over, Crowley!" Daniel yells, shouting Jared's surname out the window of the silver car he's driving, and Donny's smug face pops into view from the passenger seat.

Dee answers for her boyfriend by flipping them the bird.

"You mute bitch! I'm gonna have fun showing you what it's like to have a train run on you!"

"Motherfuckers!" Jared roars before swerving his ute hard into the side of their car.

I scream. Dee raises her gun, and Jared white knuckles the wheel as he tries to run them off the road.

Oh my God, we're going to die.

I clutch onto my stomach, fear gripping me at the thought that I might not be able to keep my unborn baby safe.

With a sudden jerk, Jared swerves his ute hard in the other direction, tyres squealing as the back fishtails before he guns it up the freeway on-ramp, trying to put distance between us and Daniel.

Glancing over my shoulder, my heart sinks as I see the silver car gaining on us, headlights glaring through the darkness.

"They're coming!" I screech.

"I see them," Jared mutters, tossing Dee his phone without taking his eyes off the road. "Call Ayden."

She nods, tapping the screen, and a moment later, the phone rings through the car speakers as Jared weaves across four lanes of light traffic on the freeway.

"You got her?" Ayden's voice booms through the cabin, rough and urgent.

"We got her, but we can't shake Stone and Allen. We're about to hit the tunnel," Jared grunts, eyes flicking to the rearview mirror.

"Fuck. Okay. I'll call for reinforcements," Ayden replies, but as we shoot into the tunnel with Daniel on our tail, something else catches my attention.

A distant rumble. Like a storm rolling in. Only this rumble doesn't stop. It just gets louder.

"Uh, who were you going to call?" Jared asks, still focused on the mirror, his voice tight.

"You know who," Ayden barks, and Jared snickers.

"No need. They're already here. Gotta go."

Dee ends the call, glancing over her shoulder, and for a long moment, as we race through the tunnel, I just sit there frozen as my heart flips over in my chest.

It can't be? Right? I'm imagining something that isn't real.

There's no way there is an entire pack of motorcycles entering the tunnel behind us… right?

I don't realise my left leg is jittering up and down until Dee's hand comes to rest on my knee, giving it a squeeze.

My eyes flick from her hand to her face, and she offers me a small smile before mouthing. *'You'll be okay.'*

I don't know how true that statement is, but as the thunder-ous roar of engines gets louder and closer, something inside of me settles. Like just knowing who might be in that pack makes me feel a little safer.

"Fuck, hold on!" Jared yells right before the ute lurches for-ward from being hit from behind.

In an instant, Jared's and Dee's arms shoot out protectively, one from each side, holding me back against the seat. It's such a simple, instinctive act, but it ignites a storm of emotions inside me. Like maybe, just maybe, there are still people besides Lexi who care about me despite everything I did wrong. Despite how I pushed them all away.

"Pricks." Jared sneers, slamming his foot on the accelerator harder and swerving into the middle lane as we descend under the Yarra River. "Are you both okay?"

Once again, Dee gives a thumbs-up, and I manage a squeaky "Yes" before they both relax their hold on me.

When I glance up at Jared, he's wearing a wicked grin, eyes fixed on the rearview mirror, which is when I notice how loud the roar of motorcycles has become—deafening, like a tidal wave crashing down behind us.

When Jared rolls his window down, I stiffen, the noise roaring through the cabin like a freight train before a motorcycle rum-bles up beside his window, and I see a familiar face.

"Hey there, Charity. Good to see you're still in one piece."

A laugh bubbles up my throat at Smitty calling me "Charity", and I slap a hand over my mouth to stifle it before he shoots me a wink and turns his focus to Jared.

I have no idea how Smitty's not crashing his bike right now. It can't be easy riding at this speed through a tunnel while casually chatting through a car window.

"You look like you could use some help," Smitty's voice is clear despite racing through a tunnel. "And since you're carrying some very fucking precious cargo, I'm gonna cut through the shit and just tell you, straight up. We're helping whether you want it or not."

Jared nods, his grip on the wheel steady. "Fine with me, man."

"Good fucking answer." Smitty nods again, raising his hand and giving some sort of signal to his club brothers riding behind.

Glancing over my shoulder, I watch each of them mimic the gesture in unison, like it's some kind of code. Or maybe it's just a thing they like to do. Who knows.

Jared rolls up his window, keeping his ute in the middle lane as the tunnel starts to ascend, and he chuckles to himself, shaking his head.

"Wanna see Daniel Stone look like he's about to piss his pants?" Jared asks, his tone smug. "Take a look behind us."

Brows shooting up, I shuffle in the seat, craning my neck to peer out the back window. The silver car is falling back, and just like Jared said, Daniel looks panicked.

His eyes are wide, lips moving frantically while Donny looks to be barking into his phone from the passenger seat.

A wicked smirk tugs at my lips.

I like seeing fear in Daniel's eyes. I like that, right now, the tables are turned and he's realising that maybe, this time, he's the victim.

My gaze shifts from the silver car to the horde of motorbikes surrounding both vehicles. Even with their helmets on, I spot JD, Murf, and Spud riding alongside Daniel's car, with many more riders flanking us on either side and behind.

My heart flips as I scan each rider, hoping to spot one person in particular.

Desperation claws at me as I search for him, needing to know if he's here, wanting to help too. But unless he's way in the back, I can't see him, and my heart stops flipping and starts sinking.

A gentle tap on my shoulder pulls my attention back to find Dee's soft eyes, understanding etched across her expression before she points out her window, giving me a knowing look.

Following her direction, I glance up, my heart stopping entirely.

Ringo.

He's right there.

And his dark gaze is locked on mine.

3

RINGO

There she is. Those big doe eyes. Those rosy cheeks. Those plump lips.

My Angel.

The last time I saw her was in my shitty bathroom back at the Western. She'd been in there cleaning up someone else's vomit off her clothes. Wendy had found her first and I'd been instantly pissed because that bitch couldn't seem to grasp basic fucking boundaries. But then Wendy stepped aside, and my eyes found Abbey wearing less clothing than I'd seen on her since I'd stolen her from her parents, and naturally, I took her in.

My gaze dropped, taking in the heavy set of her tits straining against the fabric of a tight white tank. And then my eyes moved lower, which is when shit got confusing, because the moment I saw the swell of her tummy… well somehow Abbey morphed into something else. Someone else. A person I never wanted to see again.

"Ringo! Let's round them up!"

Smitty's yell severs my connection to those big brown eyes staring back at me, and I nod over the hood of the ute Abbey's in, rolling my shoulders back and taking in a deep fucking breath.

For weeks, I've been searching for her, desperate to see her again. But my time's been eaten up with our hunt for answers.

Who the fuck killed our prospect, Morris, and left him to rot in the trunk of Casey's car?

And where the fuck is our missing prospect, Cookie?

Not to mention the warehouse breach and the men killed alongside some of the Marx crew from warehouse four.

I've barely slept two hours each night, not knowing where my Angel went. If she was safe. If someone was hurting her.

The loud rumble of our Harleys brings me back to reality. To why we're here and what we're doing.

Despite Lexi's fury over me letting Abbey run off, Ayden reached out earlier to request that we go on standby. Said they'd located Abbey, but so had the corrupt cops, so our help might be needed.

But I didn't just sit back and fucking wait. No way was I leaving Abbey's safety in the hands of a bunch of Catholic kids from Fox Pines. So I called Liam Marx, who let me know his brother Griffin and cousin Devon were already on their way to get her for the Angel sisters.

I'd been pissed that now, Bec and Amanda Angel were finally stepping in, even after I'd already asked for their help. But fuck, shit with the pandemic has made everyone's lives hard, so I let it slide and convinced Liam to give me the location.

Leather and Lace Gentlemen's Club.

Fuck. Has my Angel been stripping? Showing her body to horny men?

I squeeze the hand grip tight, not able to help myself as I take another look at Abbey travelling in the ute next to me.

She's fucking beautiful.

Easing off on the throttle, my speed drops and Trunk shifts to the side, letting my ride fall back next to him and the silver car that fucking rammed into the back of the ute carrying Abbey only minutes ago.

Maintaining my speed with the silver car, I glance in through the passenger window to see a guy sneering back at me, chatting on his phone, like the fucking glass between us can protect him.

What an idiot.

I already know who he is. I know who they all are. Those sick fuckers that hurt my Angel.

This here is Donny Allen. Nephew to the prick cop, Ian Allen. The same arsehole who somehow had a hand in disabling our security cameras at our warehouses, luring us out of the compound a few weeks ago.

While most of the men were out investigating, that bastard and his officer prick mates stormed in and fucked with our women and some of our remaining men.

We don't let shit like that slide in the Southern Sadists MC, and soon enough, that fucker will learn that lesson.

With the tunnel exit up ahead, I bide my time, wanting to be away from the CCTV cameras before I make my move, and I subtly slip the glass breaker from my cut, and grip it tightly in my hand.

The moment we're clear of the tunnel and the night sky is above us again, I curl my lip at the fucker still staring back at me and shift my hog closer.

Donny frowns.

I smirk.

Then I lift the glass breaker to the window and press the button.

The glass explodes, and the car swerves as the dickheads inside yell like little bitches. I veer away for a moment, making sure the fuckers don't hit me with their car.

My men around us roar with laughter, hooting and yelling teasing remarks at the pricks inside the car before JD copies my move on the driver's side, smashing the glass.

Daniel, the fucking little prick, starts yelling like a yabbie has latched onto his pin dick. I can tell the fucker's never faced this level of ruthlessness before. I can't fucking wait until he realises it'll never end until his cold, dead body is six feet under.

"Ahhh stop! What are you doing, you crazy bastards!" Daniel yells, and I shift my ride closer, watching as the ute carrying my Angel guns it out of here while we take care of business.

"I hear you like to rape women," I snarl into the open window, and Daniel's eyes go wide as Donny just smirks.

I see fucking red!

My fist snaps out and cracks against his nose. Blood bursts from the split in his skin from the impact, and he starts fucking screeching like a hyena.

"Not fucking smiling now, are you, Donny Allen?"

Even as he cups his bleeding nose, his eyes widen at hearing his name fall from my lips.

"Leave us alone!" Daniel yells, so forceful his voice cracks, and my men just laugh, those nearest his car kicking their boots into the side.

"Stop!" Daniel shouts again, but it's then that we hear sirens, and I know our fun will have to wait.

My eyes flash to the road ahead, catching the taillights of the ute as it exits the freeway.

Thank fuck.

"Stay in place!" I yell for my club brothers to hear, and the message gets passed on so everyone knows.

We can't let these fuckers follow Abbey, so we stick close to them, blocking their path, making sure they have no choice but to stay on the freeway as the sound of sirens gets closer.

We're lucky, given the time of night, that the freeway isn't congested. People see and hear us riding in a pack, and they either speed up or hang back, but it also means that the cops can gain on us faster.

"You wait until my uncle gets you!" Donny yells out the window, blood still pissing from his nose.

"I can't fucking wait to meet your uncle Ian. Be sure to tell him Ringo's coming for him!" I yell over the roar of the engines, my rage bubbling up.

I want to pummel these fuckers now and be done with it.

But not yet. Not while an entire police precinct is ready to ride our arses.

A sharp whistle cuts through the noise from over the hood of Daniel's car to where Smitty is, motioning ahead.

It's time to ditch Tweedle-fucking-Dum and Tweedle-fucking-Dee.

Moving in sync, my club brothers veer left, our bikes slicing through traffic like a pack of wolves closing in on a kill before we take the exit while Daniel and Donny keep gunning it down the freeway, thinking they got away.

The second our wheels hit the metro streets, cops swarm like they'd been waiting for us.

Lights flash. Sirens wail. They were prepared and we rode right into this shit.

"Fuck!" Smitty shouts. "Split up! Stay with your partner! Meet in eight hours!"

We don't hesitate. We know the drill.

Some of us will get nabbed tonight. That's inevitable, but better a few than all.

We all have a designated wingman, and as mine, JD speeds up beside me, his grin wide and reckless.

"Time to have fun?"

"Yeah." I chuckle, feeling that familiar rush kick in. "Time to have fun."

4

ABBEY

Jared snakes an arm around me, steadying me as we stand in the lift, and I watch as he punches the button for the top floor.

"Where are we?" I ask, hating the tremble in my voice that matches the way my body is shaking.

I've been like this ever since I lost sight of Ringo. Ever since we left the freeway and Jared tore through the streets, weaving us back towards the city.

"We're somewhere safe," Jared offers vaguely, and I glare up at him, unimpressed.

Dee snickers beside him, and I lean forward with a raised brow. She just shrugs, then glances up at the numbers climbing on the screen.

I don't know if I can handle any more surprises. The last hour has been a lot, and now my pelvis is sore, like I may have strained a muscle running.

Shit. Will running hurt my baby?

I don't even know. I barely know anything about pregnancy, let alone childbirth. The only thing I do know is I want to keep my baby safe.

As we near the top floor, I shift away from Jared's hold and lean against the handrail.

He frowns down at me, his lips parting like he's about to ask if I'm alright.

I shake my head and wave him off before he gets the chance.

While the lift ascends the last few floors, I finally get a proper look at my childhood best friend and his girlfriend.

It's only been a couple of months since I last saw them. It was at the worst graduation ceremony of all time, thanks to the pandemic restrictions limiting everything. But that was the last time I saw them.

So why do they look so different in only a few months?

Then again, I guess the same could be said for me.

Jared's blond hair is messier than usual, but that could just be from tonight's chaos. His blue eyes, though… they look harder. Like he's had to toughen up fast. Like he's carrying something heavy.

And I suppose he is.

He knows loss.

He knows what it's like to be at the receiving end of a fist.

He knows violence.

But there's more. So much more.

The last eighteen months have changed us all.

Dee, on the other hand, looks anything but stressed. Her mousy brown hair is long, her huge brown eyes relaxed. She's still short, and still has a smattering of freckles across her nose that makes her look younger than her eighteen years.

Despite her innocent looks, she held a knife to that man's throat tonight. A huge knife.

She also held a gun. And she didn't even flinch when the bullets rained down on us.

It's almost haunting how calm she is after everything that just happened.

Who are these people?

The ding of the lift arriving on the top floor has me dragging my gaze to the doors as they part, and I peek out to find a small passage with a stairwell leading up to another door.

Jared gestures for me to step out, and as much as I want to hesitate, I force my feet to move as Dee follows before rounding me and making her way up the stairs first.

I have no clue where we are, but I follow anyway, because I'm with my friends and they wouldn't harm me… right?

As I trudge up the stairs, Jared's presence looms behind me, close enough that I can feel the warmth of his body at my back.

Nerves coil around in my chest, squeezing tighter with every step. The unknown waits beyond that door, and for the second time tonight, my grip tightens on the strap of my backpack like it's a lifeline, as my pulse hammers in my neck.

Pressing her hands to the door, Dee pushes it open revealing the night sky, and a warmly lit rooftop alfresco area.

The second I step out onto the rooftop, the cool night fans over me in a refreshing relief after the suffocating tension in the passage.

Jared and Dee move ahead, Dee gesturing for me to follow, and as we move, I take in the space around me.

A rooftop garden stretches out, with hidden nooks partitioned by bamboo walls and each retreat housing cocoon-shaped loveseats.

It's an oasis. A place to escape.

A place to breathe.

Soft voices drift to me as I trail behind my friends, weaving through the maze of greenery, and unease prickles at the back of my neck as I still don't know what I'm about to walk into.

Jared rounds the corner of the last partition with Dee on his heels, and suddenly, the voices cut off.

Silence.

Then I hear a voice. Urgent and desperate.

"Where is she?"

A sob catches in my throat, my feet moving before I can think as I rush forward, rounding the corner before I freeze.

They're here.

All of them.

My friends from back home.

"Abs!"

Lexi's scream shatters the moment, my eyes instantly finding her as she leaps over a low table, arms outstretched, blue eyes glossy with unshed tears.

But then... she skids to a stop, her gaze dropping down my body.

My noticeably pregnant body.

"I didn't know how to tell you," I whisper, but she's close enough to hear, and her tears finally spill over as her lips part to speak.

"Oh, Abs," she cries, closing the distance and wrapping her arms around my neck, pulling me into a hug I've been longing for, for months.

Burying my face in her neck, I inhale the familiar scent of my best friend, and fall apart.

My knees buckle and Lexi follows me to the ground, not letting go for a second as she holds me tight, letting me break in her arms.

She shouldn't love me after everything I did.

She shouldn't even like me.

She shouldn't be here.

But she is.

She's the one who sent Ringo to take me.

She's the one who sent Jared and Dee to find me.

She's still fighting for me.

Unconditional.

That's the way Lexi West loves me despite everything.

That's the type of love Lexi West has to offer those she cares about, and apparently, I'm still on her list.

"I'm so glad you're safe," she sobs into my ear, her body trembling with emotion.

Strong arms wrap around both of us as a familiar weight presses against my back.

"Thank fuck you're alright, Yeb."

Marcus.

His voice, his words, the childhood nickname they called me, shatter whatever control I have left.

The dam breaks, my sobs spilling out harder, louder, buried pain rising to the surface and spilling over.

His grip tightens, keeping me and Lexi firmly in his warmth, and I let myself collapse into the love I never thought I'd have again.

I don't know how long we sit there, tangled together, sobbing on the deck-like floor of the rooftop. Eventually, our tears dry up, and Marcus' hold loosens as Ayden steps in to help Lexi stand.

Marcus shifts, straightening, then turns to face me, his hand outstretched.

I take it, my fingers curling around his as I watch his familiar brown eyes rake over me.

By the time I'm on my feet, his gaze is trained on my bump, the worry etched into his face almost suffocating. His dark gaze flicks to mine, searching my expression.

"Abs, you're…"

I snicker, but there's no real humour in it. I'm too drained, too emotionally wrecked to feel anything other than the pain I've been shoving down for months.

Licking my lips, I take in a steadying breath and drop Marcus' hand, stepping around him to look over the rest of the group.

My friends.

Well… most of them.

I can't claim all of them. Specifically Lexi's new best friend, Rhys.

I can't fault her for that. She was there when I wasn't. She was there when I hurt Lexi.

"Uh hi." I wave awkwardly, not entirely sure what sort of reception I'll get from them.

Do they still hate me for what I did?

"I don't mean to state the obvious…" Simon, the playful class clown of the group steps forward, hazel eyes flicking from my face to my belly. "But, Abs, you're pregnant."

A laugh bubbles up from my throat this time as I watch his eyes widen like his brain just short-circuited.

"Super observant, Hastings," Garrett scoffs, clapping Simon on the shoulder before stepping towards me. "You've had us all worried, Abs."

His voice is softer than expected, matching the warmth in his blue-grey eyes.

He towers over me, and I have to crane my neck back to look up at him.

Garrett is such a big guy. Not just tall but broad, thicker with muscle than the last time I saw him. But underneath all that size, Garrett is still a teddy bear.

He reminds me of Ringo.

My heart clenches at the thought of Ringo. The ache is immediate, but then Garrett bends, pulling me into a hug that momentarily helps the pain to ease.

"Hurry up! My turn." Simon bounds forward like an overexcited puppy, shoving Garrett aside the second he lets me go, and takes his place, yanking me in for a hug.

I giggle. He gasps.

Simon's hands grip my upper arms as he shoves me back.

"Did I just hurt the baby? Was I too rough?"

"Sy, calm down," Rhys soothes, stepping up beside him as she slides her hand over his, prying his fingers from my arms. "Hugging Abbey won't hurt her baby."

Simon exhales, his shoulders relaxing. "Good." Simon nods firmly before flashing me a wide, cheesy smile. "That would suck if you can't hug anyone until your baby is born."

"Yeah. It really would." I smile back, but my attention shifts to Rhys.

She's like a dark goddess.

Confident.

Stunning.

And a queen to her men.

Literally. She has like four boyfriends.

Wait, no. Five. There's an older guy too, I think.

I don't know what I expected from her. She's been right there with Lexi a couple of the times Lexi wanted to help me. Even when our standoffs were tense, I knew she took her cues from Lexi.

And if Lexi thought I was worth saving, then Rhys must have believed it too.

How wonderful it must be to have friends like that.

Rhys would never betray Lexi the way I did.

Even though she's taken my place, I'm glad Lexi has her.

"It's so good to see you, Abbey. We'll have a girls chat later."

Her black-painted lips curl into a smile as she reaches out, giving my arm a gentle squeeze before leading Simon away.

A girls chat.

Shit.

That would be nice.

The thought makes my chest tighten, reminding me of Jols. When I stayed at the Western, Jols and I had a couple of girly chats. She reminded me of Lexi. They both have the same kind of warmth. They both care the same way with all of their hearts. I missed Lexi even more because of it.

I smile and nod at Rhys, letting her know I'd like that, just as Shaun steps forward.

Shaun Bossier was known as the Spanish Casanova of our school.

He's a smooth talker. The guy who could get any girl he wanted.

Well, until Rhys claimed him as one of hers.

Sweeping me up in a hug that includes a spin, I laugh lightly before Shaun plants me back on my feet.

"You had us all worried, Abs. I'm fucking glad you're okay."

"Thanks, Shaun." I smile just as Ayden shoulder-bumps him.

"Bossi's right," Ayden says, using Shaun's nickname. "All of us have been worried, and Lex has been beside herself. I don't know what happened at the Southern Sadists' compound, but Ringo is on our shit list."

My brows shoot up. "Oh… ummm." I glance around, feeling the weight of every stare. They are either locked on my face or my bump, and my hand drifts over it protectively.

"He didn't tell you?"

Ayden frowns at my question, his blue gaze flicking to Lexi, who steps up beside him.

"He said you ran off. That was it."

My brows shoot up at Lexi's words.

Of course he didn't tell them the whole story. Their reactions to my pregnancy alone prove that much.

Shuffling awkwardly, my cheeks heat as I try to figure out how to explain what happened, mainly because I still don't really understand it myself.

"Did something happen?" Ayden asks, and I can feel my friends closing in around me.

They are doing it because they care, but it's making me feel claustrophobic.

The urge to run is palpable.

"Well, umm..." I lick my lips, my gaze dancing between Ayden, Lexi, Marcus, and Garrett.

"Did someone hurt you?" Lexi snaps, now a little panicked.

My gaze flicks to hers, and I quickly shake my head.

"No... no. Not on purpose."

"What the fuck happened?" Jared snarls, and I shrink in on myself, wanting to hide.

"Oh for fuck's sake, back off her, you psychos." Rhys shoves past Marcus and takes my hand, leading me out of the pack to one of the cabana loveseats.

I look at her, searching for something.

I don't even know what, but it's like she sees more than she should, because Rhys takes my hand and deadpans, "Who broke your heart?"

My lower lip wobbles.

Shit.

A fat tear spills over before I can stop it, but I quickly bat it away, so sick of crying. Sick of feeling like I can't control my own damn emotions.

"Shit." Lexi exhales, sitting down beside me. "You and Ringo did get close, didn't you?"

All I can do is nod.

"Did he fucking touch you?" Marcus snarls, and Ayden scowls at his cousin.

"Dude, Ringo isn't like that."

Marcus scoffs. "He's a fucking criminal. She's a pretty damsel. As if someone like that wouldn't fucking try something."

"Marcus!" Lexi snaps, her voice sharp as she levels him with a glare. "Just because he's on the other side of the law doesn't make him a monster."

He was my monster.

I want to tell her that but I don't.

Because this… this is just another thing they won't understand.

How could I be attracted to a man after what Daniel and his friends did to me?

How could I be attracted to a criminal?

How could I be attracted to the kind of man who so easily broke into my home, stole me away in the night, and left no trace?

How do I explain that even knowing how dangerous he is… I still felt safe with him?

"You're blinded by the way he helped you, Lexi," Marcus snaps, his voice thick with frustration. "But don't forget why he had to help you. Don't forget what his brother, Muz, did to you and Ayden at that party. Don't forget how Muz held a gun to your head in my fucking driveway!"

"Forget! How can I ever forget?!" Lexi explodes, springing off the loveseat like she's ready to throw hands.

She doesn't get far though, Ayden moving fast to hook his arm around her, dragging her back, even as she fights against his hold.

"I will *also* never forget that when I was being attacked, when I thought I was about to die, Muz was there! Have you forgotten about that part Marcus? Because I sure as shit haven't! Or how about the fact that he died BECAUSE OF ME?!"

Tears stream down Lexi's face, her body wracked with sobs as Ayden turns her into his chest, wrapping her up in his arms.

I can't watch this.

I can't listen to this.

Pushing to my feet, I clear the lump in my throat.

"Please don't fight because of me."

It doesn't matter how much love they've shown me tonight. Doesn't matter that I truly feel it. Because deep down, I'm still an outsider. Someone who drags toxicity with them wherever they go.

And the last thing I want to do is cause a rift between them.

"Fuck, sorry, Abs." Marcus sighs, raking his fingers through his thick dark hair. "I'm just worried." He steps forward, guilt lining his face, brows furrowed in concern.

"I understand that. Thank you. But Lexi is right. Ringo isn't the bad guy you think him to be, he—"

My words are cut off by the loud clang of the rooftop door bursting open, rattling on its hinges.

Angry male voices cut through the air, sharp and dangerous.

We all stiffen, freezing in place momentarily.

Jared moves first. Gun out, raised as Dee slinks off into the shadows, unsheathing her knife.

5

RINGO

“I don’t have a problem with spilling Marx blood tonight, Griffin. Get the fuck outta my way!”

Griffin smirks, completely unfazed by the gun I’ve got trained on him, even as he walks backwards.

“You’re standing on the rooftop of a Marx building, pointing metal at me. You really think there’s not at least four snipers ready to pull the trigger on you right now?”

Fuck.

That has me hesitating.

He could be bluffing.

But this is the Marx family I’m challenging here. They are the type to have traps set before you even realise you’ve stepped into one.

“How about you just step outta the fucking way then, so we don’t traumatise the poor girl even more, hey?” JD sneers from my side, his gun aimed at Devon Marx, who looks like he doesn't have a fucking care in the world.

Cocky fucker.

"How about you leave us alone to do what we were paid to fucking do?" Griffin snaps, spinning on his heel and stepping around the corner of the bamboo partition.

What the fuck kind of rooftop is this?

As I step around the corner, I nearly slam straight into Griffin's back, because the fucker has stopped dead in his tracks.

That's when I see it.

A gun pointed our way.

"Crow. It's only us. Lower your weapon," Griffin suggests, his tone edged with caution.

I recognise the guy holding the gun as the driver of the ute that had my Angel in it.

"Can't do that, boss," Crow answers, his hard gaze flicking between the four of us.

"Well, isn't this fun?" Devon drawls, stepping to the side and dropping himself into a sun lounger, stretching his legs out and tucking his hands behind his head like he's a lazy fucking king about to summon the fucking sun to rise in the dead of night so he can get a suntan.

Crow curls his lip at Devon, but I ignore their exchange and look past him, taking in a bunch of familiar faces.

Fox Pines kids.

Lexi's friends.

Only, they're not really kids anymore, are they? They've all grown into themselves, and judging by the way they're standing behind Crow, arms crossed, not looking remotely fucking impressed, I'd say they've got as much balls as he does, daring to point a gun at his fucking boss.

A Marx boss.

On second thought, maybe that's just dumb.

"Where's Abbey?" I demand, stepping forward and shoving Griffin aside.

The fucker just chuckles, but given his gun is still in his hand, I'd say he's a little concerned about the loyalty of his own crew member.

"None of your concern," Crow responds, which is when Lexi pushes through the wall of her male friends, stepping up like she's ready to fight me herself.

"What did you do?" she snaps, cheeks flushed with anger.

"The fuck do you mean?" I snap back, my gaze bouncing between her and her fucking posse.

"You were meant to keep her safe, Ringo. I reached out to you because I trusted you. Then you call and say she ran. But why did she run? Why wouldn't you give me answers? What did you do?!"

I jerk back at her yell, her anger hitting me like a punch to the gut.

"What the fuck are you accusing me of?" I growl, and another fucker, one I recognise as Ayden's cousin, steps forward, eyes burning with the kind of rage that means he's two seconds from swinging fists.

"If you fucking touched her, I'll—"

"Please stop this bickering."

The new sharp voice cuts through the tension like a blade.

I turn, and my stomach sinks to find the Angel sisters strolling around the corner.

Fucking hell.

Am I really standing on the rooftop of a Marx-owned building in the middle of Melbourne, surrounded by two of the most notorious Marx bastards, a pack of Fox Pines teenagers, and the fucking Angel sisters? The same women who have a little black book of killers that they send out to hunt down abusers and carve out their retribution like modern-day fucking assassins?

What fucking bullshit is this?

"Jared, lower your gun," Amanda insists, giving Crow a look that says she's not in the mood for his bullshit.

"Not until they toss their guns aside," Crow bites out, and Amanda smirks, turning her raised brows to her sister, Bec.

"You heard him, Griff." Bec holds out her hand like she's expecting a fucking gift, and Griffin scowls, clearly not happy.

Even so, he surrenders his weapon.

The fuck.

"You too, Devon." Amanda gestures to the lazy fucker on the sun lounge, his gun not drawn anymore.

The smug prick gasps dramatically, feigning terror.

"Oh no, whatever shall I do?" he mocks before stretching like a lazy cat, plucking his gun up between two fingers like it's a dirty sock, and tossing it to Bec.

Bec catches it with ease and rolls her eyes as he flops back down like the world's laziest warlord.

Fucking Marx family.

"JD. Ringo." Amanda turns to me, her hand outstretched and I grit my fucking teeth.

"You want me to fucking trust you after I asked for your help with Abbey and you turned me down?"

Amanda sighs. "We were in lockdown. And we were at capacity. I offered Devon's help."

My glare snaps to him.

"You really think sending her to him was the best fucking option?"

Devon smirks. "What's wrong, Ringo? Scared she'd like me better than you?"

I snarl, taking a step towards the cocky fucker, but Lexi shoves her way between us, holding up a hand.

"Either get rid of the gun or leave, Ringo."

Damn.

She may be a sweet-looking thing, but she's got the spine of someone who's been through hell and came out swinging.

Eyeing JD, I give him a nod, and we relinquish our guns to Amanda, who hands them off to Bec.

"Lower your gun, Crow," Griffin snaps, and this time, the blond guy with a huge fucking chip on his shoulder does as his boss asks, lowering his gun and slipping it into the back of his jeans.

"Hush. You too," Bec calls, and I frown, looking amongst the Fox Pines teens.

Who the fuck is Hush?

Everyone looks around like they are trying to spot someone, but Bec's gaze doesn't falter off Griffin as she sighs.

"Lower the knife, Dee."

Griffin's whole body stiffens, his eyes wide before he spins, and a strangled gasp floats past his lips.

Holy fuck.

There's a girl. A five-foot-nothing girl with dark eyes, sharp as fucking daggers, mere inches away from Griffin. Her gaze is locked on him like he's already dead, and in her hand is a massive fucking blade, an inch from his face.

Hang on. I recognise her.

She's the girl that was in the ute with my Angel.

Dee. Crow's chick.

"Fuck. Where did she come from?" JD mutters quietly, but it's loud enough for Dee, or Hush, or whatever her name is, to hear.

Her dark gaze cuts to him, head tilting in a way that sends chills right up my fucking spine.

This girl is a killer. I'd bet my hog on it.

If she really wanted Griffin dead, he would be already, and judging by his ready to flee stance, he fucking knows it too.

"Come on, Dee. Put it away and let's all take a breath." Amanda insists, and I wonder, just for a moment, why this little lethal killer would listen to the Angel sisters.

But she does, which means she works for them.

"Right, now that we have all calmed down..." Bec claps her hands together, now free of the weapons, as the little assassin shoulders past Griffin with a glare and moves to stand by Crow's side. "Let's get this situation sorted so I can go back to my date."

Amanda throws her head back, laughing. "A bottle of red and a book is not a date."

"When a book can give me more pleasure than a real, living man can, then hell yes, it is." Bec shrugs, and I just shake my fucking head, my patience running out by the second.

"Where's Abbey?" I snap, cutting through their bullshit.

Bec's glare sharpens. "She's not your concern anymore, biker boy. You were given a job, and you failed. So now we're stepping in."

"The fuck you are," I snarl, stepping forward, but the little assassin is quicker, moving between us and cocking her head in challange, those dark, unblinking eyes locked on me like she's measuring exactly how much effort it would take to put me down.

"Ringo," Ayden steps forward, cutting through our standoff, and just like that, my tension eases a fraction.

I stare at him, the guy I spent years protecting from my brother, Muz, before he finally died. Ayden is taller than the last time I saw him. More built too, packed with strong muscles that he didn't have as a teen.

"Let's just relax a little and sort this out, yeah?" Ayden suggests, and I fucking grind my teeth, because I fucking hate getting pulled into line by a guy that was a teenager a year ago.

Even so, I suck in my fucking pride and give Ayden a nod.

He's right of course, but it doesn't mean I have to like it. But since my goal is my Angel, and I'll be fucked if I'm letting anyone keep me away from her, I take a step back, roll my shoulders, and try to shake off the rest of the tension clinging to me like a second skin.

"Ringo, Bec is right," Lexi snaps, stepping up beside Ayden. "I asked you to keep her safe, and instead, she ran from you. I want to know why."

"Did you ask her why?" I snarl, and just like that, another fucker steps forward.

He's built like a fucking tank, fists balled at his sides, body practically vibrating with aggression.

I remember this guy from my little brother's funeral.

Garrett Cole.

"Lexi is asking *you*!" he fucking bellows, his voice so deep that it shocks me for a moment.

"Stop!"

The single shouted word has everyone freezing, and for the first time in what feels like months, my fucking pulse stutters.

The group before me shifts, bodies moving aside to let someone through… and there she is.

My Angel.

Every ounce of anger drains from me in an avalanche of white noise.

"I appreciate everyone trying to help me. Really I do." Abbey's sweet voice sounds sure and strong as she draws closer. "But no one has asked me what *I* want, and to be frank, I'm fucking sick of it."

Fuck.

"Did she just swear?" JD murmurs next to me, and I nod absently, a smirk tugging at my lips.

My Angel has a pure heart, but it's wounded and scarred, and the woman standing before us now with her hand running over the swell of her stomach is the same woman I caught glimpses of at the Western.

The same woman who, no matter how many times she's been knocked down, keeps clawing her way back up.

"Sorry, Abs," Lexi steps closer to my Angel. "I just thought because you wouldn't accept our help last year, we kinda had to take matters into our own hands."

I realise now what I hadn't before.

They were all protecting her, standing in a line so we couldn't get to her.

I can respect the fuck out of that kind of loyalty, because I know what it's like to care about Abbey Delany.

"Things have changed now," Abbey continues. "You got me away from my family and Daniel, and now I need to do what's right for my baby."

Now standing before Lexi, I notice my Angel is a little taller than her friend, but as I watch them together, it's easy to picture them as kids, growing up together, side by side, getting into mischief.

I wonder if Abbey realises that what her and Lexi have is more than friendship.

It's unbreakable.

Like family.

Like sisters.

Lexi's eyes fill with tears, and as usual, Ayden is right there to soothe her, running his hand down her back, keeping her grounded.

"Of course." Lexi's voice is thick with emotion. "What do you need, Abs? What can we do? We'll do anything."

Smiling, Abbey reaches out to squeeze Lexi's hand before finally turning in my direction.

And fuck, I feel it.

Her caramel orbs lock onto mine for a few long beats before darting away just as fast.

Her head drops, chin lowering… And fuck me, the way she shifts into her submissive pose has my blood rushing straight to my fucking cock.

"Angel?" The word is out before I can stop it, and of course someone just has to fucking pick up the pet name I called her.

"Why the fuck are you calling her Angel?" Crow snaps, but I don't spare him a second fucking glance, my eyes remaining locked onto the woman who's had me on the edge of insanity for over three fucking weeks.

"Eyes up," I demand, and just like usual, she obeys, her gaze snapping to mine.

The thing with Abbey is, she was raised in a controlling environment. She likely didn't even notice it until all the shit with her and Daniel happened. Until her parents' control tightened to near suffocating.

She was raised to submit. To obey. To take direction and orders, fall into line, and never speak up.

That sort of submission is a turn on in the bedroom, but even in that environment, she'd have all the power with the simple use of a safe word.

Her parents never gave her that.

She's never had the luxury of making her own decisions. Even now, after that little outburst, she won't say what she wants because she's spent her life terrified of how people will react.

How will they punish her? How will they make her feel bad for speaking up?

So she's not going to say what she wants now, unless I demand it.

"The fuck?" someone whispers as they witness Abbey's obedience to me.

"Tell us what you want, Angel."

She parts her lips, but snaps them shut, her uncertain gaze darting to Crow and the little assassin.

"Eyes on mine," I snap, and again, her gaze returns to me and she licks her lips. "Tell us, now."

"I need to speak with Ringo alone," she rushes out, and the Fox Pines crew move as one, shuffling at the unexpectedness of her request.

My fucking heart, which I'm sure stopped minutes ago, kicks back into action with a force that nearly takes me to my fucking knees.

Is it possible that I haven't lost her after all?

Because she bailed really fucking fast from me. From the Western.

And yeah, I get that she didn't understand what was happening when I lost my shit. I'm still fucking pissed that she fled before she could learn the truth.

But she's here now, right in front of me, and I need a fucking minute alone with her without all these eyes on us. Without all these fucking opinions coming from every fucking direction.

"You sure, Abs? You don't have to. If he's forcing you…"

Abbey's wide eyes snap back to Lexi at her words, her expression tightening like she's been slapped.

"Ringo would never force me to do anything."

Lexi hesitates, looking between us. Her brows pull together, and I can practically hear the gears turning in her head.

"Uh… okay… ummm." She flicks a glance at Ayden, looking for backup.

I get it. To her, it must look like I forced Abbey to tell us what she wanted a moment ago. And maybe, in a way, I did. But all I was really doing was giving Abbey permission to be honest without making her feel like she had to take responsibility for it.

Amanda, watching the whole exchange, steps in smoothly to assist.

"If that's what Abbey would like, how about we give her some privacy?"

There's a heavy pause.

Abbey's hometown friends hesitate, their reluctance thick in the air.

Their instincts are screaming for them to stay. To protect her. But one by one, they finally start moving, dragging their feet as they go.

A few of the guys size me up as they pass, and I grin.

I like those fucking kids.

Devon, ever the smug prick, takes his sweet time, cracking his neck and finally peeling himself off the sun lounger like a man with nowhere important to be.

He saunters past giving me a slow, knowing smirk that makes my fists twitch.

Ignoring him, I watch my best mate, JD turn back to Abbey.

"I'm glad you're okay. Jols will be relieved to hear it as well."

Abbey's lips kick up in a small, warm smile, and JD turns and claps me on my shoulder before following the others inside.

And just like that, it's quiet, the sounds of the city almost muffled as my gaze travels up from Abbey's feet to take her in properly for the first time tonight without an audience.

Fuck me.

Her hair is a soft pink shade now. It's pretty on her. Really makes her dark eyes pop. She's wearing black boots. A knockoff version of Docs. The grey skirt hugging her hips stretches over her bump stopping just above her knees. And her top, a red, white and black tee, is tied in a knot at the front, sitting below tits that are fuller than I remember.

Fuck.

It doesn't really look like her style, but considering she's been hiding out at Leather and Lace, I bet these clothes came from the girls there. They are the type of clothes that despite her condition, would have helped her blend in.

But fuck, I'd spot her in a heartbeat. My Angel doesn't blend in.

Not to me.

When my eyes find hers again, I take a step forward, moving close enough that she has to tip her chin up to hold my gaze.

"You fucking ran." My voice is rougher than I mean for it to be.

But I can't help it. Being here with her after all that time apart. All the fucking doubt and frustration and sleepless fucking nights.

And here she is. Just standing here.

Safe.

Whole.

Looking at me like she's not sure if she wants to run again, or stay.

Hooking my finger under her chin, I lean down, hovering my lips achingly close to hers as my voice drops, low and firm.

"What did I tell you about running from me?"

6

ABBEY

The deep gravel of his voice sends a tremor through me, and I'm not so sure it's from fear. The pull to launch myself into his arms is demanding, but I don't know where I stand. I don't understand what happened back in his motel room three weeks ago.

So instead of falling into him, I force myself to step back.

"You said there was nothing I could say that would make you turn your back on me." I remind him of the words he spoke that night when I was scared to admit the heinous things that had happened to me at the hands of Daniel and his friends. "You said nothing would stop you from wanting to protect me."

"That hasn't fucking changed, Angel," he snaps, and I take another step back. "Stop. Don't take another fucking step. You know I'll never hurt you."

Won't he?

Maybe not physically, but we both know physical pain is nothing compared to the damage emotions can do.

"You were angry when you saw…" My voice falters, a lump forming in my throat as I gesture to my bump.

"No… Yes… Fuck!" His whole body tenses before he spins, giving me his back.

Tension sparks in the air between us, like it's alive. A cell or being that you can feel and see.

Ringo shoves his hands through his hair, his chest rising and falling like he's trying to keep himself from breaking apart.

The muscles in his shoulders strain through his tee, his leather vest hiding the rest of his back.

I've never really studied his vest before. But now, with the hue of the city lights glowing over us, it picks up the white design on the black leather, and I'm surprised at the beauty in it.

The skull is anything but perfect, and I think that's where the beauty lies.

It's imperfection.

With the motorcycle tyre behind the skull and the wings fanning out at each side, I get a sense of freedom from it.

Or maybe, my hormones are making me see shit that isn't there.

I really don't know.

Ringo exhales sharply, tugging at his dark strands before tilting his head back, looking up at the sky.

My eyes follow, the twinkling stars above so dull compared to how brightly they shine back in Fox Pines.

A perk of country living I guess.

"I'm sorry." His words float to me, soft yet heavy, before he drops his hands and spins back to face me.

For a long moment we stare at each other.

And it's then that I see something different behind his whiskey eyes.

Pain.

It's not the kind of pain that comes and goes. It's the kind of pain that settles deep. The kind that makes you feel like you're drowning.

I know that kind of pain.

As hard as I try to stop it, my lip wobbles, my reaction visceral.

"Abs, I need you to know my reaction to seeing you pregnant wasn't because of something you did." His voice is rough, taking on a husky tone.

It's incredibly sexy, but there's no room for thoughts like that right now.

I shake my head, swallowing hard. "I don't understand," I admit, and he chuckles, although there is no humour to it. Just bitterness.

"Shit, I don't even want to have this fucking conversation."

His words are like a slap, and I jerk back, instantly throwing up my walls.

"Then don't!" I snap, my feet already moving to flee.

"Wait. Abs. That came out wrong."

He reaches for me, gripping my arm as I try to move past, but I wrench free, heart hammering, my instincts screaming at me to get away.

"I don't think it did," I bite out. "Your words were pretty clear."

Storming off, I don't get far before his strong hands grip my waist and slip around my middle, his large, warm palms settling over my belly. Over my baby.

"Don't run from me, Angel."

His breath fans across my ear, and for a moment, I relax back into him.

It's instinct.

It's what I crave.

To melt into him.

To believe him.

But I have more than myself to think about now. I can't let my emotions dictate how I handle things.

"Abs, please," he rasps, his lips brushing close to my ear, his beard grazing my skin, making my breath hitch. "Remember how you needed to tell me something from your past, but it was so hard? How you really didn't want to take yourself back to that dark place in order to have the conversation?"

I stiffen, because I remember exactly how that felt.

I remember the fear, the shame, the way my stomach had twisted into knots. How I wanted to throw up.

"The reason I don't want to have *this* conversation," Ringo continues, "is because *this* is *that* sort of conversation."

Shit.

The pain in his tone slices straight through my chest.

"But I will, Angel." His grip around me tightens ever so slightly. "For you, I will… if you'll just let me explain."

Shit. The agony lacing his tone matches the pain I saw in his eyes moments ago, and all I want to do is turn in his arms and wrap mine around him and never let go.

But that's my emotions trying to rule me. I need to be smart.

Shifting in his hold, he loosens his grip, allowing me to take a step away to face him, and the moment I see his face, I regret it.

He looks so shattered. Torn. Like he's barely keeping himself together, and hell, it hurts seeing him like this.

Ringo gestures to the loveseat nearby, so I take in a calming breath, and move over to it, lowering myself down and trying to get comfortable despite the thick tension between us.

Glancing around the space, Ringo's gaze lands on the low coffee table Lexi jumped over earlier to get to me, and he moves to it, dragging it closer until it's right in front of me.

Then he sits on it.

It brings us close, his legs manspread, his thighs brushing mine as he rests his forearms on his knees.

God, I've missed him.

I don't understand how that can be. I was with him for a little over a week, yet it felt like a month or longer. Maybe even a lifetime.

For a long beat, Ringo just stares at me. The weight of his gaze makes me squirm, before a warm smile tugs at his lips, but never reaches his eyes.

"When I saw you…" he starts, his voice quiet and strained.

He inhales deeply, as if he needs to brace himself.

Then his gaze flicks to my baby bump, and he clears his throat, preparing to speak again.

"When I saw you pregnant, I didn't see *you* anymore, Abs."

I frown. "I don't understand."

He nods, like he expected that. Like he's already bracing for the next part.

"I didn't see you, Angel. I saw my ex. Kylie."

My eyes widen.

Kylie?

His ex-girlfriend.

It takes me a moment to figure out why, but then it clicks.

"She was pregnant?"

"Yes." He nods, his gaze dropping to his hands, his fingers clasped so tightly I can see his knuckles turning white.

"She was happy about the pregnancy for about five fucking minutes before she realised how it would affect the lifestyle she lived."

"How so?" I ask, and those whiskey eyes lift to meet mine again.

"She had to quit using."

Using?

Oh.

"Drugs?" I ask, just to confirm and he gives me a sharp nod.

"Meth. Coke. When I met her, she just indulged during the occasional party, but somewhere along the way, while I was out on runs, her partying never stopped." He holds my gaze as he speaks, his voice flat, like he's forcing himself not to feel the weight of it.

"I dragged her to rehab three times before she fell pregnant. We'd already broken up, but then one night, I hit the whiskey too hard and woke up with her back in my bed." He clenches his jaw. "I'm a fucking idiot for taking her back, but she claimed to be clean. She seemed better. So I gave her the benefit of the doubt."

He looks away then, breaking our connection, and I hate it.

I could drown in his eyes.

I know I shouldn't think like that, but I'm not strong enough to deny how he makes me feel.

Admitting it and acting on it are two different things, though.

"Kylie fell pregnant that night." His voice grows quieter. "We didn't find out for a while. By then, I'd already booted her to the curb again because she loved lines of coke more than, well, anything. But when she came crying to me, showing me the positive pregnancy test… fuck, I dunno. It changed something inside me."

His dark gaze returns to mine then, and I don't just hear the truth in his words.

I feel it.

"You wanted the baby?" I ask and he nods.

"I wanted the baby. I wanted to be a dad. I wanted to leave the MC, live a simple life with my ma and my sisters. I wanted to do something good for once."

His shoulders tense before he shrugs, like he's trying to play it off, but his voice betrays him.

"I had it in my head that even though I couldn't be a good big brother to Muz, that perhaps, I could be a great dad to my baby."

My stomach twists and dread begins to settle heavily in my gut.

The fact that I didn't see a kid around the club… The fact he's never spoken of one, has me pausing.

Because that can only mean one thing, right?

My voice drops to a whisper.

"What happened?"

I lean forward without realising it, and Ringo takes advantage of my nearness, weaving his fingers with mine.

We're not really holding hands, but we are connected. Our skin is touching, fingers intertwined at the tips. I should probably pull away, but I just can't make myself do it.

I've missed his touch.

I've missed him.

"Kylie couldn't lay off the gear." Ringo's voice cracks a little as he answers my question. "She was skin and bones, much like you'd been when I stole you. Only, her malnourishment wasn't because she was locked away or denied food. It was because she barely ate and pumped her body full of chemicals to stay high."

He blows out a frustrated breath and shakes his head, the truth of his story taking him back to a place I know he never wanted to return to.

"I gave her an ultimatum. If she wanted to stay with me and have the baby then she needed to go back to rehab and get clean for good. Otherwise, she needed to get an abortion and leave me the hell alone."

My stomach twists.

If she aborted the pregnancy, then he wouldn't have reacted the way he did at seeing me pregnant, right? She wouldn't have been showing at that early stage.

"She chose to keep it?" I ask, and he nods solemnly.

"Yes. And she agreed to rehab."

"Did she go?"

"She did." He exhales, and I don't like the way his whole body tenses again before he speaks. "She lasted eighteen days and then disappeared. I searched for her. Followed every lead. Heard rumours about her selling her body for cash or drugs, even while her belly grew with my child inside it."

"Oh my God," I gasp and his lips thin.

The air shifts and our fingers break apart as he leans back, putting space between us. His muscles ripple with tension, his hands curling into fists as his breathing grows shallow. Sharp, like he's holding himself back.

I don't say anything, not wanting to pull him deeper into something he's barely holding together. I already know this isn't going to be a good story, and I'm not sure I'm strong enough to hear it.

"I found her one day after a tip off," he mutters, his tone more chilling than I've ever heard it as his hard gaze returns to mine. "She was in the city gardens… passed out."

He pauses, coughing like he's trying to clear a huge lump in his throat.

"She was fucking passed out in the bushes while a John was fucking her."

My heart stops.

Tears burn the backs of my eyes.

I'm not sure I can hear anymore of this.

I don't want to picture it, but it's too late. I already am.

"All I could see was the bump where my baby was trying to survive inside her, while her legs were spread and her arms lay lifelessly in the dirt."

Tears flood my eyes before spilling over, any control on my emotions lost as Ringo blurs in my vision.

"It wasn't until we got closer that I noticed how deathly pale she was… and that the bump…" He stops. His lips part, but nothing comes out.

I swipe at my tears, angry that they dare fall when this isn't my pain. It's his.

He gulps, and blows out a slow, shaky breath, before clearing his throat again, and I brace myself.

"The bump… it wasn't as big as it should've been."

I stiffen, heat washing over me as fear sinks its claws into my heart.

"JD pulled the guy off her and that's when…"

He leaps up, standing abruptly, his movements sharp and jerky like he can't sit still any longer.

Storming away a few steps, he rakes both hands through his hair, a strangled sound falling from him as he gives me his back.

Pushing to my feet, I hurry to him, reaching out, unsure if he wants to be touched, but unable to stop myself.

"Ringo..." I trail off as my palm presses to his back, not sure what to say.

Should I even say anything?

I really don't know.

Slowly, Ringo turns to face me, and that's when I see it.

Tears.

So many tears, falling unchecked from his broken whiskey eyes.

"My little girl was lying in the dirt next to her." He chokes on a sob, and his words are like a punch to my chest, stealing my breath.

"She was so tiny. So blue. So..." Another heartbreaking sob lurches from him, like he has no more control. "That fucking John had been fucking Kylie while my daughter was still connected to her mother by the umbilical cord."

Oh.

My.

God.

I can't even begin to comprehend his words.

But I have to, because this is real.

It happened to him.

It ruined him.

A broken sob rips from my throat as I lurch forward, my arms flying up around Ringo's neck. He meets me halfway, catching me, lifting me, crushing me into him like he's afraid to let go.

I get it now.

I understand his reaction to seeing me pregnant.

It was a trigger. His mind dragged him back to that day. That place. That nightmare.

I feel his whole body shudder as he cries, the pain radiating off him in waves so powerful they have the ability to drown me.

Anger.

Loss.

Agony.

I fear I'll suffocate from it, but I refuse to let it control me.

"I'm so sorry," I cry, over and over, my hands fisting in his hair, desperate to hold him together, hoping I have the power to keep him from falling apart in an irreparable way.

Minutes pass in tangled grief, our bodies locked, our breaths ragged, our sobs mingling in the space between us.

Eventually, I feel us moving, Ringo carrying me back to the loveseat where he lowers down to get comfy, cradling me to his chest.

I never want to let him go.

The thought kind of terrifies me. I'm sure I used to think the same about Daniel once, and not for the first time, I worry that perhaps I'm someone that falls too hard, too fast, and is too naive to see the red flags until it's too late.

But I know Ringo's red flags. He wears his flaws proudly, and here tonight, he's laid his biggest wound out for me.

Maybe I should stop overthinking and just be in the moment.

Taking in some shuddering breaths, Ringo holds me tighter like he's grounding himself in my presence.

I nuzzle into his neck, inhaling his spicy, masculine scent.

"JD killed the man." His voice is quiet but unshakable, rumbling through his chest. "And I…"

Pulling back just enough to see his defeated expression, I take in his nearly empty eyes.

"You don't have to say anymore, Ringo." I offer him an out. A lifeline. A chance to tuck his nightmare back away.

But he doesn't take it.

"She couldn't live, Abs. Kylie was still breathing, barely. But I just couldn't risk someone saving her after what she allowed to happen, so I…"

He doesn't need to finish the sentence.

I already know.

He killed her.

I don't know if I feel relief or horror.

Maybe both.

Maybe neither.

Maybe… I don't care.

I already know what kind of man Ringo is. I know he's killed before. They were people who deserved it.

And Kylie?

Right now, it feels like she deserved it.

Ringo swallows hard, his voice raw as he speaks.

"Afterwards, I used my knife to sever the umbilical cord, and bundled up my baby girl." His eyes meet mine, pain swallowing every trace of light in them. "There's no record of her birth, or her death. But I named her Hope."

Hope.

My breath catches in my throat.

"That's a beautiful name, Ringo," I whisper past my tears.

Reaching out, Ringo swipes at my falling tears with his thumb.

"I named her Hope because for a short time, while she was growing inside Kylie's belly, she was the only thing that gave me hope of a different future."

Shit.

Fuck.

My heart shatters into a million pieces.

"Her name is even more beautiful now that I know the meaning behind it," I manage to say between sobs, and a slight tug pulls at the corner of his mouth as he nods in agreement.

This is so heartbreaking. The pain he's suffered is unthinkable. I can't imagine it. I don't want to either.

"I buried Hope under the Jacaranda tree on my property," he rasps, his voice so thick with emotion it barely escapes, "and ever since I've forced myself to forget that Kylie ever existed."

A part of me wishes he never had to tell me this story. That I didn't have to hear his pain.

But the other part of me? The part of me that aches for him… well that part is glad for it. Because as horrible as it is, it explains so much about this man.

About the way he carries himself.

About the way he protects those he cares about.

The way he protects me.

As Ringo swipes at my tears again, I reach up and cup his bearded jaw, my thumb brushing over the rough stubble.

"I'm sorry that happened to you, Cameron," I say softly, using his real name.

A flicker of something crosses his eyes. Something I can't quite name.

"You're a good man. You didn't deserve that. *Hope* didn't deserve that."

"Fuck." His chest rises sharply, his breath catching before he leans forward and presses his forehead to mine. "You being pregnant doesn't change the way I feel about you, Angel. Seeing it unexpectedly was a trigger I guess, but now…" His lids fall shut, hiding those intense whiskey eyes.

When he opens them, he pulls back, his gaze shifting to my pregnant belly.

"Fuck, it all makes so much sense now."

"What does?" I frown.

"You feeling sick. Not being able to handle eating meat. Fuck, even how horny you were."

I blanch, heat rushing to my cheeks as I scramble from his lap.

"That's not why I was—"

Ringo smirks, and damn if his eyes don't look a little lighter than they did a minute ago.

"No? Then what made you so horny, Angel?"

I narrow my eyes at his teasing tone.

"It was the orgies."

Throwing his head back, his deep laughter fills the skyline, and damn, it's the best sound in the world.

If all it takes to make him laugh is saying stupid shit, then I'll do it a thousand times over. If I could erase the pain he's suffered, and take away even a fraction of the weight he carries, I'd say the dumbest shit on repeat until he never remembered it again.

But I know that's not enough.

"Okay, *sure*," he draws out the words, patting the loveseat next to him. "It was the orgies."

Poking my tongue out at him, I move back to sit on the loveseat, tempted to tuck myself deep into the cabana-styled shell of the outdoor furniture and hide away with him forever.

I wish.

God, how I wish.

Angling himself towards me, Ringo reaches up and brushes some of my pink strands behind my ear, his gaze dancing from my eyes to my lips and back again.

"I'm sorry for how I reacted that day, Angel. When I was able to calm down again, you were gone." He shakes his head in frustration and hooks his finger under my jaw. "Why did you run? Did you think I was going to hurt you?"

The memory hits like a spear lodging itself into my heart.

His furious face. The tension in his shoulders. I'd been sure he was rejecting me.

And then I remember Wendy, and her cutting hate towards me. The slicing words she spoke.

"He doesn't want damaged goods, Charity Case. You need to fuck right off and take your bastard pregnancy with you. He has no interest in raising someone else's kid."

I swallow hard.

He might not be angry at me like I thought, but she was right. Especially after finding out what happened in his past, Ringo doesn't need this. Me. The worry of an eighteen-year-old, soon-to-be teen mother and her kid.

He doesn't need me, making his life more difficult.

Wendy was right.

I *am* damaged goods.

He deserves better.

"No…" I shake my head, pulling myself back to the present and remembering his question.

He wants to know if I thought he would hurt me.

Do I?

"I don't know." The truth falls past my lips, my voice barely a whisper.

Shifting back to the coffee table, Ringo moves so we're face to face again, reaching for my hand and entwining our fingers. The warmth of his palm seeps into mine, grounding me.

"I'd never hurt you, Angel. Never." His voice is steady. Unwavering.

I nod, because I don't know what else to do.

I understand why he killed Kylie, but also… he killed her and while I don't mind given the situation, I have to think about more than myself.

I have to think about my baby.

I'm so far out of my depth with Ringo and the Southern Sadists. We live completely different lives. Come from different walks of life.

It's not that I think I'm better than him. It's not that at all.

I'm just… different.

He lives in a MC compound with men who spend their days drinking and fucking, and on some of those days, probably killing.

He's so much older than me. A real man, and I'm… well despite the fact I'm about to become a mother, I still feel like a naive girl.

And, in a few months, I'll be having this baby.

A baby that needs a home.

A safe place.

And an MC is not a safe place to raise a child.

As brutal as that truth is to accept, I push down the pain of it and stare into Ringo's whiskey eyes.

"Thank you for coming to clear the air."

He frowns, studying me, brows pulling together as he tries to read between the lines. Then, as my words sink in, those furrowed brows shoot up.

"You're fucking dismissing me?"

7

RINGO

"It's been a long night. I should get some rest."

Is she fucking kidding me right now?

It's been a long night?

The urge to hoist her in my arms and kidnap her all over again is strong.

Sure, I have to get past the Marx fuckers and her friends, but I'll shoot their kneecaps if I have to.

But fuck it, no. I can't do that. She doesn't need a fucking caveman controlling her like that anymore. She needs to feel safe. Like she has some say in what happens.

I just need to figure out a way to convince her.

"You're not safe here, Abs," I point out, my eyes pleading for her to see reason.

"I'll be fine." She waves me off like I'm overreacting, already shifting like she's about to stand.

No way will I let her walk away from me.

Not again.

"No, you won't," I snap, my fists balling as frustration burns through me. "Daniel. Donny. His uncle. They're all gunning for you, and they won't stop until they get you. And in case you missed the fucking memo, over my dead fucking body will I let that happen."

Abbey throws her hands up. Exasperated. "What am I meant to do? Go with you?"

"Yes."

She fucking scoffs.

"Why the fuck are you scoffing at me?" I snap, my patience hanging by a thread.

She stares at me, defeat clouding those caramel eyes.

"You can't keep me safe from them, Ringo. No one can."

"Like fuck!" I slap my hand against my chest, stepping closer. "I'm the *only* one that can."

"He's right."

We both stiffen, our heads snapping towards the intruding voice.

A chick leans against the partition, arms crossed like she's been watching this whole time.

Dark hair. Black lips. A smirk that tells me she knows way too fucking much.

"Lexi asked for his help for a reason, Abbey. And it isn't because he's easy on the eyes."

"Who the fuck are you?" I snap before I can stop myself, already irritated that we're no longer alone.

Abbey shoots me a glare, and the dark-haired girl giggles, her hand outstretched as she approaches.

"I'm Rhys, but you can call me Kitten."

"No, he fucking can't."

The deep menacing voice comes from behind her, a tall man, blond, and fit as fuck, steps around the partition.

Abbey's eyes widen as she leaps up from the loveseat and squeaks.

"Mr Foster."

Mr fucking Foster?

"And who the fuck are you?" I snarl.

The tall fucker just smirks, stepping forward to press his palm to Rhys' still outstretched hand, pushing it down.

Rolling her eyes, Rhys waves him off.

"Shoosh Ty. Let me work my charm."

Ty smirks, before sliding his hand to her back, tugging her into his side.

Okay... so he's not her dad, not that I thought he was since he looks closer in age to me, but he's obviously her fella.

I wanted alone time with my Angel, but maybe a buffer will help.

After all, Rhys was kind of on my side, right? Maybe she can convince Abbey to come with me.

"I'm Ringo," I offer, turning down my fucking psycho for a moment.

"Tyler." The guy nods and when I glance at Abbey, I find her gaping at him.

"Miss Delany. Nice to see you again."

Miss Delany?

Now I'm fucking confused all over again.

Why the formalities?

Why not just call her Abbey?

Rhys giggles. "I'll fill in the blanks for you so you don't have an aneurysm." She flashes me a grin, her black lips stretching in a smile as she juts her thumb at Tyler. "Ty is Mr Foster. Our old sports teacher, and now he's my daddy."

"Jesus, Rhys. Really?" Tyler sighs like he's used to dealing with this kind of shit from her, daily.

Rhys shrugs, unbothered.

"Anyway, back to you." She winks at me before turning at Abbey. "He's a badass criminal. He's not scared of the law, Abbey, and with the way he looks at you, well," she waggles her brows. "There isn't anyone on this Earth that'll fight harder for you than someone in love with you."

"He's not—"

"I'm not—"

Abbey and I say in unison and Ty and Rhys laugh.

"Uh-huh. Okay sure," Rhys snickers. "Let me know when you realise I'm right."

Right?

Is she fucking right?

I've known Abbey for, what? A week before she ran off, so no, this chick is not fucking right.

"Well, now that I've done the dirty work and made you aware of what's clear to everyone else, I'll leave you two to have rooftop makeup sex." She grins unrepentant. "I gotta tell you, though. This rooftop has seen a damn lot of action."

My brows shoot up while a strangled sound falls from Abbey, and I try not to laugh when I see her eyes widen in horror.

"Get your arse back inside." Tyler spins Rhys before slapping it.

While I grin, Abbey blushes so hard she could light up the whole fucking city.

I watch their backs as they leave, waiting until their voices fade before I turn back to Abbey, raising a brow.

"Friends of yours?"

She nods, but then shakes her head, before finishing with a shrug.

"Rhys is Lexi's friend. She was there for her when I wasn't."

Damn. There's so much pain in Abbey's tone.

"Don't forget, Angel, at *that* time, you were also going through your own hell, too."

She offers me a small smile, but it doesn't reach her eyes as she nods, her gaze dropping to her awkwardly shuffling feet.

Fuck.

I hate this.

I feel so out of my depth with this situation. Especially now that I'm not on MC turf. But maybe that's exactly what this situation needs.

Distance from the craziness. Somewhere quiet where we can both find our bearings and try to fucking think straight.

"Look, you don't have to decide tonight," I say, trying to keep my voice as soft as a thug like me can, stepping forward and hooking my finger under her chin, forcing those doe eyes back to mine. "Take some time to think about it. You should be safe here for a bit, but staying in the city isn't a good idea long-term. Too many CCTV cameras. Far too many eyes."

She nods, exhaustion darkening her gaze before she sighs.

"I just want this to be over, but I feel like it will never end."

Her voice is just above a whisper. So small and timid and far too beaten down.

"I promise you, it will come to an end soon enough," I murmur, my voice rough. "I'm sorry I haven't gotten to the list of names you left me yet. The club has been reeling after finding Morris dead in Casey's car trunk."

She cringes at the reminder. That wasn't a pleasant fucking discovery, and it's why she ended up with puke all over her.

"And, there's also been the hours upon hours I've spent scouring the streets, looking for you."

She stiffens. Her big caramel eyes flare, like my words both shock and please her.

"You've really been looking for me?"

"I told you not to run from me, Angel." My voice drops with the reminded anger it caused me. "I fucking warned you there would be consequences."

She rolls her eyes. "And yet, you still haven't punished me."

Fuck.

That little bit of defiance has my cock twitching as heat licks up my spine.

I'm getting hard just thinking about the ways I could punish her. She has no idea what she's inviting.

Sucking in a sharp breath, her sweet scent wraps around me, distracting as fuck.

Shifting my fingers from under her chin, I graze them slowly down the front of her throat, before gently, wrapping my hand around it.

She stiffens.

Her breath hitches.

Her eyes flare wide in panic.

I completely fucking expected it.

I bet those fuckers did this when they raped her. They probably choked her not even knowing the safe way to do it. Or, they
knew and didn't care if they asphyxiated her to death.

Staring into her eyes, I hold the connection, and ignore the
way her breathing picks up, and how there's a slight quiver in
her body.

She's scared of me, but also she isn't. Which is probably what
is actually scaring her.

I bet she's asking herself why she's so drawn to me.

How can she be attracted to someone like me?

I know she likes what she sees. I remember the sear of her
hungry gaze in the privacy of my shitty room at the Western. I
remember the feel of her hand wrapped around my cock as she
jerked me off in fascination.

I remember the way she used my fingers to make herself
come.

Fuuuck, I'll never forget that.

Never forget how fucking wet she was… or how she tasted on
my fingers.

So yeah, she's confused.

I'm not the type of guy she should go for. And fuck, I know
I'm probably not the type of man that'll get down on one knee,
propose to her, give her a house with a white picket fence, three
kids, and two fucking dogs.

I let myself believe I could have that once too, but people
like me, we don't get the easy life. We don't get the big family
dinners with everyone talking over each other, laughing as food
is passed around.

We don't get the sweet woman who sees all our scars and fucking worships us anyway. We don't get the arms that hold us each night, or the morning kisses that keep us sane.

Fuck.

I want that.

But crims like me. We don't get that.

We live a ruthless life, and die a ruthless death.

Shaking the truth of my reality from my thoughts, I focus on my Angel in front of me.

"Why did you fucking run?" I ask her again, needing to understand what was going through her head. "Why didn't you wait and see what the fuck was happening? Did you really think I was going to hurt you?"

Something in her shifts and I see the warrior in her rise to the surface.

Her chin lifts, stretching her neck as she leans into my hand, even as her eyes turn glassy.

"I didn't understand what was happening," she admits, her voice quiet yet strong. "I'd been lying to you. I kept the pregnancy from you and everyone else."

My grip tightens slightly, but this time she doesn't flinch. She doesn't react.

"I was biding my time until I could figure out what to do, because the truth of it is, I don't know who the father is. However, I *do* know the father is a vile human, but it could be any of the six arseholes that…"

She trails off, her throat bobbing against the press of my hand as she swallows hard.

She can't bear to say the words, so I make her.

Giving her neck another little squeeze, firm enough that she feels it, I remind her, from that action alone, that I won't let her run from this.

"Say it."

Her lip trembles, and she takes in a shaky breath, but when she speaks, her voice is firm and sure.

"The father could be any one of the six arseholes that raped me."

Good girl.

"So you don't know who the father is. What does that have to do with you running from me?"

She looks at me like I'm an idiot, scoffing in frustration. "I chose to keep this baby, Ringo. I chose this baby despite the fact it was created in such vulgarness and violence. I'm not foolish enough to know people are going to think I'm crazy for doing that. Why would any sane person willingly have the baby of their rapist?"

Easing my grip on her neck, I let my hand slide to her nape, fingers tangling in her hair. Fisting the strands, I tug slowly, tilting her head back just enough that she has nowhere to look but at me.

"What does your choice to have this baby have to do with you fucking running from me?"

"What do you mean?" she cries out, frustration cracking her voice. "I thought you took one look at me and were furious that I lied. That you knew there was no way you'd want to be involved with someone in my condition."

My jaw clenches so hard my teeth ache.

"Why the fuck would you think that?"

Her expression shifts, confusion swallowing her anger, "Wendy said…"

"Wendy? Wendy said fucking what?!" I yell, probably a little too loudly, but she doesn't flinch back. No, she does the opposite, pulling against my hold of her hair, getting right in my face, caramel eyes flashing with something fiery and fucking unbreakable.

"She said you don't want damaged goods or have any interest in raising someone else's kid. And then she said…"

Red hot rage pulses through me like a fucking live wire.

"Abbey, I swear to fucking satan if you don't tell me what that bitch said, right fucking now, I'll kidnap you all over again." I lean in impossibly close, my voice dropping to a deadly rasp. "And this time I'll keep you chained up."

Angry tears dampen her eyes, but despite them, her chin lifts in defiance. "Do it."

Fuck.

"Don't fucking tempt me, Angel." I tighten my grip just for a second, knowing her scalp must be burning from the pain. "Now tell me what she said."

Her hands come to my chest, shoving me away, my fingers barely releasing her hair in time to not fucking hurt her.

But she's angry, furious. So fucking alive with the emotion of it that it sparks something inside me.

Mine.

Fuck. I want to keep her.

Trying to walk off her rage, Abbey starts pacing, her body wired tight, her breaths coming too fast.

Her fury is like a wildfire, and I can't say it's a bad thing.

She's going to need it.

Some days it'll be the only thing that keeps her standing.

"Angel." I warn again, waiting for her to fucking tell me what that bitch of a woman said to her.

Wendy had been in my bathroom with Abbey when I found them. I'd thought it was weird at the time. I'd wondered why Wendy had turned to me with smug satisfaction written across her face before she spoke.

"I thought you should see this."

Fucking bitch was practically frothing at the mouth to throw Abbey under the bus. Not only that, Wendy fucking knew what I'd been through with Kylie. With Hope.

So she fucking knew my reaction wouldn't be good.

She fucking knew it would trigger me.

Fuck.

"She said if I don't run, then you will kill me."

I stiffen at Abbey's words.

"She. Said. Fucking. What?"

Abbey throws her hands up again.

"What was I supposed to think, Ringo? You went crazy. All my fears came true right before my eyes, and all of a sudden, I didn't feel like a single person in that place would fight for me, so I ran. Okay? I ran like a coward, but you know what, I'm not trying to keep *me* alive. I'm trying to keep my baby alive. I'm trying to do the right thing for him or her because they deserve a chance at life."

I'm vibrating with so much anger, I can't see straight.

I'm ready to kill someone.

Not Abbey.

Never Abbey.

But Wendy? Fuck, yeah, I could kill that bitch in a heartbeat.

Wendy better be fucking gone when I go back to the Western, or that cunt will fucking wish she'd never been born.

Spinning, I give my Angel my back, because I don't want her to see the fucking rage written across my face and think it's directed at her.

Linking my fingers behind my head, I pace past the partition to the high ledge of the rooftop and look out over the city.

Everything is a fucking mess. It's my fucking job to deal with it, but I can't fucking fathom dealing with anything but Abbey right now.

I can't explain it. I don't understand the pull she has on me. I get that I'm all kinds of fucking wrong for her, but I can't bring myself to walk the fuck away.

"Cameron?"

Fuck.

The way she says my name. My real fucking name. It does something to me.

Dropping my hands to my sides, inhaling deeply, I try, and fucking fail to calm down.

"For over three weeks I was scared you would find me." Her voice is soft behind me. So fucking broken that I feel it burrowing inside my chest. "But I was also scared you wouldn't even try."

I turn.

Because that?

That fucking wrecks me.

As she stands with the evening breeze kicking up her hair, her arms wrapped over her bump as she curls into herself like she's trying to hold herself together, I know, without a doubt, that I'll do everything it takes to protect her and her child, even if it kills me.

"The moment I realised you had run, I was out looking for you." The words leave me like a confession. "And I wasn't looking because of any favour to Lexi. I was looking because I fucking care about you. I was looking because I was terrified something bad would happen to you. That those fuckers would get their hands on you and do all of those…" I choke on my own fucking words, not able to say the horrendous things my mind conjured up that could have been happening to her while I couldn't fucking find her.

Dropping my chin to my chest, I fight for control. I fight back fucking tears. Tears I haven't let fall since the day I buried Hope.

Until tonight.

Abbey's small booted feet step into my line of sight, and I glance up to see her right before me.

"I'm sorry I worried you." Her fingers tremble slightly as she hooks them with mine. "All I'm trying to do is keep my baby safe."

My eyes drop to her bump, watching how her other hand rubs over it protectively.

Fuck.

I understand that need.

So fucking much.

"Then let me help you keep him or her safe." I flick my gaze back to her caramel pools. "You don't have to *be* with me. I know lines got blurred in my motel room, and I probably shouldn't have acted on the way I fucking crave you, but I can be man enough to control myself around you if it means keeping you safe."

Her lips part as a silent breath rushes from her.

"You crave me?"

I smirk, just a little, some of my worry falling away because, fuck, I'm touching her.

Nodding, I lift our entwined fingers and press my lips to the back of her hand, hovering there for longer than I probably should. "I crave you in ways that fucking scare me, Angel."

Her brows shoot up at that.

"Do tell."

I chuckle, shaking my head. "Now's not the right time."

She sighs at the reminder, her gaze drifting to the rooftop door.

"I should go to my friends."

I nod. "Lexi will be up here any moment, ready to throw me over the ledge if you don't go to them soon."

She smiles. "She's pretty pissed at you."

"Yeah well, I let her down."

Her smile fades.

"It's all my fault though. All of this is my fault." She huffs, shooting a worried glance at the rooftop door.

"Nope." I shake my head. "No more thinking like that, Angel. We're all here fighting for you because we care. That's what happens when you need support. Your family and friends rally to help."

Her expression shutters slightly.

"I don't have any family here." Her voice is flat, but I just grin.

"Don't you?" I tilt my head, watching her. "Because when I saw you and Lexi earlier, I could have sworn you were sisters. Just remember, it's not just blood that makes someone family."

Her eyes shine.

"Stop it. You're going to make me cry again."

I chuckle. "Okay, I'll stop, as long as you promise not to forget that everyone here tonight cares about you."

"Fine." She rolls her eyes, giving me a glimpse at her playful side. "I guess you should go back to the Western now?"

I scoff, even as I gesture to the rooftop door. "Nope. Where you go, I go."

"But I'm staying here with my friends."

I nod. "Then I am too."

"Ringo. I don't think that's a good idea. The guys… Well, I'm sorry to be blunt, but I don't think they like you."

Throwing my head back, I laugh as we start for the door.

"Angel, I don't particularly care whether your teeny bopper friends fucking like me. All I care about is your safety. I'm not taking my eyes off you for a fucking second."

"What about if I have to pee?" she asks, and I smirk down as I pull open the door.

"Like I said, where you go, I go."

"Like fuck!"

The words barely register before a fist slams into my face.

8

ABBEY

There's so much blood. And that's not even the scary part.

It's Ringo. How his eyes darkened so much that I could no longer tell that they were brown anymore. Instead, they were nearly black as his muscles bunched, stalking after Marcus like he was going to rip him apart.

"Keep him the fuck away from me, Peter, or I'll fucking kill him!" Ringo's voice booms as we step inside Ayden's dad's apartment.

If it wasn't for Griffin and Devon stepping in as they loomed in the passage near the lift, watching everything unfold, I'm almost positive my childhood friend would be dead right now.

"Just try it!" Marcus snarls, straining against Ayden and Garrett as they hold him back. "I'm not scared of you!"

"Is it bad that this is turning me on?" Rhys' voice cuts through the chaos like a party grenade, all heads snapping in her direction, locking onto her with glares. "Okay. I guess it is." She shrugs, completely unbothered.

I'd laugh if I wasn't terrified someone was about to get murdered in front of me.

"Let's all just calm down." Ayden's mum, Andrea, steps into the middle of the room, lifting both hands in a calming gesture.

"Agreed." Lexi's voice carries over the tension. "All this dick swinging can't be good for Abbey's stress levels. Or the baby."

As if her words are laced with magic, the energy shifts, and the guys in the room start to relax, nodding as the reality of the situation sinks in.

I take that as my cue.

"Marcus, what the hell?"

His brown gaze shoots to me, worry etching lines into his forehead.

"He's controlling you, Abs. I saw the way you responded to him up on the roof. You're being manipulated."

"Oh please," Ringo scoffs, holding a wad of tissues to his nose.

I have to admit, I'm surprised Marcus punched him, and with such force.

Ringo isn't a small man. He's tall and built like a weapon, packed with muscles I didn't even know could exist on the human body.

He also has dangerous energy surrounding him. You can't look at him and wonder if he's a lethal man or not. It's visible in every part of him.

My face heats as Marcus' words echo in my head, but before I can come up with a response, Rhys beats me to it.

"Marky Mark." She strolls up to him, unfazed by his tension, and reaches up, brushing his mussed brown waves back off his forehead. "Baby. He's not trying to control her. He's her daddy."

"Jesus," Garrett mutters, gripping the back of his neck awkwardly as his eyes shoot to Ayden's mum in discomfort.

"Ahh. We should get you cleaned up," Peter interjects, clearly feeling just as uncomfortable with the conversation, gesturing to the passage off the kitchen.

Ringo grunts, giving him a nod, and the tension in the room doesn't disappear. It shifts.

Stepping aside, my friends make a path for him as Andrea speaks up.

"What do you need? I can get the first aid kit."

Ringo stills, only a few steps past Marcus, Garrett and Ayden, before turning back to face me. Slowly, he lowers his hands from his bloody nose, a trickle of blood trailing down, catching in his beard.

Even through the mess, I can tell he's smirking.

"There's only one thing I need." His voice is a low rasp as he lifts his hand before crooking his finger. "Be a good girl, Angel. Come and clean up your daddy."

My mouth falls open as I stare at him, but before I can react, Marcus lunges.

Ayden and Garrett leap into action again, yanking Marcus back before he can land another hit, and through it all, Ringo doesn't even flinch, his hard stare still zeroed in on me.

"Really?" I quip, raising a brow, and he nods.

"Really."

My eyes flick to Lexi's to find her smirking, her amusement contagious as my lips kick up in a grin.

I have no idea what's happening between me and Ringo. He was asked to protect me, but somewhere along the way, it turned into something else.

I don't know what that something is. But even as my mind scrambles for clarity, my body moves forward, ignoring the burn of Marcus' gaze as my other friends watch on with curiosity.

Taking my hand as soon as I am close enough, Ringo leads me down the passage and into the small bathroom.

My head is spinning as he locks us in, the bright white tiles surrounding us feeling too stark for the mood.

"Was that really necessary?" I ask, crossing my arms over my chest.

He nods without hesitation, moving to the sink and leaning closer to the mirror, checking out the damage.

"Ayden's cousin has a mean right hook." He wipes some of the blood away, examining his nose. "Not mean enough, though. My nose is still straight and barely bleeding now."

I roll my eyes. "You're such a brute."

He chuckles.

"So you want me to help patch you up?" I step up beside him, checking the damage in the mirror.

"Nope," he mutters in response and I stiffen.

Shifting to face him, I frown. "No? Then why did you bring me in here?"

Turning on the tap, Ringo leans down, washing the blood from his nose and beard.

So, I wait. Patiently, I might add, leaning back against the bench so I don't have to look at my own reflection in the mirror.

I got a glimpse already, and I really don't like what I see.

These clothes are not me.

I don't actually mind the pink tint in my hair. It's already faded a lot since I first did it, and in a few more washes I bet it will hardly be noticeable.

Even so. What I see isn't me.

Shutting off the tap, Ringo dries his face using a hand towel before finally turning to me.

Widening his stance, he crosses his arms over his chest, his eyes raking over my face, my hair, and then down my body.

It's like he's seeing me for the first time tonight under these bright, unforgiving lights.

"You remember how you were wearing my hoodie and didn't want to take it off, but couldn't explain why?"

I frown at his question, nodding slowly.

"I remember."

"Well, I need you in here with me for the same reason." He unfolds his arms, stepping closer and crowding me against the vanity. "I can't explain it. It doesn't make sense. I just know that's what I need."

Reaching up, he pinches a few of my pink strands between his fingers before running them down to the ends.

"You look really beautiful with pink hair, Angel."

I can't breathe.

Like I actually think my lungs have stopped working.

"I'm not sure the clothes are you though." His smirk breaks the moment, and finally, I remember how to breathe.

"I hate the clothes. So bloody much."

Ringo chuckles. "Let's see if Lexi has some you can borrow."

I scoff.

"I doubt Lexi has anything that'll go over my fat tummy."

Ringo growls. "It's not fat." His gaze drops to the bump between us. "It's beautiful."

My cheeks burn and my gaze drops to his lips, remembering the times he kissed me. The way he kissed me. The way he owned me.

My tongue darts out, wetting my lips and my gaze shoots back to his, to find him studying me.

He knows exactly where my mind just went.

Would he kiss me again if I asked?

A loud thump on the door shatters the moment, and Ringo takes a step back, irritation flashing across his face.

"Stop fucking like rabbits and get out here, Ringo. We need to talk strategy."

My brows shoot up and Ringo mutters under his breath, something that sounds a lot like *'fucking Devon'* before he reaches for the door, jerking it open.

"Fuck off, Devil."

Devon grins, leaning lazily against the door frame.

"Naw, don't be like that. You can get your dick sucked later."

Ringo tenses, his fists balling, his body coiled like it's gearing up to swing.

Before he can do anything of the sort, I shove past both of them, going back out into the main living area.

The room isn't as crowded with my friends now, only Jared and Dee remain, sitting at the round dining table with the two blonde women, Bec and Amanda.

Griffin is here too, leaning against the kitchen island, swigging from a beer.

"Where's Lexi?" I ask, moving towards Jared.

"The others are back down the hall in the other living room." Jared smirks. "Well most of them are. Rhys said she needs to service Marcus to help get rid of his pent-up anger."

Griffin chuckles at that, as Ringo and Devon join us in the kitchen, and all eyes turn to Ringo.

"She stays with me. That's non-fucking-negotiable."

His voice cuts through the room like a blade, and Jared sneers.

"How about we let Abbey decide?"

The tension thickens as Dee stands from her chair, before calmly lowering herself onto Jared's knee.

The action is a silent message. Don't start another dick swinging contest.

"I think that's a great idea," the taller blonde woman, Amanda, cuts in. "Abbey. You're still in a lot of danger. The fact that Daniel's friend Donny is the nephew of a corrupt cop makes your situation ten times worse." She glances around the room. "We've all shown our hands tonight. The fact that the Marx brothers were there will imply our involvement. And simply just seeing Devon's involvement will cause trouble."

My brows shoot up, and I turn to Devon who smirks and winks.

Cheeky bugger.

"Devon is known for making victims of abusers disappear so their attackers can't find them," Bec explains, reading the confusion on my face. "He has a safe haven for women and children. In fact, one of Ian Allen's old girlfriends is hiding away thanks to Devon, so Allen's going to start looking into him again."

"I'll have to stay away from Hell for a little while longer I guess." Devon smirks, like being on a corrupt cop's radar is no big deal. "I wouldn't want to lead those fuckers back to my palace."

Hell?

Palace?

This guy is weird.

Very easy on the eyes though. But still, he seems a little crazy to me.

"I'll give my staff a heads up that the Red Room will likely get raided," Griffin adds, and my heart sinks.

These people are going to pay for helping me.

"That's probably wise," Amanda agrees before glancing at Devon. "Feel free to take Ian Allen on a wild goose chase."

Devon grins, wickedly. "My favorite kind of chase."

"As for you two." Bec's firm tone has me glancing her way to see her glaring at Jared and Dee. "What the hell were you thinking?"

"That's what I'd like to know," Griffin mutters before tipping his head back to get the last dreads of his drink.

Jared smirks and Dee rolls her eyes before she starts moving her hands around in what I recognise as sign language.

Huh. Did I know she could communicate through sign language?

I don't think I did.

"Jesus, fuck. How are we meant to know what she's saying?" Devon whines, and Jared snarls.

"You're not. Shut the fuck up."

"Griff!" Devon growls. "I swear to God if you don't pull Crow into line I'm gonna put a bullet between his eyes."

Before anyone can react, a knife flies through the air, embedding deep into the plaster wall right next to Devon's head.

I gasp, my eyes wide as I look back to see Dee ready with another knife, body tense, standing next to Jared.

What the hell just happened?

Everyone is silent. Devon chokes on his own saliva before coughing, pointing a sharp finger at Dee, but it's Amanda who speaks first.

"You know she never misses, Devon. Consider yourself lucky. That was just a warning."

I stare, my mouth opening and closing like a fish. Am I awake right now?

"Uhhhh," I clear my throat. "I appreciate all the help, and I'm sorry it's going to cause you all trouble, but if you don't mind, I'm just going to sort this out with Ringo."

Bec and Amanda nod, as Dee puts her knife away and returns to Jared's lap like nothing just happened.

What. The. Hell.

"I will keep Abbey safe." Ringo's voice breaks through my haze. "We'll leave the city. I'll talk to my Prez and work out a few things…" he frowns, pausing. "Where the fuck is JD?"

"Doing a perimeter sweep and checking the security on-site." Griffin rolls his eyes. "I told him this is a Marx owned building, but he still doesn't fucking trust my word that it's secure."

Ringo grins. "The Southern Sadists are fucking thorough."

"Yeah, yeah." Griffin waves a dismissive hand. "We still have an open investigation into the warehouse breach, so we'll see how fucking thorough your club is then."

Ringo rolls his eyes.

"Let's not get off track." Amanda reminds them, and I sigh, feeling the weight of exhaustion dragging on my limbs like dead weight. "Do you know where you and Abbey will go?"

My heart flips at the thought of Ringo and I going somewhere. I don't know why. What do I think will happen? He'll fall madly in love with me and we'll live happily ever after?

That's a load of BS. That stuff doesn't happen.

Even as I think it I consider Lexi and Ayden. Rhys and her... five guys. And Jared and Dee.

But I'm not *just me* anymore. I come with a baby. A baby created in hate and brutality. No one wants an emotionally damaged single mum. No man wants to raise another man's child.

"I have an idea of where we'll go," Ringo's voice is gruff as his gaze dances to me. "But that'll stay between me and Abbey. The fewer people that know, the safer she'll be."

The Angel sisters nod, and a few more words are exchanged before they leave with the Marx men.

Ringo's gaze catches mine, his expression softening, and it's obvious he's noticed how tired I am.

Without a word, he leads me back to the others where Lexi has set up mattresses on the floor for her and Rhys, while the guys have built their own makeshift beds out of cushions and blankets throughout the living room.

The moment Lexi sees me, she jumps up.

"Let's get you changed. You can't be comfy in those clothes."

I sigh in relief, because she's damn right I'm not comfy. "I'd love that. Thank you."

Taking my hand, she ignores Ringo's looming presence and tugs me back out into the hall, leading me to the open door at the end.

"This is Ayden's room. I made sure Rhys and Marcus didn't leave a mess behind." She grins before her eyes dart over my shoulder and it falls away. "You don't need to follow her everywhere she goes, Ringo."

Glancing back, I find him walking lazily behind us, his expression neutral, no words in response.

Lexi rolls her eyes, pulling me into the room.

"Bathroom is through there." She gestures to the other door in the room. "I left a pile of clothes for you on the bench. There are a few dresses that should still fit you…" she trails off, her eyes dropping to my bump and her face falls. "Shit, Abs. I wish you'd told me. You must have been so scared."

"I'm sorry," I whisper in response as a lump forms in my throat, taking in her glassy blue eyes. "I wasn't sure how to tell you I was carrying the child of…" I can't finish the sentence because I haven't told Lexi everything. Right now, she probably assumes this baby is Daniel's.

If only it were that simple.

"Was Daniel the one who told your parents that you were pregnant? Is that why they moved up the wedding, because he knocked you up?"

And there it is.

The assumption.

Of course, she'd never even imagine any other truth, since it's so unfathomable.

"Maybe you should sit down, Lexi," Ringo suggests, leaning against the wall with his arms crossed.

My frantic gaze snaps to him as panic coils in my stomach.

I don't know if I can do this again. Take myself back to that place. To put my nightmare into words.

"What's going on?" Lexi frowns, her gaze darting between us.

"I don't think I can say it again," I admit to Ringo, and he pushes off the wall and closes the distance, his big strong hands cupping my cheeks.

"I'll say it if you really can't, Angel." His voice is steady, his touch grounding. "But I really think Lexi should hear it from you."

"Hear what?" Lexi's voice sharpens and panic flickers in her wide blue eyes.

I stare at my best friend. The one who never gave up on me even when I told her to walk away.

She hasn't stopped fighting for me.

If anyone deserves the truth, it's my Lexi.

"Ringo's right. You should probably sit."

Lexi's face pales, and she nods, absently lowering herself to the mattress, never taking her gaze off me.

"Do you want me to wait outside?" Ringo's voice is so gentle it makes my heart hurt with something I don't understand.

"No." I shake my head frantically. "Please don't leave."

"Of course, Angel."

When I glance back at Lexi, her gaze flicks between us, studying how we interact. How we talk to each other.

Ringo moves to a chair at the edge of the room, giving me space to talk to Lexi while honouring my desire for him to remain close.

To think, the first night I met him, I thought he was a real prick.

Ringo can be, I've seen it, but not to me. Not even when he's mad.

How is it that I feel like I know him so well, even though I really don't?

Nervous over the place I have to take myself back to, I start pacing at the foot of the bed, ignoring the way Lexi watches me like she's trying to see inside my soul.

What I'm about to tell her will hurt her, because she loves me. Which is why she needs to know.

"For a couple of months I'd suspected I might be pregnant," I begin, continuing to pace because it's easier to watch the grey carpet at my feet as I walk than look at my best friend's expression.

"I wasn't sure how to confirm it. I couldn't go to the doctor and risk my parents finding out. They never gave me much money, and Daniel was always around. I never had the opportunity to duck into a pharmacy and buy a test."

Blowing out a breath, I risk a glance at Lexi to see her listening attentively.

"I had to steal a pregnancy test," I admit and Lexi's eyes widen.

"You stole something?"

Her shock pulls a smirk from me.

"Yes. From the supermarket. Mum sent me and Maggie in for a few things.

I sent Maggie off to get the milk… and then, I shoved it down the front of my shorts."

"Oh. My. God. Abbey Delany stole something?"

I poke my tongue out at her, but then her smile falls. "That's when you found out you were pregnant?"

"Yes. At home. I did the tests when I was meant to be showering. It's literally the only time my parents gave me privacy. I only took one of the tests, and I didn't even have to wait the full time for the result. It was obvious pretty quickly. I mean, I was already getting a little bump by then."

"Shit. So did you tell your parents or did they see you getting bigger?"

I scoff, shaking my head. "Nope. It was only a few weeks until I was due to leave for Nursing school in the city, so I just kept wearing the baggy clothes and was biding my time, but then somehow, Maggie found the test. She would've had to go through the rubbish to find it, but she did, and then she took it straight to my parents."

My eyes dart to Ringo, his legs manspread and his forearms resting on his knees, silently taking in this part of the story I never shared with him.

"Anyway, we all know what happened that night." I wave a hand in Ringo's direction, and Lexi nods, even though her brows are pinched with worry.

"What aren't you telling me?"

Oh yeah. I left out the part about how I got pregnant.

My teeth sink into my bottom lip as my heart starts pounding a nervous rhythm.

Just spit it out, Abbey.

I clear my throat.

"Any chance you were wondering why Donny Allen and his uncle came after me tonight?"

At that, Lexi straightens, frowning. "I assumed since Donny is mates with Daniel, he was helping him out."

"That's not why." My voice is flat, and her brows hitch.

"Is… Donny the father of your baby?"

I glance nervously at Ringo and he gives me a reassuring nod.

"I'm not sure if Donny is the father. Or if Daniel is, or…"

"Or? Or *what*?" Lexi shoots up off the bed like she's just been bitten by something. "What do you *mean,* or?"

"Well, honestly Lexi… this baby could be Craig's. Or Michael's. Or Tim's. Or even Darnel's."

Lexi freezes. Her eyes are locked on mine, wide and unblinking, and the only reason I know she's still breathing is the way her chest rises and falls.

"Are you saying…" she whispers, her voice barely there.

She can't say the words. Can't even bring herself to finish the sentence.

But I can. I have to. Because it happened to me, and because this is *my* baby.

I said the words earlier, up on the rooftop. I can do it again.

"They *all* raped me, Lex. On my eighteenth birthday. And again over the long weekend in November."

I drop my gaze to my belly, running my hand over the bump as fresh tears finally break free.

"It was the November weekend. That's when my baby was made."

When I glance up again, tears track down Lexi's face, her cheeks flushed, and her face is twisted with a storm of emotions.

Grief.

Helplessness.

Rage.

"Abs…" she chokes on a sob, before her expression hardens, fury overtaking everything else as she whips her head towards Ringo.

"You have to kill them. I *know* it's something you do. I'll pay you."

Ringo's voice is pure steel. "Already in motion, Lex. No need for payment. But first, I'm taking Abbey somewhere safe. Somewhere they can't touch her. Then, one by one, I'll hunt those fuckers down and torture them until they die. Mark my fucking words."

"Who are you killing?"

I whip around with a sharp gasp to find Marcus eavesdropping in the doorway, eyes burning with rage.

"For fuck's sake," Ringo snaps. "Is there no fucking privacy around here?"

RINGO

My lids shoot open with a start as I feel someone watching me, only to find my pretty Angel hovering at the foot of the armchair I claimed as my bed for the night.

"Angel?" I whisper, watching her fingers nervously twist at her sides as she glances over her shoulder to her sleeping friends spread throughout the living room.

When she turns back, the faint light from the corner of the room is enough to show me how anxious she is. Not just from her fidgeting hands, but the tight pull of worry across her brows.

"I can't sleep," she whispers, before sighing and shaking her head. "Shit, sorry. I shouldn't have woken you. It's not your problem."

She turns to leave, but I sit taller in the chair and grasp her wrist, giving it a gentle tug.

A gasp escapes her, but before she can react, I have her on my lap, cradled against my chest as I lean back again and get comfortable.

She remains quiet as I settle us into the recline of the chair, her big eyes peering up at me through the dark fan of her lashes. She's clutching the hem of my t-shirt, the one I insisted she wear to bed, as if to try and cover herself up.

I don't know if this is what she wanted, to end up here on my lap, but it's what's fucking happening. I hated that I couldn't sleep beside her tonight. But as much of an arsehole as I am, I won't be the prick who comes between her and her friends.

Especially after Marcus overheard my admission about planning to kill someone. The nosey, perceptive fucker instantly clocked that something deeper was going on, especially with how rattled Lexi was after Abbey's confession.

Fuck. Hearing the pain in her voice as she spoke the words for the second time tonight nearly wrecked me. I'm not sure why, but it seemed more painful for her to tell Lexi.

Maybe it's because she never reached out to Lexi for help.

"Why can't you sleep?" I ask in a low murmur, and Abbey shifts on my lap, nestling into me, her hand coming to rest on my chest just under the neckline of my cut.

"I don't know. I guess I'm just not used to having so many people around."

I smirk at that.

We are surrounded by her friends.

As soon as Abbey gave Lexi permission to share with their friends what happened to her and her rapists, with the condition that no one talk to her directly about it, her friends rallied. Each one of those fucking fellas was as smothering as Lexi and Rhys, bringing their makeshift beds closer to where Lexi, Abbey and Rhys were to sleep, completely surrounding them.

The exception is Jared and Dee. They seem quite content just across from me in the other armchair, keeping to themselves. But the others? They fucking engulfed Abbey.

The blond cheeky fucker that reminds me of an overexcited puppy even had the balls to start massaging her feet.

Took every ounce of restraint in me to not pull out my fucking gun and shoot him between the eyes.

"Where'd you sleep for the last three weeks?" I ask the question that's been clawing at me for days, wondering if she was alone, on the street, scared… or worse.

"On the lumpy sofa in the dressing room at Leather and Lace."

My brows shoot up at her quiet reply.

"You slept in the club?"

She nods against my chest.

"Every night?"

Another nod, but this time she tilts her head to look up at me.

"It wasn't so bad. I was safe. They've got a TV in there, and Ariel had her boyfriend drop off a pillow and blanket. The women fed me, and Freddie gave me a job cleaning and stuff." She shrugs like it's nothing, but fuck, it's a big fucking deal.

Because I can't fucking hold back, I graze my fingers across her cheek, feeling how warm she is under my touch.

It's too dark to tell if she's blushing. Maybe she is. Maybe being this close to me affects her.

Fuck, I hope so.

I hate that I missed the signs she was pregnant. They were there, I just didn't want to see them.

I hate that she didn't feel like she could tell me, but honestly, I know she would have eventually. And truth be told, I probably would've reacted the same way, regardless, because my head's been fucked up since Kylie. Since losing my little Hope.

"I'm so fucking sorry, Abs. Maybe if I'd told you my own fucked-up baggage, you'd understand why I flipped. Even holding you now, knowing you're safe… it doesn't stop the sick feeling I've been carrying for the last three weeks at not knowing if you were okay."

She offers me a small smile, her fingers playing with the fabric of my shirt.

"I was scared for a day or two, but the girls at the club took me under their wing. Helped me blend in, and made me feel like I belonged. Like I was one of them."

My brows shoot up. "They treated you like a stripper?"

She giggles a little too loud, slapping a hand over her mouth as her wide eyes dart over her sleeping friends.

"Whoops," she whisper-giggles before melting back into my chest. "They didn't treat me like a stripper, silly. They treated me like a friend."

I smile at that. "Guess I owe them a thank you."

"No need. I'll thank them once everything settles down… if it ever does."

"Hey." I pinch her chin gently, lifting her face so she has no choice but to look at me. "It *will*. I fucking promise all of this will all be over soon."

She nods, but her eyes say otherwise.

She doesn't believe me.

And I get it. Everyone she's trusted has let her down.

She doesn't know it yet, but I'm not going to be one of them.

Alright, so *technically* I already let her down when I lost my shit over seeing her pregnant for the first time, but damn… I should get a pass for that. Right? Given what I've also been through.

"What do the patches mean?" Abbey asks softly, and my eyes drop to where her finger traces the small three-lined arrow patch with our club death head beneath it.

"That one means Sergeant at Arms," I say, and her brows shoot up.

"Oh yeah. You're like the enforcer or whatever. Jols told me about that."

"Hmmm. Did she now?"

Abbey rolls her eyes. "Yes, and you'd better not tell her off for it."

My lips twitch into another grin. "It's my job to pull people into line, Angel. Don't think I won't use my authority on you."

She scoffs quietly. "I'm not part of your gang, Ringo."

"Not a gang. A club."

Her eyes narrow. "Your 'club'," she uses air quotes with one hand, "has a name, has an identifying logo, has colours. Sounds pretty much like a gang to me."

"Do you follow football, Angel?" I ask, throwing her off by my abrupt change in subject.

"I guess," she answers warily. "I haven't really followed footy for a couple of years. But before that, I barracked for Essendon."

"Okay, so Essendon is a club. They've got colours. Red and Black. An identifying logo with the bomber jet on it. So, are *they* a gang?"

She grins. "I see where you're going, and no, it's not the same. They don't go around wearing this." She jabs her finger against my one percent patch.

My brows shoot up. I wasn't expecting her to clock that. I mean, it's no fucking secret, but Abbey doesn't strike me as the type to binge outlaw biker docos in her spare time to know what the one percent patch means.

"And how do you know about the one percent patch?" I ask, more amused than anything.

"Charlie Hunnam." She sighs, and I roll my fucking eyes.

"Really? *Sons of Anarchy*?"

She shrugs. "Lexi and I binged it when we were fifteen. She was more into it than me, but when Jax Teller wasn't being an arsehole, I kinda liked him. Just a bit."

I can't fucking help the wide grin spreading across my face. "So you know a little from a fictional Hollywood production. It's very American. MC's operate a little differently here in Australia."

"How so?" She shuffles higher, nestling her head into the crook of my neck.

Fuck. When her hot breath fans over my skin, I get movement in my cock.

"You really wanna know this stuff?" I ask, instead of answering. It's purely selfish, because once she knows, there's a chance she'll look at me differently.

"I do. Will you tell me? Please?"

Shifting so I can see her face, her big doe eyes lock onto mine.

She wants the truth. For me to open up. I barely spoke about this shit with Kylie, but then again, Kylie never asked. She just partied, took what she wanted, and didn't care to understand.

But Abbey… she's not here for the chaos. She wants to know me. Understand what she's caught up in.

"Will you be pissed if I don't tell you?" My eyes drop to her lips. They're so fucking close. I could easily lean forward and claim them.

Fuck, I want to.

Her gaze dims a little. "Not pissed. Just disappointed." She shrugs, and fuck me, I don't want to be another person to let her down.

"Do you know much about cartels?"

Her brows shoot up, and she shifts on my lap again, trying to see my face better.

"Like, drug cartels?"

I nod. "In the US, the cartels are predominantly run by South American outfits. But here in Australia, we're a fucking island in the middle of nowhere. It's a lot fucking harder to smuggle shit in. So most of the drugs come through outlaw motorcycle clubs and a few top-tier crime families."

"Mafia?" she asks, and I grin.

"Not your classic Italian or Russian mobs, but yeah. We have mafia here. Mostly run by foreign nationals."

"Griffin and Devon… are they mafia?"

"They are part of one of the most notorious crime families in this state. So yeah, I'd call them mafia if you want to put a label on it."

Her mouth falls open. "Let me get this straight. Tonight I had dirty cops, mafia, and an outlaw motorcycle club all chasing me?"

"You did, Angel." I nod, and she sighs, her eyes dropping to my chest.

"I don't know if I should feel special or just plain terrified."

"Hey," I grip her chin, redirecting her gaze back to mine. "Terrified is normal, but mostly, you should feel important. Because despite the guns and suits, the Marx men are good people. If I wasn't a selfish prick, I'd tell you you're better off going with them."

Abbey remains quiet for a few long beats, her big eyes tracking over my face, shifting from my eyes, to my forehead, down to my nose, before settling on my mouth.

She licks her lips, and my fucking heart stalls.

Why the fuck does my body have such a visceral reaction to something so innocent? Just the lick of her lips, and there goes my fucking brain.

Jesus Christ. No one has ever knocked me off balance like this girl.

Reaching up, Abbey's fingers graze my longer than usual beard, a result of not fucking looking after myself lately.

"I don't want to go with them," she whispers, her eyes flicking back to mine. "I want to be with you."

"Fuck, Angel," I breathe, leaning forward until our foreheads touch. "I don't know if I'm the better option."

"I don't care. I know it doesn't make sense," she whispers, voice low so we don't wake the nine other teens sleeping in the room, "but I don't feel safe unless I'm with you."

I ease back, cupping her face, our noses brushing.

"You're right. It doesn't make sense. I kidnapped you. Brought you to an outlaw MC compound. Made you sleep in my bed. Threw you into a world of booze, orgies and drugs. And fuck, let's not forget the violence. There's nothing safe about that."

"And yet," she breathes, leaning in closer, her lips hovering over mine, "the only time I've felt safe is with you."

Our breathing grows shallow, lips barely apart, but still not touching.

I should pull away. Should stop blurring the lines. Focus on protecting her, killing her attackers, and then, walk the fuck away.

But the thought of that, of leaving her, makes something in my chest twist so tight, I can barely fucking breathe.

"Angel," I rasp, and a broken sound as small as a whimper escapes her lips, ghosting over mine.

"Please kiss me," she begs, so soft, but still loud enough for every single fucking cell in my body to hear.

"I shouldn't," I whisper back, my fingertips searing where they touch the delicate, smooth skin of her cheeks.

"Why?"

"Because I'm not right for you," I admit, laying out the raw truth, and she leans in closer, so close that even through the roughness of my beard, I feel the lightest brush of her lips as she breathes her next words.

"If you're not right for me, then why do you *feel* so right?"

"Fuck, Abs." I practically fucking pant, needing her like I need fucking oxygen.

If we were alone right now, she'd already be mine.

"Kiss me, Cameron."

That.

Her saying my real fucking name does me in.

A growl rumbles from deep in my chest as I barely stifle it. We're not alone, but that doesn't stop me. I give in, crossing that blurry fucking line, and press my lips to hers.

She moans softly into the kiss, her hands fisting my leather cut like it's the only thing tethering her to Earth. Her tongue brushes mine, and fuck, she tastes like temptation wrapped in innocence.

She's so soft, so sweet under my touch. So fucking pure despite the horror she's been through.

She's everything I'm not. Maybe that's why I crave her like this. Maybe I want to mark her. Ruin her just a little. Know that I pulled her into the dark with me.

My cock is hard. Fucking solid as a rock. I've got no hope of controlling it now. It has a mind of its own and it wants her, even though it's not going to have her, maybe ever. But shit, she is the fucking sun breaking through the darkest storm clouds.

She's my Angel.

I've never been like this with anyone before. Abbey isn't just some piece of arse I want to conquer.

Fuck, she feels like the very air I breathe.

My oxygen.

As our tongues dance, her whimpers fall into my mouth, and I drink in the sound like it's something fucking holy, because this moment, this girl with the fire in her soul and softness in her eyes, is the only place I want to be.

She really fucking is.

I didn't realise it until she ran, but when she did, she took a piece of me with her. And it still fucks with my head how that's even possible when we've only known each other such a short time.

"Oh," she gasps suddenly, pulling back, her eyes wide, a smile tugging at her lips. "My baby just kicked."

This time it's my eyes that go wide, as we both glance down at her belly, hidden under my grey tee.

"He moved?"

She rolls her eyes at me. "You don't know it's a *he*."

I shrug. "Sounds better than calling your baby *it*."

"True." She smiles again, her gaze falling to her hand now stroking over the swell of her stomach.

"Can I..." I trail off, unsure of myself. What the fuck am I doing?

Abbey's dark eyes snap back to mine, brows raised. "You wanna feel?"

"No... that's weird, right? Just forget—"

"You can feel it," she rushes out, and my gaze drops to her bump again.

I shouldn't do this.

It's emotional torture.

What if I touch her and my PTSD kicks in again and I have a flashback?

What if all I see is Hope, lying dead in the dirt?

What if I hurt her?

Sweat prickles along my brow, my heart hammering so fuck-ing loud it's all I can hear.

"Cam, if it's too soon, I totally get it," Abbey whispers, and fuck, her soft voice slices straight through my panic, grounding me.

She's like a siren.

"I would never expect you—"

I cut her off with a finger to her lips. My eyes drop to where I touch her, and she gives me a gentle smile, like she's telling me, without words, that it's okay. That everything is alright.

"I'm gonna touch you now, Angel," I rasp, and fuck, you'd think I was talking about touching her intimately by the way her nostrils flare and eyes heat.

I feel it too, my body reacting like we're about to cross another line.

Sliding my hand away from her lips, I shift my focus back to her belly.

She's not overly big, but it's obvious she is pregnant.

She's undeniably beautiful.

Shifting her hand out of the way, like silent permission, I hover my rough hand over the fabric of the tee before gently pressing it to her.

"You might not feel it," she whispers. "It's obvious to me, but I don't know if it'll be to you."

I remain silent, my hand splayed across her pregnant swell. The sight alone is enough to remind me just how fucking fragile she is.

Then I feel it.

My eyes snap up to hers, and her smile, fuck, it's the most genuine thing I've ever seen.

"You felt it?" she asks, and I nod.

"Yeah. It wasn't strong, but it was there. Unmistakably."

She glances back down, placing her dainty hand over mine.

"I know it's hard to fathom why I'd want to keep him or her... after how I conceived," her big doe eyes flick back to mine, "but I have to give this baby a chance, Ringo. I just *have* to."

"I know." I offer a small smile, knowing she means every word, and knowing she'd do anything to protect that kid. No hesitation.

Abbey drops her head back into the crook of my neck, yawning.

"Sleep, beautiful," I murmur against her forehead, pressing a kiss there, and she sighs, melting into me.

Not even two minutes later, I hear her breathing even out, and my Angel is finally asleep.

"If you hurt her, I'll kill you myself."

The words come from the armchair across from mine, two sets of eyes locked onto me.

Fucking hell. Privacy really is a myth in this house.

I give Jared, AKA Crow, a nod, but he's not really the one I need to be afraid of.

It's the little assassin curled up in his lap, much the same way Abbey is curled in mine. She's the one I need to keep an eye on.

She'd slit my throat in my sleep if I so much as make Abbey cry.

And something tells me I wouldn't even hear her coming.

10

ABBEY

One of the annoying things about being pregnant is that I have to pee more frequently now. It's driving me a little crazy to be honest. I swear I'm peeing more out than I'm drinking, and I can't make sense of it.

Maybe one day, if I'm lucky to do my nursing degree, I'll figure it out. I think I'd like to be a midwife. I feel like I'd be good at that.

Whispering has me hesitating to step back into the living room we all crashed in last night. I can hear Ringo's deep voice floating down the hall from the kitchen. He's talking with Ayden's parents and JD, I think. And maybe Mr Foster.

I still can't wrap my head around that one.

But the whispering inside the living room gives me pause, because I kind of suspect it's about me.

Just the thought has my gut twisting, and it has nothing to do with my baby.

Leaning closer to the door, I try to catch what's being said, and it's Marcus' voice rising above the others that gives away his anger.

"Why would she willingly have her rapist's child?"

The words hit me like a backhand, hard and sharp.

Before I can stop myself, I barge into the room, every fear I had about people's opinions now slapping me straight in the face.

"Tell me you didn't just say that?" I snap, and all eyes whip to me.

All nine of them are huddled on the mattresses in the centre of the room. No doubt, the second Ringo and I left, barely five minutes ago, they started gossiping.

Whispering.

Judging.

"Abs," Lexi starts, standing quickly, but I shake my head, locking my glare on Marcus.

He's someone I thought of as one of my closest friends for years. But I guess my choices burned that bridge, and now here we are.

"I'm not talking to you, Lexi. I'm talking to Marcus," I bite, stepping further into the room like I'm readying myself to face a firing squad.

"I'm not trying to be insensitive, Abs. I just don't understand it," Marcus admits, standing too.

I can at least appreciate his honesty. If he'd made up some excuse about being caught out, I'd never trust him again. But even though I hate his question, I can see the concern etched across his expression.

"Here's the thing. You don't have to understand it. It's not happening to you. It's happening to *me*. All you need to do is support me." I drag my gaze across all of my friends watching on.

"Part of being a friend is looking out for each other, though," Simon chimes in.

He didn't grow up with us, but he's always had a way of making me laugh. Whether it's with one of his really bad jokes, or by taking the piss out of himself. But this serious version of Simon? It's new to me.

"So you think making me feel like shit for making the biggest decision of my life is looking out for me?"

"No." Simon jumps up, leaping over Garrett's legs to reach me. "I'd never want to make you feel like shit for that, Abs."

"Look, I'm not saying I agree with Marcus' opinion that this is wrong," Shaun adds, standing to give his two cents, "but it might help us support you if we can understand how you came to the decision."

I glare at Shaun Bossier, with all his pretty-boy Spanish charm, but right now, it's the first part of his sentence that has my rage bubbling over.

"So you think me having this baby is *wrong*?" I snap, eyes flicking back to Marcus, who sighs and throws a dagger in Shaun's direction.

"I just worry that once you have it, you'll resent it. That's no way to raise a kid."

He's not wrong. It's something I've thought about more times than I can count.

"I'm only gonna have this conversation once. After that, if you still have a problem with my decision, feel free to stay the hell out of my life." I swallow hard, trying to clear the golf ball sized lump lodged in my throat.

Now is *not* the time for tears. Now is the time to prove to them, hell, even to myself, that I am more than just a broken girl that needed rescuing. That I'm more than what was done to me.

I *am* strong. I know that now.

And they need to see it too, if they're ever going to believe I can be a good mum to this baby.

Stepping over the bodies on the mattresses, Lexi moves to my side and takes my hand. "You don't have to explain anything to me, Abs. I'm with you, no matter what."

Dammit. Here come the tears.

No.

NO!

Back off, you salty little buggers. You don't belong here.

Giving my hand a squeeze, Lexi rests her head against my shoulder, while Rhys leaps up and comes to my other side, offering me a smile.

"I've always wanted to be an aunty."

I can't help but smile back.

This girl is quirky as hell, but she's loyal and caring, and I can see why Lexi adores her.

Turning my attention back to the boys, and Dee, who doesn't seem to be paying much attention, yet I get the feeling she's watching every single move and taking in every single word, storing it away in her vault.

"I've thought a lot about what I should do. For weeks, I knew I was pregnant, well before I could confirm it. And in that time, I've asked myself over and over whether I should go through with it... or abort."

Marcus slowly lowers himself back down to the mattress, his brown eyes glued to me like I'm the only person in the room.

"Not that I could've aborted," I continue. "Not without asking my parents for help, and we all know how that would have gone. Especially with my mum trying to force me to marry Daniel, even after I told her what he did. I didn't tell her about all of them, but she knew what Daniel was doing, and still, she was adamant that I marry him."

My cheeks flush with shame, and I shuffle my feet, my flight mode testing my resilience.

What happened to me isn't my fault, I know that. But shame lingers, carved into my bones, etched into my soul like it's permanent.

"So yeah, I was on my own. And I knew I'd have to go through with it unless I tried to abort it myself. But you know what? I never once looked up how to do that. Not once. I never really considered it. I just knew I was going to have this baby, whether I wanted to or not."

Lexi gives my hand a squeeze as my voice wobbles. It's hard saying this stuff out loud. For so long, it's been just me and my own thoughts, running loops around each other.

"So what are my options then? Would I give my baby up? Keep it and raise it alone? What if my little baby resembles his or her father? What if every time I look at my child, all I see is my rapist?"

I pause, clearing my throat, pushing my emotions down deep where they can't touch me right now.

"The thing is, it doesn't matter the way I conceived this baby. What matters is the life I choose to give him or her that means *everything*."

"But the father..." Marcus blurts out, and I glare at him.

"Means nothing." I slap my free hand against my chest. "*I* am this baby's mother. It doesn't matter who the father is, because *I'm still the mother*, and I will love this child with all of my heart and raise it right, without any taint from a sperm donor who's gonna be dead soon enough."

A few of the guys look surprised at that last part, but not Marcus.

Even if he's not on board with me having this baby, I know he'd tear Daniel and his scum mates apart with his bare hands if he got the chance.

"So the question is, can *you* put your feelings aside and support me, Marcus? Or is this where we part ways?"

His face falls, and shit, there are even tears in his eyes as he steps over his mates, beelining straight for me.

"Parting ways is not an option, Abs. Never. I'm just worried about you. But if this is what you want, then count me in."

He pulls me into a hug, and I sink into it, his familiar scent wrapping around me like a memory, taking me back to simpler times. Back when it was just me, him, Lexi and Jared. Back when dreams still felt possible.

Back before everything turned to shit.

In a matter of seconds, I'm wrapped in a full group hug, everyone but Dee and Ayden.

They are the newer additions to my group of friends, and I guess their part in this is really just supporting the ones they love, since they hardly know me.

Still, I have to give it to Ayden. He arranged for us to stay in his parents' city apartment. He didn't have to do that, and yeah, it was most likely to keep Lexi happy, but I'll take it.

A throat clears from the doorway, and we all break apart. Ringo and JD stand there, filling the frame like giants, rough and rugged compared to my cleaner cut friends.

Hmmm. When did I start preferring the rough-around-the-edges look over clean cut?

"Andrea wants to take you to a private clinic to get a full checkup," Ringo announces, and my brows shoot up as I glance at Lexi, whose eyes widen with excitement.

"She's a nurse and has solid connections," she beams. "It's a great idea."

Nodding, I turn back to Ringo to gauge if he thinks it's a good idea too, but he just lifts a hand and crooks his finger.

Like the damn puppet I've become, I step away from my friends and move into his space, peering up at him.

"Shower and food," he gives me a wink, "then we go to the clinic."

"I like the sound of the food part." JD grins, peeking over Ringo's shoulder, and I laugh.

I've missed him. Jols too. The Western never felt like home, but some of the people there wormed their way into my heart before I realised.

Wendy though... If I ever see her again, I'll... Well, I don't know exactly what I'll do, but I'll do something.

Maybe.

Surely.

Ugh, who am I kidding. I'm not the type of girl to throw down. Not while pregnant, anyway. Maybe after, though.

Yes. Wendy better watch out once I pop this baby out. I'm coming for her.

Maybe...

Taking my hand, Ringo leads me out of the lounge and up to Ayden's bedroom where he leads me straight into the bathroom and turns on the shower.

"Wash," he commands, arms crossed over his chest as he leans against the vanity.

I lift a brow.

"You gonna step out so I can do that?"

He shakes his head. "Nope."

"But—"

"Nope. Get in."

I scoff, shutting the bathroom door and flicking the lock so no one else can barge in.

Turning back to him, I prop my hands on my hips.

"I'm not showering with you."

He smirks. "No?"

My mouth drops open. "What is going on here?"

His eyes travel down my body, slowly and deliberately perusing me, as I stand there in his oversize tee and nothing else but a pair of undies underneath.

"What's going on is you're having a shower."

I roll my eyes. "I'm not getting naked in front of you, Ringo."

He chuckles, pushing off the vanity, stalking towards me like a predator.

"Aren't you? Why not?"

I back up instinctively, until my spine hits the cold white tiles, before my eyes dart nervously down to the door handle.

"You're not afraid of me, Angel," he rasps, stopping an inch from me. If I so much as breathe, my small bump and boobs will brush his chest.

His words make me pause.

Is he testing me?

Lifting my gaze to his, I catch the smirk tugging beneath his beard.

Am I afraid of him?

No.

Not even a little, but… am I afraid of something?

Yes.

"Expectations," I blurt out, and he frowns.

"What?"

"I'm afraid of expectations." He still looks confused, so I try to explain. "We kissed again last night… and I know you're used to women who… you know… sleep with you easily, but—"

His finger presses to my lips, silencing me.

"I don't expect anything from you, Angel."

I raise a brow, and he chuckles softly, dropping his finger.

"Okay, so maybe I expect you to wash."

"Oh… do I smell?"

He shakes his head. "No. But if I have to keep looking at you in nothing but my t-shirt, I'm gonna need some alone time in here."

Even as my cheeks heat, I can't help but smile. I love how he makes me feel wanted without making me feel pressured.

"Just so you know, I *do* have undies on under the shirt."

His eyes narrow. "Not undies, Angel. *Panties*."

Shit! Now my cheeks are on fire.

"Panties," I breathe, agreeing without thought, and just like that, I'm almost ready to let him touch me again, the way he did in his bed that night. Letting me use his hand. His fingers.

Ringo's whiskey eyes drop to my lips as he leans in closer, caging me in against the wall with one hand braced on the tiles above my head.

"Tell me to leave the room, Angel," he rasps, his breath warm against my ear.

Oh dear lord, how am I meant to do that? I'm aching, probably worse than I was at the Western, and that scares me because I'm not ready to take another man into my body.

As much as I crave that connection, I know I'm not mentally there yet.

Still, I can't find it in me to tell him to leave.

Steam fills the room from the shower I completely forgot was running, making my skin sticky and damp.

"I don't want you to leave, but…"

"But?" he asks, easing back to lock eyes with mine.

"I'm not ready for you to see me naked."

"Hmmm," he hums, grazing the backs of his fingers down my cheek and along my throat. "I'm not ready for that either. When that happens, it'll be somewhere we can't be disturbed."

My heart flips.

"But I want you to know, it wasn't just my heart that ached when you ran from me, Angel. I've got enough pent-up tension filling my nuts to explode a fucking building. I'm looking forward to giving you another show some time soon."

Ooooohhhh. I've missed this side of Ringo. The ruthless man. The same man who told my mum I was his and he'd do with me as he pleased. The very man who shamelessly stroked himself in front of his Southern Sadists brothers and half naked Doxies, all while his eyes stayed locked on me.

Is it wrong to be turned on by that kind of behaviour after everything I've been through?

Maybe.

Or, maybe not, because if there's one thing I've come to appreciate about Ringo, it's that he's open about who he is.

Daniel. Donny. All those vile animals who took from me against my will, they walk through society like they're decent humans. Like they give a crap. Like they are law-abiding citizens.

But really, they are worse than the outlaw members of the Southern Sadists. Because guys like Daniel Stone and Donny Allen hide who they really are.

Ringo? He lays it bare with every word. Every look.

Some might call it crude. Perhaps the old me would have too, because she was a naive little goody two-shoes.

But now? Now I'm drawn to his brutal honesty. Especially when it comes to sex.

If I'm ever going to get past what happened to me, I need that.

I need sex not to be taboo or something wrapped in shame.

Even though I like this version of Ringo, it doesn't stop my breath hitching at his mention of another 'show'.

My mind flashes back to the night he stripped in front of me, hand wrapped around his dick, giving me one hell of a show.

I touched myself under the sheet so he couldn't see, but he knew what I was doing, and the moment he came, shooting his seed over the bed, I came too, for the first time in what felt like forever.

"Angel, what's going through that head of yours right now?"

Dammit. I've been staring this whole time.

Can he see the hunger in my eyes?

"You don't want to know," I breathe, and he lets out a low, raspy growl that makes my knees weak.

"I've got a feeling I do. But since we are *where* we are, it'll have to wait." He pulls me from the wall and slaps my arse, and I squeal as he points to the shower. "Now, get your cute arse in the shower."

I shoot him a challenging glare, and all he does is raise a brow, crossing his arms over his chest, feet planted wide.

"All that look is doing is making me hard, Angel."

I roll my eyes. "At least close your eyes or turn around, or I'm not taking your shirt off. I'll wash in it if I have to, and then you'll be stuck wearing a wet t-shirt all day."

This time, when he growls, it's laced with danger, and I worry he might actually pounce with the way he drops his hands from his chest.

"Get in the fucking shower, Angel. Now."

And with that, he spins around to face the white tiled wall.

I giggle, because this is what I love about Ringo.

He's dominating without making me feel small. If anything, I feel the opposite.

I feel alive.

Desired.

Worshipped.

And the crazy thing is, he's barely even touched me.

God, I've missed him.

Running from him felt like torture. I didn't want to, but I couldn't make sense of what was happening… and Wendy?

Yeah, I've changed my mind. The next time I see her, I'm going to tell her exactly what I think.

While Ringo is still facing the wall, giving me a fraction of privacy, I slip out of his tee and toss it at the back of his head.

He chuckles, dragging it off, but remains facing away, honouring my request.

When I step out of my *panties,* as he likes to call them, I brazenly toss them at his head too before darting into the shower and pulling the door shut, letting the frosted glass obscure my nakedness from him.

"Angel, you're pushing my fucking limits," he growls, and I giggle, already lathering shampoo into my hair.

Looking down at my bump, which seems to be getting a little bigger each day now, I wonder if he'd still find me attractive.

Surely this rounding belly isn't sexy to him.

My boobs, though? He'd probably be into them. They are heavier, fuller than they have ever been. They make me feel womanly. So much less of a teenager, even though that's exactly what I am.

As I rinse off, I hear Ringo talking to someone just outside the door, before he taps on the glass.

"Lexi has left some pants that Andrea ducked out to get for you. You should find them more comfortable than squeezing into the skirts you got from Leather and Lace."

"She did?" I call over the sound of the running water, a wave of emotion rising in my chest from the unexpected kindness Ayden's parents have shown.

"She did. The Mitchells are good people, Angel."

"How did you meet them?" I ask, turning off the tap and tugging the towel down from the top of the screen to start drying myself.

"It was because of Muz. He was deep into gang life. Managed to work himself up the ranks. People were scared of my little brother, and with good fucking reason. He could flip like a switch. Was unpredictable as fuck. Was far too controlling of those under him."

Ringo pauses, and I stop drying my skin for a moment to listen as he clears his throat.

"Ayden got sucked into that world because of a chick he was seeing, and when she died, mainly thanks to my dickhead brother and the hard drugs he pushed on everyone, Ayden lost it and beat him to within an inch of his life."

I shove the door open, towel now wrapped around me, and stare at Ringo in disbelief.

"Ayden did that?"

He nods, his eyes briefly flicking down to the towel covering me.

"He did. I never blamed Ayden for it. Hell, it was deserved, if you ask me. Ayden ended up in juvie for a while... but Muz? He didn't go down for a thing and spent his time plotting Ayden's death. He didn't take well to having his pride hurt."

"Oh my God. Did Muz try to kill Ayden?"

Ringo nods as his eyes flick back down again like me standing in only a towel is a distraction.

I have to say, I'm thankful my baby bump isn't much bigger or the towel may not have fit and I'd be flashing him more skin that I'm ready to expose to him.

"Muz tried. More than once. But I stepped in. That's how I met Andrea and Peter. They had my number on speed dial, and any time Muz went after Ayden, I'd get a call and I'd drop everything to stop that little shit before he could finish the job."

"Shit," I breathe, my brows lifting as I finally notice Ringo's not wearing his leather vest anymore. When did that happen?

He's standing in the steamy bathroom in nothing but his jeans, sitting low on his hips. No shirt, no shoes. Just tanned, tattooed skin and sooo much muscle.

"Eyes up, Angel," Ringo chuckles, dragging me out of my daze with a knowing smirk, and I blink fast, shaking my head.

"Sorry."

God, I feel like a creep.

"Don't be sorry. Just maybe work on your poker face, because the way you were eye-fucking me isn't helping this situation."

That's when he pops the button on his jeans, shoving the denim down to his knees, freeing his thick, hard erection.

I gasp and slap a hand over my eyes as he laughs.

"Sorry, Angel. Couldn't help myself."

He brushes past me and opens the shower door before stepping in and turning on the water.

What's the female version of an erection?

Because whatever it is, I've got it.

I'm hot. Achy. Slick between my thighs. The temptation to open that door and join him is damn near unbearable.

Biting my lip, I stare at the shower, gaze locked on the dark silhouette of him standing beneath the stream of water.

Shit. Even though it's blurry, I can still see enough that I can make out the dark patch of hair between his legs, and the curve of his butt as he turns under the water. I can still see the shape of him.

Oh my... could he see my outline?

My breasts?

My bump?

My arse?

Did that sight make him want me still? Or did seeing it kill the mood?

"I can feel you watching me, Angel," he rasps, and I gasp at getting sprung and spin to face away.

11

ABBEY

S ince sharing the bathroom with Ringo this morning, I've felt nothing but hot and bothered. He knows exactly what he's doing when he teases me. I enjoy it way more than I should. But now, I'm beginning to regret not getting in the shower with him.

"The gel will be a little cold," says the sonographer, a middle aged woman with short, spiky purple hair.

She smiles warmly as she lowers the towel draped across my bump, revealing it to herself, and everyone else in the room.

As usual, my cheeks flush.

At this point, I'm starting to wonder if I've got an underlying medical condition, because surely no one blushes this much and survives.

My gaze darts to Ringo, leaning casually against the wall by the door. The room isn't big, so he's not far, but right now, he feels worlds away, and I don't like it.

Lexi is beside me, holding my hand, and Andrea is standing behind the sonographer, watching on with quiet support.

My heart races as Ringo's whiskey eyes drop to my stomach. It's the first time he's seeing my bump in the flesh, and I can't help but worry he's picturing Kylie, lying in the dirt while some random man…

No. I can't bear to think about it.

"If this is too much…" I start, but Ringo's eyes snap back to mine and he shakes his head, a frown tugging at his brows.

"I'm not going anywhere, Angel."

"Dad can come closer if he likes," the sonographer offers.

Oh.

Shit.

She's not to know Ringo isn't the dad, and my cheeks practically burst into flames in mortification.

"Oh he's not…" I trail off, completely thrown as Ringo pushes off the wall and strides forward, dragging a chair up next to Lexi like he belongs there.

"Yeah, Dad would like."

Wait, what?

My wide eyes dart to Andrea, who is smothering a laugh, then to Lexi, who is grinning like the devil herself.

I blink a few times wondering if Lexi and Ringo planned this given their matching smirks, before I'm distracted by the sonographer pressing the probe thingy to my skin.

All eyes turn to the screen.

It's nothing but black, white and grey at first. Nothing really resembling much until…

"And there's your little bub." The sonographer's words have me blinking a few times to see past the tears blurring my vision.

But I see it.

The shapes… the round of a head. The bud of a nose. And oh my gosh… even lips.

I giggle as a little hand moves, looking like it's waving.

"Holy shit, Abs," Lexi cries. "Look at your little baby."

I laugh through my tears, seeing even Andrea is getting emotional. I look at everyone but Ringo.

I can't.

I'm too scared.

What if I see pain in his eyes? What if I see regret, or even worse, resentment?

"Do you want to know if it's a boy or girl?" the sonographer asks, and all eyes turn to me.

Do I?

I hadn't even thought of that. It's probably something I should have considered. I guess that and thinking of names, but I've been too busy trying to stay alive. Too busy running.

"I don't," I say quietly, clearing my throat. "I'd like it to be a surprise."

She nods, giving me a warm smile, and Lexi squeezes my hand, pressing a kiss to it before she holds my hand out, offering it to Ringo.

I don't know why she does that, but he takes it, and when I finally glance at him, his whiskey eyes are softer than I've ever seen them.

Resting an elbow on the bed, Ringo leans in to press his lips to my fingers. The tenderness of it steals my breath, making me forget a complete stranger is currently probing my stomach.

This soft side of Ringo is almost jarring.

We barely know each other.

I'm eighteen. He's thirty-three. That's like fifteen years difference.

He walks on the wild side and brushes shoulders with criminals. I go to church and confess my sins to a congregation of perverted men.

We're polar opposites.

Fire and water.

Chaos and calm.

And yet… we've been thrown together. A broken girl and her dangerous protector.

On paper, in society's eyes, we don't make sense.

So why does it feel so damn right?

Why does Ringo, holding my hand during my first ultrasound for a baby that isn't even his, feel like the safest place in the world?

It makes no sense.

Should I care?

Probably.

Is this just another heartbreak waiting to happen?

Most likely. Nothing good lasts, right?

But maybe… just maybe, the good things, no matter how fleeting, are still worth having.

"Let's listen to the heartbeat," the sonographer cuts through the emotions swarming through my head, and I don't even get a chance to respond before the room fills with a fast-paced, rhythmic thump-thump-thump.

Holy shit! That's my baby. That sound! It's my baby's heartbeat!

A laughing-sob falls from me as Lexi wraps an awkward one-armed hug around me, pressing her cheek to mine. At the same time, Ringo gives my hand a gentle squeeze, and when I glance at him, there's no mistaking the smile tucked beneath his bushy beard.

Happiness. Pure and raw.

Something I haven't felt in so long, I almost don't recognise it.

But it's good, and this moment is everything.

It's the confirmation I needed to solidify my decision to keep this baby.

I will have him or her.

I will raise this baby on my own, and never let myself dwell on how it came to be.

The sonographer does some technical stuff, taking measurements and letting me know that the gestation is around twenty-four to twenty-five weeks, but that bub is a little smaller than they'd like.

That turns into a discussion on prenatal vitamins, eating properly, and all the things I haven't been able to do.

And just like that, the lightness drains from me.

I've already let my baby down. He or she is smaller than they should be.

Andrea and the sonographer keep chatting about my care, but I zone out, sinking under a feeling of self-doubt.

Am I really the right person to raise this baby? I'm already doing such a bad job.

"Can we have some privacy please?" Ringo's voice cuts through my spiral, and my attention snaps back to what's happening in the room.

His eyes are on me now, sharp, yet worried, and everyone in the room gets up and exits, leaving just the two of us.

"What's happening inside that head of yours right now?"

I frown at his question.

"I don't know what you mean."

"You were glowing just a minute ago, Abs." He wheels his seat closer, taking my hand between both of his. "Then it was like someone turned off the light in your eyes. Tell me what changed."

I don't want to say it.

I don't want to give it breath, but shame creeps back in, familiar and cold.

"Angel. Don't make me demand it."

Part of me *wants* him to demand it. To pull that submissive side out of me so I don't have to be the one responsible for admitting to the thoughts running through my head.

But, I also don't want that to be the foundation of whatever this is between us.

Every time I can't find the courage to speak my truth, do I really want to rely on him to force it out of me?

No, I don't want that, so I lick my lips, draw in a calming breath, and shift my gaze to my still exposed baby bump.

"What if... what if I'm making the wrong decision for this baby?" I ask, too scared to look at Ringo. Too scared I'll find the same uncertainty on his face. "I'm already failing this baby. I should have gotten medical help sooner. He or she is too small. I haven't fed my baby enough. I haven't protected it enough."

This time, I can't stop myself. I glance at him, and shame hits hard as tears fill my eyes.

He's already shaking his head, his features softening with a kind of gentleness that cracks something inside me, and he reaches up and brushes his fingers over my cheek, swiping at the salty drops.

"Angel, just the fact that you're worried about this proves you're the right person to be this baby's mum. It's the good mums that always think they aren't doing enough."

A sob slips free as I press my hand to his over my cheek, leaning my head into his touch like I need it to breathe.

"How do you always know exactly what to say?"

He scoffs. "That's not the right thing to say. That's just the truth, Abs."

Abs. I swear I could melt every time he says my name like that.

"Why aren't you running?" I whisper, and he frowns, sitting taller which puts far too much space between us.

"Why would I need to run?"

I stare at him for a long moment, tears still clinging to my lashes.

Ugh. I'm so sick of crying.

Is it a pregnancy thing? The hormones? Is that why I'm so emotional?

Maybe. Maybe not.

"I'm having a baby," I deadpan, and he frowns, nodding slowly like he's struggling to follow my train of thought.

"I know, Angel. I can see that." His gaze flicks to my bump before returning to my eyes.

"I'm eighteen… and having a baby. A baby that's a result of being raped."

He growls, his eyes turning dark with anger.

"I am *very* aware, Angel."

"Then why…" I shake my head, swiping at my cheeks. "I guess I'm just trying to understand what you're doing here. I mean, I know you're trying to protect me, and I do appreciate it, but…" I trail off, and he arches a questioning brow.

"Have you already forgotten what I said last night on the rooftop?" he snaps, clearly annoyed with me.

"I haven't forgotten," I admit, and he narrows his eyes.

"Are you sure? Because I told you I went looking for you because I *care* about you, Abs. *I care.* I told you that I crave you."

"Yes, I know but—"

"But what?"

Jesus. Is he really going to make me say it?

Fine.

Whatever.

"Look, I'm not saying there's anything between us. I don't know the first thing about relationships. But I don't really understand what *this* is." I gesture between us. "And since I'm going to be a mum soon, and my life will no longer be mine anymore, I don't get why you're here… holding my hand while I get my first ultrasound. Telling the sonographer you're the dad."

He smirks. Like this is some kind of joke, but it's not.

There's no humour in this for me. Just pain. The deep, dragging kind of pain that sits heavy in my chest, squeezing until I wonder if my heart is going to stop beating altogether.

"Yes, I said I was the dad, because the sonographer looked like she was about to start asking questions. Questions you don't need."

"So, you were just lying to protect me," I murmur, mostly to myself.

I mean, it makes sense. There's no way after such a short time he'd actually step in and claim my baby as his with the intention of taking care of it too.

Not that I need him to.

I know I don't need a man in my life to be a mum, but the truth of it is, if I'm ever to have a relationship with someone ever again, I'm not just me anymore. I'm me *and* my baby.

Us.

I have to remember that. Not just for my sake, but for my baby's.

"You know it's more than that," Ringo snaps me out of my thoughts, his voice low and sharp.

When I meet his eyes, I notice a war going on behind them.

His dark brows are drawn tight, jaw ticking beneath his beard like he's struggling to hold something back.

"I'm here because I fucking *care*, Angel. I don't know anything beyond that."

He fucking cares.

If I had to guess, I'd say he's just as confused as I am about whatever this thing is between us.

"Okay," I whisper, letting it be enough for now.

If he wants to protect me, I'll let him. Even if it's just for the sake of my baby.

Relaxing back in his seat, Ringo's eyes drift down to my bump. The gel has been wiped away, but my bare skin is still exposed, the towel sitting low, barely covering my panties.

"Can I touch it?"

My brows shoot up, and when our eyes meet, whatever he sees in my expression makes him smirk.

"I mean your tummy. Just to be clear."

I stifle a giggle, my lips tugging into a closed-mouth smile, and nod.

Rolling his eyes like *I'm* the one being inappropriate, he places his large hand over the swell of my stomach and his lids flutter closed, as if feeling the life growing inside me, skin to skin, just knocked the air out of him.

"Are you thinking about her?" I whisper, unsure if he wants to talk about Hope ever again.

I want him to, though.

Hope was… *is* important to him, and he should speak of her. Remember her. Even if he never got to know his little girl, she still matters.

"No… Yes…" His lids flicker open and his gaze shifts back to me. "I'm sorry. I don't know why I lied. Habit, maybe."

"It's okay."

Reaching out, I slide my fingers through his thick, unruly hair, which, just like his beard, has grown untamed since I saw him three weeks ago.

He really hasn't been looking after himself… because of me.

"You know, it's okay if *this* is too hard." I gesture to my bump. "I don't expect anything from you. The baby… Well, it's a lot."

"It's not too hard, Angel. I just wish the circumstances were different. I fucking *hate* knowing what you've had to endure."

I sigh at his words, because yeah, we've both been through hell.

Our experiences may have been different, but we've both suffered unimaginable pain.

"I feel the same way about you…" I clear the growing lump in my throat. "What you told me on the rooftop last night. I'm so sorry that happened to you."

He offers me a warm smile, and chuckles. "We are a fucking pair, huh? Damaged goods."

I giggle, liking that he can joke about it, even though it's still heartbreaking.

Running his hand gently over my bump, he leans forward and presses his lips just below my navel. My breath catches, the intimacy of it sending heat surging through me, and his eyes flutter closed, like he's savouring the moment.

Before I can even figure out what to say or do, the door flies open.

"Oh, fuck, sorry, I…" JD freezes like a deer caught in head-lights, eyes wide as he stares at Ringo, who lifts his head from my stomach and glares over his shoulder.

"What is it?" he snaps, and I can tell by the way JD is looking everywhere but at me with his lips twitching, that he's trying not to laugh.

He probably has no idea what he just walked in on, but since it's also none of his business, neither of us rush to explain.

"Ahhh… thought you'd want to know, our spotters reported seeing the Stone and Allen kids nearby."

I stiffen.

Daniel and Donny are nearby?

How the hell did they find us?

12

RINGO

I insisted on driving Andrea's bloody mum van back to the apartment. It wasn't that I doubted her driving skills, but I knew if we ended up being followed or chased, I was the one built for that shit. Not a nurse who'd worry about hurting others on the road.

Sure, I don't *want* to hurt bystanders, but I'll do what I have to in order to protect what's mine.

We make it back to the apartment without any issues, but I'm fucking wired, certain the longer we stay in the city, the higher the chance that Officer Allen and his corrupt pig mates will show up and raid the fucking building.

"The instructions are in the bag." Andrea smiles at Abbey, handing over a bag filled with information and some prenatal vitamins the sonographer and doctor recommended.

Given Andrea is a nurse and knows the doctor running the private clinic, they worked together to gather everything Abbey will need while I was busy in the sonographer's room, staring at Abbey's stomach.

Fuck.

My first instinct was to bolt, because the second I saw her bare skin and the swell from her baby growing inside, I was hit with memories I've fought hard to bury.

But then I shifted my focus to my pink-haired Angel, watching the sonographer with wide, nervous eyes, and I couldn't fucking leave.

"Thank you for your help." Abbey gives Andrea a small smile, and Lexi hugs into Abbey's arm as we travel up to the apartment in the elevator.

"Anytime, hun," Andrea smiles warmly. "And if you ever want to know anything about nursing, if you decide to go ahead with training in that field, just ask."

"She'll be going ahead with it," I cut in, and two annoyed stares hit me hard.

Lexi and Andrea.

Abbey just rolls hers.

Back inside the apartment, we're swarmed again by Lexi and Abbey's friends, everyone dying to know how the scan went. I hang back, leaning against the kitchen counter with Ayden and Tyler, itching for this interaction to be over.

It's not that I don't want Abbey to have this moment with her friends, but we need to get the fuck out of here.

She doesn't know that yet, so I bite my tongue and give her a little more time with her friends.

"If you ever need somewhere to lay low," Tyler murmurs beside me, and I glance over to see he's mimicking my stance. Arms folded over his chest, one ankle crossed over the other. "I've got a house at Redfield Lake. It's across the other side from Griffin's. It's quiet. Private. The Marx crew has eyes and their own covert security cameras all around the lake."

He gives me a one shouldered shrug. "Happy to help, whether it's for Abbey or something else."

"Appreciate it." I nod, understanding why Abbey's friends mean so much to her.

These people, her people, they're her family, the way my club is mine.

"You leaving soon?" Ayden asks from my other side, and I glance at him, now so much more of a man than the first time we met years ago.

"I've gotta get her out of the city," I admit, and Ayden nods.

"You'd die for her, right?" he deadpans, stone-faced like anything less simply won't cut it.

"You know I would."

He watches me for a long beat, blue eyes scanning mine, looking for a lie. But he nods when he doesn't find one.

"If anything bad happens to her, it better be because you're dead and couldn't stop it."

I smirk. "It's always a pleasure, Ayden."

He grins in response.

There's always been this push and pull between us, like he wants to hate me but can't. For a long time, my brother was his worst nightmare. But Ayden knows who I am. He knows I'll do what it takes to protect those being done wrong by.

We watch Abbey and her friends for a bit longer, but then a message comes through from Trunk, notifying me that there's raid-style activity happening at the local precinct, and shit, I know our time is up.

"Cops are likely to hit this place in the coming hours," I inform Ayden, and he nods like he's been expecting it.

I bro-slap him on the shoulder, and offer Tyler a nod before heading for my Angel, who looks so at peace right now surrounded by her friends.

"It's time to go."

Her brows shoot up. "Go?"

"Yeah. Just got word the cops are gearing up for a raid. We gotta move, Angel."

She pales, but it's Lexi who jumps into action, ordering Rhys to grab Abbey's bag and urging everyone to say their goodbyes.

One by one, the fellas hug Abbey. I hate every fucking second of it, but I'll have her to myself soon enough, so I stand a few feet away, arms crossed, glaring daggers at each of them, while forcing myself to remain in place, keeping my fists to myself.

"I'm sorry," Marcus says as he pulls her in close. "I didn't mean to be a prick. I'm just worried about you."

Abbey hugs him back. "Caring isn't a bad thing, Marcus. I appreciate it."

They hug again, longer this time, and I grit my teeth and fucking bear it, waiting for Marcus to step the fuck away from her before Jared takes his turn.

Jared Crowley, Abbey's other childhood friend, and a Marx crew lackey.

He's got a fucking chip on his shoulder, and even though he glares at me as he steps up to my girl and whispers something in her ear, I can appreciate his protectiveness. He cares enough to give a fuck, and that's exactly the type of people Abbey needs in her life.

I don't have to be a genius to know he's promising my death if I hurt her as he whispers in her ear. Whatever he says makes Abbey snort and she slaps his shoulder playfully, before they share a knowing smile and she turns her attention to the girls.

While Rhys hugs Abbey, I glance at my phone, checking there's no new threat headed our way.

Since my MC split up last night, JD has been feeding info to Smitty and Spud, who put spotters out on the streets. They are loyal to our club, some hang-arounds plus some of Riggs' security from the Marx crew.

Meanwhile, some of my club brothers are flying under the radar in our tradie vans, spying on the local police stations, watching to see if Officer Allen shows his ugly fucking mug.

That's how we know they're gearing up for a raid. But Allen is a slippery bastard. We can't be too careful.

"Thanks, Dee," Abbey says quietly, gaining my attention.

The little assassin who doesn't fucking say a word smiles and hands Abbey something.

A knife.

It's a butterfly knife, and Dee shows her quickly how to flick it open, and close it again.

The way Dee demonstrates it is efficient and deadly, but when Abbey tries, it's sloppy and untrained.

I have a right fucking mind to take it off Abbey so she doesn't end up stabbing herself, but that can wait. The last thing I need right now is a group of fucking teen protestors snapping at me.

Lexi is last to hug Abbey, and it's one of those long, lingering hugs you feel long after it's over.

I know that feeling. Feel it every time I visit my ma and have to leave again. And fuck, saying goodbye to Abbey would be the same.

Maybe worse.

The second they break apart, I've got Abbey's hand in mine, dragging her out of the apartment and rushing us into the lift.

"You're scaring me." She clutches the strap of her backpack, so I take it from her and hand her a leather jacket.

It's one we keep handy for Jols, which for some fucking reason, JD had with him.

Makes me wonder what's really going on between those two.

"Sorry, Angel. Just wanna get you out of the city as fast as possible."

She nods, but there's still a crease in her brow as she lets me slide the jacket over her arms, adjusting it as best I can over her growing bump.

"Is someone picking us up?" she asks, glancing at the floor numbers descending on the screen.

"No. JD is down in the garage waiting. We're riding out together."

"Riding?" Her gaze snaps to mine, wide and full of panic. "Like… on your motorcycle?"

"Yeah." I nod, jaw tight, hating how fucking slow this lift is.

"I—That's—No. I don't think that's a good idea."

I raise a brow, watching her stumble over her own panic, and finally the lift dings open.

"We don't have a choice," I deadpan, grabbing her hand and the backpack before pulling her into the garage.

JD is already there, bike rumbling low, and he tosses me the spare helmet he usually keeps for Jols.

"Ringo. I can't get on a motorcycle. I'm pregnant."

Ignoring her, I brush her pink strands off her face and fit the helmet onto her head.

"I know you're pregnant, Abs. Doesn't mean you can't ride on the back of my bike."

"But they're so dangerous…" she murmurs, eyes darting to my ride as I fasten the helmet and pass her the bag.

"Put it on."

She slips it on quickly, and I turn just in time to catch the pair of leather pants JD throws me. Kneeling, I slip them over Abbey's feet, dragging them over the maternity gym pants Andrea gave her.

She's dead quiet while I get her ready, and when I'm done, I realise she's trembling.

"Abs, look at me." I grip either side of her helmet gently, locking eyes through the open visor. "I won't let anything happen to you. I swear I'm a fucking safe rider. I'd never put you or your baby at risk if I wasn't sure I could keep you both safe."

"Where are we going?" she whispers, eyes flicking back to my hog, even though she's clearly not convinced.

"We're going home, Angel. My home."

"Gotta go, man. Pigs are on the move." JD cuts in, and that's all it takes to have Abbey hurrying to get on my bike.

I've had Jols on the back of my bike a couple times. Kylie, too. But Abbey? Fuck. There's something about having her pressed up behind me, her arms locked tight around my waist, fingers digging into my abs, that makes me feel like a real fucking man.

I go over the basics with her. Where to hold me. How to lean with me. And to never fucking let go.

Thank fuck her bump isn't too big yet, or this would be a helluva lot harder.

A minute later, we're tearing through the streets of Melbourne, Abbey's grip tight as hell as we ride. Not that I give a shit if she draws blood. Having her behind me like this is fucking everything.

I'm on edge the whole ride through the city, sure there will be a police blockade waiting around every fucking corner, but within minutes, we hit the freeway heading east, the city fading behind us.

We don't encounter any problems as we head towards the Dandenong Ranges. As time ticks by and the countryside opens up, Abbey's hold starts to relax, and at some point, she rests her helmet-covered head against my back.

Even though I can't see her, I can feel her easing into the experience, starting to enjoy the ride.

The freedom of it is fucking epic. The life I've carved out for myself isn't just about the club and the brotherhood.

It's my hog. The wind tearing past my face. The raw, wild feeling of flying down the road, weaving between cars, heading straight into the sunset.

Fucking poetic, aren't I?

The fresh scent of gum trees and grass has nostalgia wrapping itself around me, making me even more desperate to get home. To see my ma. My sisters. Even the ducks, and just fucking breathe.

A little over an hour out of the city, we wind along dusty roads and thick bushland. My eyes track the hidden CCTV cameras I installed. I don't technically own this road, but the other locals don't care. They let me set up cameras and I pay them to keep watch.

No one slips past them. Not with how they look out for my ma and sisters like they are their own.

Why would they do that?

Money of course. I take care of them.

When Old Joe's brother needed round-the-clock care, I fucking paid for it.

When Darcy next door couldn't afford more IVF rounds, I covered it.

When Andrew and Paul couldn't find a celebrant willing to marry them, I fucking found one.

I look after them, and they look out for what's mine. It's a win-win.

Abbey straightens as we slow, turning off the main road and heading down the long, winding driveway. The big steel gates are shut, and I use my remote to open them, riding through with JD at my side.

As we take the last bend, the thick bushland opens up to a clearing with lush green grass, my house, and a barn coming into view.

I fucking love this place. I worked closely with the builder to ensure it was as fire proof as possible, with rammed earth, solid brick, and structural steel. Plus all the extras someone like me needs like bulletproof windows, explosion-proof security shutters, and a state-of-the-art security system.

Only the best for my ma.

As we pull up in front of the large house, stopping just at the edge of the pond where a family of ducks are enjoying the cool water, the front door swings open, and my sisters, Alana and Millie, come bounding down the steps, grinning wide.

"About time, big brother. I was beginning to think you'd dropped off the face of the Earth," Lani snickers, doing her best to push my buttons as I kill my engine.

"Shut the fuck up, Lani," I mutter as I pull off my helmet.

"I see you brought the riff raff with you," Millie snaps, glaring at JD, even as Lani flutters her fucking lashes at him.

Fucking hell.

My sisters are total opposites in personalities, but both absolute bad arses.

I usually need to keep an eye on Lani to make sure she doesn't land herself in fucking trouble, while Millie, I'm more worried she'll snap and kill someone for looking at her wrong.

Judging by the way she's trying to murder JD with her glare, Millie's my biggest concern out of my two sisters today.

Millie's not a fan of the life I lead, which is fair enough. She's already lost one brother. She doesn't want to lose another, but she knows my way of life is what pays for everything she has.

She's not ungrateful. She just gives a shit about me. I can respect that.

"Good to see you too, darlin'." JD grins at the snark in Millie's tone, tugging off his helmet.

Then he shoots her a fucking wink.

Fucking hell.

I'm gonna have a word with him. The last thing I need is him stirring up my sister.

Lani giggles again, and I catch her twirling the ends of her long dark waves and batting those fucking lashes at him again.

For fuck's sake. I need uglier mates.

"So, who is this then?" Millie asks, honing in on my little leather-clad passenger behind me.

Millie has dark hair like Lani's, but it's shorter and messier. She often ties it back. You could say Alana is the princess and Millie, well, she's more like a drill sergeant.

Reaching down, I give Abbey's thigh a gentle squeeze.

"This is my old lady."

At my words, Abbey stiffens. Millie's brows shoot up. Lani gasps. And JD damn near chokes from laughing.

Fucker.

"Ringo!" Abbey scolds by my ear, her voice muffled through the helmet she's still wearing.

I can't stop the smirk that spreads across my face. We never spoke about this. For some reason, I fucking enjoy catching her off guard.

Hell, even I wasn't expecting those words to come out. But they feel right. Maybe they are just another ruse. Maybe they aren't. I can't fucking tell yet, but it's a declaration I know my sisters will understand.

It means Abbey is my property.

It means Abbey is someone that we protect no matter what.

It means she's important to me. And that's all they need to know.

"Since when do you have an old lady?" Millie snaps, her gaze laser-sharp, already dissecting Abbey.

Striding over to us with all the cocky swagger he can muster, JD helps Abbey down off my hog.

I know the exact moment my sisters clock her baby bump, their sharp gasps are theatrical as hell, but exactly what I expect from them.

"Well, you certainly didn't tell us about this," Millie snaps, but my attention isn't on her. It's on Lani as I quickly dismount.

Her gaze is locked on the swell of Abbey's stomach even though it's partially hidden by the leather, and big fat tears spring to my sister's eyes.

"Lani," I rasp quietly, and her eyes, the same shade of brown as mine, dart to me before she launches herself at my chest, wrapping her arms around my waist.

Fuck.

Hope.

Lani thinks this is my kid.

It makes sense. I just called Abbey my old lady, so it's an easy assumption to think the baby is mine.

It's not common in my club for a brother to claim another man's kid. Especially not this early. A few have taken on the role of a stepdad when the kids are older. Potty trained and all that shit.

I awkwardly pat my sister on her back as she sobs into my chest, blubbering something I can't make out while JD helps Abbey out of the helmet, setting her pink hair tumbling free.

"Do you have a name?" Millie asks, ignoring my glare as she sizes up my Angel.

"Yes, sorry." She nods, offering my sister a small, nervous smile. "I'm Abbey." She glances at me, like she's not sure if she should've used her real name.

I shoot her a wink, hoping it calms her nerves, before she turns back to Millie.

"Hmmm, you seem too sweet for the filth that trails behind my brother."

Abbey scoffs, unzipping the leather jacket. "Normally I'd agree, but the shit I've seen over the last few weeks... Well, let's just say, I think it scared all the sweetness right out of me."

Millie snickers.

Damn. My sister doesn't usually take kindly to strangers, but is it possible my Angel is already winning her over?

"Hang on a sec." Millie frowns, eyes narrowing on Abbey's hot pink tee as she peels off the leather pants. "You mean to tell me he knocked you up, and *then* dragged you into the club's fold? That must've been a real eye opener."

I roll my eyes as Abbey giggles and nods.

"That's enough, Mills."

She just joins Abbey, rolling her eyes at me, but I ignore their tag-team bullshit and turn my focus to my oldest sister, still latched onto my waist.

"Lans." I ease her back off me so I can see her face, and when she drops her gaze, I cup her cheeks so I can get a good look at my little sister.

She's loud, and reckless, and brave as hell, but has the biggest heart of anyone I know,

Well, until I kidnapped Abbey.

"Enough of the tears. It's not what you think."

Lani frowns, the action making her look so much like our dead brother.

"What do you mean?" She pulls back glaring at me before flicking her gaze to Abbey. "Looks to me like you've come home with your pregnant old lady. Is that not the case?"

"Alana May! Give them a moment to breathe. They've just arrived."

Ahhh. There she is.

My ma.

"Hey Ma," I call, glancing over Lani's head as I release her face.

"Get your butt up here and give your mother a hug." She waves me over, her dark greying hair a little messy like she's been busy cleaning or doing something she shouldn't be doing.

Giving Alana's shoulders one last squeeze, I shoot Millie a warning look before climbing the steps, two at a time, to reach my ma.

She's shorter than Abbey, so I have to practically fold myself in half to hug her, pulling her close as her arms squeeze around me. Even with all the muscle I'm packing, my ma's hugs feel a thousand times stronger than I'll ever be.

"Cameron Eugene, I've missed your face."

"Ugh, Ma. Don't call me that," I protest, pulling back as she tuts.

"That's your name. Of course I'll call you that. Don't think I'm about to call you that god awful name your biker buddies use."

"Just Cameron then. Can you lay off the middle name?" I whine like a little fucking bitch, and my ma slaps my arm.

"You don't call. You don't visit. What's a mother supposed to do?"

I chuckle at her dramatics, her hands waving around, her frown serious, but her eyes are nothing but loving.

"Sorry, Ma. You know how things can get in the club, and then with the lock down."

She scoffs. "Those lockdowns are nothing but hogwash if you ask me. A way for our government to control us. I swear it's a test to see how far they can go."

I chuckle because the conspiracy theorist inside my ma's head is always entertaining.

I mean, she could be right. Who fucking knows. Crazier things have happened.

"I'm with you, Mrs Musgrove." JD snickers, and my ma fucking beams at him.

"It's so nice to see you again, Jimmy. How's that little brother of yours? Still causing havoc?"

"You have no idea. I swear that kid is going to be the death of me."

Ma giggles before she shifts her gaze to Abbey.

I watch her studying the woman I've claimed, her assessing eyes turning to me briefly before she holds out a hand towards Abbey.

"Come here, sweetie. Let me get a look at you."

Fuck, I feel fucking nervous. It's like high school all over again, only now I'm a grown arse man, and the woman I'm introducing to my ma actually matters.

I shoot JD a quick look, and then one to my Angel, but she's already moving, walking up the stairs, her smile soft, yet confident despite the way she's white knuckling the strap of her backpack.

"Well, aren't you just a delicate little thing?" Ma says as Abbey reaches her, their hands meeting between them.

"Uh, hi, I'm Abbey."

"Abbey. What a beautiful name." Ma squeezes her hand gently before her gaze drops briefly to the swell of Abbey's bump.

One thing about my ma is that she's not rude. She doesn't like to make anyone feel uncomfortable unless they deserve it and since she doesn't know Abbey, unlike my sisters, my ma is already willing to give her a chance.

"Let's get you inside, love. You must be exhausted after the ride."

My Angel nods, glancing my way.

I get the sudden urge to reach out and take her hand in mine. Pull her close and kiss her.

I don't fucking get it. I've never been into PDA. Not in front of my family.

Club life is different. It's sex, not affection. Territory, not tenderness. And hell, even then, I've abstained mostly, only ever using my own fucking hand to get off in front of an audience.

As Abbey follows my ma inside, my sisters barrel past me, Mills deliberately shoulder-checking me before my phone vibrates in my pocket.

Pulling it out, I pause to check it as JD comes to my side.

"Fuck," I mutter, reading the message.

"What is it?" JD asks, stepping closer as I glance up at my best mate.

"Ayden just messaged. The cops are there now, raiding his parents' apartment."

13

ABBEY

I can't tell if Ringo's sisters like me or not. As soon as I step inside the impressive house made of stone and steel, Lani hooks her arm through mine and leads me in deeper.

I'm awestruck when we enter a generous open plan living, dining and kitchen area, lit by natural light streaming in through the towering windows that must be at least three stories high. With all the sunlight shining in, I expect the room to be hot, but it's surprisingly cool.

Maybe the glass is tinted.

"My brother was talking in riddles before. I couldn't quite make sense of half of it," Lani rambles, leading me to a stool at the kitchen counter before slipping the strap of my bag off my shoulder.

Dammit. I want that back.

I feel oddly protective of the bag. It's all I have, even if most of what's inside isn't even mine.

Lani drops it beside the softest looking couch I've ever seen, before turning her attention back to me.

Glancing away, I feel the weight of her judgement roll over me in waves.

Where the hell is Ringo? I thought he was right behind me.

Glancing back towards the wide hallway leading to the front door, I find it empty.

Did he seriously just ditch me with his sisters?

"So, you're his old lady?" Lani asks, appearing right in front of me.

Did she run back across the room?

"Lana, give the girl some space to breathe," Ringo's mum scolds, and when our eyes meet, she offers me a warm smile before returning to her chopping board, dicing up vegetables.

"No, let her speak. I want to know what our darling brother has gotten himself into." Millie smirks, but there's nothing friendly about it. Her eyes rake over me, my pink hair, my make-up free face, the hot pink tee I'm wearing.

Shit.

The. Hot. Pink. T-shirt!

I was too distracted by the possibility of the police turning up at Ayden's parents' apartment to think fast enough when Ringo said he was bringing me here. I can't believe I'm meeting his mother and sisters for the first time wearing the t-shirt I borrowed from Shandi.

Like my ass?
Imagine it grinding on your lap.
Leather & Lace Gentlemen's Club Melbourne

My cheeks flame as Lani giggles and Millie glares, both of them taking a moment to read the damn t-shirt.

Mortified.

That's the only word for what I feel right now.

Okay, ground. You can open up and swallow me now.

Please!

"Well, I guess we know where he found you," Millie scoffs as Ringo finally strolls in, a frown tugging at his brows.

"And where's that?" he asks, his gaze bouncing between us.

"A strip club, Cam? Really?" Millie crosses her arms over her chest, unimpressed, and Ringo's frown deepens until he spots my tee.

Then he laughs.

"Yep. Apparently I've got a thing for half naked, pregnant strippers."

"Cameron!" his mother snaps, but he and his sisters ignore her.

"She was already pregnant?" Lani squeaks. "You mean to tell me, you made a stripper your old lady and the baby's not even yours?"

She makes it sound like a scandal, talking about me like I'm not even in the room.

Ringo's sisters are confusing me. One second I think they like me, and the next I feel like I'm the enemy, and all Ringo can do is shrug like it's just another typical Friday.

I can't just sit here and listen to this.

The old Abbey would have, but I'm not her anymore.

"Whoa, hold up." I slide off the stool, hands raised. "First of all, I am *not* a stripper. Don't listen to your brother. He's talking shit."

JD bursts out laughing, while Ringo's smile falls.

"You're swearing now?"

"Damn right I am, Mr!" I snap back before swinging my glare at the sisters, who both look like they have a front row seat to a reality show. "If you *must* know, your brother kidnapped me, kept me locked in his room, and then claimed me as his in front of his barbarian biker buddies."

"Hey," JD pouts. "I'm no barbarian."

"He kidnapped you?!" Lani gasps, just as Ringo's mum slams her knife down on the stone benchtop.

"She'd better be joking, Cameron!"

Cringing, I glance at Ringo, and his jaw ticks as he levels me with a glare.

"Thanks for throwing me under the bus, Angel."

"Angel?" Lani echoes, so softly I almost miss it.

Sighing, Ringo pinches the bridge of his nose before raising his hands.

"Everyone just stop. Give me a second to think."

"You'd better be thinking fast, boy. Don't think you're too old for me to give you a good hiding."

Ohhhh. I like Ringo's mum.

"You call her Angel?" Lani is hyper focused on that part for some reason.

"How about we all sit down, and I'll explain the situation," Ringo suggests. "Then you can decide if I still deserve a hiding, Ma."

Biting back my smirk, I glance at his mother, such a petite yet fierce woman giving her grown son *the look*.

I shouldn't find it funny, but watching him get scolded by his mum and bicker with his sisters makes him more real… more human.

It does something to my heart.

"Fine." His mum nods. "Let's all take a seat and hear how my boy plans to worm his way out of this one."

This time, my giggle slips free, and even though Ringo shoots me another glare, there's no fire in it.

His mum heads towards the plush couch, the sisters following behind, but not before Millie slices a finger across her throat at her brother, and Lani pokes out her tongue.

"You want me here for this?" JD asks, and Ringo shakes his head.

"Nah, head over to the barn and get it set up for us. Call Smitty too. See if there are any updates from the spotters on the streets."

"Will do." JD nods, and as he passes me, he shoots me a mischievous wink.

I have no idea what Ringo means about spotters. But the tension in his tone makes my stomach twist.

This mess and all of this chaos is because of me. I hate the thought of anyone suffering for me. It makes me want to crawl out of my own skin.

"I should spank you for being a brat, Angel."

Ringo's hushed, deep voice brushes against my ear as he passes, and I swear I stop breathing. But when he glances back and points to the couch where his mother and sisters are already seated, I gulp.

There's no way anyone looking could miss it. The lump in my throat is the size of a tennis ball, only this time, it's not caused from holding back tears. It's something else entirely, and whatever it is sends a flush over my skin from the tip of my toes all the way up to the crown of my head.

Ringo waits patiently, his gaze never leaving me until I move, joining his family on the couch.

I feel completely out of place. Like maybe he should be having this conversation without me, where judgemental opinions can't break through my walls.

"Abbey wasn't lying. I did kidnap her," he starts, holding up his hands before anyone can jump in. "But before you chew me out, I did it as a favour for a friend. Abbey needed help. She was in a bad situation. She needed to get out fast, and taken somewhere her family and the cops wouldn't find her."

Slowly, three sets of eyes, so similar to Ringo's, slide my way.

"Holy shit. Your hair is actually blonde, isn't it?" Lani's gaze tracks over my pink strands. "You're the girl from the news."

"So she wasn't lying about you taking her and locking her in your room?" Millie asks Ringo, and he shakes his head.

"And that's not my brother's?" Lani asks, pointing to my baby bump.

Instinctively, my hand cradles the swell of my stomach like a shield as I shake my head.

"No."

"Whose is it?" Millie presses, but Ringo cuts in before I even part my lips to reply.

"That part is none of your business. Abbey has been through... a lot, and the people who hurt her are still out there. You will respect her privacy."

"Of course we will." His mum stands, moving to Ringo and giving his arm a squeeze before turning to me. "I'm sorry you've been through such a rough time, sweetheart. I hope your stay with us will be peaceful."

"I'm sorry," Millie snaps, standing, her face contorted in anger. "Is no one gonna mention the fact that whoever's after Abbey might show up here?"

My heart sinks.

She has a right to be concerned. What if I'm putting them all in danger? They don't deserve that.

"Shut up, Millie," Ringo growls, but I'm already standing, shaking my head.

"She's right. I should go."

I barely make it two steps before Ringo's big hand closes around my wrist, his voice a growl, low and rough, not even trying to hide his warning from his mum and sisters.

"Don't you fucking run from me again."

I spin to face him, my jaw clenched tight, letting him see my anger. I'm trying so hard not to lose my shit in front of his mum, but my voice still comes out sharp.

"You know the last thing I want is to be a burden. To put everyone in danger."

"And *you* should know by now, Angel, that I'll do whatever it takes to keep you safe. So how about you let me?"

His eyes are wild, like his monster is lurking beneath the surface, the storm brewing within him barely contained.

"You're kind of bossy, big brother." Lani tuts, which is Ringo's tipping point.

"For fuck's sake! Will you all just lay off for one goddamn minute?!" He explodes, spinning to face them, his face redder than I've ever seen it.

Shit. He's *properly* pissed. Not the haunted, grief-fuelled anger I've witnessed before. This is different.

This is raw frustration.

"I haven't slept in fucking days." He drags his hand through his hair, pulling on the long strands. "Actually, scratch that. I haven't slept in *weeks*," he grits through clenched teeth. "I came here because we needed somewhere to lay low and take a god-damn breath. Can you all just let us do that please?"

Silence.

For a long drawn out beat, no one says a word.

I don't dare look at his mum or sisters. The guilt is already crushing me, reminding me I'm not worth this much trouble.

"Of course we can do that," his mum says softly, stepping up to him and slipping her hand into his.

I stare at them for a moment. At the way she looks lovingly up at him. At the way he softens for her. This fierce man, unravelling with tenderness in front of his mum.

Damn.

Why is seeing Ringo like this so…. attractive?

If I weren't already pregnant, I feel like I would've just con-ceived right this second just from watching the way he respects his mother.

But then, his mum rears back, and brings her hand down hard on his in a loud, echoing slap.

I jump at the sound, dumbfounded as she jabs her finger at his chest, and Ringo gasps… like *actually gasps*… and yanks his hand back, no match for his mother.

"You will do well to remember that I don't tolerate foul language in this house, Cameron." Her finger wags like a weapon in front of his face. "You're more than welcome here, since this is *your* home. But you will show respect and remember we *do not* speak like that around here, Cameron Eugene. Are we clear?"

"Geez, yes, Ma. Did you really have to slap me?"

"You're lucky I didn't still have my knife in my hand, boy."

Oh my...

I suck in my lips, biting down to keep from laughing.

If there's anyone on this Earth who can keep Cameron Musgrove in line, it's his mother.

"Right, well now that that's settled," she forces a smile, regaining her composure and gesturing to me, "why don't you show Abbey around? I'm sure she's going to love it here."

Whiplashed.

That's the only way I can explain how I'm feeling right now.

I still don't know if I'm truly welcome. His mum is being kind, but his sisters? Well, their eyes are still sharp when they fall on me.

I can't blame them. I'm a stranger in their home. They don't know me from a bar of soap, so it's only natural to be wary of me.

As Ringo's mum returns to the kitchen, his sisters leave the room, whispering something to him on their way past. I don't hear it, and honestly, I'm glad. I already feel like such an intrusion.

"Come on, Angel. Let me show you around." Ringo gestures to nowhere in particular, so I nod, quickly picking up my backpack, not wanting to leave it alone given the cash tucked away inside.

As Ringo shows me through his home, I don't say much, my eyes and mind too transfixed on the towering man doing such a mundane, domesticated thing like giving me a tour of his house.

I would never have pictured him in a place like this. It's so different from the rough, banged up filth of the Western. There's so much pride in his expression as he shows me around, a lightness to the way he walks, his shoulders relaxed and at ease.

I chew on my lip, and my eyes fall to his as they move, explaining something about this house that I'm simply not hearing. Not when he's such a distraction. This hulking man, covered in tattoos who rides a motorcycle that I can only compare to a steel road demon with how loud it is and how powerful it felt between my thighs.

Ohhhh. That sounded dirty, didn't it?

I inwardly smirk.

As strange as this sounds, even though I feel out of place, I feel closer to the old Abbey than I have in years.

The old me, she had dreams. She had fun. She didn't have many boyfriends, but that's okay, she had Lexi, and together, they got into mischief.

This version of me that's been dormant for a couple of years, is still alive, still has dreams, but has needs she never used to.

I would have shocked the old me with how fascinated I am by the contradiction walking beside me. The menacing brute wrapped in muscle, who dotes on his mum and probably feeds those cute ducks I spotted out on the pond.

The house is three storeys, and when we reach the top floor landing, I pause by the tall windows, gazing out over the peaceful pond.

The tranquility of this place doesn't match Ringo's energy at all, but maybe I only think that because I barely know him.

Maybe, this is where he planned on raising Hope. Maybe he would have married Kylie. Maybe he planned to quit the club and be a family man.

Whatever the reason, it's a shame his ex was the way she was. She missed out on something truly beautiful by giving in to the drugs.

But what do I know?

All I know is a girl could get used to this.

Is it bad that I want this tour to hurry up and end?

I mean, the house is stunning. Don't get me wrong. But being so close to Ringo again, after longing for him night after night as I tried to sleep on that lumpy couch at Leather and Lace… well, it has that ache returning tenfold. The same ache he helped me with at the Western.

"This is my room." Ringo's deep baritone snaps me out of my thoughts, and I turn to see him keying in a number on the keypad.

"You keep it locked?" I smirk and he nods, pressing his palm to the heavy timber door before pushing it open.

"Absolutely, I do. Can you imagine my sisters? They'd take over my space. Touch my shit. I don't fucking think so."

I burst out laughing, because that is the most brotherly thing I have ever heard.

I know what it's like to have sisters going through your stuff, helping themselves.

God, I miss that.

What I wouldn't give to have little Tahli bugging me about borrowing something.

Maggie, though? She can bugger right off.

Following Ringo through the door, we step into a long hallway that opens up into another living space. There's a small kitchenette and a plush charcoal couch, similar to the one downstairs, but smaller. Cosier. The kind that only fits two people.

My attention shifts to the side of the room where a number of guitars are hanging on the wall. Some are electric. Some are big and others are small, and I think one may be a banjo.

I don't know for certain since instruments have never been my thing but its circular body looks like it to me.

"I don't get much time to enjoy them these days." Ringo's deep voice is right behind me, and I want to turn and face him, but I don't.

Instead, I enjoy the heat of him at my back, so close I swear I can feel his breath on my neck.

It's strange how comfortable I am with him now. A month ago, I would have felt uneasy having my back to him, not able to watch if he was gearing up to pounce.

We'd gotten close back at the Western. I even got intimate with him.

Shit. Is intimate the right word to use when you let a guy touch your… coochie?

"I guess there's not much time for luxuries like playing a guitar when you're with your club." I breathe, my skin prickling with little zaps of static electricity, reacting to every tiny shift of his body behind me.

"Not so much," he agrees, right at my ear, the sound sending a shiver up my spine. "You cold, Angel?"

My cheeks flame, heat licking across them like they do so often when he's around, but I can't lie to Ringo, so I shake my head.

"Not cold."

"Hmmm."

Oh dear God, he's so close. Too close, yet not close enough.

Touch me.

Wait… do I want that? For him to touch me.

He's touched me numerous times since he found me again, but they were nothing but innocent. Not the sort of touching I'm anticipating.

Just this morning we were locked in a bathroom together, and I thought I wasn't ready to have him completely. My body feels ready though. I'm practically on fire, burning for him. His touch. His lips. His… dick.

Shit, is that what I want?

"Turn around, Angel."

My breath catches at his low rasp, and I do what he says, slowly turning to take him in. I have to crane my neck to meet his eyes, and my deep shallow breaths make my breasts brush against his vest.

Staring down at me, his fingers are gentle as they reach out to brush some of my pink strands behind my ear with a gentleness that weakens me.

Then his gaze drops to my mouth.

My tongue darts out to wet my lips, having a mind of its own, and I wait, barely breathing, to see if he's going to kiss me.

His lips part, and his eyes flick back to mine.

"Let me show you my bed, Angel."

14

RINGO

Having Abbey in my personal space is doing something to me. Something I'm sure she's not fucking ready for if I don't get a fucking grip, and fast.

"Oh wow," she gasps as she rounds the corner behind me, her big eyes locking onto my massive bed.

My room at the Western might have been a dump, but here, I live like a fucking king.

Turning away, I hide the smirk tugging at my lips, feeling a little smug that she's impressed by my moody, oversized room.

My four poster bed was custom made to accommodate a big prick like me, and it suits the space with the dark charcoal panels stretching up the wall at the head of the bed, and the gold-framed mirror centred on top. I've imagined Abbey on top of me, riding me, watching herself come undone in that mirror.

Fuck. Now I'm hard.

I should have left her to explore my room alone and made myself scarce out in the fucking barn.

That would have been smarter. Safer.

Instead I'm pacing like a caged lion, because part of me is ready to pounce. Pin her down. Claim her with a brutal thrust.

But fuck, the other part of me, a part I don't fully understand, just wants to hold her. Much like last night in the chair, when she curled up on my lap and fell asleep.

As much as I want to taste every inch of her with my tongue, and hear those soft little whimpers spill from her lips like they did that night at the Western, before everything went to fucking hell… I'd also just be as happy to simply keep her safe and protect her with everything I've got until my last damn breath on this Earth.

See? Fucking confusing.

Ringo, the fucking Sergeant-at-Arms of the Southern Sadists MC doesn't fucking snuggle.

Until now, apparently.

And it's all because of an angel I shouldn't want like I do.

"I take it my bedroom gets your seal of approval?" I tease, biting back my smirk as I eye her again.

"Duh. Who wouldn't like this?" she deadpans, a grin tugging at the corner of her plump lips.

Even though she's still too skinny for my liking, she's filled out more now. The apple of her cheeks are a closer match to her portrait in her parent's house. Her tits… well, they are hard to miss now, the pregnancy obviously contributing to her already plump melons.

And then there's her baby bump.

Fuck.

I've finally stopped seeing ghosts of Kylie's gaunt strung-out face now. And all I see is Abbey. A fighter. A survivor. A mum to be, willing to risk it all to protect her child.

She's fucking beautiful.

As she moves to the bedside table, I watch her scan over the book resting on top, before flicking her gaze back to me.

"Hypothetically speaking, if I were to snoop in your drawers here, am I going to find the same thing I found at the Western?"

Even as the words leave her mouth, her cheeks flare to life with a rosy tint.

She's referring to my fleshlight. Probably remembering how I caught her touching it. How she slid her finger inside it.

Jesus.

"You will," I confirm, my voice low, and those caramel orbs flare as she shakes her head.

"Sorry. That's none of my business. I don't even know why I asked that."

Chuckling, I close the distance, noticing how she doesn't back away. She doesn't stiffen. She even angles herself towards me, like she's welcoming me into her space.

Fuck. I wish she'd retreat. I wish she'd give me a reason to stay away.

"I've missed your curiosity, Angel. Don't hold back with me."

What the hell am I saying?

She *needs* to hold back, because I'm not sure I've got enough strength left to be the decent one.

For a long drawn out beat, she simply stares up at me.

And then, a slight frown puckers her brows.

"What's that for?" I reach up, smoothing it with my thumb.

"I…" she murmurs, then shakes her head, dropping her gaze to the carpet between us.

Submissive.

Shit.

I shouldn't crave the thing that's made her such a victim for so long. But I fucking do. I'm so tempted to tell her to kneel, just to see if she'll do it.

But I won't take that from her.

If she wants it, then she has to be the one to decide it.

"You need me to demand it, Angel?" I growl instead, my voice rough with want.

My pulse is thundering, waiting to see if she'll say yes, but like always, Abbey surprises me.

Clearing her throat as she shakes her head, her big doe eyes lock with mine.

"I don't think I should stay here. Your sister wasn't wrong. I could bring danger to their doorstep."

Okay, so I don't hate her speaking up. Not one bit. I'd like not to spend my time trying to figure out what's going on inside that head of hers, so her honesty is welcome.

"Would it make you feel better if I said, you *don't* have a choice?" I ask. "I've stolen you again, Angel. You can stay willingly, or as my little captive. Your call."

Her eyes burn with anger, but underneath it, there's a flicker of something else.

Desire, maybe?

Hunger?

"Wow. So many options to choose from," she quips, full of sass, and fuck me if it doesn't drag a growl from my chest.

In one swift move, I grip her arms and shove her down onto my bed.

She gasps, wide eyed, but I don't know if it's from the force or the surprise.

"I think we'll go with you being *my little captive*," I growl, wedging my knees between hers, forcing her thighs to part as I cage her in.

"Why?" she breathes, biting her lower lip, drawing my attention there.

Fuck, I want to kiss her again. Bite down on that lip too, and draw blood.

"Because I like it when you submit to me." I lean closer, my voice raspy as fuck. "And I think you *crave* being controlled, even if you don't understand why."

Her lips part, as if she's gearing up to argue, but then snaps them shut, her big doe eyes flickering with uneasiness.

"Is there something wrong with me?" she whispers. "You know… for being like that?"

It's as close to an admission of acceptance as I'm going to get from her.

She knows she's a submissive. I've told her as much. But given the way she was raised, I can see it doesn't sit right with her.

She wants to fight against the way she was brought up. Wants to be something else. Someone else. But honestly? I think it's just who she is. Her mum likely saw it too, and she fucking abused it. Bent Abbey's nature into something ugly so she could control her.

"There's absolutely nothing wrong with you, Angel. You're fucking perfect."

Shit. I need to stop saying what's in my damn head.

Her face softens, lips parting just a little as she speaks a quiet truth of her own.

"I don't know that I'm perfect, but when you look at me like that, I feel it."

Fuck. I want to kiss her.

I want to kiss her, press her into this mattress, and grind my cock against her soaked core until she's begging me to finish what I started.

"Shit," I rasp, leaning in and pressing my forehead to hers, eyes squeezing shut as I breathe her in. Her scent, her breath, the fucking *warmth* of her lips hovering so close to mine.

She's right there.

So close.

I could just do it. Step over the line and…

Rearing back, I shove off the bed, leaving her wide eyed as I put distance between us.

"Bathroom is through there." I point to the open door across the room. "You should find everything you need."

Moving to the wardrobe, I scoop up a couple of sleeping bags and some spare clothes for JD. When I turn back to Abbey, she's sitting up on my bed, her cheeks flushed and confusion etched across her pretty face.

"What are you doing?"

"Grabbing a few things for me and JD," I tell her casually, already moving back into the living area.

"Aren't you staying here with me?" she calls after me, before quickly backpedaling. "I mean… you don't have to. I guess it just seems weird that you'd give up your bed. Because I can totally sleep somewhere else if you want your own space, Cameron.

The little nook under the stairs with the bookshelves is kind of perfect, actually. I can sleep there and—"

I spin back to her, cutting off her nervous ramble.

"You're sleeping in *my* bed. You're staying in *my* room. And I'm staying out in the barn. That's all there is to it."

Her mouth drops open as she frowns.

"But why? Did I do something wrong?"

I shake my head, closing the space between us, the sleeping bags and clothes still clutched to my chest.

"You didn't do anything, Angel. I just think my ma would prefer it this way."

Lies. Fucking lies. I told her I'd never lie to her, yet here I fucking am, lying right to her face.

But what am I meant to say?

If I stay here, I'll fuck you. I'll drive my cock so deep inside you, you'll forget any man has ever touched you.

Yeah, nah. I can't fucking say that.

Abbey isn't ready to be fucked. Not yet. Not like that.

When she decides to part her thighs for someone—and fuck, I hope it's me or there'll be hell to fucking pay—it can't be anything but soft, caring, and worshipping. But eventually, she'll let me wreck her. Let me fuck her hard and rough in a way that reclaims her as mine each and every fucking time.

"Oh. Of course." She nods, her frown still in place, like she's annoyed at herself for not considering what my ma would want.

I'm a fucking prick.

"This is your mother's house. We need to respect her wishes."

"It's mine actually, but yeah, it may as well be hers."

Nodding, Abbey's hands fidget in front of her bump, vulnerability bleeding out of her.

Fuck.

Tossing the stuff in my arms down, I step into her space, cupping her face.

"I'm sorry, Angel. I should've said something sooner."

"It's fine," she breathes, lips twitching into a small smile.

I can't help myself, and graze my thumb over her bottom lip, tugging it down just enough to catch a glimpse of her teeth.

Fuck, I want her on her knees while I do that. I want to watch the tip of my cock press past her lips and—

"What are you thinking about right now?"

Her voice snaps me out of my depraved thoughts, and I blink, as I come back to reality.

"You don't want to know."

She bites her lip. "What if I do?"

"Fuck, Angel. Stop," I growl, dropping my hands from her face and taking a step back. "You're dangerous."

Her grin grows.

"Do you want your sex toy? You might need it," she teases, a wicked glint lighting up her eyes.

"I should spank you for that."

She shrugs. "I'm beginning to think you're all bark and no bite, Cameron Musgrove."

My eyes fucking narrow. "Don't poke the fucking bear, Angel. You might not like the consequences."

Her smile fades a little and she nods. "True. Even so… do you want your thing?" She juts her thumb over her shoulder, gesturing to my bedroom, and I know she's referring to my fleshlight.

"You think I'm gonna whip it out in front of JD and go to town on it?"

She shrugs. "I don't know what you're into. But you did… you know… *wank*," she whispers the last word, "that night in the courtyard in front of everyone, so I figured…" she trails off, not finishing that thought.

"I like to watch JD fuck." I shrug, like it's no big deal. "It's like live porn. But me and my toy? We've got a private thing. She doesn't like an audience."

Abbey's face turns crimson. The flush creeps up her neck, painting her cheeks and bleeding into her temples.

Stepping closer, I lean down, lips brushing her ear.

"She'd love *you* to watch me fuck her, though."

A strangled gasp escapes Abbey's lips as I pull back, smirking at her stunned expression.

"There are snacks in the cupboard," I say casually like I wasn't just talking about fucking a toy in front of her. "Cold drinks in the fridge. I'll restock it later and give this place a clean since it's been left untouched for nearly six weeks." I pick up the sleeping bags and clothes again, straightening, my eyes lingering on her beautiful face. "In the meantime, settle in. Have a bath. Take a nap. You can relax here, Angel. You're safe."

She nods, not saying a word as she stares at me, so I shoot her a wink and haul arse out of there before I give in and strip her bare and eat her cunt for fucking lunch.

I leave out the back door, dodging my ma and sisters. I need a fucking minute so I can switch gears and deal with MC business.

"Update?" I call as I step into the barn, the aircon already on, the chill prickling over my skin.

From the outside, this place looks like a regular barn. Maybe a place for livestock. But inside, it's a biker's paradise.

I lived out here while the house was being built, back before the fucking pandemic shut the world down. The barn is fully equipped, has a number of small bunk rooms, which have on occasion lodged some of my club brothers.

When the lockdowns first started, some of the Southern Sadists hunkered down here, but I wasn't a fan of my ma witnessing my club's chaos. Doxies, booze, and club brothers with zero shame.

Once restrictions lifted, Smitty made it his mission to make sure we were never separated again which is when the Western became our shared home.

The truth is, living twenty-four seven at the club isn't my thing.

Yeah, they are my family, but I'm a solitary bastard. I like space and privacy.

But given the situation, and the fact I didn't have an old lady or kids to keep me away, I couldn't fucking refuse.

How would that look to my club brothers? To our associates?

"Cops are raiding the Western now."

JD's voice comes from behind the bar, and I veer that way, watching him swig on a beer.

"Fuck," I snap. "On what grounds?"

"Amber alert."

I freeze mid-step. "What the fuck do you mean, Amber alert?"

JD frowns. "You know… a kid's been taken."

"I know what an Amber alert *is*, JD. I'm asking what the fuck it's got to do with us?"

I toss the things in my arms onto the old black leather couch and approach the bar.

"They are looking for, and I quote, a young, underage missing teen. Abbey Delaney from Fox Pines."

"The fuck! She's not underage."

"You sure? Could she be lying?" JD arches a brow, and I slam my fucking fist down on the counter.

"She's not fucking lying!"

Even as I say it, the doubt creeps in.

I haven't exactly seen her birth certificate or driver's licence.

"Fuck," I mutter, yanking my phone from my pocket and calling the burner Lexi has.

It rings twice before it picks up and Lexi's anxious voice meets my ears.

"Tell me she's safe."

"She's safe," I snap, always the arrogant fucker. "Now you tell *me* why the fuck the cops are raiding my club under an Amber alert saying Abbey is underage?"

"I don't know," Lexi huffs. "They said the same thing when they raided Ayden's dad's apartment and recording studio. But Abbey *is* eighteen, Ringo. Her birthday is in August. In less than five months she'll be nineteen."

"Jesus fucking Christ. Either Allen's got friends in high places with the ability to forge records, or the Amber alert raids aren't even fucking legal."

JD's phone starts ringing then, and he holds it up to show me, Prez flashing across the screen.

"Gotta go, Lexi. I'll have Abbey call you later."

"Okay, thanks."

She hangs up, and JD accepts Smitty's call, putting it on speaker.

"Hey, Prez. We're both here."

"You reach your destination?" Smitty barks, voice tight like he's been smashing up more fucking furniture.

"We have." I step closer to make sure he can hear me. "Tell me the raid on the Western wasn't too bad."

"Can't fucking do that," Smitty snaps. "Six of our men got hauled away for possession. Darla and Casey got roughed up. And, they *fucking shot Molly!*"

My fucking eyes bug out of my head as JD gasps in a way that sounds more like he has a pussy and not a cock.

"They shot Molly?" I growl, needing fucking confirmation, because surely I heard him wrong and the cops didn't shoot a fucking dog.

"THEY FUCKING SHOT OUR QUEEN!" Smitty roars, and something crashes in the background.

"She's in surgery now," Spud cuts in, our VP taking over. "Allen fired the shot after Molly went for his leg. The bullet clipped her side. Passed clean through, but she lost a lot of blood. The vet and his team are doing everything they can."

"Fucking hell," JD mutters, before Smitty rejoins the conversation.

"Tell me why we are protecting this girl," he snaps. "Why the fuck are we bleeding for a stranger who isn't even club?"

I fucking stiffen.

This is what I've been afraid of. It's why I claimed her as mine.

"What the fuck, man?" I snarl. "We spoke about this. Three fucking weeks ago. I claimed her as mine. You said you fucking liked her. You told me to do what I had to in order to keep her safe."

"THAT WAS BEFORE THEY SHOT MY DOG!"

More smashing echoes through the line, and I rake a hand through my hair in frustration.

"Tell me why my Queen is bleeding out because of a knocked up runaway teen?!"

I. Fucking. Snap!

Snatching JD's discarded beer bottle off the counter, I hurl the fucking thing at the wall with an exploding shatter.

"I fucking *told* you what happened to her, Nate!" I roar, using his real name. "You were on fucking board with protecting her. And now you're fucking backtracking?!"

"I guess I fucking am, given the shitstorm she's dragged us into!" Smitty bellows so loudly that the speaker on the phone crackles.

I glare at the fucking phone, picturing his face and my fist caving it the fuck in.

"I've given this club *everything*, Smitty! You fucking know I have. And now, when I need backup, you're gonna leave me hanging?"

For a long fucking moment, there's a heavy silence before Smitty clears his throat.

"We have fucking rules for a reason. To protect everyone in our club. And now, because of your *little piece of arse*, my whole club is in fucking jeopardy. If I keep backing her as an outsider, our brothers will doubt my fucking ability to do my job!"

His words make me pause, and I run them through my head a few times before responding.

"What the fuck are you saying?"

"You've got two options, man." He clears his throat like he's gearing up to drop bad news. "Toss her aside… or make her yours."

My brows hitch.

What the fuck!

"I *have* claimed her," I point out, and Smitty scoffs.

"You said some fucking words to keep your brothers from copping a fucking feel."

"I said the fucking words to make her my old lady. That makes her part of the club."

"Not enough anymore." His words send my heart crashing into my gut. "If you want our men to rally and lay down their fucking lives for her… If you want to repair the fucking damage done to our club's reputation, then something has to fucking give."

Another crash of what sounds like a glass echoes through the speaker as Smitty's already short tethered temper makes another appearance.

"Because right now, we look fucking weak. Like a loose end they don't fucking need. And all because we're too busy playing vigilante for some nobody, who just led the pigs straight to their front fucking doors."

The phone crackles like it's being moved, and when Smitty speaks again, I can tell his lips are practically pressed to the phone.

"As President, I can overrule her old lady status if she's dragging our club down."

My eyes flick to JD's, his wide with panic as he shrugs.

"Is that what you're doing?" I growl, my fists balled tight on the benchtop, ready to destroy something.

"I will… unless you seal the deal in the one way I *can't* fucking undo."

I frown hard, my mind fucking reeling at what he's implying, but JD chimes in before I get another word out.

"Uh, Prez… can you spell it out for us? We're not quite following what you're saying."

"For fuck's sake," Smitty snarls. "Either marry her. Or bounce her. I want your answer now."

15

ABBEY

Moving quietly through the house, I feel like an intruder as I head towards the sound of chatter, the smell of delicious food coaxing me from the comfort of Ringo's room. By the time I'm one step from rounding the corner into the main living area, I'm tempted to turn tail and retreat back upstairs.

Not because anyone is talking about me, but because of how familiar they all are with each other, reminding me that I'm an outsider.

"What do you think?" Ringo's mother's voice floats to me before his deep tenor follows.

"Delicious, Ma."

Ma.

I've never known anyone who calls their mum that.

Is Ringo from a different background? Australia is a young country, so it's more than possible his parents weren't born here.

And where is his dad? Is he dead? Alive and just not in the picture?

It's another reminder of how little I actually know about the brute who kidnapped me. Which seems strange, considering every time I look at him, it feels like we've known each other for years.

As my thoughts spiral, I sneak a peek around the corner, only to get busted by the man himself.

Those whiskey eyes lock onto mine instantly, and I swear I can feel my heart do a flip inside my chest.

And… cue the blush.

Lexi and I have that in common. Our blushing disorder. And yes, I'm calling it a disorder because it basically rats me out to everyone.

Oh look, Abbey is embarrassed, or humiliated, or angry, or about to cry, or horny.

I bite my lip at that last one, because honestly, it's all I seem to feel when I'm around Ringo.

Horny.

It's just your hormones, Abbey. You're not a deviant.

Ticking his head in that classic *come here* gesture, Ringo waits for me to obey, his brows lift when I don't move right away.

I like annoying him like this. Not obeying him, just because I can.

It's like some part of me knows I can push him, and still be safe.

Like earlier, up in his room when I dared ask about his sex toy. I could barely believe the words flew past my lips, but it's like my soul knows something my brain is still playing catch up with.

Whatever it is, I know I'm safe with him. He'd never lie to me. He'd never hurt me. He'd never force me into anything. Not like my parents did.

I mean, aside from kidnapping me and making me his captive, but that was with good intention. I can appreciate that.

His little captive. That's what he called me.

Why do I like the sound of that?

His words from earlier pop into my head.

"Because I like it when you submit to me. And I think you crave being controlled, even if you don't understand why."

The submissive stuff has me a little rattled, to be honest. Not because I don't like it, but because I really think he's right.

I do like it.

Which is confusing as hell, given what I know now about how I was raised.

The moment Ringo steps towards me, I sigh, pushing my thoughts away, and move into the room. His mother spots me instantly, a toothy smile flashing my way.

"Ahhhh here she is. Beautiful Abbey. You must be starving."

I nod, spotting the massive spread of food across the kitchen bench.

"She loves veggies." Ringo grins, shooting me a wink. "How about meat? Still making you queasy?"

He remembers.

It's such a simple thing, and I don't know why it affects me so much, but knowing he remembers how I'd been struggling to consume meat, sends warmth through my chest.

"Not so much now." I smile. "As long as it's cooked right through, I should be fine."

He looks genuinely pleased to hear this, taking my hand before leading me to the bench. He loads up a plate with marinated chicken skewers, grilled corn, jacket potatoes, and a generous heap of mixed grilled veggies.

The whole meal gives off serious Mediterranean vibes. Not that I'm an expert, but maybe it's a hint at his heritage.

We sit around a large, round table to eat. It's nothing like the Western where you ate off your lap, or squeezed in beside someone at a flimsy trestle table.

This one has a round glass centrepiece filled with floating flowers and tea candles, and is big enough to seat another four people comfortably.

Even with all that space to spread out, Ringo sits close enough that his knee brushes mine under the table, and I enjoy the constant contact.

It's grounding and calming but does nothing to douse the building ache I've had since the moment we laid eyes on each other again.

Despite his nearness, Ringo stays pretty quiet during dinner. His sisters do most of the talking, mostly to JD, and while they glance my way a lot, they don't pull me into the conversation.

I don't particularly mind, too scared they'll pepper me with questions.

I'm guessing Ringo told them to back off, but that doesn't explain *his* silence.

Is he uncomfortable with me here?

Maybe I should've eaten upstairs so he could have dinner with his family without me hanging around.

"I'm sorry. I need to know," Millie says suddenly, her eyes snapping to mine. "If Ringo isn't the dad, then who is? Because if you think you're going to trap him into raising some other man's—"

"That's enough!" Ringo booms, launching up from his seat and slamming his palms onto the table. "I asked you for one thing, Millie! One. And you couldn't even give me that!"

I can't breathe.

"You can do the dishes tonight, Millie," his mum snaps and for a brief moment, I can breathe again, but Millie's not done.

She shoves her chair back, stands, and slaps her own hands down on the table.

"After what Kylie did, do you really think I'm just going to sit here and watch some pink-haired stripper wannabe wreck you too? It nearly killed you, Cam!"

This time, I nearly choke from the invisible boulder in my throat, but no one seems to notice.

"This is *not* the same situation, Mills. Just drop it!" he yells, but she shakes her head.

Finally air rushes back into my lungs, Ringo's unwavering support for me, reminding me that someone cares.

"No. I won't drop it." Millie jabs a finger in her brother's direction. "Because you're about to take her and her unborn kid as your own, and then what? What happens when the baby daddy shows up? Hey?"

"I hope your brother kills him."

The words are out of my mouth before I can stop them, and three sets of shocked eyes snap to me, while JD just nods in agreement. It takes a beat before Ringo finally looks down, realising it was me that said the words.

"Oh sure. So he can go to prison for you, and you run off with his money, or take all of this as your own."

Shoving my chair back, I stand, my eyes remaining locked on Millie since she's the only one in the room brave enough to challenge her brother.

"Firstly, I'd never do that. I know you don't believe me, since I'm a stranger. But perhaps you should have a little more faith in your brother, and respect the choices he makes for his life."

Ringo reaches for my hand, but I step away, shaking my head. I can feel his piercing stare in my peripheral, but I refuse to look at him right now. Not when Millie is the one that needs my attention.

"To answer your question, and I hope it satisfies your concerns, although, I'm sure it will raise many more questions, none of which are any of your business," I take a beat and clear my throat, mentally preparing myself to admit my truth out loud, yet again. "This baby's sperm donor is a rapist. *One* of my rapists. I don't know which one impregnated me, but it doesn't matter. There were six of them. But none of them are, or will ever be, this baby's father."

The silence that fills the room is almost deafening.

With a trembling hand, I lift my half eaten plate of food and finally tear my gaze from Millie's paled expression. My emotions are waging a war inside me, and I'll be stuffed if I let the salty tear demon win this time.

"Your brother saved me," I say, my voice thick again. "He's been protecting me, and despite what happens next, I'll always be so grateful that he kidnapped me from my parents, who were hell-bent on forcing me to marry one of the bastards who raped me."

My eyes flick to Lani, her eyes flooding with tears, before I shift them to Ringo's mother.

"My apologies for disrupting your household, Mrs Musgrove. Dinner was lovely. I'm sorry I can't finish it. I've lost my appetite."

"Abs…" Ringo murmurs softly as I pass him, but I don't look back. Not at him, or anyone else as I carry my plate to the kitchen. Since I don't know where to scrape off the scraps, I just leave it on the bench and quickly slip out of the room.

"I'm sorry," Millie calls after me, but I don't stop. I head straight to the only place I know I can disappear.

Ringo's room.

As soon as I'm through the door, the first tear spills free, but I keep moving, hurrying into the bathroom, to lock myself inside.

There's shouting coming from downstairs, Ringo's familiar boom louder than any.

Staring at myself in the mirror, I really *hate* what I see.

Will I always have to explain myself to people?

Why is it any of their business?

I guess it's not. I could probably just refuse to talk, but for some reason, I always feel like I have to explain. I have to fight for everything I do and every decision I make which seems to disappoint, disgust, or confuse everyone around me.

Maybe I should take a page from Dee's book. Stop talking altogether. Keep my voice in and not share it with anyone. I know it's something that annoys people about her, and they give up trying to get answers from her because she simply doesn't speak to them.

Dropping my gaze from the mirror, I peel off my clothes and run the shower.

It's a huge double shower. I could easily lay down on the floor, it's so long and wide.

"Angel?"

Ringo's voice comes through the door as he knocks, and I freeze, one foot inside the shower as I watch the doorknob jiggle.

"Abbey?"

"I'm taking a shower," I call over the rushing water, feeling a little exposed standing here naked while he's on the other side of the door.

"Can we talk first?" he calls through the timber separating us, his voice laced with concern.

"I'll come find you later," I call, the confidence I had downstairs slipping.

There's a pause for a few long beats, before there's a light thud on the door.

My heart twists like a hand is crushing it as I picture Ringo on the other side of the door with his forehead against the timber.

Shit.

Slapping my hand over my mouth to muffle my whimper, I hold everything in for as long as I can, not wanting him to hear me break again.

It seems to be all I do these days.

Cry.

Shatter.

Fall apart.

"Promise you'll come find me?" he calls after a long while, and even as silent tears stream down my cheeks, I somehow manage to keep my voice level as I call back.

"I promise."

I hold it in for a few more minutes, until I'm sure he's gone, and then I sink to the floor of the shower and cry.

Like *really* cry.

The emotional agony that's been haunting me every minute of every day spills from me, and I try and fail to fall apart quietly. But I *need* to purge it, get it out and hope like hell it doesn't come back.

I'm sick of feeling like such a helpless damsel. I don't want to be that girl.

I don't want to need anyone but myself. I don't want to rely on anyone.

I can't bear to go through the pain of someone failing me again.

But I'll be there for my little baby boy or girl. I will love my baby. Nurture it. Give my bub everything my parents didn't give me and more. And I will do it all on my own.

Somehow. I know I can do it.

I just have to figure out how.

I stay under the raining water for what seems like forever. It's ice cold by the time I drag myself out, and take my time drying off, combing my wet fading pink strands, and digging through my backpack until I find a dress that stretches over my bump.

When I finally go looking for Ringo, the sky outside is streaked with pinks, purples, and oranges as the sun begins to set.

The house is quiet as I pass through the living area, spotting Ringo's mum dozing on the couch with the TV on and the volume down low.

Outside is still warm, but a light breeze hints that it might cool off a little more through the night as we move deeper into autumn.

Over by the barn, I spot JD working on his motorcycle, but there's no sign of Ringo.

"You looking for Cameron?"

I startle at Lani's voice, spinning to see her behind me, a basket propped on her hip with what looks like grapes or some sort of fruit inside.

"Ahhh, yeah," I mutter, suddenly feeling awkward after my outburst earlier until I notice her red rimmed eyes. Has she been crying? "Are you okay?"

She studies me for a moment, and then points towards the rows of vines she must have come from, completely ignoring my question.

"He's spending time with someone special. You might want to leave him alone."

"Oh." My heart sinks at her words.

I don't know who he's with, but it's clear she doesn't want me encroaching.

When I part my lips to speak, she turns and walks away, her behaviour, paired with her sister's from earlier, adding to how unwelcome I feel here.

As unwanted as I feel, I don't feel unsafe, which is the only reason I haven't tried to leave yet.

I need to be smart, for my baby. So for now, I'll endure their judgement.

Glancing at the rows of vines, I decide to go for a wander. Ringo did make me promise to come find him, after all.

The air is thick with the scent of grapes and rich earth, the vines so pretty I almost forget I'm trespassing on someone else's world.

I don't think the vines are big enough to be a full-blown vineyard, but maybe this is like a hobby farm, and they make their own wine or cider or whatever it is you can make from grapes.

The sounds of the birds chirping are loud out here. I can hear cockies squawking somewhere not too far away, and as I glance up, a flock of sparrows zip overhead, like they are racing home for supper.

As I reach the end of the vines, my eyes widen at the sight of a large tree, and it isn't until I spot Ringo kneeling beneath it, his head bowed before a small gravestone that I realise, this must be the Jacaranda tree Hope is buried under.

The sight punches air from my lungs.

Before me, is a man so fierce... so brave... yet completely broken.

I shouldn't be here.

Spinning, I turn to leave, which of course is when I step on a twig, the snap of it loud under my foot, making me freeze in place.

"Come here, Angel."

His voice is rough, thick with emotion, and even if he'd told me to go away, I wouldn't have been able to leave.

He's suffering right now, and he needs someone to drown in his pain with.

Hesitating only for a moment, I spin and move to him, closing the distance to stop beside him, my gaze flicking to the small headstone… too small.

Slowly, Ringo lifts his gaze up to mine before reaching out.

"Come and meet Hope."

As overwhelming grief slams into me, I slip my trembling fingers into his big palm, feeling his heat around them as he tugs me down to kneel beside him.

Taking in a steadying breath, I finally let my gaze fall to the headstone.

Hope Angel Musgrove
Never walked on Earth
But will forever fly in our heavens

I have no control over my tears at this point. Between the two of us is so much unimaginable pain that I can barely stand it, yet know I don't want to share it with anyone other than him.

I can't help but picture the day he buried her here.

Did he dig up the soil himself? Lower her tiny casket into the earth and bury it here for her eternal resting place? Did he etch the words into the stone himself?

I can't bear to ask him, and there's no need to take him back to that day.

Still, to think that Cam's little baby girl's remains are buried right here under this soil… It's too unbearable to comprehend.

"I know I never knew her," the gravel in Ringo's voice breaks as he speaks, "but I do know she would have loved you."

I don't even know what to say. This pain is too much. Too brutal.

What if this were *my* baby? I don't know what I'd do if something were to happen to him or her.

How does Ringo get through everyday knowing that his little girl died?

How does he face every day with the images he likely still has in his head of little Hope, probably not even fully developed lying in the dirt next to her horrid mother?

"I d-didn't mean to d-disturb you," I stammer, hating the tremor in my voice.

"You're not disturbing me, Angel."

Angel.

I didn't know that was Hope's middle name. Not until now. Not until seeing it carved into stone.

"Why do you call me that?" I whisper, glancing up at him.

His gaze meets mine before flicking to my lips where they linger a little too long, before shifting back to my eyes again.

"I call you Angel, because no one has mattered in this life until you came into it. No one other than my Hope."

His words are raw. Honest, and confusing as hell, even while they are as clear as day.

"But you've got family. Your sisters. Your mum. JD. Jols. The club..." I remind him, but he shakes his head, shifting his gaze back to his daughter's headstone.

"I've been lost in the dark for so long, Abs. It wasn't until I found you that I finally started living again." He turns his gaze back to me. "I swear the moment I saw you in your bedroom, covered in blood... my cold dead heart started beating again. That's the only way I can explain it."

"Shit." A sob lurches from my throat, even as a warm smile lights his face.

"Yeah. Shit." He reaches out and wipes the tears from my cheeks with his thumb. "I think Hope sent you to me, Angel. So I could finally breathe again."

I open my mouth, but nothing comes out. The words just won't form.

A small grin tugs at his beard, and he gives my chin a gentle pinch.

"It's okay, Angel. You don't have to say anything."

"I... I just don't understand any of this. We only just met, and—"

"Sorry to interrupt." JD's voice cuts through the moment, and every part of me wants to scream at him, but given the way Ringo snaps to attention, I know JD wouldn't interrupt unless it was important.

"What is it?" Ringo asks over his shoulder.

"The Marx estate has been raided. Cops are still looking for the... uh... same thing."

I frown at JD's words as Ringo stands.

"They raided Ewan Marx's mansion?"

JD nods. "Yeah. Your phone's blowing up. Griffin. Devon. Conrad. Even Barrett has tried to call."

"Fuck." Ringo drags a hand through his hair, and JD's gaze flicks to me for a beat.

"Smitty rang too. Said they'll see you tomorrow for the, uhhh... thing. Then said, and I quote, *'we need to seal this deal and fast before Ewan Marx fucks me up the arse.'*"

I stare at them trying to piece things together, but it's clear JD is deliberately holding back.

"Uhhh, who is Ewan Marx? And why is he fucking Smitty up the arse?"

JD snorts, amused at me swearing again, but Ringo just shakes his head.

"Nothing for you to worry about, Angel."

My brows hitch, because even if JD hadn't frowned at that, I already know, just from the way he danced around his words, that this sure as shit is something I need to worry about.

16

RINGO

This is all one big clusterfuck!

"Look, my brothers didn't tell you everything," Liam Marx admits on the other end of the phone. "But you know I've got your back, man."

"What the fuck didn't they tell me?" I snap, my voice raw from spending the last three hours on the phone, trying to convince the oldest Marx brothers that I've got shit under control, when in reality, I fucking don't.

"You should know," Liam continues, "Officer Allen name-dropped you directly. Puffed his chest out like a big man in front of my dad. You know we've been trying to keep the Southern Sadists off Dad's radar, but Allen threw you and your club right fucking in it. Claimed you were into kidnapping minors, which goes against our treaty."

"You know that's bullshit!" I roar, and Liam chuckles.

"Relax. *I* know it's bullshit. Most of my brothers know it too. But you know how my dad is."

"Yeah. I fucking know how Ewan is," I grumble, hating that Smitty was right earlier when he said the reputation of our club is on the line.

Ian Allen is gunning for us.

"Allen mentioned Abbey's name so many times that it's now ingrained into my dad's brain," Liam says. "He know's Allen is dirty as fuck, but it doesn't matter. Being associated with an MC accused of trafficking, especially minors, is not part of Dad's business model."

I'm about ready to hurl the phone at the wall when JD cuts in.

"Has your team dug up anything else on Allen or his family?"

"Nah. Not yet. That bloke must have deep fucking pockets, because our informants have gone dark. We've got hackers working around the clock, but men like him don't leave a paper trail."

JD and I lock eyes, our concern mirrored.

"Why does Allen have such a hard on for you, Ringo? How'd he even know you were involved?"

I consider Liam's words for a moment before it hits me.

I know exactly how.

Back on the freeway, when my MC surrounded Daniel and Donny's car so Crow could get Abbey away... I fucking poked the bear.

The bear being Ian Allen and his nephew, Donny.

I punched Donny in the nose, and threw my name in his face.

"I can't fucking wait to meet your uncle Ian. Be sure to tell him Ringo is coming for him!"

It doesn't take a genius to find out who I am. We didn't hide our cuts, so Donny and Daniel saw our Southern Sadists death heads on our backs. And there's only one Southern Sadist that goes by Ringo in Australia.

The hunt for Abbey is now more than personal.

I'm the real reason my club is in the firing line. Not Abbey.

So while they are still hunting for Abbey, they've basically put the Southern Sadists on notice by dragging our allies into it, shaking up every partnership we've built.

It's smart.

Stir up shit with our people, drop my name, and suddenly we're not just dodging cops. We're dealing with a hoard of organised crimers who don't want their business getting fucked by the police.

Fuck.

Not only have I put a bigger target on Abbey's back, but I've put one on the club too.

No wonder Smitty was so pissed.

"I may have punched his nephew in the nose," I finally answer Liam's question. "But let's not forget, Donny is a rapist cunt, along with his prick mates. They're all going to die. I won't fucking stop until I see to that."

"Damn. You're in deep with this chick, huh?"

"Shut up," I snap while JD chuckles.

"He sure is."

I punch his shoulder, but he takes it with a grin, tossing a peanut into the air and catching it in his mouth like a cocky bastard.

"Come on, man." Liam sighs, the sound of a lighter clicking in the background. "You're talking to *me*. No need to lie about your girl."

My girl.

"Not my girl," I snap, not wanting that attention.

"Well, if you're about to feed me some shit about her being *just a job*, then I'm getting in my car now so I can personally deliver you a swift fucking cock punch."

"She *is* a job. I'm helping her as a favo—"

"Let me stop you there." Liam cuts me off. "Smitty's been running his mouth about her being your old lady. That you've claimed her or some shit. And as much as I *love* that for you, my old man doesn't give a single fuck about your love life. He wants to know why we're all paying the price because you've got a fucking crush on an eighteen-year-old."

"Be very fucking careful with what you say next," I warn, my fists balling on the bar top, about ready to start smashing shit.

"Look, you fuckers might do old ladies *plus* have a citizen wife, which by the way, why the fuck would you want to juggle that shit? But as far as Ewan Marx is concerned, in the real world, there's only one fucking relationship that counts. A wife. So to him, all this drama is just you chasing pussy and dragging the rest of us through hell."

"Fucking come here, Liam! I fucking dare you to say that shit to my face!"

Liam chuckles, and JD smirks, not even pretending to be worried about catching a flying fist.

"You know what you've gotta do, man," Liam says. "Only one thing's gonna give her proper protection, and repair your club's reputation."

"Hate to say it, but Liam's right." JD holds up his hands as I step towards him. "Club rules don't mean shit to the underworld. An old lady is nothing but an inside club title. Outside the MC, the only thing that matters besides money is family."

"Exactly," Liam agrees. "So why the fuck haven't you seen to that?"

With every word Liam spits, my blood fucking boils.

But, fuck. The bastard's not wrong. Neither is JD. And neither is Smitty.

If I want Abbey safe, like really safe... I have to marry her.

Only then will the club protect her.

Only then will the Marx family stand behind her.

And only then will the rest of our allies back us up.

"Jesus fucking Christ, would you two back off," I hiss. "I *know* what I have to do. It's happening tomorrow."

"Well, fuck," Liam scoffs. "Why didn't you tell my brothers that?"

"Because Abbey doesn't even know it's happening yet," JD snickers, and this time I grab a handful of peanuts and hurl them at his smug face.

"Uh... not to be the bearer of bad news." Liam sounds fucking amused as he speaks. "But you *do* know, for it to be legal, she actually has to agree with it."

"I fucking know that," I growl, "but how the hell do I ask her to do something that her parents were gonna force on her? She's fucking traumatised, man. I can't just drop it on her and expect her to fall in line."

"Remind her there's this thing called *divorce*," Liam says casually. "And once this whole mess is behind you, she can ditch you and live her best life however the fuck she wants."

"Fuck," I hiss, raking my hand through my hair again.

I hate the part about divorce, because deep down, I don't want to let her go, and I still don't understand why.

"Fuck's right. She's really got you twisted in knots. Never thought I'd see the day."

"It's a beautiful fucking sight," JD adds unhelpfully.

"Both of you, shut the fuck up," I snap, and they just laugh.

"Look. It's not ideal," Liam continues, still sounding more amused than serious. "But the people after her aren't messing around, man. Get hitched. Consummate or don't. I don't give a fuck. Just make it official. Then the club's associates will know she's important enough to be properly *owned* by the Southern Sadists. It's a win-win. And once everyone's back on your side, you'll have all the fucking backup you need to wipe those cunts off the face of the Earth."

"Will we actually have that help?" I ask, my jaw so fucking tight I'm starting to get a headache. "Because word is your dad has blown a fucking gasket and ordered Riggs to burn down the Western with everyone still inside."

Liam huffs. "Riggs won't do that. He'll stall for as long as he can until this shit is resolved. But my old man has every right to be pissed off. He's worked hard to build our reputation. We haven't been raided in over eight years, and all of a sudden they get hit with no warning, and it's got nothing to do with our business."

"Yeah I fucking know," I mutter, the exhaustion catching up with me, wrapping around my shoulders like a thousand weighted blankets.

"Right. So get fucking hitched, and let me know if you want to use one of our penthouses for your honeymoon."

I roll my fucking eyes. "Like fuck I'm taking Abbey to one of your penthouses. You probably have them rigged with cameras."

"Of course. Why pay for porn when I can watch my brothers' conquests in high def?"

We chuckle, and JD cuts in. "Any chance you can send me one of your home-made pornos? I'm out here in the middle of bum-fuck nowhere with nothing but my hand for company."

"Sure. Five grand and you can take your pick." Liam laughs. "Well Ringo. Good fucking luck with your marriage proposal. Make sure you get down on one knee. I hear chicks dig that shit."

As Liam laughs at my grunt, the call ends, and I sit at the bar numb as fuck over what I have to do.

JD tries to chat with me for a while but he quickly realises I'm not good fucking company tonight, so he wanders outside to sit around the open fire with my sisters.

I should join them, but I can't bring myself to look my sisters in the eye yet, after the way they treated my Angel at dinner.

Rounding the bar, I flick the sound system on, needing to drown out my sisters flirting with JD.

I don't know where Abbey is. Probably back inside after I stormed off and left her under the Jacaranda tree.

With Hope.

Fuck.

Pain slices through my chest just thinking about my little girl. The little girl I never got to meet.

I never got to see what colour her eyes would have turned.

I never got to hear her cry or coo, or speak that gibberish babble babies make.

What I did get was the feel of her light, lifeless body as I scooped her up from the dirt. So tiny. So fragile, her skin almost translucent. Her miniscule fingernails, and how blue they were underneath.

It's one sight I'll never forget.

Her little fingers, limp and cold, curled around nothing while I held one with my thumb.

That image is seared into my brain.

Doc said she was likely stillborn. Said Kylie's shit lifestyle killed her and expelled little Hope before bleeding out.

Some days I wish I didn't kill that fucking bitch just so I could have made her suffer. But really, that's just me wanting to punish someone for what I lost.

Getting rid of Kylie was the best thing for everyone, yet still, I wear the anger like a fucking crown. It's in everything I do.

It built my ruthless reputation and cemented my future with the Southern Sadists, because when my world fell apart, and my fury unleashed, my fucking club brothers were the only ones that stood by me.

They didn't tell me to calm down.

They didn't force me to go to a therapist.

They didn't tell me to take some time away to heal.

Normal society does that shit. But not my club. They handed me the matches and helped me burn it all down.

Some call that fucked up.

Me? That's the best therapy a man can get.

Fuck.

I need to figure out how to bring up marriage with Abbey. And I need to do it tonight.

Will she understand?

Will she feel trapped again, like she did with her parents?

Will she flat-out refuse?

The barn door creaks open and JD strolls in, carrying a few empties, tossing them in the bin as he passes, moving to the fridge.

"You wanna come sit by the fire?" he asks, eyeing me over the open fridge door.

"Is Abbey out there?" I stand, stretching my neck from one side to the other.

"Nah, man. Think she went up to bed a few hours ago."

I nod, considering whether I should go to her, even after I lied and told her Ma wouldn't want us sharing a room.

Would she let me touch her like she did back at the Western? Maybe she'd let me taste her pink flesh this time.

I could run the marriage thing by her as she comes apart on my fingers, while she's in an orgasm coma.

Fuck. I want all of that except for the part where I try to seduce her into something she'll likely say no to under normal circumstances.

"I think I'll enjoy the quiet in here for a bit," I mutter, and JD frowns, a six-pack now in hand.

"Everything okay?"

"Bout as okay as it was before," I deadpan, and JD cringes.

"What can I do?"

"Nothing." I shake my head. "Just don't stay up too late. I'll need all hands on deck first thing in the morning to get this place ready for the club."

"You got it." He nods, then leaves me to wallow in this fucked up mess.

Oddly enough, my misery isn't about the fact that I'm being railroaded into marrying Abbey, because honestly, I like the idea of her being my wife.

My misery is because I hate taking this decision away from her.

She deserves better than this. Better than me and this fucked up life I live.

She's not a club wife or an old lady. She's too good for that life.

"Fuck," I hiss to myself.

"Are you talking to yourself now?"

I fucking jump at Lani's voice.

"Jesus fucking Christ. Make some noise when you enter a room," I snap at my sister, who just smirks and pulls out the bar stool beside me and takes a seat.

"I wasn't quiet, Cam." She rests her arms on the bar. "So, what's going on? You've been off ever since you got home."

Sighing, I pinch the bridge of my nose.

"There's a lot going on, Lans."

"With Abbey?"

I nod.

"You call her Angel." Her eyes search mine, studying me.

"Yeah. I do."

"She means that much to you?"

"Yep. She does." And somehow, saying it out loud again, makes me feel a little lighter.

"How can she mean so much when you barely know her?"

I frown but answer truthfully.

"Can't explain it."

She half scoffs, half giggles. "You really are a man of many words."

"Yep," I mutter, smirking down at the coaster I've absently torn up into little pieces.

"You sure about her? Maybe your brain is just trying to replace what you've lost."

My head whips in her direction so fucking fast I nearly throw my neck out.

Biting my tongue, because that fucker wants to rant obscenities at my sister for saying such a thing, I try to rein in my clawing fury.

"If anyone else said that to me, I would've fucking stabbed them by now."

Lani just waggles her brows. "I'm not just anyone. I'm your favourite sister."

"Hmmm. That's fucking debatable," I mutter, dropping my gaze back to the ruined coaster.

"Seriously though, are you sure that's not what this is?" Lani pushes, and I sigh, squeezing my eyes shut for a fucking beat.

"I'd like to think not," I rasp.

"But you're not sure?"

Her words have me shoving back from the bar and pacing.

"I'm not sure about anything, Lans. How the fuck am I meant to explain this?" My gaze flicks briefly to hers to see she's watching me. "I've known her for four weeks, and only one of those weeks was real time together. It doesn't make any fucking sense, but there's just something different about her. About me. About how I am with her. About us. I can't explain it. I don't fucking know, okay?"

Throwing my hands up in the air, I stare back at my sister, her long chocolate hair now twisted into a pile on her head, making her look more her age of thirty-one.

"Okay," Lani holds her hands up like she's trying to calm a wild animal. "Just for the record, I think she's really nice."

My hands drop to my sides.

"She's too nice for someone like me."

"Probably." Lani nods with a growing smile before it falters. "What she said... about the baby's father... I hate that she's been through that. I can't even imagine what her life has been like. I'm sure I don't even know the half of it."

"Nope, you don't." I cut in. "That's *her* story to tell, though."

Lani nods. "She's strong. Incredibly brave. I know you wouldn't be doing all of this if she didn't mean something."

"She does. She's *everything*."

That lightness returns at my admission, and Lani smiles as she slides down off the bar stool.

"In that case, I'll have a word with Mills. Make sure she backs off."

"I'd appreciate that." I offer her a small smile, since it's all I can fucking muster right now. "Hey, before you go."

She pauses and turns back to me.

"Ma dozed off on the couch straight after dinner. Has she been doing that a lot lately?"

"Most days. She hasn't had a flare up in a while, so she's bound to have one soon."

I nod, feeling like shit for adding to her stress.

"Did JD tell you what's happening tomorrow?"

Her brows lift. "No. What's happening tomorrow?"

Taking in a deep breath, I glance at the door to make sure no one is slipping in unnoticed.

"The club is rolling in for the night. If you and Mills can be up early to help set up tents and shit, I'll talk with Ma about the food and letting the Doxies have access to her kitchen."

Lani scoffs. "You do remember who our mum is, right?"

Grinning, I nod. "I'll try to alleviate her stress. The last thing I want is to trigger a flare up."

"Okay. You coming outside with us?" she asks and I shake my head.

"No, I'd actually appreciate some alone time to be honest."

Stepping closer, Lani gives my arm a gentle squeeze.

"Alright. I'll keep JD out there for a while."

"Just don't fuck him please."

She giggles, wagging her brows. "That, I *can't* promise."

I shake my head as she laughs all the way out, and once she's gone, I round the bar and study the top shelf whiskey. I find myself a single malt, and take it and a glass to one of the old tables, pouring myself a decent portion.

I can't remember the last time I had a drink. It was some time after Hope died. After I dug her grave with my bare hands, clawing at the earth until my nails bled.

That was three fucking years ago.

I've been sober ever since. Too paranoid I'll end up like Kylie. Dependent on substances that do nothing but destroy lives.

But now, as I stare into the amber liquid in the glass, knowing I'm about to destroy Abbey's life, I accept that I'm too much of a fucking coward to do it sober.

17

ABBEY

The fact that I can't sleep in this luxurious cloud-like bed is nothing but infuriating. It smells like Ringo. He's everywhere in here, his scent clinging to the sheets, which usually brings me peace, but instead, is teasing the ache between my thighs, making me beyond restless.

"Ugh!" I practically yell, kicking off the sheet and lurching out of bed with way too much energy.

I start pacing, back and forth. Again and again. Needing something I don't know how to get.

Stopping mid-step, I bite my lip as I eye the bedside drawer. I barely give myself a chance to think better before I'm there, opening it to find Ringo's sex toy. The thing that looks like a flashlight, only the top is a silicone vagina.

I snort a laugh, then immediately moan as an image of Ringo sliding his dick inside this… thing, flashes through my mind.

I've already tried three times to touch myself tonight. Each time I do, I feel absolutely nothing. It's like my body won't co-operate, and I have a feeling that even if I used a vibrator, my body would have the same response.

I'd still go cold. Numb.

Because it's not him.

Shit.

Dropping the sex toy back into the drawer, I decide that maybe I just need to go for a walk. Maybe if I find Ringo and just be near him, the intensity of the ache will soften. And, honestly, I'm lonely in this big room all by myself.

I search through my backpack, looking for pants or shorts to put on, but then I catch sight of myself in the huge gold framed mirror propped against the wall.

I'm wearing one of Ringo's t-shirts. It's huge on me. The neck-line hangs wide, slipping off one shoulder, and the hem stops mid-thigh.

Turning from side to side, I study my reflection. Do I look ridiculous or… not?

My hair is pulled into a messy pile on my head, stray wisps of hair softening around my face, the look making my exposed neck seem longer.

With the way the t-shirt falls, you can only see my bump when the fabric clings in the right spot. My boobs, which are so much bigger now, kind of create a tent with the fabric.

I'm only wearing undies underneath. Or, as Ringo likes to call them, *panties*.

Do I still appeal to him now that he knows I'm pregnant?

He did kiss my stomach this morning.

God, was that really this morning? It feels like today has gone on forever.

Glancing at the digital clock on the bedside table, I note it's a little after 11pm.

I guess it's nearly Saturday.

Taking one last look in the mirror, I shrug at myself.

"Stuff it," I mutter.

I'm going to find Ringo as I am, and if he doesn't like it, well… I don't know but he'll like it, right?

Ugh. Why am I so insecure?

Oh I don't know, Abbey. Maybe because you grew up in a household full of coercive control and had an arsehole ex who got off on raping you and passing you around like a toy to his rapey friends.

Okay. I think I have cabin fever. I need to get out of this room and my own thoughts for a bit.

Shaking my head at my own stupidity, I slip out of Ringo's room and pad through the house quietly, noting only a few dim lights are on downstairs.

I don't come across anyone as I creep quietly, until I step outside and hear laughter coming from the direction of the barn.

My heart sinks a little at the lack of invitation to whatever it is. Not that I deserve one, but I miss friendship. Being at the top of someone's list of invitations. Someone thinking, hey, I really want to hang out with Abbey today.

I miss the laughter and feeling of lightness you get from being around people you feel so comfortable with, you don't have to worry about being someone you're not. Having deep conversations about the important stuff, as well as the less important things that you enjoy and love.

Like One Direction.

That makes me smile.

Ringo hated me playing their songs on his phone. I actually think he was pretending but I liked that he gave me shit for worshipping a boy band. It was light and carefree and reminded me of the banter I used to have with my friends.

Following the sounds of chatter, the closer I get the more I'm able to make out that JD, Millie and Alana are sitting around a fire, music playing in the background as they sip on some drinks. But Ringo is nowhere in sight.

I hesitate, not really wanting to get into it with his sisters again. I get that they are protective, and I'm still a stranger, but it doesn't mean I have to expose myself to their judgement.

What would Lexi say?

That's a *them* problem.

I grin, wishing she was here with me.

"Oh hey, Abbey," JD calls, spotting me in the shadows.

Dammit.

I give him an awkward wave and approach as Alana and Millie glance over their shoulders to see me.

"Hey. I'm just looking for Ringo." I offer a half smile, my gaze locking on JD, waiting for him to respond, but it's Lani who speaks.

"He's in the barn. He's a bit mopey so I'm sure he could use the company."

I blink a few times at Lani's tone. It's… nice. Warm. Dare I say, friendly?

"He's mopey?" I ask, and JD scoffs.

"Probably stressed about tomorrow."

I frown. "What's happening tomorrow?"

"Oh… uhhh." JD shifts, sitting taller as he cups the back of his neck, giving it a squeeze. "The club is coming to visit."

My brows shoot up.

"They are?"

He'd mentioned earlier that Ringo would see Smitty tomorrow, but I didn't think it meant *here*.

JD nods. "Yeah. I think Ringo was hoping to get a break from them."

I'm confused. Not by JD's words, but by the flicker of something else in his expression before he masks it. Like he's not telling me everything.

Nodding, I jut my thumb towards the barn door. "Guess I'll go find Mr Mopey."

Alana and JD laugh, but Millie doesn't. Her eyes follow me until I reach the barn door.

Stepping inside quietly, a deep male voice sings through the speakers, the music soulful. Almost sultry.

Taking in a breath of courage, I snip the latch on the door, locking myself in, and step into the room.

Scanning the space, my heart thrums with anticipation, and then stops for a beat as my eyes land on him.

Longish dark hair. A dark beard to match, threaded with a few flecks of lighter brown. Eyes just as dark, staring into the glass of what looks like whiskey on the table, one thick finger lazily circling the rim.

He's lost in thought, brows puckering in the centre like a war is waging inside his head.

A moment later, he lifts the glass and takes a long sip, his lids fluttering closed like he's savouring the taste, or perhaps the burn as it goes down. When he lowers the glass back to the table, his lids part again as he resumes staring into his drink.

"I thought you said you don't drink alcohol."

Ringo's gaze snaps up, instantly locking on mine as I hover near the doorway, suddenly wondering if I've made a mistake by coming here.

"Normally, I don't. But since I'm off the clock, I decided to have one."

His voice.

Damn.

There's no other voice on this Earth that can induce such a visceral reaction in me. I feel it, like sound waves rippling over my skin, soaking into my blood, and shooting adrenaline through my veins.

Not just adrenaline… but something else, too.

Red. Hot. Lava.

I nod, feeling the weight of his stare, suddenly hyper-aware that I'm only wearing his t-shirt, one shoulder exposed to him and the cool air.

"I couldn't sleep," I say, stepping slowly into the room, lazily dragging my finger along the edge of a table as I pass by it, glancing around the place to see that it doesn't resemble a barn at all.

It's more like a bar. Or a clubhouse. Something way cooler than a barn.

Something so *him*.

"My bed not comfy enough?" He smirks, and I shake my head.

"Your bed is heaven."

"Then why can't you sleep?" he presses, before sipping his drink again.

As I step closer, only a few feet from his table, I shrug and change the conversation.

"I like this song. What is it?"

"Tennessee Whiskey." He smirks and my brows shoot up as my hands grip the back of the chair across from him.

"I didn't take you as a country guy."

"I've got eclectic taste. I'm a mood listener." He shrugs.

"Oh… so that means you're like…" I trail off, my cheeks flushing as they tend to do when I get embarrassed.

"Like what, Angel?"

I shake my head, waving my hand to brush it off, but he leans forward on his chair, gaze pinning me in place, his tone deep and expectant.

"Answer me."

Biting my lip, I consider why I came here.

If I can't say the words then how the hell am I going to… what? Seduce him? Ask him to touch me?

Am I really that bold?

The way he leans back in his chair, relaxed but watching, one hand wrapped around his glass, his other hand coming to rest on his thigh as he stares up at me… it sends a pulse of heat straight to my core.

I want him.

Wetting my lips, his eyes track the motion, dark and locked in like he's just as affected by me as I am by him. It sends a flare of power straight to my heart.

"Are you horny?" My voice is husky, and my bold question has his brows shooting high, clearly not expecting those words to fall from my lips.

"Am I horny?" he repeats, amused. "You think this song is a *horny* song?"

I grin. "No. But it's sexy." I shrug before I somehow find some huge lady balls and start swaying my hips to the music. "Don't you think it's sexy?"

He sits taller.

"I didn't until now." The look he gives me sets me on fire. "Is that why you couldn't sleep, Angel? You feeling horny?"

I try not to blush at his words, but it's a battle I'll never win when it comes to this man and the way my body responds to him.

"Maybe," I say, letting my lids fall closed as I move to the music, trying to channel every bit of sensuality I've ever seen in movies.

God, I hope I don't look ridiculous.

What if I look hilariou—

"Come here, Angel." His rasp is gravelly yet demanding, interrupting my insecurities, and my eyes snap open to meet his. "I want to see how horny you are."

A swarm of butterflies rush through my chest and into my stomach at his words.

He wants to *see* how horny I am... like actually *see*?

I should probably be questioning my sanity at this point, yet my body, having its own agenda, moves with the music as I round the table. My heart is hammering as he shifts his chair back, angling himself to face me as I near, his gaze hungry, devouring me with every step.

"Did you try touching yourself?"

I nod, biting my lip, eyes dropping to his boots as my swaying slows, and I wait to see what he'll do.

"Eyes up."

Ohhh. His tone. The demand in it hits me hard, need pooling between my legs.

"What happened when you touched yourself?"

I shrug. "Not much. I feel nothing when I do it."

"Do you want me to touch you, Angel?"

"Please." It's practically a beg, the word leaving me so fast I never had a hope of stopping it. I ache for his touch so much that I don't even feel ashamed, especially when his lips kick up in a wicked grin.

"Are you wearing panties?" he asks, and I nod. "Take them off."

My heart slams against my ribs at his demand, my fingers obeying him as they slip beneath the hem of the t-shirt. Without a second thought, I hook the fabric of the panties and shimmy them down, letting them pool on the floor.

After tossing back the last of his whiskey and discarding his glass on the floor, he leans forward, scooping up my panties and brings them to his nose.

Then he drags in a deep sniff.

He moans and I whimper, my whole body shuddering with need just watching him.

How can he make me feel so cherished when he hasn't even touched me yet?

"Fuuuck, Angel," he growls. "I really want to taste you again."

I'm not sure where Abbey Delaney went, because this person standing here with her legs trembling and heart ready to explode, has way bigger lady balls than I ever thought she did. Especially when I reach between my thighs, sliding my hand under the fabric of his t-shirt until I find the wet heat waiting for me.

His eyes flare as he watches, his head tipping to the side to hone in on my fingers as I graze them through my slickness.

His expression is something I've never seen before, and it hits me that he's never actually *seen* me down there.

He's touched me. But not *seen* me.

The thought of exposing my bare flesh to him…

Oh, Jesus, more heat pools inside my core at the thought, and I find myself lifting the fabric of the tee with my free hand, baring myself to him.

"Fuuuck, Angel." His tone is rough and sexy as all hell. "You're letting me see now?"

His dark gaze flicks up to mine, and I nod, sliding my fingers free from between my legs, holding the two digits up, wet and glistening.

"Taste me."

I can hardly believe the words come from my mouth, but I don't have to say them twice. Ringo's gaze turns drunk, almost feral, as he leans forward in his chair.

"Put them in, Angel," he rasps, parting his lips, and I lean in, my eyes zeroed in on his open mouth and slide them in.

Oh… there's something wickedly intimate about the wet feel of his tongue as it curls around my digits, licking, tasting, then sucking like he's starving for me.

I whimper, another wave of heat rolling through me, and his hands snap to my hips, dragging me closer, and my fingers make a popping sound as he releases them from his mouth, his gaze never leaving mine.

"Do I have permission to touch you tonight, or would you rather I do it like last time?"

Last time… he let me use his hand. I was the one in control, guiding his fingers where I needed them.

It was on my terms. It was thoughtful. And I felt safe.

But… I don't need that tonight.

Not with him.

Ringo won't hurt me. I trust him.

If I ask him to stop, he will. No shaming. No guilt.

"I don't want to do it that way," I whisper, my gaze dropping to his lips. "I want you to touch me how *you* want to."

A low growl reverberates in his chest, his fingers digging into my hips, almost bruisingly.

"No, Angel. Not yet. Don't give me that much freedom. Until you're *truly* ready, I need you to be more specific. I don't want to risk triggering something."

"Specific how?" I ask, feeling my stupid cheeks flush.

"Well…" he starts, voice thick and low as he urges me a little closer to stand between his manspread legs. "Do you want me to touch you just on the outside, or would you like my fingers *inside* you this time?"

My knees almost give out at the thought. That image, his big fingers, deep inside me, sends a surge of hunger I didn't expect.

"Both," I whisper, my chest rising and falling with so much anticipation that I fear the moment he touches me, I'll come apart and it'll be all over.

With another wicked smirk, his eyes darken, and his voice drops another octave.

"How about my tongue, Angel? Can I lick you? Fuck you with it?"

Another needy whimper escapes me, and there's no hiding the plea in my eyes, or my voice.

"Yes. Yes to all of that."

A low growl vibrates through him again as he leans forward. "Are you ready to get naked for me yet?"

Am I?

I consider that, but shake my head quickly, already knowing that tonight, I'm not quite there yet, not quite ready for that vulnerability.

He nods. There's no disappointment. Just understanding and respect, and I know there's no other man on this Earth that I trust more than the one before me.

"Widen your stance, Angel," he demands, and like his willing puppet, I obey. "Any moment you don't like what's happening, you say stop. Or red. Okay?"

I nod, shifting my legs further apart as he slides his chair closer.

"Let's fix that ache for you, beautiful."

I nod a little too eagerly, desperate for his touch, yet I still flinch the second his hand starts gliding up my inner thigh.

"This okay?" he asks, and I nod, heat rushing up my neck, embarrassed that I flinched. "Are you sure? You're trembling, Angel."

"Ignore that," I rush out. "I'll tell you if I need to stop."

"Alright," he rasps right before his fingers brush over my folds.

I jolt again, my hands flying to grip his shoulders for balance, as his fingers begin to explore me.

"You're soaked, Abs. You should've come to me sooner."

"Sorry, I…" My voice trails off as he finds my clit, and a moan bubbles up my throat.

"You what?" he growls, circling me, spreading my slickness over my nub.

"I was nervous," I admit in a whisper, my trembling legs starting to relax as heat licks over my skin.

"You never have to be nervous coming to me for anything, Angel." His gaze is piercing as we lock eyes. "Now, I want to kiss you. Maybe touch those fucking *perfect tits* over the top of the shirt. Is that alright with you?"

I whimper, leaning my pelvis into his touch as I nod desperately.

"Yes. Please."

Cupping the back of my head, his touch gentle, he presses his lips to mine, and the moment we connect, I relax even more.

At first his lips nibble mine, the tickle of his facial hair adding to the heightened sensation. Then, he deepens the kiss, his tongue gliding into my mouth, making me picture it between my legs, and I swear I stop thinking. The only thing that matters is where his lips, hands and fingers are.

I buck against him as he works over my clit, little whimpers flowing from my mouth and into his before his digits slip between my folds, and I hold my breath.

"Relax, Angel," he groans into my mouth as I tense, but I don't pull away.

Instead, I widen my stance. I want to feel him. His fingers inside me. Desperate to rewrite the memory of what the pain felt like when...

No. Don't go there.

Those thoughts don't belong here.

His finger teases my entrance, his tongue sweeping into my mouth, fueling the fire in my veins as he starts to ease his digit in.

It's thick. Thicker than…

No.

It doesn't matter, it's just thick and it's his, gentle and skilled and… I cry out as he hooks his finger inside me, pressing against my inner wall.

"Fuck, Angel. You're dripping all over my hand."

"I'm sorry," I pant, and he chuckles against my lips.

"Don't ever apologise for that. That's my reward. It means I'm doing everything right."

The heel of his palm grinds against my clit, the friction so addictive that I know I could easily become an addict when it comes to this man. And as if to reinforce that thought, he eases his finger out before adding a second and sinking them both in, giving me the most intoxicating stretch that has me gasping.

"Fuck my hand, Angel. Take what you need."

His words spur me on, my lids fluttering open as he releases my head to palm my breast over the t-shirt.

Tipping my head back, I arch into his touch, his thumb easily finding my already pebbled nipple as he rolls it between his fingers.

I moan, I whimper, I mule, my legs trembling again, but this time for another reason.

"That's it." He groans as his fingers work faster inside me. "Come for me, Abbey. Come all over my fingers. Fucking drench me."

It's the dirty talk combined with his curling fingers, his palm grinding against my clit, and the pinch of my nipple that sends me careening over the edge in a tidal wave of ecstasy.

My lips part as I scream, yet there's no sound as I shoot straight to oblivion in a ripple of spasms that feel like they last an eternity.

It's endless. Blinding. And euphoric.

I ride out each wave until they float away, and I realise he's lifting me, my feet no longer on the floor.

Before my axis can make sense of what's happening, my back meets the surface of a table.

"W-what are you doing?" I pant, blinking through my lusty daze as his strong hands pry my knees apart.

"I want fucking dessert."

My breath catches, my brain not processing fast enough to understand before his head disappears between my legs and his hot tongue glides over my slick folds.

I cry out, my back arching as my hands shoot to his head to push him away, but the moment his tongue finds my clit, I'm a goner.

My fingers delve into his hair, anchoring him in place like my body refuses to let him go.

He laps at me, gentle yet deliberate, then sucks my clit into his mouth, while simultaneously using his tongue to flick it.

Ohhh, he's going to ruin me.

And I want him to. Completely.

I don't even realise it's coming until I'm in the thick of it, and another orgasm rips through me, fast and brutal. I scream as my body explodes again, so intense it borders on euphoric pain.

If I died in this moment, I'm certain the power of that orgasm would resurrect me.

"Fuck, Angel," Ringo pants, coming up for air.

I should feel embarrassed, laid out with my coochie on full display, but right now, I really don't care.

"Marry me?"

I snort lazily at his words, a half smile lifting my lips as my body melts into the table like I've been drugged.

The drug is him.

"Sure," I coo lazily, barely able to form the words as I slur. "I'll be Mrs Abbey Musgrove."

Before I can even register the shift in the air, I'm scooped up into Ringo's arms, and he cradles me to his chest as he starts walking.

"In that case, Angel, you need to get some sleep before your big wedding day tomorrow."

I giggle again, my lids heavy as I nuzzle into his neck, my lips brushing over the hot skin there.

"Sure. Tomorrow," I mutter against him. His scent and the rhythmic motion of him walking sends me into a deep, dreamless sleep.

18

ABBEY

There's this smile on my face that just won't budge.

It's there the moment I wake, the sweet sting between my legs taking me back to last night and the way Ringo gave me exactly what I needed.

It only grows when I roll over and see the sheets on the other side of the bed are crumpled, the pillow still holding the shape of his head. And when I reach over and run my palm over the sheets, I find them still warm.

Ringo.

He slept next to me last night.

I'm a little bummed I missed it, but considering I don't remember dreaming or having any nightmares, I know I must have slept soundly for the first time in… well, years.

My smile sticks with me while I shower, while I get dressed, and while I take my time enjoying the calm.

I feel so safe here.

Like I can finally breathe again.

The stresses of the last month, and longer, feel like a distant memory. This place has that effect on me. Or maybe it's just Ringo that affects me that way.

Squeezing into the only summer dress I have, I slip on my shoes and leave the sanctity of Ringo's bedroom in search of something to eat.

The first thing I notice is the music playing in the background, followed by the aroma of food.

Downstairs, I find Ringo's mum in the kitchen, cooking up a storm.

There are so many different things happening, like she is cooking ten different meals and I wonder if this is for the club members.

"Oh! Abbey. Good morning," she coos, spotting me as she flicks a tea towel over her shoulder.

"Good morning, Mrs Musgrove." I smile awkwardly, and she immediately shakes her head.

"Please, call me Doreen. 'Mrs Musgrove' feels so formal."

"Oh." I giggle. "Okay."

Stepping around the counter, her arms are wide as she approaches, and I let out a slow breath, relaxing into the comfort of her embrace.

"You look so well rested, dear," she says, pulling back to cup my shoulders. "I take it you had a good night's sleep?"

"I had the *best* sleep I've had in years. Thank you."

She beams. "Wonderful. That's just so lovely."

Reaching out, she cups my face, her eyes, the same shade of whiskey as Ringo's, fill with nothing but love. "Let's feed you. You have a big day ahead. You'll need to fuel your body."

"Uh… okay?"

My brows pinch, but Doreen doesn't seem to notice my confusion, passing me a plate of bacon, eggs, and grilled tomato and gesturing to the table.

As I sit, she lays out cutlery and juice for me, serving me with a smile as she chatters away about the lovely weather, and how I'm going to look beautiful today. I'm completely lost as to what she's talking about, but the food is so delicious, I don't bother interrupting her to ask.

By the time I finish eating, I'm satisfyingly full, but in need of some fresh air, because breakfast in the company of Doreen has been exhausting to say the least.

Making my escape, I hurry outside, taking a moment by the pond. The ducks paddle in slow circles, some dipping under the surface foraging for food. It's so beautiful here. Maybe later, I'll ask Doreen for some bread to feed the ducks.

Wanting to lay eyes on Ringo, I go in search of him, quickly spotting him, JD, Millie and Alana in the clearing on the other side of the barn, putting up tents.

"Here she is," JD calls out as I spot him walking my way, his lips spreading into a toothy smile.

"Hey, JD. You guys look busy. Need help?"

He shakes his head. "No way are we letting you lift a finger."

Stepping close, JD sweeps me up in a bear-like hug, spinning us before planting my feet back safely on the ground.

"Whoa." I laugh. "Someone is happy today."

He shoots me a wink. "It's a day worth being happy about."

"Yeah?" I ask, my smile matching his energy. "You excited to see your buddies?"

"Eh… not exactly. Being in lockdown with them twenty-four seven has a way of making me want to strangle my club brothers. But having them here today, for this, will be worth it."

I frown, but JD's attention snaps away, and a glance in Ringo's direction has him mimicking JD.

It takes me a moment, but then I hear it.

A low rumble.

A thunderous never ending rumble, drawing closer, yet still off in the distance.

Alana squeals, clapping excitedly, while Millie scoffs and rolls her eyes at her sister.

"Jesus Christ, Lans. You'd think you'd never met Cam's heathen mates before."

"Shut up, Millie. You're just jealous they give me all the attention."

"Yeah," Millie deadpans. "That's *definitely* my problem."

"Both of you better fucking behave," Ringo barks as he strides past them, jabbing a stern finger their way. "Lans, keep your fucking legs shut. And Millie, no fucking punch ons with the Doxies. Think you can both manage that for one fucking day?"

"I'm not making any promises." Millie rolls her eyes, but when she looks my way, she winks.

Wait… what just happened?

What was that wink?

Was it a friendly wink or a conspiratorial one?

Or worse, a promise that she's gunning for me?

"I'm thirty-one years old, Cameron. I'll spread my legs for whoever the hell I want," Lani calls, as Ringo continues my way, a low growl rumbling from his chest as frustration rolls off him in waves.

Regardless of his frustration, he looks good today.

Not that he doesn't normally, but there's something different about him today.

His hair is pulled up and knotted on top of his head, but he often wears it like that, although it looks a little tidier than usual.

It's not until he gets closer that I realise he's trimmed his beard. Like a lot.

He looks… groomed.

"Come on you two, let's get these tents finished." JD moves away as Ringo reaches me, giving us some privacy.

"Angel. You look radiant today."

Ringo's smile is warm, his eyes trailing over me like I'm something precious. When he reaches out and pulls me to his chest, I melt into him, peering up in time for him to claim my lips.

The chatter of Millie, Alana and JD fades away.

The storm of motorcycles fast approaching turns into nothing but a distant hum.

Right now, all that exists is me and Ringo, and his lips on mine.

Before I realise what's happening, I'm lifted in his arms, my legs wrapping around his hips as he carries me. Our mouths are molded together in a heated kiss that speaks of so much want, I can feel it pooling between my legs.

"Ringo," I whimper against his lips, right before he presses me against a hard surface.

My eyes fly open as he breaks the kiss to stare into my eyes.

"Thank you for trusting me last night, Angel." His thumb brushes over my lip as he pins me to the outside wall of the barn. "Are you feeling okay after what we did?"

"I feel wonderful." I nod easily, biting at his thumb playfully.

"That's good. I look forward to doing it to you again tonight."

His promise, and that deep rasp in his voice has me grinding against his hard length, and he grinds right back.

"Fuck, Angel. Now's not the time." He chuckles and I pout.

"But I'm needy."

"Don't I fucking know it." He smirks. "Just hold on to it. The longer you let it build, the better it will be," he promises, before slowly lowering my feet back to the ground.

I'm about to protest when I realise the thunderous rumble is so loud now, that I can feel it vibrating through the wall of the barn.

"The riff raff has arrived," Millie snides as she walks past us, followed by an overexcited Alana, while JD shakes his head at her enthusiasm.

"Shit." Ringo frowns as he starts tugging out his top knot. "I was hoping to go over what we spoke about last night before they got here."

"What did we talk about?" I ask watching his dark hair tumble free.

The first rumbling steel demon appears through the thick trees then, stealing his attention.

Trunk leads the pack, with Smitty just behind, and the rest of the club cruising at the rear. Celina is on the back of Smitty's motorcycle, and the VP, Spud, is just behind them with one of those sidecars carrying Smitty's dog, Molly.

"What do you mean?" Ringo asks, and I drag my confused gaze from the Southern Sadists rumbling closer.

"What do *you* mean, what do *I* mean?" I frown. What had we been talking about?

"I asked you—"

"Fuck, man. Why does Trunk look so good in my position?" JD appears between us, cutting Ringo off. "You think he does a better job than me?"

Ringo sighs. "There's only one Road Captain, JD. Calm down. Prez isn't looking to replace you."

I'm so damn confused right now. What the hell is a Road Captain?

I could ask, but the roar of the motorcycles is too loud now as they fill Ringo's property.

Shit. I forgot how many members there were. Not to mention a lot of them have women on the backs of their bikes. Most are Doxies, but there are some I don't recognise as well.

Suddenly, the peace I'd had this morning evaporates.

As they park their rides, the thunder of engines slowly lessens as one by one, they shut them down and start pulling off their helmets.

"Here's the lucky couple!" Smitty yells and cheers ring out from the men un-straddling their motorcycles.

Even though I'm smiling, I'm reeling, because what the hell is happening?

I knew the club was coming today, but everyone seems a little too cheery, like they are here to celebrate something.

"What's going on?" I ask loud enough for Ringo and JD to hear, and it's JD that looks mortified when he glances my way, before he shoots a glare Ringo's way.

"You didn't fucking tell her?"

"Tell me what?" I snap, and Ringo groans, tipping his head back to stare up at the sky as club members close in around us.

"Fuck, man." JD shoulders past Ringo, walking straight into the fold of club brothers where he disappears into a swarm of man hugs and back slaps.

I open my mouth to ask Ringo for answers, but Smitty steps in, shaking Ringo's hand, his dog getting wheeled to his side in a pram… what the?

A new level of confusion hits me when I take in Molly's bandaged leg and body, and when I meet Celina's eyes, standing behind the pram, she smiles, like there's nothing wrong.

What happened to Molly?

"Beautiful Abbey." Smitty's rough voice drags my attention away from his dog, and I blink up at him. "Or would you prefer we still call you Charity?"

I roll my eyes. "Abbey. Please. I killed Charity. She's dead."

Throwing his head back, Smitty laughs, directing his attention to Ringo.

"I forgot how sassy this one can be."

"Hmmm." Ringo's lips thin, but then he shoots me a wink.

Smitty grins. "We're all so happy to share today with you."

I frown. "What's happening today?"

Smitty blinks in confusion before turning to Ringo. "What am I missing?"

Ringo sighs.

"There's been a little… uhh… miscommunication."

Now my frown just plain hurts, and then the edge in Smitty's voice has me stiffening.

"You know the fucking options, Ringo."

"Yeah, I *do* know the fucking options. Just give me a fucking minute. I need to speak with Abbey."

My heart races, a lead weight of dread settling in the pit of my gut as my mind whirls.

What the hell is going on?

It's then that the crowd parts, and a familiar face comes into view.

One I'd be happy to *never* see again.

I don't know what comes over me, but I move before I can think better of it and shove through Ringo and Smitty, barging past club members, and storming straight towards the woman who has had it in for me from day one.

Wendy's smirk is lined with a familiar smugness that instantly has my shackles up, and she crosses her arms over her chest, popping her hip as she watches me approach like everything about me is amusing.

And maybe it is.

Maybe I look ridiculous, all five foot six of me with pink hair and a bump that looks like I'm smuggling a tiny cushion under my dress. But I don't give a shit.

I'm angry she's even here.

I'm angry she still has the audacity to look at me like I'm beneath her.

And I'm angry she did what she did to drive a wedge between me and Ringo.

Yeah, at the time, it had worked. I'd been devastated, but not anymore.

He came for me.

He chose to keep protecting me.

He chose *me*.

And now this bitch can eat shit. Because no matter what happens, she will never win the affection of *any* decent man.

"Oh fuck," someone mutters from behind me as I shove through the last cluster of people and come to stop right in front of Wendy.

"Looks like you get the wedding after all, *Charity*," she sneers. "Just don't forget who he'll be balls deep in when you're stuck at home playing house."

Something inside me *snaps*.

A war cry bursts from my throat as I lunge, my hand swinging hard and fast. The slap cracks through the air, connecting clean with her cheek, and Wendy's head whips to the side, as she stumbles, barely catching herself before turning her fury back to me.

She moves to pounce, and in a blur of movement, several bikers step in between us, two seizing Wendy with rough hands, while a solid wall of muscle shields me.

For a moment I think they are here to protect her, until one of them, Mex I think, growls.

"You even think about raising a hand to Abbey, and I'll slit your fucking throat."

I stumble back in shock, right into a soft chest. Spinning around in a panic, I come face to face with Jols.

"Hey, it's just me." She holds up her hands in peace, her smile soft and warm, and I collapse into her arms.

An *umph* flies from both of us as I latch onto her, happier than I realised I'd be to see her soft blue eyes and welcoming smile, and that silky dark hair that flows halfway down her back.

"I missed you," I whisper, and she gives me a squeeze.

I don't quite understand the reaction I'm having. I knew Jols for a week.

She was one of Ringo's crew that kidnapped me. But she showed me kindness and cleaned me up in that murky rest stop bathroom. She also opened up to me, sharing her heartbreaking secret, so similar to mine.

I only knew Ringo for a week too, but maybe, some souls just recognise each other.

Or maybe, my pregnancy hormones are messing with me again.

Ugh, I don't know.

All I know is having Jols here means I have a friend.

"Shit, Abs. I missed you, too." Jols pulls back, her blue eyes locking with mine. "I've been so worried. I looked for you, day and night. When Ringo had club business, I *still* looked for you."

"You did?"

"Fuck yes I did. I'm sorry I didn't find you sooner."

She looked for me?

We hug again, emotion swelling thick in my chest.

"Alright. Enough lovey dovey shit. Save it for the ceremony."

Smitty's voice has us breaking apart, and I turn to face him.

"What ceremony?" My gaze dances between him and Jols, before shifting to Ringo by Smitty's side, looking nervous. "Is this a biker club thing? Are you like, patching someone in, or something?"

"Or something," Smitty mutters, glaring at Ringo.

"Wait..." Jols looks frantically between me and Ringo. "She doesn't know?"

"Look, I thought she did, but clearly I'm fucking mistaken," Ringo snaps.

"I don't even know how you can fuck that up," Jols scoffs.

"You're fucking overstepping, Jols!" Ringo snaps and I throw my hands up, sick of being kept in the dark.

"Oh my *fucking* God. Would someone just tell me what bloody ceremony you are all talking about?"

A hush falls over the crowd around us, who had, up until now, been minding their own business.

"She swears." Ringo's brows shoot up, and I roll my eyes.

"You're *pissing* me off. So yeah, I *swear*."

Jols snickers and Smitty smirks before he reaches out and gives my shoulder a gentle squeeze.

"We're talking about your wedding ceremony."

For a moment, I just blink dumbly at him.

Did Smitty just say… my wedding ceremony?

A laugh bubbles past my lips, but it dies quickly when I realise, they aren't laughing too.

Then I stop breathing.

"My *what?*" I squeak.

"Maybe we should give you and Ringo a minute," Smitty suggests, before raising his voice to the crowd. "Let's finish setting up!"

What. The. Hell.

"Did I…" I turn my wide eyes to Jols. "Did I hear him right?"

Her panicked eyes flick in Ringo's direction, before she cringes and spins on her heel, stepping away.

I shake my head, sure I must be confused about what I think he said. Or maybe it's Smitty that's confused, because for some stupid reason, he thinks Ringo and I are getting married.

Staring up at Ringo, I see a flash of guilt whip across his expression and the dread I felt earlier gets heavier.

"You better start explaining," I snap, surprised by the steel in my tone.

The crowd dissipates around us like they don't want to be anywhere near while we have this conversation, and Ringo steps closer, keeping his voice low.

"You really don't remember me asking you last night?"

"Asking me what?" I snap, hands on my hips as I glare up at his towering height.

"Shit," Ringo mutters, dragging a hand down his face before his gaze darts over my head, and he gestures for me to start walking.

But stuff that. I'm not going anywhere. So instead, I shoot him a steely glare as I shake my head, and he sighs.

"Fine. We can do this here if we must." He crosses his arms over his chest. "Last night, I asked you to marry me, and you said yes."

I frown. Then blink. The frown again. Before I laugh.

Ohhh. I get it.

They are all messing with me. This must be a club joke or something.

"Yeah I remember that," I snort. "You were mucking around..." When his serious expression doesn't falter, I start to panic. "Right?"

He shakes his head.

Oh... shit!

My hands drop to my sides, all my sass now gone.

"I thought you were kidding," I whisper, my heart thumping an irregular rhythm in my chest.

"Angel, I'd never joke about that."

My mouth opens... then snaps shut.

Is this really happening? Is his club really here to witness us get married?

Panic crashes into me like a wave, drenching me in cold, choking dread.

"I'm not marrying you."

"Why the fuck not?" he snaps, brows knitting together like my denial has hurt his feelings.

"You're kidding right?" I scoff.

"Do I look like a fucking joking man, Angel?"

For a long moment I just stare up at this man I have so quickly become enamoured with in utter disbelief.

He blinks at me, and I blink at him, but nothing changes. He remains serious, and I… *I can't do this.*

Spinning on my heel, I storm away.

"Where the fuck are you going?" he snaps, his long strides easily keeping up with mine.

"I've told you before," I bite out, flinging him a furious glare as I stomp towards his house. "I'm *not* marrying you or anyone else. And I'm certainly not interested in being your *property*, or your side piece wife while you keep an old lady." I stop abruptly and jab my finger into his chest, hard. "I don't fucking share."

He smirks.

He. Bloody. Smirks!

"Good, because I don't fucking share either, and I have no fucking interest in anyone but you, Angel."

I roll my eyes and throw my arms wide.

"Oh sure. You say that now until you have me at home playing your little housewife, raising your six kids while you visit your *old lady* at the club and fuck her the way you used to fuck me!"

He blinks at me.

And then smirks again.

Before I can scream and punch that smug look off his face, he steps close, invading my personal space, snaking his thick corded arms around me, and yanking me flush against him.

Then he dares to give my arse a biting squeeze.

"Firstly, Angel," he growls, low and lethal. "I haven't fucked you *yet*. But I will. Mark my fucking words, I will." He fists the hair at my nape, tugging my head back sharply. "And just so there's no fucking confusion moving forward. You *are* my old lady and *will be* my wife, Angel. You are both. There will never be anyone else."

"Not *are*," I snap, pressing my hands to his chest, and trying, and failing, to shove him back. "Not *ever*."

Ringo's jaw ticks as he stares down into my raging eyes, and then he sighs and releases me.

Shooting him my best glare, I quickly straighten my dress with sharp, angry movements, making sure he sees every bit of my rage.

"Look, we kind of don't have a choice."

My brows shoot up at his words.

No… he wouldn't.

"You'd better not be saying what I think you're saying, *Cameron Musgrove*."

His eyes darken instantly. "Don't use my real fucking name around my club."

I scoff, too far gone in my anger to care.

"Oh, *I'm sorry*. How rude of me to use your *real name*. What a heinous crime."

"Don't get fucking sassy with me, Angel," he growls, and I gasp dramatically, feigning my fear as I slap a hand to my chest in overexaggerated shock.

Then I roll my eyes.

"I'm not scared of you, Ringo." I shove my hands on my hips. "And if I want to be sassy, I'll be *fucking* sassy."

His brows shoot up in surprise… then of course he smirks.

"I think I like you like this. All riled up. Swearing like a sailor."

Heat licks over my cheeks in shame, and the weight of what this actually is slams into me.

This isn't just bickering. A disagreement over something mundane.

This is real.

The anger in my arms unravels as my hands fall from my hips.

I don't understand why this is happening again.

Marriage.

No long love story with a heart stopping proposal that has bystanders in tears.

Just another person telling me what I have to do. Who I have to marry.

And once again. I don't even know why.

"You know I can't marry you," I whisper, emotion thick in my throat, and despite how I feel, I'm not prepared for the flash of pain in his eyes.

Does he actually want to marry me?

Before he can say anything else, and before I change my mind, I turn and run straight for the house.

19

RINGO

F ollowing Abbey into the house, I don't run like she is. I fucking stroll, knowing she's heading to my room, and will likely lock herself in my bathroom again.

She doesn't know I can get in there even if it's locked. I let her have the space she needed yesterday, but today, she's shit outta luck.

I ignore my ma's concerned voice as I pass through the main living area, feeling like a cunt for being so rude to her, but I need to sort out this mess I made with my Angel. I need her to understand why I'm asking so much of her.

Once inside my room, just like I expected, I find the bathroom door locked, so I find the key hidden in my wardrobe, before unlocking the door and stepping inside.

Abbey is huddled in the empty bathtub, her arms around her knees, head tucked down, her body bouncing with nervous energy.

"Angel," I rasp, stepping closer, and her head snaps up, those wide, disbelieving eyes locking onto mine.

"Of course." She throws her hands up in a huff. "How stupid of me to think you couldn't get in here."

"You're angry."

"And you must have a really high IQ to be able to figure that out."

"Ouch." I slap a hand over my heart. "You're nasty when you're angry."

Her lashes flutter as her face falls. "Shit… I'm sorry."

"Don't be sorry, Angel. Jols is right. I fucked this up."

Even as she scoffs again, I catch the smirk she tries to hide.

Fuck. I'll take her smile over her tears any day.

"Will you let me explain?" I ask, even though I'm not going to leave this room until she hears me out.

"I get the feeling I don't have much choice." She bites back.

Lowering my arse to the edge of the bath, I stare down at her, even as she shifts her gaze out through the window that overlooks the back of the property where a small stream runs.

I've seen a few different versions of my Angel since the day I stole her. There's been a lot of tears. Fear. Heartbreak. But there's also been strength. Playfulness. Sass. All brief flashes of the person I think she used to be, but none more than today.

None more than right now.

This woman here is strong, fed up, and willing to do every-thing in her power to protect her child. This side of her is *not* the submissive. This is the independent woman she was growing into before her family and ex stripped her of everything.

I don't want to smother that fire in her. I want it to burn fucking bright and blind anyone who dares challenge it. But I can't fucking do that if I can't protect her, so now, I have to somehow get her to see my reasoning behind this huge fucking ask. Because even if I don't like it, her protection requires a ring and vows.

"You saw Molly?" I ask, and her gaze snaps back to mine.

"Yes. What happened to her?"

"Well, Ayden's parents' apartment wasn't the only place that got raided, Angel. Officer Allen issued an Amber alert for you, saying you are underage. That gave them grounds to enter and search any place they 'reasonably believed' you might be. Even without a warrant."

Her eyes widen. "An Amber alert? But I'm eighteen."

"Yep." I reach out and brush my fingers over her cheek, for no other reason than I just need to touch her. "The cops also raided the Western. A few of the men got locked up for possession. They roughed up a couple of Doxies, and Molly got shot."

"Molly got shot!" Her sweet voice is loud, bouncing off the walls.

"As you can see, she's doing okay. Probably high on drugs and living her best life getting pushed around in a fucking pram."

Abbey slaps her hand over her mouth as a laugh bubbles up.

"I'm sorry. That's not funny." She looks mortified that she laughed.

"What's really funny is that Molly is getting better treatment than Celina." I chuckle, and she giggles again, shaking her head at the madness of it all.

Then she falls silent again, taking a moment for that to sink in.

"So, because of me, Ayden's parents and your club are suffering."

"Uh-uh. Not because of you, but I'll get to that in a moment, because it's not just the Mitchells and my MC. The cops hit some of our biggest business associates, like the Marx family."

Her eyes practically bug out of her head.

"You mean… Those guys in suits? Their family?"

I nod, as I stroke her pink strands behind her ear.

"Exactly."

"But why?"

"To ruin the Southern Sadists' rep," I explain. "If our allies start turning against the club, it'll weaken us. We'll have no one to back us up, and provide extra protection for you."

"So it *is* because of me," she deadpans, looking pissed like I'm lying to her.

"Angel, it's partly because of you, but the raids have more to do with me because I kind of… threatened Donny Allen and told him to tell his uncle that Ringo was coming for him."

She blinks.

And then blinks some more.

"What? So now Ian Allen has made it personal because of you?"

"Pretty much." I nod.

For a long beat she contemplates what I've shared with her, and I know the moment her confusion returns by the pucker of her brow.

"None of that explains why everyone is here to celebrate *our* wedding."

"That's the next part of this shit show, Angel."

"Of course," she mutters, crossing her arms over her chest.

"There are only a couple of ways to mend the damage done with our associates to show them we are serious about our business."

"Well, let's choose the way that doesn't mean I have to marry you," she rushes out, and fuck, why does it hurt so fucking much every time she rejects the idea of marrying me?

"You know, you're giving me a complex with how much you hate the idea of becoming my wife, Angel."

She rolls those gorgeous eyes again. "What are the options?"

Standing from the edge of the bath, I toe off my boots and step into the tub, folding myself down into the other end, bringing us face to face. She shifts a little to let my legs slide on either side of her, and her delicate hands come to rest on top of my denim clad knees, her touch alone showing me I haven't lost her, despite her anger.

"Option one, is the option I'm *not* willing to do. But, if you must know, it's casting you out and washing our hands of you."

Her eyes instantly redden, like she's fighting back the threat of tears.

"Remember. It's *not* a fucking option."

She gulps at my attempt to reassure her, giving me a nod.

"So option two is us getting married? Why?"

"Loyalty. Devotion. Family." I entwine our fingers, hoping my touch will remind her how good we feel together. "Right now, you're a nobody to our associates. Old ladies are a club thing. It's not recognised seriously in Australia's underworld, therefore we have to show them we are serious. That you are important. And the only way to do that is by making you family."

Her caramel gaze drops to her feet, the frown in her brow, deepening.

Lifting her hand to my lips, I kiss it, drawing her gaze back to mine.

There she is.

"So, in truth, Angel, my club can't protect you, because you aren't part of the Southern Sadists family."

"But couldn't you just…" I'm already shaking my head before she finishes.

"Angel. My hands are tied. I know it sounds cold, but this is club life. It's different. The club is the closest thing to family a lot of us have. It's not just about running guns and breaking laws. It's blood. Loyalty. Brotherhood. And that's something the Marx family understands."

"The club isn't just your family, though. You have your mum and sisters."

I nod. "Yeah, but I don't have a dad. I got myself into a lot of shit as a teen. The only thing that kept me in line was my band, and Toby McCullen, the President of the Southern Sadists MC, back at that time."

Abbey blinks at me. "You've never mentioned your dad before."

"That's because I don't have one. I have a sperm donor, and that's it. He left us when I was like fifteen or sixteen. Found a new woman and left the country. Turns out he owed money to a loan shark. Toby helped with that too. So for me, this club didn't just keep me out of prison. It kept my family alive and safe."

"So your loyalty is what keeps you in the club?"

"And purpose, Angel. Ain't no other fucker gonna hire someone like me. Can you see me working at Maccas?"

A grin tugs at her lips and she shakes her head.

"So, you're saying I have to marry you in order to keep *me* safe?"

"Like I said before, there's only one option I'm willing to accept, so like it or not, you have to marry me, or someone else in the club." A low growl rumbles in my chest at that. "And let me be very fucking clear," I shift forward, getting in her face, "there's not a fucking chance in hell I'll stand by and watch someone else make you theirs."

For a few long moments, Abbey just stares at me. Her chest rises and falls, fast and shaky like she's struggling with her emotions. Her fingertips dig into the denim over my thighs, pinching into my skin, her caramel stare piercing.

"So what you're saying is, you saved me from being forced to marry one man, only to be forced into marrying you instead?"

I fucking flinch at the chill in her tone, so fucking hollow.

"I guess so." I nod, my voice low. "But as soon as this is over, you can divorce my arse. Hell, you can take me for half of everything I own and set yourself up for a better life."

Her glare turns deadly. "I don't know what sort of person you think I am, but I would never do that to your mum and sisters."

She stands abruptly, stepping out of the tub, leaving me sitting there like a stunned idiot.

"I'm petty enough to take your motorcycle, though." She shrugs like my hog is no fucking big deal. "I've been around your club long enough to know how *sacred* a man's ride is."

"Bit fucking harsh," I snap, and she shoots me a look that reeks of sarcasm.

"Is it?"

Then she fucking walks out.

"Hey! We're not done." I leap out of the tub, grabbing my boots off the floor as I chase after her.

"Actually, we *are*." She storms out to my suite's living area, calling over her shoulder. "If you expect me to marry you, without my best friend by my side, I might add, then you'd better get the hell out so I can find something remotely nice enough to wear."

She stops at the mouth of the hallway, turning to me with her arms crossed and her eyes blazing.

"Abbey, come on. You know it's the only way to protect you."

"*No!*" she shouts. "It's the only way to protect *the club*."

"You fucking know it's not about the club for me."

She has the audacity to wave me off like I didn't just speak.

"Whatever. I'll *marry* you. But don't expect me to be happy about it." Jabbing a finger toward my bedroom door, she seethes. "Get out."

"It's my fucking room," I protest, and she shakes her head.

"Actually, it's *mine* now. If I have to sacrifice my maidenhood, then you can sacrifice your fucking bedroom."

My cock is so fucking hard right now. I have a right mind to shut her up with it.

I also don't have a fucking death wish.

"I'll send Jols up," I mutter. "She brought dresses."

"Fine," she snaps, her cheeks flushed with her fury, and I can tell she's holding back tears.

Pretending to move past her, I quickly grab her unawares, pulling her to my chest.

She struggles, shoving and beating her fists against me. Fighting me with everything she's got.

"I hate you!" she screams, and I hold tight, not letting her escape.

"No, you don't," I counter, feeling the fight slowly seep out of her.

"I do so," she says softly against my chest.

"You're angry, but you don't hate me, Angel." Leaning down, I press my lips to the top of her head, and she sinks into me a little more.

"What would you know?" she mutters, and this time, I release her and take a step back.

"I know that when I asked you to marry me last night, with your slick juices running down my chin, I fucking meant it."

Her eyes widen, but I spin on my heel, needing this conversation to be done.

I feel too fucking raw. Like I've been cut open and the entire fucking world can see my insides.

It's a weird fucking feeling, and not one I'm keen to get used to.

Back downstairs I apologise to my ma, where I take my scolding and lecture like a man, before heading outside where my club has now thoroughly invaded my little patch of paradise.

Jols gives me more shit for fucking up so badly, but hurries off with Lans to get the bride-to-be ready, and I spend the next two hours with my club brothers catching up before I duck off into the barn to get myself ready for my own fucking wedding.

It pisses me off that Abbey's wedding day has to be like this, because she's right. She should have Lexi here. And her other friends from Fox Pines. Hell, I bet she's torn up about her littlest sister Tahli not being here too.

I'll make it happen eventually. She'll get her dream fucking wedding after all of this shit is over and those rapist fuckers are dead.

Assuming she even wants to keep me.

Fuck.

"You almost ready?" JD steps into the tiny fucking bedroom I was meant to sleep in last night.

"I suppose," I mutter, staring at myself in the narrow mirror on the wall.

"You scrub up alright," he snickers, and I smirk at my best mate.

"I feel like a fucking pansy."

JD roars with a laugh, moving up between me and the mirror and starts unravelling the tie I just spent the last fucking ten minutes perfecting.

"You're trying too hard. The collared shirt is enough. The tie isn't you." He wags his brows at me. "Besides I doubt she wants to see you look like anything but *you* at the end of the aisle."

Fuck. I wish.

"She doesn't even want to marry me, man."

He nods, tossing the tie aside. "She's been through a lot. Don't take it personally. It's about her, not you. Everyone can see how much she's into you."

I thought she was into me.

What am I thinking? Of course she's into me. She never would have trusted me with her body last night if she wasn't.

"Why the fuck am I so twisted up about her?"

JD chuckles and claps me on the shoulders. "She's your person, man. Ain't no other way to explain it."

"My *person*," I mutter, glancing back to the mirror to see the top few buttons of my black shirt undone, and this time when I look at myself, I see me.

Black shirt, sleeves already rolled up, my cut over the top, black jeans, and my freshly polished black shitkickers.

"Hair up or down?" I ask JD, and my best mate studies me for a moment before answering.

"Leave it up. Let everyone see that gorgeous face."

"Fuck off." I go to slap him, my hand meeting fresh air as he dodges it.

"Hey, as your best man, I have to be honest."

I roll my fucking eyes.

Fuck. My Angel is rubbing off on me. Now I'm an eye roller?

Organising the wedding has been rushed as fuck. Smitty had people working all night to make sure everything was in place for this to go smoothly.

"Tell me Lewy has arrived with the documents," I ask JD as he eyes himself in the mirror.

"He has. He's got her birth certificate, and her learner's driver's licence credentials. Ace has the marriage certificates ready, too. The fucker is keen as hell to officiate today. He's ready to go when you are."

"Fuck," I whisper. "Am I really doing this?"

"You sure fucking are." He gestures to the open door. "Let's get you hitched so this party can begin, and you can consummate your marriage."

"I like the idea of that last part," I grin, before it fucking slips away. "I don't fucking know if she's going to come out of my room to marry me."

His lips spread wide in a grin. "She's already waiting down-stairs, man."

What?

My fucking heart flips in my chest, and I'm moving before I can stop myself, dead set on making Abbey mine for fucking ever.

Trunk and Murf have everything set up, yelling for everyone to sit the fuck down as I step out into the chaos.

The barn doors are wide open, letting the outside in, and I make my way over to the duck pond where Ace, our ordained brother, waits on the deck overlooking the water.

I catch Wendy's scowling face in the crowd, and wish like fuck Smitty had approved my request to fucking banish her. The problem is, Wendy is an anything goes type of Doxy, so the men fucking froth over her. There'd be a riot if she got sent packing, but at least Smitty gave her an official warning. You only get one in our club. Next fuck up, and she's gone.

Those that are sitting are on hay bales and low benches slapped together from old scraps of timber, lining the makeshift aisle, while the rest of the crowd stand around the outside, watching on.

I get a few whoops and cheers as I take my position on the deck, some of the Doxies throwing catcalls my way.

The second I spot Ma moving to her seat, I rush forward and take her arm, helping her over the uneven ground, my gut clenching at how unsteady she seems on her feet.

Shit.

Millie hurries to join us, and the look we exchange says it all. It's one we've shared more times than I can count.

Ma is close to a flare up.

"Would you two stop fussing?" she mutters as we help her to sit. "You're carrying on like I'm some old biddy."

"I'll never stop fussing over you, Ma," I tell her as she relaxes back in her seat, her hand lifting to cup my jaw.

"You're a good boy, Cameron. Even though we can't see him, just remember Bobby is standing right by your side today."

"Shit, Ma," Millie sobs. "You're making me cry before the wedding has even started."

Fuck. I wish my little brother was here.

It takes me three fucking tries to swallow the lump in my throat, and when I finally do, I press a kiss to Ma's forehead before returning to the deck.

A hush falls over the crowd as Smitty yells, "Quieten down!" And then I spot Lani hurrying out of the house, a camera at the ready as music starts playing through the outdoor speakers.

I barely register the tune, too busy waiting for my first glimpse of my bride.

Is she really going to marry me? Or will she leave me at the altar?

The male voice singing through the speakers finally registers, and I fucking stiffen, spinning to face Ace.

"What the fuck is this music?"

He shrugs, taking a noticeable step back. "It's what the bride wanted."

"What the fuck is it?" JD whispers from next to me, and fuck me, my soon-to be-wife has a set of balls on her.

"That little…" I trail off, turning my smirk to my best man. "It's fucking One Direction."

Horror flashes across his expression. "Oh."

Yeah… fucking, oh!

My fucking jaw ticks as I shoot my gaze back to the steps of my house to see Jols already doing her wedding march or whatever the fuck you call it, heading our way as Abbey's stand-in-brides-maid.

"Fuck me," JD mutters under his breath, and I sneak a glance at him.

Jesus, he's practically drooling.

I've always known he has a thing for Jols, but lately, he's not being real fucking subtle about hiding it. Especially from Smitty, Jols' step-dad.

"Keep it in your pants. Prez is coming," I mutter under my breath, and in my peripheral, I see JD stand taller, straightening his cut.

It's then that I finally get my first glimpse at my bride as she steps from inside my house.

She's wearing a grin, her lips moving as she walks, and it takes me a hot fucking second to realise she's singing along to the fucking song.

I barely register the ivory satin dress draped over her curves and baby bump, or the low neckline, accentuating her plump tits. Because all I can focus on is her shit-eating-grin as she proudly sings the lyrics to her favorite boy band like she's throwing me a big, smug fuck you.

Fucking little brat.

Jols takes her place on the far side, giving Abbey space to join me on the deck, and I shake my head at my Angel, my cock already a fucking semi just from her defiance.

"*... let these little things slip out of my mouth...*" Abbey sings, the sweet scent of berries wrapping around me, and I forget all about the fucking boy band playing in the background, or the sixty plus eyes watching us.

All I can focus on are those big doe caramel eyes, striking with the subtle makeup illuminating her skin in a glow that accentuates the one she had earlier this morning.

"Cause it's you," she sings quietly, so only I can hear, taking the hand I hold out to her. *"Oh it's you. It's you they add up to."*

When the song hits the part about being in love, Abbey stops singing and quirks a single brow as she leans closer.

"When I say our vows today, I'm going to be picturing Harry Styles instead of you."

20

ABBEY

There's a good chance I've lost my marbles. I could blame my newfound courage on hormones or just being plain fed up, but I have a feeling if a shrink got their hands on me right now, they'd probably lock me in a padded room and throw away the key.

It has to be the only explanation as to why I'm hellbent on riling Ringo up this much.

Am I pissed about being forced to marry him?

Hell yes, I am.

And it's not even because I don't want to marry him, because if I'm being honest, later down the track, when my life's not hanging by a thread and things are calmer, I could totally see myself as Mrs Musgrove.

But I'm being forced, which quite frankly, pisses me off.

"You're acting very reckless, little bride," Ringo sneers into my ear after I taunted him about picturing him as Harry Styles. "Don't forget, your actions will have consequences. Some of which you may not like."

When he pulls back to glare at me, I arch a brow.

"You mean there's something worse than being forced to marry an old man?"

A muscle ticks under his eye, and everything in me screams to take a step back.

Warning. Danger ahead. Do not proceed.

"Yeah, Angel. Maybe there *is* something worse." He grips my chin, pressing our noses together. "Like being fucked by an old man."

Oh.

My traitorous body lights up, an instant pulsing flaring between my thighs, and my nipples bead into tight buds, straining against the satin fabric of my dress.

Shit. This is not good. I'm not even wearing a bra.

Two months ago, the thought of being fucked made me feel sick.

Today, however, I'm practically salivating to find out if this man can wipe away the filth those six arseholes left behind.

Still, I'm pissed about this forced wedding. About having the decision ripped from me once again.

Am I as pissed as I was with my parents?

God, no. That was different. On a whole other level.

But, I'm still not happy.

As a little girl, I used to dream about my wedding. I imagined Lexi beside me as my bridesmaid, and my friends throwing confetti. My little sister, Tahli, sprinkling the aisle with rose petals as the cutest flower girl you ever saw.

Instead, I barely know ten percent of the people here, and none of them know a damn thing about me.

Hell, even the man I'm about to marry probably thinks my favourite colour is pink, just because I'm a girl.

Narrowing my eyes at the big brute breathing the same air as me, I straighten my spine to make myself a little taller.

"You talk a big game, old man. Be careful not to strain your back."

JD and Jols snicker at that, but Ringo looks about ready to put me over his knee.

Huh… not sure I entirely hate that idea.

"If you want to act like a little brat, Angel, then be prepared to be treated like one," he snaps, before turning his dark gaze to his biker mate, Ace. "Get started. I've got a bride who's gagging to get to the part where I fuck her."

The crowd rumbles with low laughter, and my cheeks flame to life in embarrassment, but it's Doreen's scoff that keeps me calm.

"Cameron Eugene, I'll clip you across the ears. Apologise to sweet Abbey."

Ringo's lips twitch into a smirk as he turns back to me. "Hear that, Angel. My ma thinks you're sweet." He leans in close, lips brushing my ear. "I bet she wouldn't think you were so sweet if she knew how I ate your pussy last night."

Fire.

My cheeks are blazing.

Heat races from my scalp, down my spine and into my toes.

Ringo chuckles as he straightens and motions for Ace to get things rolling, and it takes me way too long to settle the storm in my head enough to focus on what Ace is saying. He must be ordained or something because it all sounds legit to me.

I zone out so much that it isn't until Ringo squeezes my hand that I realise Ace is talking to me.

"Oh, I'm sorry. What?"

"I asked if you're ready to make your vows?"

I blink at Ace before darting my wide eyes back to Ringo.

Vows.

Of course there are vows. It's a wedding.

Shit. Was I meant to write vows?

"She's ready," Ringo answers for me when I don't respond, and I swear I must look like a total bimbo right now.

"Great," Ace beams, his silver streaked hair tied neatly back at his nape, making him look weirdly civilized for someone in a biker vest. "Repeat after me, together."

"Together?" I whisper to Ringo, and he nods.

"Together, Angel."

Clearing my throat, I try to compose myself, unsure if I've ever seen wedding vows recited together. Is that an MC thing?

I should have asked more questions before agreeing to this. There's so much I don't know. Not just about weddings and being a wife, but about marrying into a lawless biker club.

What the hell do I know about being a biker wife?

Ace starts the vows, so I force myself to listen so I don't mess them up, and when he finishes speaking, I take a big gulp and glance at my soon-to-be-husband to find his dark gaze already on me.

"Ready, Angel?"

My heart skips a beat from the tone in his voice and the way he's looking at me.

I could be standing here marrying Daniel Stone right now. Forced into pledging my loyalty to a vile, cold creature who never once looked at me the way Ringo is right now.

This wedding might've started out feeling like a prison sentence… but to say that it's forced doesn't quite fit anymore.

If I were given the option of choosing between Daniel and Ringo, there'd be no contest.

Hands down, Cameron Musgrove would win every time.

So, with emotion thick in my throat, I nod at my monster of a man.

With his hair up in a knot, his leather vest sitting over a black shirt with the top buttons undone, teasing me with a hint of his chest… well… I can't deny he looks sexy as sin, and it occurs to me now why I noticed his trimmed facial hair this morning.

He cleaned himself up for me.

Ace turns the page he's holding with the vows, offering them if we need to read along, and I scan them again, letting the words sink in, bracing myself to speak.

The moment Ringo starts, I join in, our gazes locked. His big hands cradle mine, his thumbs sweeping across the backs like I'm the most precious thing he's ever touched.

> *"Today, we take our vows of marriage before our family and friends.*
> *We will honour one another when we are together or apart, and always respect each other's differences.*
> *We will cherish the good times, and endure the*

storms. Hand in hand. Side by side. Riding this life together and always leaning into the curve."

The corners of Ringo's lips kick up like he's pleased I didn't fight him or twist the vows like the brat I was before.

Damn.

I actually like that I please him, and realise I want to do more of it.

Don't get me wrong, I like being a brat too. But there's just something about pleasing a man like Ringo, that I know I'll do just about anything to see his stormy gaze soften when he looks at me like that.

"Now, Abbey," Ace draws my attention. "Please recite this line."

My gaze drops to the paper he's holding, and the line high-lighted in pink.

Reading over it, I wet my lips before glancing back up at my monster.

"Cameron, when I say I love you, what I'm really saying is that I'll hold on tight until our ride on Earth ends."

Emotion slams into me as I finish, my voice cracking, and I find myself wanting to mean every word I just spoke.

Which makes no sense. I know this. I keep reminding myself of this. That what Ringo and I are doing is yet another ruse until this nightmare is over.

Sure, we are attracted to each other. I won't pretend the moments we've shared weren't real. They've felt more real than anything I've ever known. But I know he's just doing this to protect me. So really, I should be more grateful and at least try to be civil about what's happening here.

As if reading every thought stamped across my face, Ringo's smile widens, his teeth making an appearance as he lifts one of my hands and kisses it.

"Ringo. Please recite this line."

Ace's prompt has Ringo reading from the sheet before refocusing back on me.

His wicked grin should have been warning enough to prepare me for his next words.

"Abbey, I promise to treat you as good as my leather and ride you as much as my Harley."

A laugh bubbles from my lips as the crowd starts hooting and cheering, and tears spring to my eyes.

Oh my God.

For a moment there, I thought these big, burly bikers were closet poets, what with the vows we recited, but there it is, in Ringo's words. They are still brutes.

Funny brutes.

As hilarious as that line is, I'll admit, it's fitting for my monster of a man. I wouldn't want him to say anything else.

"JD. Do you have the rings?"

Rings?

My brows shoot up, eyes snapping to Ace before JD steps forward, placing something into Ace's open palm.

How long have they been planning this wedding without my knowledge?

Long enough to organise wedding rings, apparently.

My anger returns, but it's short lived as Ace thanks Tups, the MC's Secretary, for whipping them up last night.

When I glance at Ringo, he's watching me, amusement tugging at his lips, like he knows *exactly* how many questions are bouncing around in my brain.

"These rings have been crafted with fortified Tungsten Carbide," Ace announces. "Symbolising strength and longevity to compliment the union of marriage. They mark the beginning of your long journey together, their circle a symbol of love without end."

Ace opens his palm, revealing two sleek, black carbon bands. Smooth and polished, each one engraved.

Ringo takes the small one, and gives me a nod, so I take the large one and study it.

Abbey.

My name is engraved on it. Not on the inside, hidden away, but on the outside, for everyone to see. When people see it, they will know I'm his.

Taking my left hand, Ringo slowly slides the ring over the tip of my finger, his dark whiskey gaze locking with mine.

"With this ring, I thee wed."

My breath catches at the rasp in his tone, and given the way his eyes practically drown in mine, I know he's just as affected by what we are doing.

Slipping the ring in place, it fits so perfectly that I wonder if someone measured my ring size without me knowing.

Glancing at the ring now encircling my finger, I see Ringo's name is engraved on it for all the world to see.

Mine.

He said that he'd claim me as his, and I guess now he truly has.

I belong to him now. I am *his property* I guess, given the way the MC works.

With his hand extended, Ringo waits patiently for me to get my head back in the game, so I hurry and slide the large carbon band onto his finger.

"With this ring, I thee wed."

My voice is much the same as Ringo's, a little husky, filled with emotion I can't seem to control.

Ringo shoots me a crooked smirk, adding in a wink as he takes both my hands again while Ace continues.

"Brothers. We chant."

Before I can process what that means, Ringo drops to one knee.

My hand flies to my chest as my breath catches, quickly noticing every Southern Sadist brother doing the same. Then, in unison, they thump their fists to their chests, their gazes locked onto me, as they chant.

"May the road rise up to meet us.
May the wind be always at our backs.
May the sunshine be warm upon our faces.
May the rain clouds never be black.
We are the Southern Sadists MC.
Ride 'em high.
Ride or die."

Tears sting my eyes.

I have no idea if this is something they usually do, or if they all just pledged loyalty to me somehow. It felt like both. But whatever it was, has me choking up.

With another fist thumping over their hearts, they all rise, re-taking their positions, and Ringo stands tall, never once breaking eye contact.

My hands are trembling as he takes them in his, and just like that, his touch calms me.

"May your love grow ever stronger as you ride this life together, reflecting the promises you made here today," Ace declares before he speaks words I didn't think I'd have to hear for a very long time. "By the power vested in me by the Victorian Marriage Registry, I now pronounce you husband and wife."

Before Ace can add anything else, Ringo releases my hands, his big palms sliding around my waist, yanking me against his chest as he claims my lips like they've always been his.

Everything falls away.

The claps.

The cheers.

Even the sting of being forced into this.

None of it matters. Not when his lips crush against mine, our tongues clashing as we swallow each other's moans. Nothing else matters as my skin ignites with sparks of electricity that only Cameron Musgrove can entice.

Cameron Musgrove.

My husband.

"Fuck, Angel," he groans against my lips, before slowly pulling back to meet my eyes. "You're Mrs Abbey Musgrove now."

I smile, biting my lip at how damn proud he looks about that.

"I'm a modern woman. Maybe I don't want to take your surname," I tease, but he's already shaking his head before I even finish.

"No fucking way, Angel. You're the wife of a Southern Sadist now. We claim our women and fucking worship them. I don't care how modern you think you are. There's nothing I won't do for my wife, and every fucker who fell to a knee will protect you with their own life now. So you will carry my surname with honour, and you will do it with a fucking smile."

By the time he's done laying down the law, we're both grinning from ear to ear. If we weren't getting swarmed by bikers wishing us well, I'd be climbing this man like a tree and show him just how much I appreciate him.

My thoughts make me giggle, because when did I become so bold?

Maybe it's from being around someone who put everything on the line for a stranger. Because every passing minute I spend with him, I feel pieces of the old Abbey resurfacing.

"Woohoo, you got fucking married!" JD hoots, practically jumping on Ringo's back as music floats from speakers somewhere nearby, and the club brothers snatch my man away.

"You know," Jols bumps her shoulder to mine. "If I didn't know better, I'd think you two meant every word of those vows."

I roll my eyes rather dramatically before we both burst out laughing.

The Doxies gather around, hugging me and offering congratulations, all except Wendy. She stays well away, standing off to the side, watching on with a scowl twisting her face.

"Congratulations Mrs Musgrove." JD pops into view, startling me, and I laugh at the playful glint in his eye.

Right now, I can see the resemblance to his little brother, Brody.

Leaning close, I keep my voice low. "Like I had a choice."

"Not one second of what I just witnessed looked forced." He grins. "If you didn't want him to know how much you like him, maybe don't look at him like he hung the bloody moon."

"I did *not* look at him like that," I protest, hands flying to my hips and noticing that now, my fingers no longer dig into my hip bones, but sit out a little further, grazing the curve of my baby bump.

"I agree with Abbey," Jols backs me up. "It was more like she was *fucking him* with her eyes."

I gasp and JD throws his head back laughing like it's the funniest thing he's ever heard, so I slap her shoulder.

"Jols! I was not!"

"You weren't what?" Ringo's deep gravelly voice has me stiffening as he steps close, and I immediately shake my head in a panic.

"Nothing. We should eat. Are you hungry?" I grab his arm in an attempt to drag him away, but he doesn't budge.

"She was eye-fucking you through that whole ceremony, man." JD's shit-eating-grin has my eyes practically bulging out of the sockets.

"It may have looked like that," I scramble for a comeback, "but I was actually picturing Harry Styles."

That sends JD and Jols over the edge, collapsing into each other with full body laughter, tears glazing their eyes.

Risking a glance at Ringo, I find him smirking down at me with a single brow raised.

"I'll tell you what, Angel. If it'll make you feel better, when I spread those pretty thighs later and finally sink inside you, I'll let you call me Harry."

"What?!" I gasp, right as Jols and JD go crashing to the ground in absolute hysterics.

It's hard to ignore them and the attention they are drawing, but I force myself to focus on what Ringo just said.

"You heard me, wifey." He flashes me the most sinister smirk I've ever seen him wear as he leans closer. "We have to consummate the marriage."

My heart is racing, and my lips part to protest, but Ringo moves faster than my thoughts.

One moment I'm standing, and the next I'm in his arms, being carried away from the crowd and around the edge of the large pond.

"Now, according to Australian law, consummation isn't actually required." His gaze flicks to me as he walks, and I clutch to the front of his shirt as he moves us further away from the crowd. "But, since the law *I follow* is that of the Southern Sadists… Well, let's just say, I'm making it a thing."

"You can't do that." I giggle, and he raises a challenging brow at me.

"Can't I?"

Now nearly behind the house, surrounded by trees, Ringo lowers my feet to the ground and nudges me back against a large trunk.

My heart stutters… is he planning on consummating here? Now?

Where people might see?

What if I freak out? Get sucked into a PTSD vortex and create a scene?

Jesus, can I really do this? Have sex? Let him inside my body?

"Stop frowning, Angel. I'm not gonna fuck you out here."

"I didn't… I wasn't…" I shake my head, knowing full well I've just been caught out. "I'm sorry. The whole consummation thing is making me nervous."

"I know." Reaching out, his fingers brush along my cheeks, gentle and unhurried. "You know I'd never hurt you, right?"

My chest squeezes, and something inside me softens as I relax back against the tree, peering up at him.

"I know."

Bracing his hand on the tree over my head, he leans in, caging me between the rough bark and the heat of his body.

Once, this would have made me feel trapped.

Now, all I feel is owned.

With his attention focused on me, like I'm the only woman in the entire world, his stormy gaze drops to my lips as he wets his own. Slowly, and deliberately.

"What I *will do*," his breath fans over my face, "is make you *burn for me*, Angel. Hot. Bright. Absolutely fucking searing." His voice is thick with dark promise that has my knees trembling. "Because I'm *not* going to fuck you until you *beg me* for it. And just so we're clear. That will be happening tonight."

My lips part as a shaky breath escapes me, my skin already alight, even though he hasn't even touched me yet.

"What if I'm not ready?" I whisper, barely able to find my voice, and he cups the side of my face, his thumb brushing gently across my cheeks as he presses his forehead to mine.

"Trust me, Angel. You'll be ready."

I don't get a chance to question it before he claims my lips with his.

I moan into his mouth, surrendering to the quiet storm that is us, hidden among trees with a party in full swing in the distance.

When he presses his body flush to me, I shift my legs wider, offering him space, which he takes, without hesitation, grinding the hard bulge in his pants against me.

"Fuck, Angel. I should spank you for being such a brat earlier," he rasps against my mouth.

"I should spank *you* for springing a wedding on me," I counter, pulling back just enough to catch my breath.

Ringo chuckles. "I'm not really the submissive type, Angel. But if you want to call it foreplay, I'll let you spank me," his voice lowers an octave. "Just be prepared for what will happen after that."

My brows shoot up. "What will happen?"

I should know better by now, because his sinister smirk says it all.

I'm in trouble.

"This."

It's all he says before dropping to his knees and hitching up the satin of my dress.

"Ringo, what are you—"

My words catch in my throat as he presses an open mouthed kiss *right there*! Straight to the centre of my panties, hot and hungry.

I gasp, palms slapping to the rough bark behind me as he urges my legs wider with ravenous hands.

"Wait," I pant. "We can't... not out here."

A low growl rolls from his chest, the vibration of it igniting sparks over my clit, and I lose all train of thought.

"I'm fucking starving, Angel." He sounds almost feral. "Eating your pussy is the only thing that will sate my appetite right now."

My whimper is loud and raw, full of desperation, and I look down to see his eyes gazing up at me from behind the bunched up fabric of my dress.

The only part of his face I can see are those dark dangerous eyes, but just their intensity is enough to undo me.

"Someone will see," I point out, even as I arch against the heat of his mouth, needing to feel his lips, tongue, any part of him *right there*.

"You're my fucking wife now," he bites out, pulling back only far enough to speak. "I'll enjoy you wherever and whenever I fucking want. I don't care who's around."

I want to protest, but then he's shifting my panties aside and gliding the hot silk of his tongue over my seam and I swear, I short circuit.

21

RINGO

The way I'm fucking salivating to eat her cunt. Fuck. Nothing has ever consumed me more than this need. To taste her again. To bring her to the brink and help her crash over the edge while revelling in her juices.

Again.

It was one thing to taste her fingers that time, back at the Western, but last night, sliding my tongue between her pretty pink folds nearly fucking undid me.

I should be punishing her for lying to me about picturing Harry Styles. I know she wasn't fucking picturing him. I was the only man she was seeing. I've seen that look in her eyes before, and it's never been about anyone else. Just me… just us.

"Ringo," she whimpers from above, pressing her head back against the tree as I devour her clit like it's my favourite fucking treat.

And fuck. It is.

Her sweet nectar rushes into my mouth, and as I pull back to look at her perfect pussy, I replace my tongue with my fingers, flicking them over her swollen little nub.

"Fuck, Angel. You're so wet for me. How long have you been like this?"

Instead of answering, she squeezes her eyes shut, shaking her head against the tree.

"I asked you a question, Angel." I pull back, removing my fingers, and just like that, her caramel eyes snap open. "Answer me."

Deliberately licking my lips, I tease her with the hint of my tongue, her eyes tracking the movement before shifting to my beard, which is already glistening with her slickness.

"Ever since I woke up." Her sweet voice is fucking gravelly, her arousal wrecking her in the best way.

"Even when you were arguing with me about becoming my wife?"

Her gaze drops to the ground beside us as her cheeks flush with embarrassment.

Fuck... that won't do.

"Eyes back on me," I snap, and just like that, her pretty orbs are locked onto mine, just the way I like them. "Answer my question."

To encourage her, I slide my fingers over her wet seam, spreading her slickness around her clit and applying a little more pressure.

"Especially when I was arguing with you," she rushes out, her lids growing heavy as she watches me.

Just what I thought. My Angel gets aroused when we face off.

"You like riling me up, don't you?" I ask, and she nods, biting her lip.

I know how hard it is for her to speak the truth, so for her honesty, I decide to reward her.

Surging forward, I glide my tongue over her needy clit in one long, filthy stroke.

She cries out, arching into me, greedy for more, so I go to fucking town. Licking. Sucking. Sinking two fingers deep inside her until she's crying out so loud, there's no fucking way Ace—who's still just around the corner waiting for us on the deck—didn't hear.

Knowing he can hear me pleasure my wife makes me want to pound my fucking chest like a savage. It's a fucking honour. And my Angel is the only person I will *ever* drop to my knees for.

As she writhes, grinding her mound against my face, her tight walls grip my digits like a fucking vice. She's hot and wet and soft inside, while her clit swells under my tongue. I flick it and lick it and suck it with a hunger that has her breaking apart in seconds.

Her pulsing cunt drags my fingers deeper, and fuuuck, all I can think about is burying my cock inside her and staying there until she milks me dry. I want to fill her with so much of my DNA that it leaks out of her for hours, while the rest of it gets absorbed, claimed by her body, like it fucking belongs there.

Fuck.

There's just something about the idea of having my DNA mixing with hers, becoming part of her.

"Cam," she whimpers, her fingers fisting in my hair as she tries to push me off.

But I can't fucking stop. My tongue keeps tormenting her sensitive little nub.

I'm fucking addicted.

Her grip tightens, trying to shove me back, her hips writhing like they want to get away… but then they hesitate, like they're not sure if they want to escape.

Chuckling low, I decide to stop teasing her. We've got a fucking wedding celebration to get to, so the real fun will have to wait until later.

Easing back, my eyes meet hers, heavy with lust, and fuck me, she's so fucking stunning like this.

"You drenched my hand again, Angel." I smirk, and her eyes widen a little as her lips part to apologise, but I stop her, curling my fingers still deep inside her, dragging a squeak from her throat. "Don't you dare say sorry."

Sucking in her lips, she breathes heavily through her nose and nods quickly, so I ease the pressure off her swollen and extra sensitive g-spot, and slip my fingers free.

Her caramel orbs lock onto my glistening fingers as I hold them up, and with a shit-eating grin, I proceed to lick them clean. One by fucking one.

She bites her lip, watching like I'm sucking honey off my digits, her chest rising and falling quickly like the sight is turning her on… again.

"You know what I think?" I ask, tugging her panties down until she lifts each foot so I can slip them free.

"What?" she breathes so quietly I barely hear it.

"I think my wife is a dirty girl. I think she secretly gets turned on by the filthiest stuff, but she's just too embarrassed to admit it."

Abbey parts her lips, ready to protest, but then frowns and snaps her lips shut.

Then she shrugs.

I chuckle, using her panties to dry off my fingers.

"Fuck yeah. My old lady is a *dirty little whore*."

She stiffens, going completely rigid, her eyes blowing wide with what can only be described as horror.

Shit.

One hand raised, I stand slowly as I tuck her panties into my pocket, watching panic flicker across her face.

"Angel, I'm sorry," I rush out, realising I fucked up.

In my world, chicks *love* being called a whore, and for a hot fucking minute, I forgot Abbey's *not* from my world.

Shaking her head frantically, her eyes dart everywhere but never land on me.

I know that look.

She's gearing up to fucking run.

Trying to think quickly, I do the only thing I can and reach out, pulling her to my chest, ignoring her immediate reaction to pull away, her soft whimper breaking something in me.

"Don't run from me again, Angel. I'm sorry. I fucking forgot… for a minute there, I fucking forgot."

"Why would you say that to me?" Her words are muffled against my chest before she shoves me back, and I fucking let her. "Why would you call me that?"

"Fuck, Abs, I'm sorry." I go to rake my hand through my hair, but instead find it fucking tied back. "Chicks in my world dig that stuff. It's a turn on for them."

As I reel, Abbey's mortified expression hardens into something else entirely… anger.

"Chicks in *your* world?" she scoffs. "I can't imagine anyone wants to be called a whore, Cameron. But for argument's sake, even if they do, what the hell makes you think *I'm* anything like *them*?"

Her voice rises, sharpening with each word, her whole body vibrating with the rage she feels.

"Because I'm your wife now? Is that it?" she snaps. "Now you can treat me however you want?"

Fuck. I guess now's a bad time to admit that her anger is making me even harder than I was a minute ago.

"No, Angel. Fuck. I really didn't think. I'm sorry."

Angry tears glaze her eyes as she glares at me, fists balled at her sides like she's ready to use me as her own personal punching bag.

And fuck… I'd let her if I thought it would help.

Quickly stepping away from the tree, she gives me her back, wrapping her arms around her middle, like she's trying to shield her baby… from me.

Jesus! Fuck!

Furious at myself for being such a thoughtless idiot, I blow out a sharp, frustrated breath, hoping like hell I can make this right.

Stepping up behind her, I watch her stiffen the second she feels the heat of my body at her back.

"Did *they* call you that, Angel?"

I hate having to ask. I hate even more that I already suspect the answer. But I need to know. I need to be sure so I don't trigger her again.

A shudder rolls through her, shoulders slumping as her head dips forward, her eyes locking on the leafy ground in front of her.

Then she nods.

I. AM. SUCH. A. FUCK. UP!

I already figured they used the word, *cunt*, given her reaction that time in my bed. And now, I know the word *whore* is a trigger for her, too.

"Abs, I'm sorry," I rasp, reaching out to gently grip her hips as I lean in close to her ear. "I'm so fucking sorry. I know there's still so much I need to learn about you, but I swear, I never meant it maliciously. It was dirty talk. I didn't think. I swear to you, I'll never fucking use the word again."

So quickly, she spins, arms flying around my neck like her body needs me before her brain can catch up.

On instinct, I lift her. She wraps herself around me, burying her face in the crook of my neck.

"I'm sorry," she whispers. "I want to give you what you want. It just took me by surprise."

My arms weave around her, holding her so fucking tight like I'm scared she'll crumble away and float off in the breeze.

My hard on is long forgotten, replaced by a heavy, aching truth I can't keep pretending isn't there.

This isn't just about protecting her. This isn't just about friendship. Hell, it's not even about lust.

Abbey is quickly becoming the very air I breathe.

"No need to apologise, Angel. I just need to learn your triggers so I don't fuck up again."

"I'm sorry," she whimpers this time, squeezing my neck tighter. "I don't want to be like this."

Gritting my teeth, my rage bubbles just beneath the surface. I need to find those motherfuckers. Hunt them down and kill them, so I can bring my Angel some fucking peace.

"Hey. There's nothing wrong with you. You hear me?" I rasp, my voice laced with fire. "You're so fucking strong for surviving what you have. And look how hard you've been fighting to protect your baby. As far as I'm concerned, you're a fucking warrior."

Slowly, her death grip around my neck eases, and she shifts back just enough to look into my eyes.

"I don't feel like a warrior."

Reaching up, I stroke some of her pink-tinged hair off her face.

"I wish you could see yourself through my eyes," I tell her, my voice rough with truth. "You'd never doubt it again."

"I wish I could too," she whispers, "I'd like to feel as strong as you say I am."

My chest fucking aches at the disbelief in her tone. She really doesn't see it. Doesn't see the power she carries with every breath.

But I do. And I'll keep reminding her, every chance I get.

Deciding I want to talk to her properly, I walk us over to a large boulder by the water and sit my arse down, adjusting her on my lap so she's facing me.

"Let me ask you this," I ask, soaking in her caramel orbs and the uncertainty I see in them. "What was it that changed in your life that made you start fighting back?"

She frowns, slowly shaking her head. "I didn't fight back."

My brows hitch.

"You don't think what I walked into that night in your bedroom, covered in your own blood, and holding a fucking lethal shard of glass fully prepared to attack, wasn't fighting back?"

Her frown deepens, her gaze dropping to my chest as she thinks over this.

"Something changed, Angel. Because for months, you endured what your family did. You endured that fuckwit. You endured what his dead-men-walking mates did to you."

"Well… I couldn't let them near my baby," she deadpans, and I nod.

"Exactly. You stayed all that time. Took the pain. Lived in it. But the moment the pain of knowing you couldn't let them near your baby was greater than what you'd already endured, you started fighting back."

She blinks a few times, her frown returning. "I couldn't even do that right. I still needed help, I—"

"Needing help doesn't make you weak, Abs." I cut her off, not wanting her to fall into that spiral. "And look at how far you've come. You don't need to swing fists or wield a weapon to be strong. You just need to keep fighting. Just like a fucking warrior."

For a long moment, she just stares at me, like she's trying to see past my eyes and into the soul behind them.

"Did I marry a poet?"

Her words catch me off guard, and a laugh escapes me, the rumble of it enticing her lips to kick up too.

"No one's ever called me a fucking poet before, Angel."

She casually shrugs a single shoulder.

"I'm starting to think all you biker men are secret poets, if those wedding vows are anything to go by."

I can't stop fucking smiling, which is fucking weird. I can't remember the last time I smiled this fucking much.

"The Southern Sadists might be full of brutes and thugs and burley-as-fuck criminals, but one thing we *do* fucking well is taking care of our women."

Now she's frowning again, looking at me like I've lost my fucking shit.

"You might want to tell your President that. He's married to Jols' mum, yet spends all of his time with Celina. And *Celina* takes second chair to his dog Molly."

"The situation with Jols' mum and Smitty is different. She didn't marry him for love. It was more about protection, and keeping a watch over Jols after what happened to her." I pause, my lips twitching into a smirk. "Besides, I'm pretty sure she's batting for the same team now."

Abbey's brows shoot up, and I can't help but chuckle.

"Right, well. What about Barts? As far as I've been able to make out, he's in the dog house with his woman."

"You know about Barts and Natasha?" I ask, because how the fuck does she know that?

"Jols and I came across him one morning when we were leaving the laundry room. She was scolding him for being drunk." Abbey shrugs casually.

"Well, Barts has an addiction problem. With these fucking lockdowns, it's been hard as hell to get him the help he needs."

"And what about Brody?" she continues, determined to prove me wrong. "He treats women like they are pieces of meat."

I cringe. "Technically, he's not a Southern Sadist until he patches in. If he ever gets his shit together long enough to get a fucking invitation. So Brody is not a good example, Angel."

She opens her mouth, probably to add another club brother to her list, so I press my hand over it, cutting her off.

"Stop trying to prove me wrong," I mutter, releasing her mouth and brushing my thumb across her jaw. "You haven't seen the married members, because most of them stay home with their wives and kids. They don't need to party their days away or crash at the clubhouse. They show up when they're needed, and help run the business side of things. So trust me Angel, married Southern Sadists take care of their women."

"So, since we're married now, we don't need to go back to the Western?"

"No." I shake my head, easing her down off my lap. "The club is laying low for a while, until we sort out the Officer Allen situation. Half the men are heading to our northern chapter. The rest are moving to the new property we've just acquired."

Abbey stiffens, her eyes wide as she stares at me.

"You mean… the property in Fox Pines?"

"Yeah, Angel. The old Vixen's Lodge Estate." I rise, straightening out my clothes and brushing the dirt off my knees from before.

"Are we… going there too?"

Fuck. Her voice is so timid. I knew she'd be nervous about returning to her hometown, which is why I've made other arrangements for her.

"You will stay here with my ma and sisters."

"Me?" She frowns, confusion clouding her features, and like a fucking coward, I avoid her gaze. "You're not staying with me?"

Sighing, I take her hand, finding a slight tremble in it that wrecks me more than she'll ever know.

"I need to help my club, so I'll join them in a week or so."

"And I'll stay here?" she snaps, and fuck me, now she's pissed again.

How do I keep fucking this up? We've been married for less than an hour, and I swear I'm about to get served divorce papers.

"I'm not taking you to Fox Pines until it's safe, Angel," I try to explain. "There's nowhere to sleep there yet. My club brothers will start converting shipping containers into livable spaces. Once it's safe, we'll go together."

"Right," she snaps again, her voice sharp enough to cut. "So I'll stay here and behave like a good little wife, while you head off to Fox Pines with your club and the Doxies to do God knows what."

My frown is so deep it fucking hurts, but the second I give the smallest nod, my wife is already storming off towards the barn.

"Where are you going?" I snap, fucking annoyed, more at myself than anything.

"To find Wendy," she snarls over her shoulder.

Wendy? Did I hear that right?

"Why the fuck do you want to find *that* bitch?"

I nearly crash into her when she stops abruptly and spins back around, stabbing her finger to the centre of my chest.

"If you think I'll stand by and turn a blind eye while you fuck Wendy behind my back, you've got another thing coming!"

"What the fuck!" I bark, snatching her finger in my grip because, *Jesus fuck,* her relentless poking is starting to bruise. "What the hell are you talking about?"

"She told me all about you and her, Ringo." She snatches her hand away, eyes blazing.

"I'll ask again," I grit out, "what the fuck are you talking about? There is no *me and her.*"

The way my Angel props her hands on her hips and glares at me like she's ready to throw down, has my fucking cock twitching.

"Really? So you don't go to her begging to sink your cock into her diseased… *cunt*."

My brows shoot up so hard they disappear under my damn hairline for a thousand fucking reasons.

One being that she just said the word *cunt*, which I know is a trigger for her. I suppose it could depend on the context it's used, though.

Another is because, what the fuck is happening right now?

"Angel. You're starting to piss me the fuck off," I grit through my clenched teeth. "Why the fuck would you think I'd put my cock anywhere near that bitch?"

"She told me."

"Uh-ha." My voice drops as I lift a brow. "And what *else* did Wendy tell you?"

Her anger falters as her lips seal shut.

"Abbey. Tell me *right fucking now*."

Those caramel orbs drop to the ground between us, so I snap my fucking fingers in front of her face.

"Eyes back the *fuck* on mine." When they dart back, I snarl. "Fucking tell me."

She doesn't even flinch at my harsh tone, her own anger still there, and I fucking love seeing her fight for something she cares about.

"Wendy said you'll get bored with me. That you don't do *sweet*. That I'm too *vanilla* for a man like you."

I fucking growl. "Anything else?"

"She said you…" She shrugs, almost like she's unsure she should keep speaking, "like it rough. That you like to choke your women until they stop breathing. That you fuck them after they pass out. She said you like being in full control of their body, so you can do whatever you want, without them saying… no."

WHAT. THE. FUCK!

I am absolutely fucking fuming.

"Is that all she said, or is there more?" I ask through gritted teeth, my fists balled so tight I wouldn't be surprised if my nails are drawing fucking blood.

This time, when my Angel answers, her fire is back.

Lifting her chin, her glare burns through me, and she speaks so fucking clearly there's no way I can misunderstand a single fucking word.

"Wendy told me not to go crying to her when I marry you thinking I've nailed you down, only to find out *she's* your old lady. That while I'm playing house with you, when you go back to the club, you'll be, and I quote, 'balls deep' in Wendy's arse."

My nostrils flare, and my chest heaves, rising and falling so fast I can barely fucking breathe.

"I'm going to *FUCKING KILL HER!*"

My roar echoes across the property. Raw. Violent. And feral. And Abbey lets out a shocked squeak as I spin and storm off towards the fucking barn, ready to do exactly what I just fucking promised.

22

ABBEY

*O*h my God, he's really going to kill her!

"Wait! Ringo!" I cry, bolting after him and trying to ignore the fact that I'm not wearing any panties beneath this satin gown.

Hurrying around the corner he just disappeared behind, I catch sight of him storming past Ace, who's still on the deck, now with a table set up and some papers spread out.

Oh my... was Ace there this whole time? Did he hear us? Hear me?

"Hey, wait up, Ringo. You've gotta sign the marriage papers," Ace calls, and Ringo grinds to a stop before stalking to him.

"Where?"

By the time I reach them, Ringo's already scrawling his name along the dotted line. Literally.

"Oh good. Abbey. You need to sign, too."

I nod, but my gaze is glued to Ringo as he finishes signing and slams the pen down on the table before storming off again.

Eyes wide, I glance at Ace, who looks apologetic, and I'm not sure if it's for Ringo's outburst or for having to interrupt his furious club brother.

"Uh… just sign here, please." He points to the papers, so I quickly snatch up the pen, scribble my name, and toss it down before hurrying after my husband.

Oh wow.

I have a husband.

A husband that is angrier than I've ever seen him.

"Wendy!" he bellows, storming across the yard towards the barn, where the thick crowd mingles, and soulful music plays quietly in the background.

All eyes swing to him as he barrels through, then snap to me as I rush after him, probably looking like a hot mess as I try to run in these strappy heels, and a satin gown while holding my damn boobs, because I couldn't wear a bra with this dress.

"What's going on?" JD hurries to Ringo's side, while Jols bee-lines for me.

"Wendy is what fucking happened," Ringo hisses, loud enough for everyone to hear, and just like that, a heavy silence falls over the crowd.

"Oh shit," Jols whispers, taking my arm to slow me down. "Babe. You don't want to see this."

"What?" I squeak, my panic spiking now even more certain my husband is about to kill Wendy. "No. You have to stop him."

Sympathy washes over Jols' features as she looks at me, so I shove her off, charging for Ringo, pushing through the crowd in a blind panic, desperate to reach him before it's too late.

"Why would you say those things to Abbey?!" Ringo's voice booms, loud and menacing, as I shove through the closing-in crowd. I burst into the barn to find him towering over Wendy, his face inches from hers as she flinches back. Smitty and Spud lounge nearby, unfazed, like this behaviour is just a typical day in club life.

"I didn't say anything to her!" Wendy cries, arching so far back in her chair that she looks like she's about to snap in half.

"One thing I do know," Ringo growls, "is my wife is not a fucking liar. And you've been caught out in more lies than I can fucking count. So tell me why the fuck I shouldn't kill you right now!?"

"You don't have the balls," Wendy sneers, and just like that, Ringo's hand snaps around her throat.

Behind me, Jols mutters a curse under her breath, but none of the men move a muscle.

Hell, even Smitty is too preoccupied picking something out of his teeth as he pats his dog.

"Cameron!" I snap, the name coming out louder than I meant it to, but it does the trick, and Ringo's wild gaze whips to me. "She's not worth it."

"You don't think she should die for feeding you those lies?" he growls, and I shake my head.

"She's jealous. And pathetic. But my guess is she's hurt because she's had her eye on you for so long and you haven't given her the time of day. So she may be a liar, but she doesn't deserve to die for it."

Taking a step closer, I reach out and snake my fingers around his wrist, tugging gently, urging him to release Wendy's neck, and he does.

She gasps, her face flushed, eyes leaking tears, and even though she's been nothing but a bitch to me, I feel a flicker of pity for her.

She just wants to be loved.

I know what that's like.

"I want her gone," Ringo snaps, turning to his President, who shrugs, like he doesn't care either way, before addressing Spud.

"You can take the bitch with you up north. See if you can find her an old man so she stops being a cunt."

Spud chuckles. "Sure thing, Prez."

"Does that appease my Sergeant-at-Arms?" Smitty asks, smug as hell, and I have the urge to slap him.

"As long as I don't have to see the bitch again, then yes," Ringo glares at his President, his fists balled in anger.

"Then consider it done. Now stop fucking whining and let's celebrate your nuptials. Let's get fucked up!"

The crowd erupts in cheers.

Everyone but me and Ringo.

And I guess Wendy too, but as far as I'm concerned, she doesn't exist.

As the tension eases, I realise my heart is still thrashing in my chest, each beat sharp and uneven, leaving me short of breath.

"You okay?" Lani's voice cuts through the haze, her concerned eyes suddenly in front of me, blocking my view of my husband.

I nod, pressing a shaky hand to my chest.

"I kind of wish I could drink wine right now. I need something to calm me down."

"I know the *perfect* thing to calm you down." Lani waggles her brows just as Millie steps up beside us.

"What are you cooking up, Lans?"

"All this drama has Abbey on edge, so I think it's time for the first dance."

"Uh… how is *that* going to calm me down?" I ask, my gaze darting across the crowd of leather-clad bikers filling the room and spilling out the open barn doors.

"His neck," Alana states flatly, and at Millie's cringe, I can't help but giggle. "I know. I know. It's kinda gross, but apparently, you two have something going on. And before you say it's just about my brother protecting you, save your breath. Cam has *never* looked at anyone the way he looks at you."

"Unfortunately, I have to agree," Millie admits, catching me off guard.

Wait. What? I thought she hated me.

"Never thought I'd see the day Cam would fall *hopelessly* in love, but here we are." Millie shrugs and it takes me a second to catch up.

"He doesn't love me," I blurt, but they each hook an arm through mine, leading me back towards Ringo, who's deep in conversation with JD.

"If *that's* not love, then I'd hate to see him when he *is* in love." Millie smirks, curling her lips as Alana nods in agreement.

"I don't think I can handle that."

I open my mouth to protest again, but before I can spit out a word, Millie casually kicks the back of Ringo's boot, and he whirls around, rage contorting his expression, until he sees me.

Then, like magic, it falls away as if it were never there.

"What are you two doing with my wife?"

"Looking after her, which is something *you* should be doing, since she's your wife," Millie deadpans.

"All the drama made her nervous, so now you need to fix that," Lani explains as they both release my arms and nudge me into him.

Without hesitation, Ringo slips his arm around my waist, tugging me into his side.

"You okay, Angel?"

"She'll be better once you have your first dance," Alana explains and Ringo's brows shoot high.

I bet he wasn't expecting his sister to say that.

Biting down on my lip, I only just manage to stop myself from laughing as Ringo asks his next question.

"Why will dancing with me make her feel better?"

"Besides the fact it'll be hilarious watching you try to dance, big brother," Millie teases before Alana finishes her thought.

"She *needs* to smell you."

Heat explodes across my cheeks, my gaze dropping to the floor the moment Ringo's gaze snaps to mine.

He doesn't say anything. Just stares.

I can't bear to look up at him as his sisters giggle.

Before I realise what's happening, I'm swept up in his arms, a squeak flying from my lips as he cradles me to his chest.

"Take a whiff, Angel. I'm all yours."

Alana and Millie burst into laughter, and Ringo's club brothers nearby start cheering before Ringo calls out to JD.

"JD, be the DJ, will ya? It's time for me to have my first dance with my wife."

Hoots and hollers erupt around us as Ringo carries me to the centre of the room, where only last night there were tables and chairs filling the space. The same table he laid me out on and... instantly my cheeks bloom at the memory.

"Are we really doing this?" I whisper, trying and failing to bite back a smile, and he looks down at me, a smirk kicking up his lips.

"I married you, so yeah, we're fucking doing this."

My heart flips in my chest at the fire in his eyes.

Is he actually excited about this?

The dance? The wedding?

Both, maybe?

Lowering me onto my feet in the centre of the room, I feel too many eyes on us, but I don't look at anyone but Ringo. My husband.

The moment music blasts through the speakers, everyone cheers, and Ringo chuckles, his smile broad as he takes in his family watching on.

It's not just his sisters and mother. It's the club members as well.

All of them watching… waiting.

It doesn't take long for me to recognise the song, and I can barely contain my smile as Ringo pulls me in, sliding one hand around to rest on my lower back, and the other lifting mine as he stares into my eyes.

"Really? *Aerosmith*?" I giggle, and he nods, proud as hell.

"Club tradition, Angel."

I snort another laugh, mainly at the obvious generation gap there is between us and our taste of music, and then, just as Steven Tyler's voice spills through the speakers, Ringo starts to sing along.

It's low. Raspy. And just for me.

And I melt.

I barely register all the eyes on us as we sway together, like our bodies already know this rhythm.

This man.

His voice.

Only for me.

Is this a dream?

Is this really happening?

Is the most lethal man I've ever laid eyes on seriously singing the lyrics to *'I Don't Want to Miss a Thing'* to me as we dance, surrounded by his club and family?

A tidal wave of emotion hits me hard, my eyes stinging, tears threatening to fall, but somehow, I hold them back.

I desperately want to deny my feelings for this man, because if I let myself fall… if I let myself love him… My heart will never survive when he walks away.

I've been trying so hard to fight it. To keep it buried deep. But right now, as he tugs me a little closer like he can't stand even an inch between us, I know I'm already losing.

Maybe, I never stood a chance.

"I could stay lost in the moment," he sings, "forever."

My bottom lip starts to wobble, so I bite the damn thing, not wanting him to see how weak I am when it comes to him.

"Where a moment spent with you," he leans closer, pressing his forehead to mine as he sings, "is a moment I treasure."

Suddenly, the whole room erupts, belting the chorus, the sound loud, wild… and perfect.

A laugh bursts from me, even as a few tears escape, my gaze taking in the bikers surrounding us, all of them holding up their beers, yelling the lyrics with zero shame.

Ringo spins us suddenly, and more laughter spills from me as his playful side kicks in.

Before I know it, Doxies and Southern Sadists are joining us on the makeshift dance floor, the chaos electric around us, yet all I can focus on is him.

Dropping my hand, Ringo pulls me in close, so tight I can feel exactly what kind of effect this moment is having on him.

He's hard. And he's not even trying to hide it.

"Do you feel better now, Angel?"

I nod, my gaze slipping to his lips, catching the satisfied grin that tugs at them.

"I'm sorry for scaring you before." He leans in close to my ear, voice low. "That shit with Wendy… well, it makes me fucking wild."

"Yeah. I noticed." I relax into him, letting his arms completely claim me.

It's a mix of hard and soft. Like the brutal beast of a man is still right here in this room, but his gentleness is just for me.

And God… that does something to me.

"I'll fuck up anyone that tries to hurt you, physically or emotionally, Angel. I don't care who they are."

My brows lift. "What if it's your ma?"

He grins. "My ma would never treat you badly. No matter what. She's got a golden heart."

I open my mouth to give him another example, but he silences me by pressing his lips to mine.

The sound around us fades away, muffled, like we're trapped in a bubble. Just me and him. Nothing else. No one else.

He deepens the kiss, and my stomach flutters, but it's not from my heart or butterflies.

It's my baby.

A sob lurches up my throat, but Ringo swallows it, squeezing me closer like he wants to crawl under my skin and stay there.

Do you like him, little corn?

Do you feel safe around Cameron?

Do you feel how much he cares?

He or she can feel him. I just know it.

Breaking the kiss, Ringo pulls back just enough to swipe his thumbs across my cheeks, and that's when I realise. I'm actually crying.

"I got you, Abs," he rasps, his whiskey eyes locked onto mine, so intense that I want to look away... but I can't.

"Must be my hormones," I lie, and he lets out a soft, knowing chuckle.

"Yeah. Must be."

Then, like the universe knows we need a breather, the smell of food hits us. We glance around to see the Doxies carrying trays of food, being bossed around by Ringo's mum as she tells them exactly where to put everything.

"Come on, Angel. It's time for me to feed my wife."

My heart flips again at hearing him call me his wife, and it does something to me.

I want to question my reaction, since I've been so against marriage. Against the whole idea of being someone's wife. Someone's property.

But things feel different now. With Ringo, everything is different.

The way he looks after me, the way he sees me. It's the kind of care I've craved for longer than I want to admit.

Maybe I just need to stop overthinking everything and just be in these moments with him.

We spend the next couple of hours eating and chatting, Ringo never once letting me out of his reach.

He keeps me seated at his side, tugging my chair so close we're practically one person. Always touching by the brush of our thighs, or our hands, or his arm curled around my back.

There are no speeches like the weddings in movies. No cheesy toasts or dramatic declarations. It's just a big, loud, slightly unhinged party, and honestly, I'm okay with that.

As the day rolls on, the Southern Sadists and Doxies overindulge in their drinks, getting rowdier by the minute.

I'm quietly grateful that Millie took their mum back to the house earlier, because the energy is shifting, and there's some not so savory activities starting up that are definitely not mother-approved.

"What are they doing?" I ask, now perched on Ringo's knee, pointing across the room to a group of men, sitting around a table, their laughter louder than any others.

"Oh, the prospects are playing Russian Shot Roulette," JD answers casually, like that's supposed to mean something to me, and Ringo chuckles, seeing the confusion written across my face.

"You know the gist of normal Russian Roulette, right?" JD asks, and I nod.

"A gun. One bullet. Right?"

He nods back. "Well, Russian *Shot* Roulette has six shot glasses, and six prospects. Each glass has something different. Only one actually has alcohol."

"What's in the other glasses?" I glance at Ringo and catch his smirk.

"You don't want to know." Ringo chuckles, and I whip my head back towards the group of guys.

"Stop treating her so precious." Jols rolls her eyes at Ringo, and then tells me what he wouldn't. "One is a fireball shot, which isn't so bad. One is a Worcestershire and wasabi mix. One is castor oil with chocolate syrup. One is unflushed dunny water. One is raw egg with hot sauce and vodka. And then one is a lucky dip."

By the time she finishes, my mouth is hanging open.

"What's in the lucky dip?"

"Not exactly sure, but given what I saw earlier," Jols cringes, "I think the last one will have a prospect walking around with a boner for a fucking week."

My brows hitch into my hairline. "Viagra is in it?"

"A lucky dip is usually laced with some sort of drug that will fuck you up in one way or another," Jols explains, and I shoot panicked eyes to Ringo, but he looks completely unfazed.

"They do this kind of shit to the prospects all the time," he mutters with a shrug.

"And you're not concerned about your brother?" I ask JD, but he shakes his head, totally chill.

"I just hope the horny fucker doesn't get the Viagra one. I'll be locking up the goats if he does," JD snickers to Ringo, who grins in return.

I make the mistake of watching the prospects downing the first shot, and a jet of vomit erupts from one prospect's mouth like a fountain, splashing across the table, before another one hurls too.

I gag.

"Okay. That's enough of that." Ringo stands abruptly, dragging me out of the barn.

My stomach churns as I try to shake off what I just witnessed, and I hear JD and Jols behind us, howling with laughter at whatever fresh hell just unfolded.

Outside, the sun has dropped lower in the sky, casting a golden haze over the yard, its beauty totally wasted on the craziness happening out here with more of the club brothers getting up to no good.

A couple of motorcycles roar to life before two guys line them up side by side, their engines like a rumble of thunder.

"Fucking hell," Ringo mutters, coming to stand with Stocky, Murf, and Trunk. "If someone dies on my property, I'm not digging the fucking grave."

"Why would they die?" I ask, feeling like I'm missing something, but then I see two other men put blindfolds on each rider, before climbing on the back of each motorcycle, and Ringo just gestures to the unfolding madness.

"You're about to find out."

The next thing I know, the bikes tear off down the driveway, zigzagging like lunatics as the blindfolded riders try to steer blind, the men on the back yelling directions over the roar of the engines.

I gasp, slapping a hand to my chest as one of the bikes loses control, skidding across the gravel before tipping onto the grass with a thud.

The yard erupts in cheers and hoots, while I'm nothing but shocked, and at best a little amused at their craziness.

When I glance at Ringo, he's not watching the chaos. He's watching me, one side of his mouth kicking up as he shrugs.

"Alcohol makes them dumb."

I burst out laughing, doubling over at the unfiltered madness of it all, yet knowing I love every second.

Well, except maybe the vomiting part. I didn't like that.

Ringo's deep laugh joins mine, and we fall into each other, breathless and leaning on one another as we both try to compose ourselves, and I realise, we've never had such a shared lighthearted moment.

"Ringo, man. I'm all set up," a tall lanky looking biker calls from behind us, and Ringo nods over his shoulder.

"Thanks Vender. We'll be in in a sec."

Nothing about this day so far has been predictable, so curiosity instantly sparks me, and I open my mouth to ask, but Ringo beats me to it.

"It's time to get our ink."

"Our ink?" I blink, turning my gaze to the tall man walking away.

"Come on. I'll show you."

Taking my hand, Ringo weaves us through the crowd, heading back into the barn, but this time, Ringo gives the chaos across the far side of the room a wide berth.

Heading down a passage and into a brightly lit room, I see some sort of instrument I'm not familiar with.

"I'll go first," Ringo states, guiding me gently to a nearby chair before taking the one next to it.

He slides off his wedding band, shooting me a wicked wink, and places his hand flat on the table. The other guy, Vender, sits across from him and picks up the instrument before a buzzing hum fills the air, making me flinch.

Ringo squeezes my hand with his free one, steady, solid and reassuring, and I watch as he gets my name tattooed around his finger, where the ring would normally sit.

Oh.

"So you'll always be there, even if the ring isn't," Ringo rasps softly, our eyes meeting for a flicker of a moment, and I swear, I can feel my heart swelling in my chest.

It takes no time at all, and once it's done, Ringo shows me my name etched permanently into his skin, and my heart races with something unfamiliar.

Mine.

That's what my brain is saying.

He's mine.

"I have hypoallergenic ink for you, Abbey," Vender states, snapping me out of my Ringo daze as he adjusts something on the table while Ringo leans back in his seat. "It's safer while you're pregnant. I'll just do it light, and once you've had your baby and finish breastfeeding, we can touch it up properly so it doesn't fade too fast."

I nod, blinking in surprise. I didn't even know that was a thing.

I'm nervous as hell. I've never thought about getting a tattoo before, and no one asked me if I wanted this. But there's something about having Ringo's name on me permanently that has me tugging the wedding band off and shifting forward to give Vendor my hand.

It's over quickly. It stung a little, and I have to wear my ring on my other hand while it heals, but the whole experience is cathartic, and I find myself smirking as Ringo leads me back out to the party.

My mum would hate everything about today.

Maybe that's why I've secretly loved every minute of it.

As far as wedding celebrations go, I've really enjoyed myself. Way more than I expected, and even though I felt like this was just another thing being forced on me this morning, now, it feels like the most right thing I've done since deciding to keep my baby.

More food is served as the sun goes down, and this time, we eat with Ringo's mum on the porch as she shares embarrassing stories about Ringo as a young boy. She even promises to get his baby albums out tomorrow, and I'm actually excited to see Cam as a little boy, full of mischief and dreaming big.

With the stars now in the sky, and Ringo's mum safely back inside away from the shenanigans, there's more dancing, drinking and wild games, which almost always guarantees someone will get hurt.

The Russian Shot Roulette lucky dip winner *wasn't* Brody. Thank goodness. But judging by the young prospect passed out on the sofa across the room with a very upright hard-on tenting his pants, I'm going to guess he's the one that won it.

"Whiskey blood oath," Murf murmurs as he sets a tray of shots on the table, and Stocky slaps a sharp knife down on the table in front of Ringo.

"Ahhh, what's a whiskey blood oath?" I ask, eyeing the blade with concern, but one look at Ringo's warm smile, and my panic instantly lessens.

"It's a toast to the groom with his closest buddies," JD grins proudly, and Ringo chuckles at seeing my confusion.

"Come on. Let's get this done. I'm about ready to consum-mate my marriage."

The guys around the table hoot, as you guessed it… my cheeks heat, and Jols grins, her eyes falling to her lap where she's texting someone on her phone.

Then, one by one, Ringo, JD, Murf, Trunk, and Stocky, each pick up the knife, slice a bloody line across their palms, then squeeze their fists, letting a drop of blood fall into each shot glass.

I watch, wide eyed as the whiskey swirls with the blood like something straight out of a cult ritual, and before I can even process what's happening, they lift the glasses and chant, *"Til death do us part."*

They shoot them back, and the moment they slam the empty glasses back on the table, Ringo stands, fire in his eyes as he holds out his hand to me.

"Come on, wife. Let's get to the fun part of the night."

23

RINGO

S he's nervous. There's a slight tremble in her hand as I lead her towards the open barn doors where my club brothers are already moving into line.

Earlier, she called us ruffians poetic, and while I don't really agree with that, I will say, we do shit like weddings, fucking well.

The rumble of demons fills the air, a sound that speaks to my fucking dark soul. I can feel it in my chest, lighting a spark of mateship that can only be found in families like this.

My club.

"What's happening?" Abbey asks quietly from beside me, so I give her hand a gentle squeeze, as she watches the men line their rides up on either side of the entrance, their headlights lighting up the centre, illuminating a path for us to take back to the house.

"It's an aisle of honour," I explain, gaining the attention of those caramel eyes I'm so at risk of fucking drowning in.

Something that looks a helluva lot like awe washes over her face, her gaze shifting back to take in the path.

"See," she speaks softly and I can only just hear it over the rumble of the bikes. "Poetic."

Chuckling, I drop her hand and sweep her up in my arms, ignoring her gasp as I carry my bride up the illuminated path.

The men cheer. The women clap. And I keep my focus on the steps at the end of the path and the door beyond it, knowing I'm finally going to claim my woman properly.

Abbey giggles as my sisters leap out of nowhere showering us in confetti, before my ma makes an appearance beside the front door to our home.

"You're a good man, Cameron." She reaches up and cups my face. "I'm so proud of you."

I smile at my ma even as guilt sits heavily in my gut.

I'm not a good fucking man. Not even close.

Her pride is wasted on me, since this wedding is nothing but a way to protect Abbey.

So why does it feel like more?

Fuck. I want it to be more.

"Thanks Ma. We'll see you in the morning," I offer, and she nods, patting my cheek before stepping back and letting me pass.

The moment we disappear inside, my club cheers behind us, some crude obscenities flying amongst them as the chaos fades with each step I take.

My Angel's hands are fisted in my shirt, gripping tightly like she's afraid to let go, and the closer I get to my bedroom, the more noticeable her trembling becomes.

Shit.

I'm a patient man. We don't have to consummate the marriage tonight or ever if she doesn't want to. Hell, I'll fuck my fleshlight for the rest of my miserable existance if I have to, but fuck, I want her. So fucking bad I ache with it. I want to sink inside her, feel her milk me. Stare into her eyes as we shatter together.

So, even though I know I can wait, I still want to push her a little to see how far she'll let me go.

"Angel," I rasp, stepping up to my door and entering the code, unlocking it. "Take some deep breaths for me."

She nods, gripping my shirt tighter, her chest rising and falling like she knows what's coming and has accepted it, but she's struggling to remain calm.

I don't fucking blame her.

After what she's been through, I'm surprised I've managed to get as far as I have with her already. That she trusts me. That she's here in my arms, shaking but staying.

Shit. It makes me want to protect her harder than I want to fuck her… almost.

Lingering in my doorway, I press my forehead to hers, just for a second. Just to feel her breath on my lips.

"You're safe, baby. I got you."

And I mean that more than anything I've ever said in my life.

She nods against me, a gentle whimper passing her lips, so I step into my suite, hearing the door click locked behind us and carry my wife into the living area, before lowering her to the sofa where she finally releases her death grip on my shirt.

"Here's what's going to happen, Angel." I eye her as I move to the kitchenette, taking out a cold beer and a bottle of water from the fridge. "We're going to take things slow. You're going to let me pleasure you, and do whatever it takes to have you begging for my cock."

Approaching her with slow and deliberate steps, I hold out the bottle of water, her fingers brushing mine as she takes it, her caramel gaze never leaving mine.

"You think you can make me beg?" Her voice is quiet, yet laced with heat, and I smirk.

"Fuck yes, I do," I growl, my voice thick with promise. "Angel, I can make you so fucking horny, there'll be no way you *won't* want my cock buried deep inside you."

Her lips part, cheeks flushing that gorgeous shade of pink, and I know my words are already steering her exactly where I want her.

"See. It's already working isn't it?"

"No."

"Liar." I chuckle, taking a swig of my beer as I lean against the wall by the guitars. "Pull up your dress, Angel. Show me your pussy."

Her brows hitch, and she chokes on the water she was trying to swallow, slapping her hand against her chest.

"You can't just say that." She coughs again, eyes wide.

"Why not?" I step closer, my voice rough. "You're my wife. We're in our private space. We are both insanely attracted to each other. My cock is hard basically twenty-four seven when you're around." I watch her lips part as she sucks in a breath.

"I've heard you *come*. Watched the way your face looks almost pained when it hits. I've *tasted* you. *Eaten* you." I pause, letting my words simmer for a beat. "I fucking married you even after you imagined me as one of your fucking boy band crushes."

She smirks at that, and I can't help but smirk too. Hers cocky, mine feral.

"So yeah, Angel. I want to *see* your pussy. I want to see how *wet* you are right now. I want you to hitch up that dress, part those thighs, and show me your sweet, pink *cunt*."

She stiffens at the word, just as I expected, so I move slow. Calm and deliberate.

Placing my beer down, I start shucking off my cut, keeping my eyes locked on hers.

"I know you *hate* that word, Angel, but let me ask you something." I step closer, watching her head tip back to keep her eyes locked with mine. "When I say it, does it sound as crude as the times you heard it from those dead fucking men walking?"

For a long moment, she simply watches me, her gaze falling to where I unbutton my shirt, her grip tight on the bottle of water in her hands.

"Answer me, Angel," I demand, and this time her gaze flicks back to mine.

"I'm… not sure." Her voice is soft, but not so scared now. "Say it again."

Fuck. There she is. My curious Angel.

"I want you to hitch up that dress, part those thighs, and show me your sweet, pink *cunt*."

Her lips part as a breath whooshes from her, her tongue darting out to wet her lips. Shifting on the couch, she slowly places the bottle of water on the floor, watching as I continue to tease her, peeling off my shirt.

Gathering the satin fabric of her dress, she slowly lifts it, finally revealing her bare pussy.

My cock jerks at the sight of her naked flesh, reminding me that I never gave her panties back earlier, and as I pop the button on my pants, she shifts her legs wider to open herself up to me.

"Fuck, Angel. You can be such a good girl when you want to be."

Her cheeks are glowing, but she doesn't stop, leaning back into the cushions to make sure I can see every single inch of her glistening cunt.

"You're soaked. Again," I rasp, toeing off my boots and kicking them to the side. "Are you aching, Angel? Do you need me to touch you?"

"Yes," she whimpers with so much need that I have to fight the fucking urge to lunge at her.

"Do you want me to touch you with my fingers?" I ask, holding my hand up and wiggling my digits. "Or perhaps my tongue?" I slide it out, licking my lips and noticing how her dainty hands grip her thighs tightly. "Or perhaps, you want me to use this?"

Easing my fly down, I reach into my boxers and free my rock hard cock, giving it a pump for good measure.

Her lips part, her fingers dig into her thighs, right before she snaps her legs closed.

Shit.

This might be harder than I thought… but I'm not one to back down from a challenge though.

Stepping forward, I watch how she stiffens, but she doesn't retreat, so I pump my cock again a few times, keeping her attention on it as I close in.

"You can touch it if you like. You didn't mind having it in your hands back at the Western."

She bites her lip, and I know exactly what's running through her head.

She's remembering the night I woke up to her touching me. Exploring my body with her fingers, letting her curiosity control her.

"Did you like feeling my cock in your hands, Angel?"

She nods absentmindedly, and I notice her legs easing apart again, like the idea of my cock is no longer so terrifying.

"Touch me," I demand, hoping I'm not pushing her too quickly, but then she obeys, reaching out to gently grip my cock, and I let my hand fall away, giving her all the control.

"Fuuuck, Angel. I love feeling your hand around me."

Her big doe eyes dart up to mine as she shifts forward on the sofa, her dainty hand slowly pumping me, sliding up and down my shaft, over and over.

A drop of precum beads on my tip, so I decide to push her a little further.

"Lick it."

There's a flicker of panic in her eyes, but she quickly masks it, a slight frown tugging at her brows like she's having a silent argument with herself.

Does she want to run?

Or does she want to stay and burn with me?

"Just a taste, Angel. I fucking ache to feel your tongue on me."

Those caramel orbs dart up to meet mine and I reach out, wrapping her pink ponytail around my hand.

Fuuuck. The way I could control her like this. Fisting her hair. Guiding her. Holding her in place. I fucking ache for it, but also, I've never been more terrified to take control in my life.

"You won't force it in my mouth?" she asks, her voice so small. Pained. And fuck me, I want to back down. I want to fall to my knees and tell her she never has to do anything sexual again.

The thing is… she needs this. She needs to be presented with an opportunity to do the things that were used against her with someone she trusts.

She does trust me. I know it and she knows it but her trauma sits on her shoulders reminding her of something that should never have fucking happened.

"I will never force anything on you. Remember you have all the control here. You say stop, and we stop."

She licks her lips, her grip tightening around my cock as she continues to stroke me up and down.

With a frown creasing her brow, her eyes zero in on the bead of precum on my tip.

"Should I have a safe word?" Her caramel gaze darts up to mine through the thick fan of her lashes. "That's a thing, right?"

"Yeah. It's a thing, but maybe, for you, we should use the traffic light method."

Her hand stills as her gaze meets mine again.

"Traffic light method?"

"Angel, don't stop," I growl, and she giggles, before resuming attention to my cock. "Atta girl."

Her blush returns, and it's really no surprise she has a praise kink, even though she likely doesn't know it.

"Traffic lights. Red for stop immediately. Orange for needing a break or pause. And green for everything is fucking good."

She grins. "I like that idea."

"Okay then, Angel. So, be a good girl and lick my cock."

Her chest rises and falls as a rush of air escapes her, only this time I'm certain it's from arousal.

With her gaze trained on the tip of my cock, I watch from above, my hand still wrapped in her hair, as she closes the distance and darts out her tongue, licking the clear bead off my tip.

"Fuuuck," I rasp, holding back my need to do exactly what she asked me not to do.

I want in her so fucking bad.

"You want to put it in your mouth?" My voice is rough as fuck, but she shakes her head, licking her lips as she eases back. "Do you want to put it inside you anywhere?"

Fuck, is that desperation in my tone?

Calm the fuck down, Ringo!

I already know she's going to shake her head before she does it, but that's alright. We have all night. Fuck. We have as long as it fucking takes.

Releasing her hair, I peel her hand from around my shaft, an agonising feat if there ever was one, and then I kneel between her legs bringing us eye level.

"Kiss me, Angel. I want to taste myself on your tongue."

Her eyes flare, my words doing something to her as she lurches forward, wrapping her arms around my neck to kiss me.

And I do fucking taste myself on her tongue. She makes sure of it as she sweeps hers into my mouth, moaning and shifting closer to me.

I haven't had the opportunity to fully explore her body yet.

Back at the Western, she was always covered in my hoodie, hiding herself. Hiding her bump. Only once did she let me feel her tits, the fabric of my hoodie a barrier, yet still, I felt her nipple pebble underneath.

I've tasted her fingers after she masturbated for me, and just last night I tasted her pussy for real.

Tongue to clit.

Tongue sliding deep inside her cunt.

Fuck, even my fingers felt her heat wrapped around them.

But through it all, I've never seen her completely naked. I've never been able to explore the delicate skin of her entire body with my lips and tongue. And fuck I want to. I want to taste every fucking inch of her.

When we were at the Western, I now know she wasn't just avoiding my touch because she was triggered by the idea, but she was trying to keep her pregnancy a secret.

Since the cat is out of the bag, I'm hoping like fuck she'll let me explore her now. Maybe she'll be a little hesitant the first time, but there's no fucking time like the present.

Gliding the tips of my fingers over her collarbone, I concentrate on any signs of her stiffening or faltering as we kiss, to tell me if she's not alright.

By the time I find her nipple, hard and straining against the ivory satin, we both moan into each other's mouths, her hands sliding to my shoulders before her nails dig into my flesh.

"Do you know how long I've fucking ached to touch these, Angel?" I rasp against her lips, pinching the hard peak before she arches into my touch. "Fuck. You like that?"

"Yes," she whimpers against my lips, so I release it and blindly search for the strap of her dress, easing it off her shoulder slowly, waiting for her to stop me if she needs to.

When she doesn't, I break our kiss completely, easing back to watch her lids flutter open.

"How do I get this dress off you?" I growl, and her lips kick up, like she's trying not to laugh.

"It has a side zipper." She gestures to her left, so I lift her arm to find it, unhooking the eye clip before easing the zip down.

For someone who was trembling only minutes ago, she's now noticeably more relaxed, her trust in me growing as I part the fabric, revealing a hint of her side.

Fuck, I want to see all of her.

With the zip down, I slide the other strap off her shoulder, watching the rise and fall of her chest as her nervous excitement controls her.

"Colour?" I ask, and she blinks a few times before shaking her head.

"What?"

"Colour? Are you still green, Angel?"

"Oh… yes. Green. So green."

I fucking love that she's *so* green.

Fuck.

She's my fucking wife now. For real. And yeah I know she'll likely divorce my arse once this is all over but fuck, I'm going to enjoy every second of her until then.

With a hunger that almost scares me, I peel the front of her dress down, so achingly slow, revealing more of her cleavage. The plump swell of her tits has my mouth fucking watering, and the second I see the rosy colour of her nipples appear, I have to hold myself back from diving right fucking in.

My cock aches, my fingers twitch, and my tongue is fucking salivating to suck her pebbled peaks into my mouth.

A loud breath escapes her as I free each melon, exposing her tits as my eyes take everything in.

"Fuck..." I breathe, my mind turning to nothing but mush. "Your tits, they are..."

"Ugh. I know. They are fat, right? Being pregnant has made them so much bigger."

My eyes flick to hers, and I can see she honestly believes that.

"Abs, what the fuck? They are perfect. Fucking delectable."

"Delectable?" Her brows hitch.

"Yes. I want them in my fucking mouth."

She whimpers, but arches, clearly wanting that too, so with a smirk, I shoot her a wink and dive in.

The moment my tongue flicks over her peak, she cries out, her hand coming to the back of my hair and latching on.

I moan over her nipple, the fingers on my other hand pinching her other one, the combined actions quickly making her writhe.

I swap tits, moving my mouth to the other while using my fingers to glide my saliva over the first nipple, eliciting another moan.

"Cam," she cries, the swell of her stomach pressing against my chest, her inner ache obviously getting worse.

Pulling back, I quickly start tugging her dress down over her bump, and I'm surprised at how much she tries to help, like she can't bear to be covered up anymore.

By the time I'm tugging it off her feet and tossing it somewhere behind me, my eyes are taking in her fully naked body for the first time.

For a moment… a long moment… I'm stunned.

Her breathing is rapid, her tits rising up and down, her nipples straining, and her cunt still glistening between her parted legs.

But that's not what has me stunned.

It's seeing her like this, the naked swell of her belly with her heavy tits… fuck.

"Ringo?" she whispers, and I can hear her uncertainty lacing that single word.

"You're the most beautiful thing I've ever seen," I admit honestly, meeting her eyes. "It makes me…"

She frowns when I trail off, shifting nervously on the sofa.

"It makes you what?" she asks.

"Fuck, Angel. It makes me want to be the one to make your body swell with *my* kid inside you."

Her lips part and her eyes water, a frown puckering her brow.

"You can't say stuff like that," she protests, yet her voice is weak. Pained.

"Why the fuck not? I'm only being honest."

"But… this isn't real." She gestures between us, and the sting of rejection starts to settle in.

But I know she's not really rejecting me. She's confused. By my feelings. By hers. By the way two people so opposite can mold together like a perfect fit.

"I said it three fucking weeks ago Angel, and I'll say it again. This isn't a ruse. Not to me."

For so long, she just stares at me. Her caramel eyes dancing between mine, roaming over my face like they can somehow detect a lie.

She's been beaten down too often. Her feelings have been brushed aside too many times. She's been betrayed by the people who she's supposed to trust most in the world.

So, she needs reassurance, and I'll fucking give it to her every day for the rest of my life if I have to.

"When you married me today," she says softly, worry flicking over her expression, "were you doing it to protect me or because you really wanted to make me your wife?"

"Both," I answer quickly. "Protecting you will always come first, but it wasn't a hard fucking decision for me, Angel. I can't explain it. I don't even fucking understand it. But you are mine, and I am yours and I'll fucking burn this world down to protect you, and the baby growing inside you."

A sob escapes her, and she slaps her hand over her mouth, so I lean in, running my palms up her thighs as I press my lips to her forehead.

Her hands come to my chest, and I'm half expecting her to shove me away, but then they start roaming over my pecs, the tips of her fingers pinching my nipples this time.

"Cam," she whispers, so I pull back to look into her glassy eyes. "I want you."

I smirk. "Are you already begging for my cock, Angel?"

She laughs, slapping my chest, yet nodding at the same time.

"Fine. I'm *begging* for your cock."

I growl, slipping my hand between her and the cushions, tugging her closer to me.

"Yeah you fucking are." I'm smug as fuck, but also trying to calm the fuck down, because my nuts are tightening in anticipation and I don't want to arrive too fucking early. "Let me get your greedy little body ready for me, Angel. I want to turn your pussy into a slip and slide for my cock."

She laughs, but I swallow it by claiming her lips, and quickly steering her attention to where it needs to be.

Me. Her. My cock and her cunt.

24

ABBEY

W hen I stared at myself in the mirror this morning, I was beginning to feel self conscious about my body.

Don't get me wrong, even with how unwell I've been up until recently, the idea that my body can transform and grow another human inside me fills me with pride and honour, yet still, before I slipped that satin gown on knowing there was a real possibility Ringo would be seeing me naked tonight, I stared at the swell of my stomach and felt a little… frumpy.

That's not how I feel now, though. Or before when his hungry gaze ate up every inch of me once he got the fabric off my body.

I don't really know if I'm sexy, but by God does Ringo make me feel sexy with a single look.

Those dark devouring eyes. The way his tongue darts out to wet his lips. The way his muscles ripple, cording all the way down his arms and into his balled fists like he's trying to hold himself back.

For some reason, I do that to him.

And then, to have him say that he wants to be the one to have his kid inside me… holy crap, if words could get a woman pregnant and I wasn't already, I would have immaculately conceived right then and there.

"This isn't a ruse. Not to me."

Damn. He really said those words.

Maybe it makes me gullible, but I can't find it in me to hold back from him anymore.

I know I'm going to get hurt.

I know there's no world where someone like Ringo can love someone like me and live happily ever after, but I'm not strong enough to deny what my heart wants anymore.

"Eyes on mine," he demands, two of his thick fingers stretching me as I writhe on his sofa, legs spread, a trickle of sweat rolling between my breasts as his thumb brushes over my clit.

Just like always, my body obeys, my eyes snapping to his as he watches my expression, taking in every slight reaction I try to fight.

"Let go, Angel," he rasps, curling his fingers inside me which makes my hips thrust closer. "Let me see what my fingers do to you."

"Can't… you feel it?" I pant before biting my lip, my lids squeezing tight as the pleasurable pressure builds deep in my core.

"Yeah, I can feel how wet you are, Angel. Already soaking my hand. And fuck, it's hot. I want to eat your pussy again, so fucking bad, but I also want to stretch you. Make sure you're ready to take me."

"Oh my…" I cry out as he adds a third finger, and even though it stings a little, something deep inside me ignites, and my walls shatter.

I start riding his hand, and his gravelly moan has me snapping my hand out, fisting his hair as I drag him closer for a kiss.

It's wet and sloppy and chaotic, but I'm suddenly ravenous, like I can't get enough of him inside me and I want more.

"I need your dick," I admit, any shame I might normally feel absolutely nowhere in sight.

"Soon." He chuckles against my lips.

I whimper, ripping my lips from his as I thrash my head back against the cushions, but the moment his hand wraps around my throat, I stiffen.

"It's only me, Angel," he growls in my ear, not letting up on massaging my g-spot. "You're safe. Nothing but me worshipping you is happening here."

I relax, soaking in his words that I know are true.

I'm not back in that nightmare being held down by strong hands, being choked by someone else's. Being penetrated as I scream for them to stop.

"Do you feel me, Abs? It's just me and you here. Abbey and Cameron. Angel and Ringo. Just the two of us on our wedding night."

I nod frantically, prying my lids open, not realising I'd closed them.

The sight of Ringo naked before me is a fantasy I've craved for weeks.

With one hand wrapped around my neck, his grip is firm and grounding, and not the least bit menacing. His other hand is between my legs as his fingers and thumb work me from both sides, and his intense dark gaze is locked onto mine.

"I won't apologise for the dirty fucking things I want to do to you, Angel," he rasps, his voice gritty and sinful, and unmistakingly mine. "I know those things have been used against you in the most heinous way." He leans closer, eyes burning into mine. "But I swear to you, what you and I do together, just the two of us, no matter how filthy it is… It's going to be fucking beautiful."

I nod, even as tears escape my eyes, the pleasure slowly coming back to me.

"What do you want to do to me?" I dare to ask, but knowing how much I love hearing his voice, so deep and gravelly, saying such filthy things, is exactly what I need.

His lips kick up on one side as he leans closer and breathes his words over my lips.

"I want to make you come so many times, that you're dripping with your own juices," he growls, and I whimper with so much need I can barely stand it. "Then, I want to slide my cock inside your tight pussy, and feel you clench around me as I fuck you until I unload my cum so deep in you that it drips out of you for days."

His words have the desired effect, getting me out of my head and any thoughts that don't belong in this moment, and put me straight into the most pleasurable erotic scene, where only he and I exist.

"More," I cry, gripping his shoulders as I gyrate on his hand.

"I want to mark you with my cum, Angel. I want to see it leak from your pussy. I want to paint these plump tits with it." He cups my breast, flicking this thumb over my straining nipple. "I want to watch it shoot from the eye of my cock onto your tongue and face, until you're bathed in it."

I… explode!

His words.

The images they conjured in my head.

His fingers mashing against my g-spot and clit.

They all send me hurtling over the edge.

I think I scream, or close to it anyway, my inner walls pulsing and clenching as I convulse with so much blinding pleasure that I feel like it will never end.

And I really don't want it to. I want to stay in this ecstasy with Cameron forever.

I'm incoherent for a bit. I don't know how long, but I start coming back down to Earth when I feel him slip his fingers from inside me, leaving me empty.

I whimper.

"It's okay, Angel. I'm about to fill you up again," he rasps, and I feel myself being shifted to the edge of the couch, and I try to blink through the haze to see him. "What colour are you?"

Colour?

I blink, his unwavering gaze finally coming into view.

Oh colour. He wants to know if I'm still alright.

"Green," I say lazily, and he smiles, right as I feel something nudge my entrance.

"I'm going to fuck you now, Abbey. I'm not going to hurt you, and I'll stop at any stage if you need me to, but this is happening tonight, and it's not because we need to consummate the marriage. It's because I'm fucking aching to feel you wrapped around me. Aching to show you how fucking amazing this can be. Aching to feel you come around my cock."

My lower lip trembles as my eyes glass over, but I'm not sad or scared right now.

I'm happy.

"I ache for all of that too," I admit, and his big hand reaches forward, cupping my cheek as he nods.

"Relax for me, Angel. It's time to let me in."

I gasp at his words and their meaning, as well as the feel of the head of his dick as it starts to nudge inside me.

He told me it's time to let him in, and I get the feeling he means more than his dick. It's like he wants everything inside me.

My baggage.

My pain.

My soul.

And… my heart.

As he feeds his dick in, I stiffen, realising even though his three thick fingers are big, they are no match to the girth of his cock, and a memory that I have worked so hard to bury slams into me without warning.

I stiffen, crying out, the wall of guitars, and the sight of Ringo before me morphing into something else.

I'm no longer in Ringo's room. I'm in a shed. Walls of tin surrounding me. My bare arse clinging to the leather of an old car bench seat converted into a novelty couch, my arms aching from the way Daniel and Craig hold them to the back of the seat, the weight of their bodies leaning in to pin me in place as Donny rapes me.

He's too big. Thick. And even the lube he keeps squirting between us so he can slide in and out easier isn't enough.

I feel myself splitting. Tearing. Grazes slashing me from the inside.

"NO!"

In a flash, the pain is gone, the feeling of being filled disappears, and the tin walls fall away, bringing me back to the present.

Ringo.

A sob lurches from my throat, and I slap my hand over my mouth at the sight of the man I married, standing a few feet away from me like he leaped back quickly.

"Abs," he breathes, his dark gaze a storm of emotions. "I'm sorry. I didn't mean to hurt you."

He moves to pick up his shirt, but I leap up off the couch.

"Please don't give up on me," I cry. "Let's try again. I know I can do this."

Sympathy washes over his expression as he drops his shirt and steps closer, reaching out to cup my face.

"Angel. You're not ready. We don't have to do this tonight."

"Yes, we do." I practically stomp my foot. "Don't you get it? If I don't do this, then they win. Every single time I get triggered it means they win, and I want my *fucking* life back!"

Ringo's expression softens, his other hand coming up to cup the other side of my face as he tilts my head back so I have no choice but to look into his eyes.

"I know you want to reclaim that part of yourself, Angel, but when we come together, I want it to be for no other reason but because we need each other."

"You don't think I need you? You don't think I want you?" I shove him back and his hands fall away. "I came to you last night *aching*. I've never done that before with anyone. Never so boldly put myself out there. And sure, I could have taken a cold shower and tried to douse the flames, but I didn't want to, because the thing is, I only feel this way around *you*."

I spin, tugging at the hair elastic in my hair, sick of having the tight pull of my ponytail making my head ache, and I toss the hair tie to the carpet, discarding it as I spin back to face Ringo, my strands whipping my face.

"Maybe hormones are playing a part in this insatiable hunger I have, but it's not even an issue until I start thinking about you. Until I see you. Until I hear your voice, or smell your intoxicating scent. So while I might have the need to get over this hurdle in the hopes my fucking head stops taking me back to scenes that make me want to DIE!" I scream the last word as I slap the side of my head in frustration as angry tears burst free. "It's my heart that fucking craves you Cameron. It's my heart that wants to be so impossibly close to you that I want to crawl under your skin because I don't know any other way to be closer."

I slap my chest this time, not even caring that I'm standing before him completely naked, my baby bump probably making me look ridiculous.

"The ache I have isn't just between my legs when it comes to you, Cam. It's in here. *My heart*. The thing I never thought would be whole again. So when I'm acting all bloody crazy like I am now, it's only because I don't know how else to make you understand that all I *need* right now is *you*."

Dragging his gaze from me, Ringo drops his eyes to the floor between us as he rakes his hand through his hair.

"I'm sorry, Abs. I feel like I've been fucking this up all day."

When his eyes meet mine again, I see the uncertainty in them, and I worry my lip, my teeth digging deep.

"Tell me what you need."

"You." I answer easily. "I just want you, in every way."

His gaze drops down my bare flesh then, raking over my breasts and my swollen stomach before flicking back up to my glassy eyes.

"I don't want to hurt you."

"You won't."

"But I did."

I shake my head, not knowing how to make him understand. "I don't think you did. I think it was in here." I stab my finger to my temple. "I went somewhere else."

He nods. "I'm going to need to know where you went."

I gulp. "Do you really need to know?"

"If we want this to work, I need to know some details so I know what *not* to do."

I stare at him for a long moment, more pesky tears burning the backs of my eyes, but I bat at the one that escapes, taking in a deep breath as I fight the rest off.

"This should be sexy. Erotic. Loving." I gesture between us. "Talking about that stuff isn't any of those things."

"I know, and I honestly don't think we'll have to do this every time, Angel. It might just be because it's the first time. You took my fingers so well. And my tongue. But I'm guessing the biggest weapon they used against you was their pricks, so while this isn't ideal, it's important we get this right."

I don't want to tell him that Donny's prick was really big, kind of like his. He doesn't need to know that, right?

"Okay." I concede as I start to tremble. "What do you need to know?"

"What was it exactly that happened that took you out of what we were sharing and into a memory?"

I gulp, shame coursing through me as my eyes dart to the floor.

"Eyes up," he demands, and yep, you guessed it, my eyes shoot straight back to his. "Answer me, Angel."

"It was when you were… ummm… going in. It, like, stung and then…"

He nods. "The pain of it took you back. What was happening in your memory?"

"I was being held to a bench seat. Daniel and Craig on each arm, and Donny he was…" I can't help it, my gaze drops to the floor again. "Donny was penetrating me."

The last bit is a whisper, but given the way his fists ball at his sides, I know he heard me.

"Right, so you were in a similar position then. Just without being held down. But it was the pain that took you to that memory, so I'm guessing he was being rough?"

I nod, still not willing to look him in the eyes right now.

"He was hard, and the lube he put… you know between my legs… wasn't enough. I felt myself splitting and…" I shake my head, nausea starting to roll my stomach.

"Besides the fact that you would have been tense and not enjoying a second of what they were doing, the splitting part… Angel… I need to know. Was he big?"

Blowing out a shuddering breath, I nod, staring at Ringo's feet.

There's a dusting of dark hair on top of his feet and toes. I used to think stuff like that was gross, but now, on Ringo, I love it. I wonder what it would feel like?

"Abbey." My name falling from his lips has my attention snapping up to his. "Let's try this a different way."

Gesturing to the armchair, he takes my hand and leads me over, before he sits and urges me to straddle him.

Even though I'm trembling, just having him touch me has me starting to relax despite the fact that straddling him opens me right up.

Reaching out, Ringo brushes my hair behind my ear, his gaze dropping between us as mine follows.

"You have the most beautiful tits," he rasps, and I giggle a little, my grin scaring away my frown.

"Are you a tit man?" I ask and he nods, not an ounce of shame in his eyes as they lock with mine.

"When it comes to you, hell yes. But also, everything about you has me thirsty for you, Angel. I'm not just a tit man. I'm an *Abbey* man."

Shaking my head, I can't hold back my grin.

"I'm a Ringo woman."

"You're my wife," he reminds me with a pleased smile. "So here's what we're going to do. I'm going to work you up again, make sure you're slick and ready, and then, you will be the one to fuck me."

"What?" My brows shoot high.

"You can be in control, Angel. Just like that night at the Western when I gave you my hand. Tonight, I'll give you my cock, and you will take what you need."

Oh…

Why is he so patient with me? So accommodating for my trauma?

"Will it still feel good for you?"

His grin spreads wide. "Fucking oath it will, Angel. I'll be inside you. That's all that I want. You take the reins and ride me."

My cheeks flush even as I nod, and the feel of his big palms grazing down my back, stopping at the globes of my butt, has sparks of electricity zapping in their path.

"Fuck, Angel. I love having you like this. Completely naked. Letting me see all of you."

"I feel kinda fat," I admit, and he chuckles.

"Ain't nothing fat about you." He leans in closer, pressing his lips to mine briefly. "Besides, there's nothing wrong with a woman with some meat on her bones. And there's especially nothing more naturally stunning that a woman with child."

"Did you write songs when you were in your band when you were younger?"

He laughs at my question. "Still think I'm a poet, hey?"

"Poet or a songwriter." I shrug, and he shakes his head.

"I'm not normally a man of many words, Angel. But for you, I've got so much to fucking say."

I don't know why that has me smiling so wide, but it does, and I feel his fingers dig into my backside as he closes in to kiss me again.

Before I even know what's happening, my hands are in his hair, his tongue is in my mouth, and his growing erection is pressing against my nub as our lips devour each other.

We kiss for so long. I don't remember kissing anyone for this long before, and it has me hot and flustered in no time.

Ringo's hands wander, one squeezing my butt while the other palms my breast, and when he finally breaks our kiss, he eases me back so his mouth can wrap around my nipple.

I arch into his mouth, familiar flutters of craving building between my legs, and just by this position alone, I know I have a better chance of staying in the moment with him.

He did this for me. Giving me the control, and I think I love him for it.

As I grind on his lap, his fingers shift between us, finding my clit, and a gush of slickness rushes between my legs.

"I'm so ready," I whimper as I arch into him, my head tipped back as need takes over me.

"I should have asked this before we tried on the couch, but fuck, I'm sorry. I wasn't thinking straight," he murmurs against my ear, nipping at my lobe as I become ravenous, trying to urge his fingers closer to my opening.

I need him in there.

"Asked what?" I mutter, hardly able to focus on speaking.

"When was the last time anyone was bare inside you?"

I still, my lids flying open, but his fingers start flicking over my clit like they are in a race, and I shudder against him finding it hard to think about anything but what he's doing to my body.

"Uhhh… Ummm… January," I manage.

"Good girl," he praises, slipping one finger inside me.

"Yes, that. I need that. I need you inside me."

"I will. Just one more uncomfortable question, okay?"

I nod, my lids opening lazily as I stare at him.

"Have you been checked for STI's since?"

I nod, even though I hate this conversation.

"Yes. It was the one thing my mum insisted on."

A deep growl reverberates in his throat as anger contorts his face.

He wants to kill my mum. I just know it. And I really think I'd let him if given the chance.

"Let's fucking forget about those people now, Angel. And just so you know, aside from a blowy I paid a hooker to give me two years ago, I haven't been with anyone since my ex."

The old me would have been mortified by what he just said, but the me here and now giggles, nodding, and kind of liking that I'm the one who broke his dry spell.

"Does this feel good?" he asks, one finger inside me and the others assaulting my clit in the best way.

"It would feel better if you were inside me," I admit, needing more.

"Okay, Angel, but just so you know, I'm going to cum inside you. Fill your sweet cunt to the brim with my seed. I want to know my DNA is mingling with yours and getting absorbed into your body so you know I'm always with you."

"Oh God." I nearly climax from his words, but he releases my clit and slips his finger from inside me, simmering my raging pleasure.

"Your turn, Abs." He shoots me a wink. "Put me inside you. Take what you need."

I'm so ravenous for him I barely think twice about what happened on the couch before. Rising up on his lap, my gaze drops between my legs to see him gripping his cock, giving it a couple of pumps before letting me take over. I'm glad my baby bump isn't too big yet or I feel like seeing between my legs might be nearly impossible, and hell, this sight is something else.

"Fuuuck, Angel. The way it feels to have you touch my cock."

His words. This position. It has me feeling powerful. In charge. Like this is my show and I can enjoy this without being taken over.

Rising up as far as I can, I line his dick up, his fat tip at my entrance as our eyes lock.

"You want to sink inside me?" I ask him, feeling bold, and his deep growl and the way his hands dart to the arm of the chair and his fingers dig in tells me he's desperate for it.

Everything about him, about us has me taking the next step, and I slowly insert his girth inside me.

It's not as stingy as it was before, the bite a lot less, and I guess that's because I'm not as tense. I'm practically gagging for his dick right now.

Letting go of his shaft, I let my body do the rest, slowly sinking down onto his thick rod, watching his eyes roll into the back of his head as we both moan loudly.

"Oh… my…"

"Colour," he grits between clenched teeth.

"Green," I rush out before biting my lip.

The moment I go to rise, his strong hands grip my hips and hold me in place.

"Fuck, Angel. Give me a second," he pants, clearly struggling with how good this feels. "I haven't been balls deep in a long time. I don't want to come just yet."

I giggle, watching his almost pained expression turn into a smile as he tugs me closer, our chests mashing together.

"Grind on me, Angel. Mash your pretty clit against me and feel how fucking deep my cock hits."

Oh man. His words have me about ready to explode again, but I do what he says, rocking back and forth, grinding on him, and feeling him impossibly deep.

It feels amazing. Better than amazing. I don't think there's even a word to describe it, and as I grind and he takes it, he presses his forehead to mine, his eyes boring into my soul.

"Tell me you're close," he rasps, his finger biting into my hips, and hell this time, I hope they leave marks.

"Yes. So close."

"That's good, Abbey. You are so fucking beautiful. Such a good fucking girl for me," he pants, his filthy mouth adding to my pleasure. "Fuck, I want to come inside you. Mark you with me forever."

"Yes," I gasp, grinding and letting his gravelly tone and words catapult me to the edge.

And a grind later, I come hard.

I cry out, feeling his hands gripping my hips, taking over the rhythm as he grinds me back and forth, riding my climax out longer.

Finally a roar bursts from his lips as he comes too, filling me exactly the way he wanted.

It's honestly the most beautiful moment I've ever had, yet also the most overwhelming, and before I even realise what's happening, I shatter into tears.

25

RINGO

H er tears. Those wrecked, soul-deep sobs. They're breaking my stone cold heart.

My Angel's trauma has ruled her for so long, and I've got no fucking doubt it'll haunt her for years to come. But what we just shared was a massive hurdle for her to overcome, and despite how fucking profound it was, now it's time for me to help her put all the shattered pieces back together.

Locking my arms tightly around her, I hold her against my chest as she sobs uncontrollably into the crook of my neck.

One of her favourite places on *me*.

"I-I'm s-sorry," she stutters, her tears leaving a wet trail over my skin.

I don't fucking care though. I'd drown in her tears if I knew it would take away her pain.

"No need to apologise, Angel." I press my lips to her temple, my hands running up and down the cooling skin of her back.

Fuck, seeing her completely naked is something else too.

Not only did it confirm that she unequivocally trusts me, but the sight of her creamy skin, her plump tits, heavy yet impossibly perky, and the way her sensual, womanly curves so perfectly cradle the swell of her child within her pelvis… To me, she's so fucking exotic. A rare diamond, shimmering like she was cut just for me.

Fuck.

I'm never letting her go.

"I-I d-don't know w-what's wrong with m-me."

Giving her another squeeze, I lift her hips, easing my cock from her vice-like cunt and instantly feeling warm liquid ooze from her, onto my thighs.

I can't help but inwardly grin.

I love having my cum leaking from her. I hope she doesn't mind it, because I'm going to be filling her to the fucking brim every moment I can until I have to leave.

But now, she needs my attention. She needs to feel what being cared for is like.

"What we did was a lot, Abs," I tell her, feeling her shuddering sobs increase. "I guess in a way it's cathartic for you. The whole experience is likely similar to a sub drop, mixed with the trauma you've suffered."

She slowly eases back, her tear-filled doe eyes piercing mine.

"W-what's a sub d-drop?"

Using my thumbs, I try to dry away her tears, but more come, like a never ending waterfall.

"Well, it's a term used in BDSM. In scenes between a Dom-inant and submissive." I pause to press my lips to her temple. "It's not unusual for the submissive to have an emotional break afterwards. After experiencing pain and restraint, the feel-good hormones that flood your brain can crash hard, and the drop can leave a submissive feeling drained… raw. Extremely emo-tional."

I press my forehead to hers, my big hands cupping her cheeks as another sob escapes her.

"It's a psychological response, Angel. And with everything you've been through, I'm not at all surprised." I swipe at her tears with my thumbs again, her flushed cheeks warm under my touch. "But now comes the aftercare."

Her face softens as I pull back despite the continuous salty drops.

"Is that the part where you clean up the mess you made between my legs?"

A grin splits across my face as I chuckle. "Yeah, Angel. That and a shower. Let me wash you and put you to bed."

Biting her lip, she nods, her gaze darting to my mouth.

She wants a kiss.

Nothing on this Earth will stop me from giving her what she wants, so I lean in and press my lips to hers, feeling her melt into me.

Fuck.

She really is mine.

All fucking mine.

My wife.

My old lady.

My fucking property in the eyes of the underworld.

And that child growing in her womb? Well, if Abbey is mine then that little baby is too.

When we finally break apart, I lift her in my arms, ignoring my cooling seed running down my thighs, and take Abbey to my shower.

She cries for a few more minutes before the tears dry up and exhaustion has her knees buckling, so I hold her up, letting her lean into me.

I wash her. Every fucking delectable inch, including her hair, which turns the shampoo suds pinkish as more of the tint washes away leaving hints of her blonde strands showing through.

Once she's clean and can barely stand any longer, I dry her and carry her to *our* bed.

Her naked skin presses warmth into my side as she curls into me, not even self conscious about the fact I didn't dress her in one of my t-shirts.

She might feel differently about that come morning, but for now, she's content, letting out a soft sigh as I pull her close to settle against my chest.

Then, she finally lets go, slipping into sleep.

For roughly an hour I remain awake listening to her even breathing. Loving the way she occasionally mutters incoherent words.

I've never heard that from her before. I've heard her thrashing in her sleep. Nightmares plaguing her. But never this.

I fucking love it.

My wedding celebrations still continue outside, my club brothers and Doxies making the most of why they are here, but eventually I manage to fall asleep too, far too comfortable with my wife in my arms to fight off what my body needs.

It's the sound of my phone that wakes me hours later, sunshine streaming through the windows from my living area, lighting up part of my bedroom.

Abbey remains asleep as I roll over, using my free hand to snatch up my phone, reading the message that just came in from JD.

> *You're needed in the barn, pronto.*
> *Smitty's fucking words. Not mine.*

I fucking groan.

The last thing I want to do is leave *this* bed and *my* woman to go deal with those fuckers. But I guess the sooner I get it over with, the sooner they'll fuck off and give me some alone time with my new wife.

Leaving our marital bed feels like fucking torture. Just the thought of being away from my Abbey has me on the verge of going on a killing spree. But un-fucking-fortunatley, I'm still on duty until my club brothers leave, so I quietly slide my arm from under Abbey and slip from the bed, quickly getting dressed.

Stepping into the barn, I find my Prez, VP and JD standing around the bar, looking at Smitty's phone screen.

"He's coming now," Smitty barks, clearly not fucking impressed with whoever he's talking to on the video call.

"Who dares to call me from my fucking honeymoon?" I snap before I even know who's on the call, and then want to fucking slap myself in the head when I see who it is.

Ewan Marx.

The head of the Marx Empire, and a man who doesn't like to fuck around.

"So it's true then? You actually married the girl who's dragging all this trouble to my doorstep?"

I fucking hate this man.

"Ewan. Nice to see you," I grit out, pissed no one gave me the heads up of who was on the fucking call. "And yes, I married the woman I care about. Let's not forget *she* is the victim here, and it's a corrupt cop that brought this to your doorstep. Not her."

"Hmmm," Ewan hums, unimpressed, his greying hair a little thinner than the last time I saw him.

"You're right." Leo, the oldest Marx sibling and heir to the empire steps into view. "This girl, Abbey Delaney—"

"Abbey Musgrove," I correct him, and he nods.

"Of course, Abbey Musgrove. She *is* a victim. And while it's unfortunate we've been dragged into this, we understand that Griffin and Devon are also assisting the Angel sisters regarding the situation," Leo offers, all business, a replica of his father, only younger. "We ask that you keep that side of your business strictly between you, Griffin and Devon. They're better equipped to handle it. And we'll stay out of your way, as long as you deal with the police officer." Leo glances down at a piece of paper. "Officer Ian Allen."

"Too fucking right, we'll deal with him," Smitty interrupts, and I see Ewan's jaw tick, like our very existence rubs him the wrong way.

What a pity he needs us for his operation to run smoothly.

"Any updates on the warehouse situation three weeks ago?" Ewan snaps, and it's Spud, our VP that answers.

"Everything still points to Officer Allen." Spud shrugs. "We've got nothing else to go on other than while our men were off the compound, Allen and his team showed up at the Western. They assaulted some of our men and women before making it real fucking clear who they were actually there for."

"And that's the girl, Abbey? Is that correct?" Leo asks and Smitty nods.

"Aye. It is."

"Seems like too much of a coincidence to not be related." Leo nods. "But what I'd like to know is when were you planning on telling us about Satan's Rebels' involvement?"

I swear, the fucking Earth stops spinning for a few beats.

"What the fuck do you mean?" Smitty snaps, practically shoulder-bumping me out of the way. "Satan's Rebels aren't fucking involved."

Leo and Ewan share a fucking look, and I step back into frame so they can see me behind Smitty.

"Why the fuck do you think they are involved?" I demand.

"You mean besides the fact they stole from our warehouses last year?" Ewan's face turns red as he snarls, like that was our fucking fault.

"Just because they are a rival MC, doesn't mean they hit the warehouses last year because of us." I point the fuck out. "Your warehouses had the biggest stockpile of PPE in the state. That's what made them a fucking target. Not our involvement."

Leo sighs, whispering something under his breath to his dad, before the old guy grunts and moves out of shot.

"Look, we figured you knew and were hiding it, but it's clear you have no idea." Leo pinches the bridge of his nose, taking a moment before continuing. "Riggs' team found the initials, SR, scratched just under the door handles of each warehouse that went offline that day. It wasn't picked up until later that night, but we assumed you knew about it, and were trying to cover it up."

"Why the fuck would we cover up something like that?" JD snarls, his head snapping into frame, and Ewan steps back into view, his fucking scowl so deep it looks physically painful.

"I don't fucking know. There are just too many fucking coincidences." Leo waves a dismissive hand. "Just get this mess handled and quickly. Everyone has already suffered enough because of this fucking pandemic. Let's clean shop and make sure we are all in a good position as the world reopens."

We all nod, but Ewan just glares at the screen, and I can tell he's pissed at his son for taking over the call.

When the call ends, Smitty starts swinging punches at thin fucking air.

"I fucking hate that arrogant cunt!" he yells, lashing out with a wild kick at nothing. "For fuck's sake, Ringo! Have you got anything here I can fucking smash?!"

We all chuckle at our President.

"Nope, Prez. You might have to smash Celina's cunt instead," I tease, feeling anything but fucking happy right now.

Smitty grits his teeth and jabs a finger in my direction. "Good fucking point."

Spinning on his heel, he storms from the barn, shouting for Celina.

"Jesus. Maybe someone should warn her?" JD mutters and Spud chuckles.

"Nah. She's used to getting brutally railed by Smitty." Spud smirks, turning his eyes to me. "You look well fucked."

My fucking brows shoot up, and JD steps in beside Spud, nodding like the smug bastard he is.

"He's right, man. Fuck. It's a good look on you."

I can't fucking help it. I laugh.

"Shut the fuck up."

Flipping them the bird, I walk around the bar and grab myself an energy drink from the fridge.

"What do you think? Was Leo right?" Turning back to eye my VP and my mate, I crack open my drink. "Were Satan's Rebels involved in the warehouse killings?"

"Makes sense." Spud shrugs one shoulder. "The pigs wouldn't have done it themselves. They obviously hired help to hit the warehouses while they stepped foot onto our fucking compound."

JD and I lock eyes.

Fuck.

It does make sense, which means, this isn't fucking good.

Not for our club. And not for my Angel.

"Spread the word amongst the men. We need to be on the lookout for Satans as well as cops," I tell Spud, and he gives me a nod. "So what's the plan? When are you fuckers leaving?"

"We'll hit the road in a couple of hours. Smitty has to be at the new property by mid-arvo to meet the first delivery of shipping containers. And I'll lead the others up north. Get that bitch Wendy out of your hair."

"Good fucking idea." I nod before taking a swig of my drink.

With all the fucking lockdowns happening in the city and Metro Melbourne, moving our club out to regional Victoria is a strategic move. It gives us the space to run and expand our operations without Metro Police breathing down our fucking necks, and with regional restrictions not as severe, it will save us from having to endure continuous lockdowns.

The shipping containers will be turned into those tiny fucking homes, converting the acreage into our own little estate. At least until some fucker dobs us into council, and then we'll need to worry about permits and shit, or who we need to threaten to keep living the way we want.

Some of those shipping containers will be buried underground, to help hide some of our less savoury business activities.

"How many men are you leaving here?" I ask, something which has been fucking bugging me. Especially now knowing Satan's Rebels might be hunting us as well.

Since Smitty wants me on site at the new location most of the time, I've gotta man up and do my job. But I can't take Abbey there. Not yet. Not until the new compound has somewhere safe for me to house her.

So for now, she'll stay here with my ma and sisters.

It's one thing for my club brothers and Doxies to slum it in tents, but there's no fucking way I'm letting my pregnant wife sleep on the cold ground under a piece of fucking fabric.

"We can only spare four men. That gives you two on shift at all times," Spud explains.

"Who?" I bark, and Spud raises an impatient brow.

"Tucker. Mule. Stoner and Brody."

My fucking brows shoot up. "Tucker is old and fucking slow. And Brody should have been kicked by now."

"Watch your fucking tone, brother," Spud snarls. "We are leaving who we can. Half our fucking MC has to go north because of this bullshit. You get what you get, and when Smitty can spare the both of you, you can come here and fucking check in on your girl."

"Wife," I bark and he rolls his eyes.

"*Wife*." He drags the word out, doing nothing but piss me off. "Besides, Jols will be here too."

"What?" JD snaps this time. "Why will she be here?"

"Well, Prez has got it in his head that one of the club brothers is fucking her." He glares pointedly at JD. "But he ain't got a fucking clue who it is yet. So, he wants her here out of the way."

I can't fucking hide my smirk, so I turn away hoping Spud doesn't see it, but JD picks up on it without any trouble.

"I guess that makes sense," JD agrees, his brow creasing like he's all for protecting the virtue of our President's stepdaughter.

Spud laughs. "Yeah. Thought you might see it that way."

Clapping JD on the shoulder, our VP chuckles all the way out of the barn, leaving me with my best mate.

"You really fucking her?" I ask him and he shakes his head.

"You really think she'd let me anywhere near her? I've been trying for years and get nothing but her sassy mouth."

"Uh-huh," I cluck, not believing a fucking word falling from his mouth and he waves me off.

"Fucking whatever. I need a slash."

Shaking my head, I drop into a seat at the bar and finish my drink, firing off a message to Griffin and Devon Marx, basically telling them it's time to meet to make a plan to catch and kill Abbey's attackers.

All I get is a fucking thumbs up emoji.

Sighing, I stare at my phone not really seeing anything as what Spud said sinks in.

They are leaving me with a handful of men. Two of which aren't up to fucking scratch. My surrounding neighbours are good at spotting people who shouldn't be there, but they aren't protection. Just eyes.

I have to hope my attempts at keeping this place under the radar will be enough. It's over an hour drive to Fox Pines. And the same back to the city. Getting here quickly will be hard.

As my private sanctuary starts to stir with my hungover club brothers and Doxies, I help pack things up while my ma and sisters throw together a greasy breakfast for the crew.

At some point, my Angel appears, her fading pink hair pulled back, catching the light as she carries food outside. The moment our eyes meet, her cheeks flush, and I know she's remembering our wedding night.

"Jesus. You two look more in love than you did yesterday." Jols nudges my arm with her elbow, coming to stand next to me.

Normally, I'd tell her to piss off, but today, I'm feeling less fucking moody, so I nod.

"She hates me less than she did yesterday."

Jols giggles. "Ringo, she hasn't hated you for weeks."

I don't argue with her. She's fucking right.

"Word is you're staying here with her." I glance down at Jols who blows out a breath and nods.

"Smitty is overstepping again. He's not even my dad, yet he acts like it."

This time, *I* nudge *her* with my arm. "Must be hard having people look out for you."

She rolls her eyes. "If he had his way, he'd put a fucking chastity belt on me. I know he thinks he's protecting me because of what happened, but it's suffocating. I was considering going back to my mum's for a while, but staying here seems more appealing. This place is paradise. I don't know how you bring yourself to leave."

"Duty calls, I guess."

She nods soberly up at me. "But you have a wife now. Things are changing."

"They sure fucking are."

My eyes find Abbey again as she smiles at something my ma is saying, and then they hug like they've known each other for longer than a fucking day or two.

"I'm glad Lexi called you that night asking for your help." Jols leans closer, flicking her blue gaze up to mine. "It's been a long time since I've seen you smile the way you did yesterday. You two might be complete opposites, but she's good for you, and well…" Jols flicks her gaze across the yard to my Angel. "You're good for her, too."

The smile she's talking about makes another appearance as the warmth that filled my chest yesterday returns.

Happiness.

Who would have thought it would find me?

My moment of cheer is fucking short lived as my club brothers gather for a final session of church before everyone parts ways.

It's short and sweet. One last confirmation of the club's plans while we are split between locations, and a reminder that it's strategic. With half the club building a new compound in Fox Pines, the other half bunking on the state border, it will help to ensure smoother operations.

The Marx crew will watch over the city warehouses, while they continue to investigate where exactly the stolen medical supplies went. It all sounds easy enough, but with the possibility of Satan's Rebels having a hand in stealing from us and killing our men, I have a bad fucking feeling things are only gonna get worse.

After church, we all eat, which is the first time I get to chat with my wife since leaving my bedroom earlier this morning.

Abbey comes to me easily, letting me pull her into my lap, and snuggles into me like she was always meant to be there.

By the time the rumble of motorcycles is travelling away from my property, I'm fucking relieved. It's hard to think straight with everyone here in my private fucking space.

Just as Spud stated, Tucker, Mule, Stoner and Brody remain behind with me and JD. As does Jols.

I spend a couple of hours with them going over what I expect from them, protecting Abbey, my sisters and my ma their number one fucking job. And even though looking JD's little brother, Brody, in the eye still makes me want to punch the little fuck in the face, I manage to refrain.

For fucking now.

The day goes too fucking fast. I don't get enough *Angel time*, what with walking the property line with my remaining club brothers and showing them where I have weapons stashed.

Ma turns in early, something that's concerning me, but Millie assures me that she's doing okay for now.

After a late dinner, we sit around the fire and reminisce about the chaotic wedding day yesterday. It's still hard to believe that it happened, and even harder to believe my Angel went along with it. I can't fucking hide my smile every time Abbey's face lights up when she laughs, remembering the shenanigans that took place.

My sisters have finally warmed to her. I can see how much it means to my wife for them to accept her, and I don't even get pissy when Millie and Lans gang up on me, spouting stories about how I used to torment them when we were little.

When the fire starts to die down, I figure I'll throw more wood on it and then steal my wife away, hoping my sisters, JD and Jols will leave us alone for the rest of the night.

As they laugh at something JD and Brody are arguing about, I excuse myself to grab the wood to stoke the fire.

Rounding the side of the barn, the firelight fades behind me, swallowing me in shadows. I know this place well, not even needing a light to know the wood heap is only three more steps away, but as I take my next fucking step, I hear it.

The sharp unmistakable click of a gun cocking.

And a second later, the silhouette of the barrel is aimed straight in my face.

26

ABBEY

I hate to admit this, but Brody is kind of funny when he's not trying to have sex with someone. He's been quiet most of the night, clearly afraid to speak around Ringo, but the moment my husband… yes, my husband… got up to collect some more firewood, Brody has been retelling some of the antics the men got up to last night after Ringo and I retired to his room.

Oh… just thinking about what we shared has my skin heating.

"He did not?" Jols asks, giggling at Brody as he talks about the tattoo Ace unknowingly got while he was passed out last night.

"Truth. I swear." Brody holds up his hands, wearing a huge grin. "It's a nun taking it up the arse by the devil."

We all roar with laughter, and I'm almost disappointed I never got to see the tattoo in real life.

The dark silhouette of Ringo snags my attention as he steps backwards from around the barn, and it takes me a second to figure out why he's walking backwards, with his hands raised.

I gasp, leaping to my feet, just as a gun comes into view. Everyone else around the fire follows my panicked stare, their own reactions just as shocked.

"Pointing a gun at me isn't fucking smart," Ringo snaps, his voice sharp as he keeps moving backwards, and whoever is holding the gun follows him out of the shadows.

"You forced her to fucking marry you?!"

I blink.

And then blink again as I try to make sense of what I'm seeing.

Then, before I or anyone else can stop me, I charge forward leaping between Ringo and the gun.

"Don't you dare point a gun at my husband, EVER AGAIN!" I scream at my childhood friend as his blue eyes widen.

"What the fuck, Abbey!" Jared yells at me, instantly lowering the gun even as Ringo sweeps me off my feet and spins, shielding me from the weapon.

"Don't be so fucking reckless, Angel!" he chastises against my ear, but I shove out of his hold, ducking around him to stand between two men I care about and jab a finger at both of them.

"I won't stand by and watch someone I care about get hurt *or* threatened!" I yell, my entire body vibrating with rage.

"Could have fooled me. You stood by while Lexi was getting hurt."

My mouth drops open in a gasp, but before I can speak Ringo's fist is slamming into Jared's jaw, knocking the gun from his grip.

"I'll fucking kill you for talking to her like that!" Ringo roars, another fist pummelling.

A sharp whistle from behind us snaps our attention around, freezing Ringo's fist mid-swing. My eyes go wide as I take in JD, standing there with a huge blade at his throat, held by a petite brunette clinging to his back like a monkey.

"Alright!" Ringo calls, quickly straightening, his hands up in defeat.

Jared gets off the ground, dusting himself off before spitting blood from his mouth, but I barely spare him a glance, my eyes trained on his girlfriend.

"Dee, let him go," I demand, but she just shakes her head, those big dark eyes glinting, wild and a little unhinged.

"Why don't we all just calm down and take a breath?" Jols steps in, her expression steady as she looks between Jared and Dee.

"Fine. I'm fucking calm," Jared snaps. "Dee. Let him go."

She shakes her head.

"Seriously?" he growls at his girl, rolling his eyes. "Fine. *Hush.* Let him go."

She shakes her head again, but this time, she flips him the bird.

"Really? You're going to give me fucking attitude right now?"

When she winks at him, I can't help but giggle, my heart finally starting to slow.

"Apologise to my wife!" Ringo demands, and all this testosterone is starting to piss me off.

When Jared opens his mouth to speak, I butt in.

"I can speak for myself," I snap, before addressing my childhood friend. "That was a low blow, Jared. Accurate, but still, at the time, I didn't know what else to do."

"Shit, sorry Abs. I know that. I just fucking reacted. Sometimes I don't think." Jared steps closer, eyeing Ringo as he passes by, before giving me his full attention. "Forgive me for being out of my fucking mind. But when I heard that he forced you to marry him I—"

"Yes, I married him but it *wasn't* forced," I interrupt with a lie that has me questioning myself.

Marriage isn't something I wanted, not after what my parents put me through, but I can't say I hate the situation now.

"Why is it so hard for you to believe that we care about each other?"

For a long moment, Jared just stares at me, his eyes assessing before he flicks them to Ringo. He can't tell if I'm lying, and as his eyes snap back to mine, his concern bursting to the surface, I feel guilty.

Guilty for the lie. Guilty for wanting something I shouldn't.

Stepping closer, Jared leans in, his voice low.

"I just don't want to see you get hurt again, Abs."

"What's hurting me is things like this." I gesture to him and then Ringo. "Two men I care about, ready to kill each other. I know you mean well, but how about having a conversation with me before reacting with violence?"

"You're right. I'm sorry." Honesty swarms in his blue gaze, so I nod and turn to face Dee.

"Dee, I swear to God, I'll throw down with you if you don't get that knife away from JD's throat and get off his back."

A slow, deliberate smirk pulls at her lips, before she finally removes the blade, slipping off JD's back with a grace so quiet you can barely hear her boots hit the ground.

"So much for not reacting with violence." Jared snickers, clearly amused by my very obvious threat, and I roll my eyes as Dee approaches, her phone in hand as she taps away on it before holding up the screen for me to read.

'It's cute that you think you'll throw down with me, but since you're pregnant, I know you won't even try. Still. It's cute.'

Even though she's right, I still roll my eyes, biting back a smile.

As Dee passes Ringo, she shoots him a glare sharp enough to cut, a silent promise if I've ever seen one.

"So you came here to bitch at Abbey for getting married?" JD asks, clearly feeling like he can have a say now that his throat isn't on the line.

"Actually, no. Griffin sent me to give you this burner and tell you to call him." Jared holds out a phone to Ringo, who snatches it. "But I have to fucking say, your security measures are crap. Not one of you knew we were on the property, and Dee looped the surveillance an hour ago, and no alarms were set off."

"For fuck's sake," Ringo snaps before shooting JD a glare. "Call Lewy. And take Stoner with you since he's supposed to be our top-fucking-notch security."

"On it." JD jerks his head at Stoner, motioning for him to follow.

As soon as they disappear inside the barn, Ringo's furious glare shoots back to Jared.

"So you're here because your boss sent you?" he snaps.

"He was going to send someone else, but I volunteered." Jared glares right back, his voice laced with venom. "Thought we should have a face to face about forcing my friend into something she doesn't want."

Ringo's jaw ticks and his fists ball, but he refrains from attacking Jared.

"As she fucking told you already. She *wasn't* forced."

Jared scoffs, jabbing a finger in Ringo's direction.

"You know, and I fucking know, that's *not* true."

"Someone give me a gun," I snap, stepping closer to the two men about ready to swing fists again. "I'm ready to start shooting people."

Jols laughs, catching my attention, pure joy spread across her expression. "You're a feisty one tonight."

"Well, yes I am." I give a curt nod, lifting my hand to count on my fingers. "I'm hormonal. Emotional. And quite frankly, sick of people *not* listening to me."

"Jumping in front of a loaded gun isn't smart," Jared says dryly, raising a brow. "So don't forget to add *reckless* to that list."

"Beautifully fucking reckless," Ringo mutters, and they both nod.

"Are you two done?" I snap, hands shooting to my hips.

"I'll deal with you later, Angel." Ringo throws me a look filled with wicked promises. "Just because you're pregnant doesn't mean I can't spank your arse raw."

"Fucking hell." Jared throws his hands up, spinning on the spot and doing a quick pace before spinning back to Ringo with a sharp finger in his direction. "I don't want to hear shit like that or I'll fucking cut off your hands."

Ringo smirks.

I sigh.

And then the burner phone in Ringo's hand starts ringing.

"Speak," Ringo snaps, pausing to listen before letting out a scoff. "A little fucking warning next time. Your little assassin was about ready to slice JD's neck open."

My eyes flick to Dee who smirks proudly, and I have to wonder how I never noticed just how lethal she was back in school.

Maybe because you were so busy trying to avoid Daniel's wrath for anything else to matter.

Ugh.

I hate that guy.

"Fine, I'll head inside and put you on the big screen," Ringo mutters into the phone, extending his free hand towards me.

Stepping in close, I lace my fingers with his, and the cheeky wink he throws me as he starts leading us into the barn sends butterflies dancing in my belly.

Sliding onto one of the bar stools, I watch as Ringo sets things up, and a moment later, the TV screen splits in two, a small bubble at the bottom showing the video feed of us.

The two men in suits who tried to force me into the SUV outside Leather and Lace fill one half of the screen, while the two women from Ayden's dad's apartment appear on the other.

Griffin and Devon, and Bec and Amanda.

"Let's cut to the chase," Amanda begins. "Our sources say that Daniel Stone and Donny Allen are roommates in a share house in the Eastern Suburbs near their university."

I stiffen at hearing the first two names of my attackers, and it only gets worse as Amanda continues.

"Craig McRoe, Tim Beck and Michael Berry are still in Fox Pines, working different jobs with no intention of leaving any time soon. And lastly, Darnel Rivers has been picked up by a

Darwin football club that paid to move him up to the Northern Territory."

Jols must notice how ramrod straight I've gone, because she moves to my side and starts rubbing my back, offering a sliver of comfort.

"Having them split up works for us," Ringo states, and Griffin nods.

"I agree. Hitting the weakest links first will cause the others greater distress. I recommend eliminating the three dickheads in Fox Pines first."

"I like the way you think." Ringo smiles at the screen, and Griffin grins, pretending to brush dust off his shoulders.

"The guy in Darwin can be handled by someone on our books if going up there is an issue," Bec adds, and for a moment, I wonder if the person she's referring to might be Dee. Or *Hush,* as they like to call her.

Surely not?

Then again, Darnel wouldn't even see her coming.

No one would.

This all feels so surreal. These people, most of whom I didn't even know four weeks ago, are all fighting for me. They are literally discussing killing the arseholes who raped me.

The old me would have been mortified. But who I am now is itching to see my rapists dead.

I don't know what that makes me, and I don't know if I care.

"Any update on Ian Allen?" Ringo asks, and Amanda nods.

"We know that we *don't* know much. He's a ghost when it comes to a fixed address. But what we *do* know is that the surprise police visit to the Western during lockdown, and the raids a couple of days ago were *not* sanctioned."

"The fuck. How did he manage that?" Devon barks, straightening from his slouch beside his cousin on the screen.

"Either he's got an army of corrupt cops following him," Bec answers, leaning closer to the screen, "or a friend in high places who made it *look* sanctioned, in which case he's likely using unsuspecting officers to do his dirty work."

"How do you know that?" Ringo asks, stepping back to sit on the stool next to me, his hand blindly finding mine.

"Jason Zimora," Bec responds. "He's a local cop in Fox Pines. He's pretty much got the Redfield district working for the Marx family now."

"What? No!" I shoot up from my seat, dropping Ringo's hand. "You can't trust him. He's a cop."

"Trust *us*, Abbey. He's on your side," Amanda says, holding up a folder, which could be anything, since I can't see inside it. "Jason pulled the files from the day you went into the Redfield station to make a report. He saw who the officer on duty was, and after questioning him in a way that guaranteed the truth, Jason discovered that the officer reached out to Ian Allen the minute Donny's name came up."

"Jason wants to clean up the Timber Valley District," Bec adds, "which is why he's working with us, and the Marx crew."

I roll my eyes. "The Marx crew are criminals."

"That's right, darlin', we are," Devon drawls. "But so is your sugar daddy. You haven't already forgotten who you married, have you?"

I shoot Devon the best glare I can muster, and all it does is make him laugh.

Ugh. He's infuriating.

"Have you fucking forgotten you're talking to my wife?" Ringo snaps, the lethal tone in his voice sending a chill down my spine.

Chuckling, Devon holds up his hands in surrender, relaxing back in his seat.

"Alright. Alright. My apologies, *Mrs Musgrove*."

"Let's stay on track," Amanda interjects. "Abbey, your concerns are valid, for sure. But you could also say that *we* are criminals too." She gestures between herself and Bec.

"That's right," Bec adds. "But in this case, it's about choosing the better option. Jason Zimora isn't the type of cop who breaks the law for his own gain. He does it because he knows crime will always exist, so he chooses the right side. The side that wants to wipe out child trafficking, rapists, and sick cults that prey on the vulnerable to do their bidding."

"They are right, Angel. There will always be crime," Ringo adds, his deep voice pulling my attention as his fingers thread through mine. "It's better to have some level of control over the people committing it, because it helps to police the rogue crims."

I nod, because it's beginning to make sense now.

I can't actually picture a world where crime doesn't exist, so this perspective feels clearer. It makes much more sense.

"What about the parents? Have you decided what we should do about them?"

Griffin's question has me stiffening, and I blink at the screen, before shifting my gaze to Ringo as he starts speaking.

"Hold off for now. That's Abbey's call, if *or* when the time comes."

My parents?

Are they talking about killing my parents?

I suppose they are since everyone else that's been discussed tonight has a target on their back, so why would my parents be any different?

As they all discuss logistics and plans of attack, I zone out, surprised they even included me in the conversation to begin with. I'm glad they did. But now I'm feeling a little numb with the weight of it all.

It's easy to forget the mess I left behind in my old life.

To forget about how cruel my mum could be, or how cowardly my dad was, never once standing up for me. Or how my sister Maggie, dobbed me in without a second thought when she found my pregnancy test. And how eager she was to help our parents force sedatives into me, all in the name of control.

Unfortunately, I've also forgotten my littlest sister, Tahli, is still there. Stuck in that house with *them*.

What if they've found out she was the one who told Lexi? That she set everything in motion by doing the one brave thing I couldn't.

I haven't spoken to her in weeks. One night, back at Leather and Lace, I picked up the phone, lonely and desperate just to hear her voice.

But I never dialled the number. I couldn't risk it. What if they traced it somehow? What if they were waiting, expecting me to cave and reach out in a moment of weakness?

So instead, I just sat there, staring at the phone as I cried.

"Hey. You wanna go for a walk?" Jols whispers in my ear, bringing me out of my thoughts, the image of Tahli's sweet face vanishing like a cloud of dust in my mind.

Nodding, I let Jols lead me from the room without glancing back.

The moment we're outside, I veer towards the small orchard, Jols footsteps crunching over twigs behind me as she follows.

When I reach the Jacaranda tree, I stop before the small headstone, my eyes dropping to the name carved in stone, glowing under the soft light of the moon above.

Hope Angel Musgrove.

"He'll be a good dad," Jols says, her shoulder brushing mine. "That monster of a man has so much love to give. And you're the one he wants to give it to. You know that right?"

I shrug, even though I think I do.

My track record isn't exactly stellar. Naivety has made me a fool more times than I can count, and sometimes I wonder if the same fool is still inside me, making me want to believe in something that is impossible.

"I don't understand, *why* me?" I murmur, glancing at Jols. "What is it about *me* that's got him hooked? Do I look like Hope's mum or something?"

Jols shakes her head quickly.

"I mean, you both had blonde hair and brown eyes, but she was taller. Less curvy. Unhealthily skinny, the kind that comes from living on amphetamines rather than food."

Reaching out, Jols tucks my hair behind my ear, much like Ringo enjoys doing.

"You are so much stronger than she ever was. Kylie only kept the pregnancy to hold on to Ringo, but unfortunately she loved getting high more." Jols takes my hand in hers, giving it a squeeze. "You on the other hand? Despite how you fell pregnant, you'll do *everything* in your power to protect your child."

She gives me a look that holds no space for doubt, and for a moment, I wonder if Lexi and Jols really aren't kindred spirits.

"Ringo didn't know that about you in the beginning. But he *did* know you were a fighter. He *did* know he was drawn to you, even though he didn't understand his feelings." Her smile is warm as she tilts her head, her blue eyes roaming over my face like she's seeing whatever it is Ringo sees in me. "And honestly, Abs, even though this marriage isn't ideal since you are both still so new to each other, I have no doubt this is exactly where you both would've ended up."

I consider her words for a few long moments, liking how they match the way I've been feeling. That perhaps I'm not so naive anymore. That perhaps, it's okay for me to care about a man so much older than me, living a life so opposite to the one I've been raised in. That perhaps I've found a family in him and his club.

"Sometimes," I whisper, opening up a little, "the way I feel about him scares me."

Offering me a sympathetic smile, Jols pulls me in for a hug before whispering in my ear.

"We aren't alone."

My eyes widen, and I gasp, pulling back to look behind us, spotting Jared casually leaning against a fence post, eavesdropping.

"So this thing between you and the Sons of Anarchy wannabe is real?"

Jols scoffs, giving my arm a squeeze before slowly walking away.

"If your bodyguard wasn't hiding in the shadows somewhere, I'd dick punch you." Jols shoves her shoulder into Jared's, and a giggle leaps from my lips at her biting words.

Even though I can't see her face as she moves away to leave me alone with my friend, I can tell she's grinning ear to ear right now.

"Would you still be laughing if she followed through and did it?" Jared snaps, and I nod, clutching my stomach.

"You deserve it. Why are you so damn grumpy?"

He sighs, moving out of the shadows, his face lighting up under the moonlight.

"Who's Hope Angel Musgrove?" he asks, eyeing the gravestone, and my eyes flick down to it, my smile falling away.

"Ringo's daughter."

Jared's eyes flare, snapping to mine. "No shit?"

"No shit." I nod, sliding my arm through his and resting my head on his shoulder. "It's so heartbreaking."

"Fuck... yeah," Jared mutters quietly, probably thinking about his older brother, Tim, who died when he was younger. "Why the fuck is life so hard?"

"I wish I knew." I exhale. "How am I meant to protect my child from the harshness of everyday life, let alone the monsters that walk in it?"

Wrapping his arm around my shoulders, Jared tugs me into his side, giving me a squeeze.

"Your baby will be protected, Abs. The guys back at home are stoked. Simon keeps going on about how excited he is to become an uncle."

A grin spreads my lips wide at that.

Simon has such a big heart.

But then, the reality of my situation creeps back in and I shake my head.

"I can't go back to Fox Pines, Jared. My baby and I have to find a new place to live which means we won't have you and Simon and Shaun and Garrett… and Marcus."

Pulling back, Jared stares down at me, his height so much taller than I remember him being the last time we were ever this close.

"It doesn't matter if you move to the other side of the world, Abs. No matter where you are, we'll always be your family."

"What if I've found a new family?" I whisper, emotion thick in my throat as I stare up at my friend.

Jared's lips thin, but he doesn't rage at my question.

"Then I guess we have found a new family too. I guess it's like when two people get married. Their worlds merge." He bops me on my nose and grins. "Consider us merged, Abs."

"Really?"

He nods. "Really."

"But you hate Ringo," I point out, and Jared shrugs.

"I don't really *hate* him, but I'm not about to make life easy for him. He needs to know you have people who will do anything for you. People watching and making sure you're taken care of."

"Which is why you're still breathing."

Ringo's voice cuts in from behind us, and we dart our heads towards his looming silhouette, moving closer.

Jared chuckles at the warning, stepping back just as Ringo closes the distance and tugs me to his side. Protectively. Possessively. Unapologetic.

"You'll never get the drop on me, old man," Jared teases, holding his hand out, and a moment later, Hush slinks out of the shadows.

A chill runs down my spine.

She's scary as hell. But I kind of love her.

"Your side piece won't always be hiding in the shadows," Ringo points out, his voice low and dangerous, but Jared just scoffs.

"Doesn't mean you'll ever get to me."

Ringo lifts a brow. "Doesn't it?"

I shoot Ringo a glare at his threat, and he throws back a very fake apologetic look. "Fine. I won't kill your friend."

"Not if you want sex again," I snap.

Ringo smirks down at me, while Jared curses under his breath.

"On that note." Ringo sweeps me up into his arms, and a squeal escapes me. "Fuck off, will ya? I'm still on my honeymoon."

I giggle as he spins and stalks off with me, Jared swearing behind us like a grumpy big brother who just walked in on something scarring.

"You're an animal." I laugh, clinging to his shirt as he hurries through the vines, heading back towards the house.

"That I am, Angel," he growls. "And I'm fucking hungry."

27

RINGO

"**E**yes on the mirror," I demand, a whimper falling past Abbey's lips as she slowly lowers onto my cock.

Fuuuck. The way her cunt grips my shaft is fucking everything.

Her legs tremble as she seats herself on my lap, her back to my front as I perch on the edge of my mattress facing the full length mirror in my room.

"You're too big," she pants, straining to take my dick in this new position.

"You can take me, Angel. Just like all the other times." I remind her, watching how her expression morphs with lust as she remembers the last few days and the sex bubble we've been in.

"You're so… deep," she moans, biting her lip as I grip her hips and help her slowly rise up again.

The fucking sight just about undoes me. Her legs spread wide across my thighs, her glistening, swollen cunt open for both of us to see. Half of my cock, slick with her wetness, makes a brief appearance before I guide her back down.

"You like me deep, Angel. Just relax into the new position."

She moans, louder this time, as I help her ease back down, stretching her, filling her, hitting that perfect spot deep inside.

She's been fucking ravenous since that first night—our wedding night—when she gave herself to me. Not completely. But enough to help her ease into sex after what she's been through.

She always has to be on top, unless I'm eating her sweet cunt. Then she just about lets me do anything.

Nearly.

Don't get me wrong, I don't mind her riding me, but fuck, I want to take her. Like truly *take* her.

Every instinct in me wants to own her completely.

But I can wait. I've been letting her fuck *me*. Letting her think she has most of the control.

She still needs my guidance. Still craves my voice.

That's enough to sate my dominant side for now, but eventually, he's going to demand her complete submission. And when that day comes… fuck… I hope she's ready.

Trailing kisses up the column of her neck, I nip at her lobe, watching her lids flutter closed as she gives herself over to the sensations.

I want to demand she open her pretty eyes again, but for now, until she's nearly lost to the pleasure, I'll let her drift. Let her ride the high that's building inside her.

As she rises up and down, building a rhythm she's comfortable with, I glide my hand over her growing bump, slow and reverent.

I fucking love how it looks. How it feels. Her skin stretched taut beneath my palm. The life growing inside her making her glow all over.

My fingers glide higher, until I find one of her full, perfect tits.

Her pebbled nipple hardens even more as I roll it between my fingers, and my Angel moans again, her plump lips parting as she pants, falling deeper into our connection.

"That's it. You're such a good fucking girl," I rasp against her ear, my words and touch making her grind faster.

She's found a good rhythm now, so I shift my other hand from her hip, sliding down between her legs to find her engorged, needy clit.

As I draw slow, deliberate circles around it, she whimpers, my teasing fingers *not* touching her the way she needs.

"Touch it," she cries, her lids flying open, those stormy caramel eyes locking with mine in the mirror.

"Say please," I growl, and she nods desperately, her fingers digging into my thighs as she rides me harder.

"Please. Touch it."

Her wish is my fucking command, and I give her what she's aching for, pressing the pads of my fingers to her bud and giving her the friction she seeks.

Fuuuck. She comes alive. That hood of skin like a fucking switch, powering up the raw, carnal side of her that I fucking live for.

She lets go then, her eyes not on mine but where I disappear inside her, my fingers kneading her clit as I hit her good and fucking deep.

My lips latch onto her neck, sucking as I fight not to come too fucking early, needing her to go over the edge first, because I fucking love the way she milks my cock.

I suck at her neck, roll her nipple between my fingers, and mash her clit while plunging inside her over and over and watch, as my little Angel's lips part in a silent O as her face contorts with pleasured pain, and she comes hard.

The moment her walls start clamping around my cock, I join her, releasing her neck, my roar mingling with her cries as I fill her with my cum.

Our panting breaths are loud as we both slacken, my fucking legs shaking as I shift us back more on the mattress so we don't end up on the fucking floor.

"Fuck, Angel. You're everything."

She melts against my chest at my words, my view down the front of her body ensuring my cock doesn't go entirely slack.

Fuck. She's the most beautiful thing I have ever seen.

I'll never get enough of her.

Fucking, never!

Wrapping my arms around her, we stay that way for a few minutes, both of us needing to catch our breath, still in our orgasm haze.

I feel the moment reality comes crashing back in by the way my wife tenses on my lap, and my heart sinks to the pit of my gut.

Fuck.

I have to leave today.

Everything in me wants to bring her with me, but we need to be smart.

She's safe here. Out of the way. I'm feeling a little more confident after Dee helped Stoner improve our security system, to leave her here.

At least then I can go do my job while hunting the fuckers that hurt her, seeking justice, and if my club catches heat, she won't be in the firing line.

Rising from my lap, my cock slips free of her, and if she feels my cum dripping out of her, she doesn't fucking acknowledge it.

Instead, Abbey spins, launching herself back into my arms, wrapping herself around me like it will somehow hold me in place so I can't leave.

"Abs," I groan, hating how much I know she's struggling with this. Not because it's annoying, but because I can't stand the idea of her hurting.

"If I break your leg, you won't be able to go," she whimpers into the crook of my neck, and a chuckle rumbles from my chest.

"I'll be back for Easter next weekend," I remind her but she shakes her head against me like nothing but me staying will be good enough.

Fuck.

I want to stay.

I really fucking do.

I don't know how the fuck I'll concentrate while away from her.

"I can't even call you. I don't even have a phone," she whispers, which makes me grin.

"About that. I have something for you."

She leans back, not even bothering to hide her wet, red eyes anymore.

"Is it my own helmet that I'll get to wear on the back of your motorcycle when you take me with you?"

I chuckle, shaking my head. "No, not that. But, I got you a phone. Lewy set it up. It has all your friends' numbers in it, and a secure group chat app that you can use to chat with them and me. And Tahli."

Her eyes light up. "I can chat with Tahli?"

I nod. "You can still use the game, but also, Lexi helped her set up the secure app on her iPad so you can also video call her."

Her breath catches. "I can *see* my sister?" she cries, and I nod again.

"I mean… you can also video call me… if you want." I shrug, and a devilish grin spreads across her face.

"Will you have clothes on?" she asks, and I throw my head back laughing.

"If other people are around, then yes. But if I can be alone, then I'll take every last piece off, just for you."

She nods, clearly satisfied, before her eyes widen and I feel a nudge against my gut.

"Oh." She smiles, her caramel eyes filled with joy. "Little zucchini doesn't want you to go either."

"More like little zucchini wants us to stop talking about possible phone sex scenarios." I laugh, and she giggles, reaching out to graze her fingers over my beard.

For a moment… She's happy.

The loud rumble of JD's hog starting up outside ruins the moment, my Angel's face falling instantly.

Fuck!

I swear the sight has my heart fucking cracking right down the centre.

Standing with her in my arms, her legs instantly wind around my hips, and I carry her to the bathroom where we take a quick, wordless shower. After we're out and dried, she watches me dress, wrapped in nothing but a towel, silent for so long it makes me uncomfortable.

What's going through that mind of hers?

"Was Wendy right?" she asks after a few tense minutes of brooding, and I sigh, sitting on my bed to lace up my boots, realising exactly where her mind went.

"We've been through this, Angel. That bitch was trying to plant poison in your head, and this is exactly what she wants. You doubting me."

Rising from the bed, I close the distance between us, taking her face in my hands, tilting it back until those stormy eyes are locked on mine.

"You are *my* wife. *My* old lady. *My* side piece. Every fucking thing a man could ever want is all in *you*." Leaning close, I press our heads together, breathing in her sweet scent, knowing I'm going to miss it like hell.

"I haven't looked at another woman in years. Not until you crashed into my life. And now?" I ease back, brushing my thumb along her delicate jaw. "You're it for me, Angel."

I don't realise what I've said until her eyes widen, but I don't even attempt to take the words back because I fucking mean them.

It's not an 'I love you', but it's fucking close, and I hope it's enough for her for now.

Shifting from my hold on her face, Abbey throws her arms around my neck, practically climbing me like a tree. I lift her the rest of the way, my hands slipping under her towel to palm the globes of her arse, and I claim her lips.

It's a hot and heavy kiss. The kind that makes me want to rip off my fucking clothes again and get lost in her, completely.

But a horn blares outside, cutting through our moment like a fucking blade, and I know JD's patience has reached snapping point.

Fuck!

Reluctantly, I break the kiss, carrying my wife to the bed.

"I'll text you once I arrive at the new compound." I peel her arms from around my neck and take a painful step back.

She pouts, her big doe eyes nearly breaking my fucking resolve.

"Just so you know," she starts, needing to clear the emotion from her throat. "I like the Doxies, but if I find out one of them so much as looks at you, I'm going to hitchhike back to Fox Pines and cut off her tits."

My laugh is loud as I clutch my gut, loving the way my Angel has a half smirk fighting past her angry expression.

"I'll be sure to make them aware, Angel."

"You'd better." She folds her arms over her chest.

"The phone is in the drawer." I gesture to the bedside table before leaning in and pressing my lips to her forehead, lingering there for a beat too long, because fuck, I don't want to leave her.

But I have to.

As soon as I pull back, I turn on my heel to leave, because if I don't get out of here right fucking now, I won't go at all.

I only make it a few strides when I hear her voice.

"Cam!"

I spin around, hearing the desperation in her voice, to see the raw emotion etched across her face.

It hits me like a punch to the chest.

"Abs?" I ask, using her name, just like she used mine.

"Be safe… and come back to me."

I nod, jaw tight. "Nothing on this fucking Earth will keep me from you, Angel. Absolutely nothing."

Accepting my declaration with a nod, tears spill down her cheeks even as she straightens with determination, like she's forcing herself to be strong.

The fact that we have to be apart for a while fucking sucks. But if there was ever someone with the strength to get through it, it's my Angel.

Taking one last look at her, I commit every inch to memory, before I spin and leave, feeling my mood fucking plummet with every step away from her.

"Thank God you're leaving." Millie's teasing tone fills the living room as I step in, her eye roll coming into view. "If I have to hear your sex noises for one more day, I think I'll throw myself off Coman's Bluff."

Shaking my head as I approach my sister, I lean in and press my lips to the top of her head.

"Ew." She pulls back with a cringe. "I know where those lips have been. Do not kiss me with them."

I chuckle.

"Love you too, Mills." And then I point a stern finger at her. "You treat my wife with respect or we are going to have serious problems."

She rolls her fucking eyes again.

"You're soooo scary," she mocks, walking away as my ma's smile comes into view.

"The love you two have for each other never gets old."

With her arms open, I step into them, practically bending myself in half to lower to her height as she gives me a squeeze.

"Be safe," she whispers and I pat her on the back before pulling back.

"Always, Ma."

She nods, giving my hand a gentle squeeze before giving me her back.

Fuck. I know what she's doing. She's trying to hide her tears.

She always gets like this when I have to leave. Every single time. And I always leave, yet this time, it feels different. I've never wanted to stay more in my life.

Needing to get the fuck outta here before I crack, I move to the door, grinning at Lans who's spying out the door on JD and Jols outside.

"You're being creepy."

She shrugs. "What's going on between those two? I was going to totally tap that but as soon as Jols showed up, JD has barely given me the time of day."

"Fucking hell, Lans. I don't want to hear anything about you tapping anyone."

She shrugs, wagging her brows as she grins up at me. "If I have to hear you pleasing your wife, then you can hear all about me getting some."

Shaking my head, I lean in, pressing a kiss to the top of her head too.

"Keep an eye on Ma. I think she's unwell but she's trying to hide it from me."

Alana nods. "That's exactly what's happening. As soon as you go, we'll be on nurse duty."

I sigh, hating that my ma has to suffer through her lupus flare ups.

"Don't worry, big brother. We've got this. You go do whatever it is you do, and make sure you bring me a big Easter egg next weekend. I want the biggest one you can find."

I chuckle. "Sure thing, brat."

She pokes out her tongue.

Leaving my house, I ignore Alana when she calls out to me to promise not to die, and Jols offers me a smile as I throw my leg over my ride.

"Bout fucking time," JD complains, clearly in a fucking mood, and while he won't admit it, I know it has everything to do with leaving Jols behind.

The fucker has done his nuts over her. I'm sure of it.

I fire up my hog, feeling her come to life between my thighs, and I don't miss the look JD and Jols share.

They are both worried.

Ignoring the sinking feeling that's telling me not to go, I secure my helmet and tear up the driveway, hearing JD follow, leaving the sanctuary of my home and hitting the road to Fox Pines.

The ride out of the windy roads of the Dandenongs and onto the freeway takes about thirty minutes. The rest of the ride takes another hour until we are weaving through the outer roads of Fox Pines, leading us to the old Vixen's Lodge Estate.

The property sits tucked behind others, surrounded by thick pine trees, hidden well from both the road and neighbours.

The only sign that place now belongs to Southern Sadists is the two burly ruffians flanking the entrance.

Knowing who we are, they wave us through, and we follow the extra long tree lined driveway until we hit a clearing, where a small pile of rubble rests in the middle of a wide patch of dirt. That was obviously where the main house used to be, now nothing but a haunting memory.

Off to the side stands an old barn, far more weathered than mine. The doors are thrown open, and a group of my club brothers are inside working with timber and saws.

Pulling up our rides, we stretch once we dismount before getting bombarded with club brothers wanting to tell us something about our new home, or to ask for help with something.

After a few minutes, I manage to step away, leaving JD to chat with them, and I open my phone to see a message.

> **Angel**
> *I think little zucchini did a somersault in my stomach!*

A grin spreads across my face, loving that she shared that with me, but also hating that I missed that.

> **Ringo**
> *Maybe you have a future Olympic gymnast growing inside you.*

> **Angel**
> *Maybe...*
> *You arrived safely?*

> **Ringo**
> *Yes, Angel. I'm safe at the new compound.*

I spin around, holding up my phone with the camera open, and snap a picture of my ugly mug and some of my club brothers working in the background.

I'm too fucking old for that selfie shit, but I know it will make her smile, so I send the fucking thing.

It takes a moment to send, but when it does, another message instantly pops up.

Fuck. I miss her too, and I'm about to tell her as much when a photo comes through and I nearly drop my fucking phone.

Fucking hell.

There on the screen is my Angel, laying back in my bed, a sheet just barely covering her nipples as she stares at the camera.

I hit call and it rings once before connecting.

"You've called Angel's, where we aim to please by letting our devil out."

A deep growl rumbles past my throat, and Abbey giggles on the other end.

"You're playing with fire, Angel."

"Am I? Whoops. My bad."

"Is this how it's going to be? You gonna fucking taunt me until I come back to you?" I snap, but there's no anger to it.

"You bet your cute arse I'm going to. I'm twenty five weeks pregnant, horny and emotional and you up and left me to entertain myself."

I can't help but fucking chuckle. This woman! Jesus, she does something to me.

"Angel. Do you really want me walking around here with a hardon in front of the Doxies?"

"Shit," she snaps under her breath. "Quick, think of something gross."

I throw my head back laughing, ignoring the weird fucking looks I'm getting from my club brothers since they aren't really used to seeing me fucking smile, let alone laugh.

"Do me a favour and save those pictures for when I call you late at night. I promise to help you with your horniness."

She scoffs. "You know it doesn't work when I touch myself."

"Don't rule out the power behind my dirty talk," I remind her and she giggles.

"Fine. I'll eagerly await this magical dirty talk later tonight."

"I look forward to it." I fucking grin, giving my club brothers my back so they stop looking at me like I've grown two fucking heads.

Abbey and I chat for a few more minutes, my eyes taking in the vast clearing and the thick pine forest on the other side. There's so much room here. We could build more than a little estate. We could build our own little fucking town.

When I reluctantly end the call, I know the only way I'm going to get through each day is by keeping busy, so I make myself familiar with the land my club now owns, before rolling up my sleeves and pitching in alongside my brothers.

The day is long, but thankfully not too hot, now well into autumn. By nightfall, after a shitty shower in the portable facilities, and some basic campfire grub, JD and I take one of the vans into Fox Pines in search of our first victim.

Thanks to Jared and Dee's relentless digging, we know that Tim Beck, a twenty year old loser who lives in a shack-like bungalow in his parents' backyard, spends his days gaming while his parents work their arses off to buy him whatever he wants.

He could be doing so much with that kind of privilege, yet he chooses to waste his days fucking gaming.

Their house sits on a corner block in town, with a driveway coming off the side road to the back of their property. There's a car parked at the end of the driveway, closest to the bungalow. Likely Tim's.

There are zero security cameras, which makes our job a fuck-load easier. His parents are preoccupied inside the main house, too busy watching MAFS in the living room to spot us striding across the backyard.

With gloved hands, JD swings the bungalow door open, the flimsy thing not even locked. I step inside, scanning the space in seconds.

The bed is unmade. There are take out containers on the bedside table, and a mound of clothes in the corner, which may or may not be dirty.

Who fucking knows, but it does smell like dirty socks in here.

Filthy fucking prick.

Sitting at the desk with his back to us is Tim. He's playing a fucking fighting game. It's a fucking pity the characters can't leap off the screen to help him. He's gonna fucking need it.

I don't clock a webcam but he's wearing a headset, which means people can hear him. It also means he can't hear us right behind him.

Sharing a look with JD, I give him a nod, and he darts forward, snatching up the game console, and ripping the fucking thing off the desk. The plug tears from the wall with a pop, and the screen goes black as Tim gives his best impression of a banshee, squealing like a little bitch.

"Ahhh! What are you…"

His words die off as he takes me in, pressing himself deep into his padded gaming chair, watching me sit my arse on his desk and cross my arms over my chest.

I point to his head, and he gets the message, slowly tugging off the headset.

"It wasn't my idea." He rushes out and I quirk a brow as his eyes dart between me on one side of him, and JD on the other.

"So you know who we are then?"

He gulps and nods. "D-Donny warned me to l-look out for blokes like y-you."

"That so? How's his nose?" I ask, and Tim's lower lip starts to wobble even as his hand shifts to his pocket.

The moment he reaches into it, JD grabs Tim's hand, slapping it to the desk, before smashing his fist onto it, bones cracking under the force.

Tim cries out, but the second I hold my finger to my lips to hush him, his lips snap shut as he sobs quietly.

"Tell me, Tim. Do you know what the meaning of rape is?"

"W-what?"

"You fucking heard him, cunt. Answer him." JD snarls, gripping a handful of Tim's hair and jerking his head back.

"S-sex without c-consent," Tim stutters, and JD shoves his head forward so hard that Tim headbutts his desk.

"Ahhh, fuck!" he cries. "Stop please."

Fury washes over me at hearing those words, and before I can stop myself, I have Tim by the scruff of his shirt, shoved up against the wall while I practically spit in his face.

"Did Abbey say those words, you sick fuck? Did she scream for you to fucking stop!? Did she beg and say fucking please?!"

Tim stammers, not able to put a coherent word together, so I shake the fucker, slamming his head back against the plaster of the wall so hard that it cracks. "Fucking answer me!"

"Y-yes. She d-did. She b-begged us to s-stop."

"But you fucking didn't. Did you?"

"I-I-it was mostly D-Daniel and Donny. I only did it o-once each t-time. I felt s-sorry for h-her."

"Oh boo," JD yells in his ear. "You felt fucking sorry for her, but you didn't do anything to stop it, did you, you weak cunt?!" With his own rage taking over, JD's fist slams into the side of Tim's face, his eyes rattling in his head before they roll and close, his body slumping in my grip.

Fuck.

He's out cold.

28

RINGO

It's been a long fucking month since I've seen my Angel in the flesh. I never did make it back for Easter, and every day I told her I wasn't returning home yet, was another day the light in her eyes dimmed.

I fucking hate it, but I can't leave Fox Pines. Not now with Tim Beck locked away in what used to be a sex dungeon in the old house that burnt down a few years back.

I could've killed Tim that first night, but that little fucker was chattier than a four-year-old being offered candy, and he filled in so many blanks about what they did to my Angel… so I kept him alive to make sure he spilled every fucking secret.

He's worse for wear, but I have fucking plans for him, and the screaming coming from the back of the van right now is part of it.

"Tell Zimora he can put his officers back in place," I bark to Griffin, who's on the phone while JD tears through the dark, quiet streets of Fox Pines.

"Will do," Griffin grunts. "This fucker was a hard one to get to."

"Sure fucking was," I mutter, gripping the grab handle as JD takes a sharp corner. "I don't like having to ask for help. You know that. But I appreciate it." I relax as JD straightens the van again, breaking the speed limit. "Michael Berry couldn't hide out at his girlfriend's place forever, thinking the patrolling cops would keep him safe."

"I'm kind of jealous I won't be there to witness their end."

I grunt, kind of annoyed Griff won't be there to witness it as well.

"It'll be slow. Feel free to drop by."

Griffin chuckles before hanging up.

"You really gonna make it slow?" JD asks, glancing my way. "I thought you'd be antsy to get back to Abbey."

Fuck.

He's right. I am.

"Maybe not *that* slow. It's taken long enough to get our hands on this fucker." I jut my thumb towards the back of the van. "I'll see how it pans out, I guess."

After Tim Beck went mysteriously missing from his bungalow a month ago, our other targets went into hiding.

Daniel and Donny are still in the city, and word is that Donny's uncle Ian is watching over them with a fucking security team. Darnel hasn't changed his routine up in Darwin, probably thinking he's safe all the way up there.

Idiot.

And Michael Berry and Craig McRoe have been hunkering down here in town.

Craig is the hardest to get to. He comes from a big family. Lots of younger siblings, and he's been playing sick for weeks so his parents don't force him to go anywhere.

Unfortunately there are always some of his younger siblings around, so getting to him has been put on hold until we can smoke him out.

As much as my Angel wants these fuckers dead, I know she'd never want innocent bystanders to get hurt.

Michael on the otherhand, is now in the back of the van, and as we pull off the main road and up the driveway of our compound, my fucking heart starts to race with anticipation.

Vengeance.

It's going to be fucking sweet.

Parking next to the shipping container that now sits above the dungeon, Murf and Trunk hurry to the back and drag a kicking and screaming Michael out of the van. A hood is over his head so he can't see, and his hands are bound behind his back so he can't fucking swing punches.

JD and I follow our club brothers down to the dungeon, where Stocky holds the door open, the stench of shit, piss and vomit assaulting us instantly.

Tim's eyes widen from where he's huddled in the corner, his body frail, some bones freshly broken, while others are a little twisted, healing wrong from breaking weeks ago.

It's not just his bones that are broken. We've well and truly shattered whatever grip he had on reality. He's basically our puppet now. Does what we say, no matter how fucked up or painful it is.

But this? What's about to happen, will really test how far gone he is.

"String him up," JD tells Murf, and Trunk steps in to help string Michael Berry up by his wrists until his feet leave the floor.

"Stop. Please. Don't hurt me," he cries, his voice cracking with fear as he hangs before us.

I fucking laugh as Murf cuts the hood off him, and Michael blinks past his tears until he can see properly.

"I love this part." Stocky snickers from beside me as Michael takes in the room and fear flashes across his face.

This is the moment he realises he's well and truly fucked.

"Please, don't do this," Michael begs JD, recognition written across his expression.

He knows who we are. He knew we were coming for him.

Stepping forward, I catch Michael's attention, his fearful sobs directed to me.

"Do you want money? I can get you so much. How about the other guys? I can give you their locations. It was all Donny's idea!"

"You're a fucking coward, Michael," I sneer, curling my lip in disgust. "But that's okay. I didn't expect anything else from a piece of shit like you." I step close, smelling fresh piss oozing from him. "Did you piss yourself, Michael?"

He whimpers.

I fucking laugh in his face.

"You know, Tim told us what you did." I tilt my head, never taking my eyes off his. "He said you tied Abbey up one night when Daniel and Donny went out to grab pizza. He said you tormented her for hours."

Michael's face pales. "Tim was lying."

I frown, turning my head to the back corner where Tim is out of Michael's sight.

"Were you lying, Tim?"

"N-no. N-no, siree. I was *not* lying." Tim hurries forward, hobbling on his broken foot, barely registering the pain now that his mind is so far gone. He rounds his mate strung up like a carcass, ready to gut. "You did it, Michael. You tied her to the pole and pissed on her. You spat on her too."

"Shut up, Tim!" Michael screams, but Tim ain't finished.

"You stuck your fingers down her throat, real deep, and she threw up." Tim nods quickly, ignoring Michael's face twisted in rage at hearing his mate betray him. "Then rubbed it into her hair."

I can't listen to any more of this.

My fist swings before anyone sees it coming, the crack so fucking loud that it's close to possible I nearly killed Michael with the impact.

Red rims my vision as I absolutely lose control.

This isn't what was planned, but now my monster is unleashed, and there's no fucking stopping me.

Michael's body is still swinging from my punch, but the moment he sobs and opens his mouth to fucking deny what he did, I lunge forward, my fingers gripping his throat and digging in until blood starts pissing out like a burst fucking pipe.

Tim is squealing like a pig in the background. I can't fucking tell if he's protesting or getting off on the chaos, but with my focus locked on the vile cunt in front of me, I let my rage surge through my arms, and explode through my fingertips.

My knuckles burn as I squeeze so fucking tight, that my digits break through skin and muscle, wrapping around his trachea before ripping it clean from his throat.

I heave, letting the chunk of flesh thud to the dungeon floor, Michael's corpse hanging lax as it swings. As the roaring in my ears fades, a low whimper reaches me.

My gaze snaps to Tim, now crumpled on the floor, wide eyed and sobbing, unable to tear his eyes away from his dead mate.

Tim divulged everything over the four weeks we've had him. Every filthy detail of what they did to my wife. Even the sick shit they planned for her wedding night with Daniel.

There's no way Abbey could ever speak of those horrors out loud, and I'd never fucking ask her to. But now I know exactly what she's been through, and I won't fucking rest until every last one of those pricks is rotting in the ground.

The moment I pull my gun from under my cut, my club brothers curse, their boots scrambling up the stairs as I level it at Tim.

His eyes don't even react. He simply looks past it to me, like the fucking barrel isn't right in his fucking face.

"It's time?" he asks, and I fucking nod.

"Well fucking overdue," I snap, and then squeeze the trigger.

The sound is deafening, my ears ringing instantly, but I don't fucking care.

Two wastes of oxygen are now gone.

There might be more to go, but I'm fucking sick of not holding my Angel when I fall asleep. So I turn on my heel, climb the stairs, and head for the shower.

I need this death off me before I go to my wife, and lose myself inside her for good.

29

ABBEY

I shouldn't be out here in the cold. Not with a storm rolling in. Winter is just over a month away, and I can't help but wonder if I'll make it through an entire season before I see Ringo again.

Tears slide down my cheeks, same as they do every night he doesn't come back to me.

Tilting my face to the sky, I let the rain mix with my tears, the clash of hot and cold a strange kind of comfort.

Over the past five weeks, I've gotten to know the men Ringo left behind to watch over me and Jols. Brody is surprisingly kind-hearted, at least when he's not thinking with his dick. Since being stuck here, he's clearly on a brutal dry spell, and I can tell as each day passes, it's wearing him down. But still, he's kept his distance, never once propositioning me or Jols.

Alana and Millie are a different story.

Not that they've taken him up on his suggestive offers, but I kinda think they enjoy the attention.

Stoner takes his security role very seriously since Jared and Dee managed to get past the measures he had in place. He sleeps less than anyone here, always out patrolling, and when he's on a break, he rarely relaxes.

Mule is a different kind of guy. He's ex-army apparently. Just like JD. Or so Jols tells me. He keeps to himself, but he's become my constant shadow.

He sleeps outside my door at night. He's always lingering just off to the side when I leave my room. And when I go for a walk through the bushland on the property, he follows. Silent. Steady. A shadow that never breaks formation.

Mule doesn't say much, but a couple of times, when I've broken down during my walks, he's handed me a tissue, always saying the same quiet words.

"It won't be for much longer."

I often wonder if he knows something I don't.

Tucker is an older guy. Not very fast on his feet, and takes a lot of naps, but, every day at four in the afternoon, without fail, he picks a handful of flowers and carries them to the porch. His smile is always big as he waves through the window to Doreen, before he lays them gently on the decking, only to retreat back to the barn.

Another loud rumble of thunder rolls through the angry clouds above, and a sudden flash tears across the sky, lighting up the Jacaranda tree before me.

"Your daddy is a good man," I tell the gravestone, my voice barely a whisper as I wonder what colour eyes Hope would've had. "He's fiercely protective. I wish he'd gotten to hold you when you cried… fed you, rocked you to sleep in his arms. I know he would have loved that," I say to a little girl that isn't here, more tears spilling down my cheeks.

"I'm sorry you didn't get to enjoy him. But I promise to love him the way he deserves." A sob escapes me and I crumple forward, begging the gravestone as if it has the ability to grant wishes. "Please, just bring him back to me."

Even though Ringo and I talk on the phone every night, over the last two weeks, a bad feeling has settled in my gut. It's heavy and cold, like something is coming for me and I can't stop it.

I fear Ringo won't return to me, and not because of another woman or stupid jealousy, but because I fear he's going to die. Or *someone's* going to die.

I don't know how to explain it, and no matter how hard I try to brush it off, the gnawing feeling digs in deeper, crippling me night after night the moment the sun dips below the horizon.

Another flash rips across the sky, followed by a loud clap that makes me jump, and I second guess my need to cry out in the rain like this.

Pushing up from the wet grass, I turn and hurry up the small hill, frowning at how long the thunder rumbles for. Until I realise, it's not thunder at all.

It's a motorcycle. Or two.

My heart flips, and my feet take over, carrying me up the hill in a frantic rush.

I can hear Mule somewhere behind me, his boots pounding the earth as he tries to catch up, but as the roar of the engine cuts off, a strangled sob escapes me.

Ringo.

I need to get to Ringo.

Hooking my hands under my belly, desperately trying to lift it so I can run faster, I clear the top of the hill bursting through the mouth of the vines, my eyes catching on a familiar silhouette in the glare of the floodlights.

"Ringo!" I scream a little too dramatically, but I don't give a damn right now, because he's here. He's finally here!

His looming shadow stiffens, his head snapping in my direction, and a second later, he tosses his helmet down in the mud, his boots already pounding towards me.

"Angel!" he roars over another clap of thunder. "What are you doing out here?"

I can't answer, my sobs are too wild as I nearly slip on the soaked grass.

Mule catches me before I hit the ground, lifting me like I weigh nothing. Even in his arms, my legs don't stop trying to race towards Ringo the whole time.

"Be careful Mrs," Mule says, calling me Mrs like he does every time he decides to speak.

"He's really here," I cry, beaming up at Mule in the downpour, and for a brief second, I wonder how his moustache is still perfectly curled at the ends, even out in this storm.

"Yes, Mrs. He is."

I giggle, bouncing on the spot, letting Ringo make his way to me.

The moment he's standing before me, I try to leap into his arms… but fail, because my huge belly gets in the way.

"Holy shit, Angel. Look at you." Ringo beams, ignoring the rain hammering down on us.

Oh wow. Look at his eyes. The way they smile without even seeing his lips.

"Bubs is basically a cabbage now." I laugh, seeing Mule slink away in my peripheral.

"Fuck," he mutters, his eyes roaming the swell of my stomach and then my face. "Come here, Angel. I need to kiss you."

Bending, Ringo scoops me up in his arms bridal style, and I don't waste another second. Reaching up, I cup his face, loving the feel of his beard under my touch as our lips meet for the first time in weeks.

We're moving as we kiss, Ringo's boots trudging across the sloshy sand driveway before he climbs the steps of the porch.

I hear voices getting closer, and when Ringo finally breaks the kiss, my eyes land on JD's wide grin, standing just inside the door already chatting to Jols.

"Didn't take you long," Jols teases as Ringo slips through the doorway, and I don't even hate how my cheeks heat at the insinuation.

"Please tell me you'll at least make it to your bedroom," Millie complains and I giggle, because while she's a very blunt person, she's been decent to me, and we've even had a few laughs over the past few weeks.

"On my way there. Where's Ma?" Ringo asks, his gaze darting around the living space as he stomps his dirty rain-soaked boots across the tiles.

"She turned in early," Alana announces, stepping out of the hallway that leads to their mum's bedroom.

I instantly feel guilty, because that's a lie.

Ringo's mum has been suffering through a lupus flare up, and while I've enjoyed learning all about it and practising some very basic care on Doreen, I hate knowing how much she's been suffering.

Ringo grunts at his sister, and I suspect he knows better than to believe her, but right now, he has a one track mind, and he's determined to get us behind closed doors.

Taking two steps at a time, Ringo has us up to his room in no time, locking us away as his lips claim mine again.

I've missed his taste. The brush of his tongue. The tickle of his beard as his lips devour mine. I know there's no way I'll handle him leaving me ever again.

I need this.

I need him.

"Fuck. I've missed your smell," he rasps into our kiss, and I giggle against his lips, because his head is in a similar place to mine.

Now in his bedroom, he lowers my feet to the floor while frantically stripping me out of my wet clothes.

"I need to taste you."

A needy whimper escapes me, but it's different from last month where I had an insatiable ache.

Now, my ache is for him.

To have him near.

To breathe him in.

To feel his deadly hands on my flesh.

I want to crawl under his skin, like it's the only thing anchoring me to this world.

Shit. If I could crawl under his skin and live there, I would.

Before I can even process what's happening, Ringo has me sprawled out on the bed, hovering over me as his lips find mine again.

It's a claiming kiss. One that screams unspoken words I've been desperate to hear fall from his lips.

"I need to taste *all* of you, Angel," he growls, breaking our kiss, his eyes so wild with lust that he looks a little drunk as they rake over my face. It's like he's recommitting every last inch to memory. Perhaps seeing something new there that wasn't present last time we were this close.

"Then I'm going to fuck you, and we aren't coming up for air until I've made you come ten fucking times."

A laugh bubbles past my lips. "Ten times. I don't think that's possible."

His eyes darken. "Oh, it's fucking possible, Abs. Let me show you."

His grin is wicked, but it quickly disappears as he lowers his head to the crook of my neck and begins his exploration.

I arch into each nip and kiss, moaning when he sucks my nipples deep into his mouth like he wants to choke on them. And I writhe when his beard tickles my skin as he trails kisses over my very prominent baby bump, before I lose sight of him behind it.

The moment his hot tongue glides up my seam, my legs fall wider, inviting and desperate, his big hands sliding beneath my butt, gripping each globe like he's settling in for a marathon.

It's not necessary. I'm so strung out with desire that the second he flattens his tongue over my clit, it's like he's flicked a switch and lit me up from the inside.

"Cam," I cry, my voice cracking with emotion, overwhelmed and ecstatic all at once, while a wave of ecstasy I haven't been able to find by my own touch, slams into me like a freight train.

"I've got you, Abbey," he rasps against my nub, his voice huskier than usual, and hearing him say my full name, something he rarely does, undoes me all over again.

Just having him here with me again makes it easy to ignore every insecurity I have about my body, or being too bold in what I want. So I let myself go, my hands fisting in his hair, gripping the strands, which are a little longer than usual, and I spread my thighs as wide as they'll go.

Instantly, he growls, the sound low and primal, vibrating against my exposed flesh. His tongue sinks inside me, so much thicker and deeper than I thought possible.

Then it happens.

Something in me snaps.

Maybe it's the filthiness of this.

Maybe it's just him.

I don't know, but I start… dare I say it… fucking his face.

I grind against his nose, trying to get his tongue deeper, the sensations somehow too much and still not enough.

With another feral growl, Ringo shifts into a kneeling position, dragging my hips up with him, his fingers digging into the flesh of my arse as he devours my pussy like a man possessed.

Whimpers, desperate and needy, fall from me. I have no control over what's happening. This man has trapped me in his vortex, and all I can do is hold on and enjoy the ride.

I'm sure he must be suffocating by the way his head is buried against my core, the thought of it shooting my pleasure so high, my world goes black, and my hearing vanishes, while I surf wave after wave of pure euphoria.

I hardly feel Ringo lowering my arse back to the bed, or him sliding off to strip out of his clothes.

I only figure that's what has happened when I find his warmth hovering over me.

"Kiss me, Angel. Taste yourself on my tongue."

I don't even hesitate, hooking my hands around his neck and pressing my lips to his.

And I *do* taste myself. It's intoxicating, the way he dives his tongue deep into my mouth, just the way he did inside my pussy. I moan as he deepens the kiss, feeling the thick head of his dick slide through my wetness and nudge at my entrance.

"Colour?" he rasps into our kiss.

"What?" I'm too far gone to understand what he's talking about as I try to suck his tongue, but I end up trying to chase it as he snatches it away.

"Fuuuck, Angel. Colour."

He's pressing into me slowly, like he's trying to hold back, and I frown, trying to see his face, but he's too close, his forehead to mine as I part my legs wider.

"Colour?" I ask, feeling dazed. Fuzzy.

Shifting back, Ringo's face finally comes into view, and I notice how he's trying to hold himself up so he doesn't press his weight against the swell of my bump.

"Fuck, Angel. Come on. Are you green? Please tell me you're fucking green."

His voice is strained and I realise he's holding back, the head of his dick the only part that has breached my entrance.

Green?

Shit. Green. Colour. How could I forget?

"Oh! Green. Yes, green, please."

A low rumble reverberates in his chest as my words spur him on, and he finally feeds his thick shaft into me.

My back arches off the bed, something close to perfect satisfaction rippling through me at the feel of him there again. Stretching me. Filling me.

"The way you squeeze my cock... I'll never get enough of it."

His words are grunted, deep and strained as he eases out slowly, and then back in again.

I don't understand how it's possible for my body to be lighting up again so soon, but every nerve ending in my body is alive, glowing brighter with each thrust of his hips. I'm lost to him. Completely caught up in everything he is, watching his face contort with a pinched frown as his eyes drop to where he enters me, and then back to my face.

Maybe it's the pregnancy hormones, or maybe I'm still just as naive as I was months ago, but it's not until this moment, as I watch him rock into me, taking the lead that I realise why he was asking if I was still green.

We haven't had sex this way before. With him in a controlling position, hovering over me while all I can do is take what he's giving.

After my freak out on our wedding night, he's let me be the one to call the shots. I was the one to lower onto his dick. I was the one to rise and fall and grind, taking what I needed while helping him over the line.

He was the one that had to hold on for the ride.

Now, without me even realising, the tables have turned, and I'm not even remotely upset about it.

Any rawness I'm feeling has to do with the fact that I wish I could have let him claim me like this sooner.

"Colour," he rasps again, obviously picking up that for a few moments, I've been lost in my head.

"Still green," I pant, feeling the way my cheeks burn with something more than desire. Then I dig deep, pulling from that bold, reckless part of me this man brings out so well... and let her loose.

"Fuck me, Cam."

This time, his growl is as ravenous as his thrusts, his fingers sliding between us to circle my clit, and I arch, my hands fisting the sheets, bracing myself as I hold on.

In this moment, there's nothing but me and Ringo.

I'm not beautifully wounded by my past.

There's no trauma between us. Just heat, sweat, and something that feels dangerously close to love.

This right here is more than fucking.

It is everything!

As Ringo works my clit like a fiddle, his dick pounding into me in a raw, claiming rhythm, I give myself over to the pleasure entirely. It surges to the surface, sending me hurtling over once again with Ringo's pleasured roar filling my ears.

"Fuck, I've missed you," Ringo groans as he sags over me, barely able to hold himself up.

Reaching up, I cup his face, running my fingers through his overgrown beard. It reminds me of when we were apart, when I ran from him. He'd let his hair and beard grow out because he wasn't taking care of himself, and now I know, he's done the same again.

"I don't want to be apart from you again," I whisper, making sure he sees the truth in my eyes.

He doesn't speak.

His lips thin, and he shifts, easing his softening dick out of me before padding across the carpet to his bathroom.

My heart sinks a little, because that's not the reaction I was hoping for.

When he returns, he has a warm washer in one hand, and a towel in the other, and he sits on the bed between my legs, shooting me a smirk.

"Open wide, Angel."

Biting my lip, I do as he asks, feeling my cheeks burn at the intimacy of being so exposed now that the pleasure part of what we were doing is over.

As he cleans me, his eyes drop to my exposed sex, and I work up the courage to repeat my words, since he didn't respond to them.

"I know you heard me when I said I don't want to be apart from you again."

Those stormy whiskey eyes dart back to mine, and he sighs.

"Just a little longer."

"Why?" I practically whine, pulling my knees closed as he finishes cleaning me.

"It's not safe, Angel."

I hate how emotional I feel. I don't want to cry. I've done that enough, especially while waiting for his call every night. Even so, the familiar burn behind my eyes warns me of an impending waterfall.

"I'm not strong enough to live so far apart from you," I whisper, too scared to speak louder in case he can hear the crack in my voice.

Lying down beside me, Ringo rolls me to face him, his fingers stroking my hair back in that way he likes to do.

"You're the strongest person I know."

I bite my lip, needing a moment to keep it together. To make sure I'm not about to start sooking like a girl that can't breathe without her man, even if that's exactly how I feel.

"It hurts, though," I admit softly. "I can't handle the distance, Cameron."

This time, it's him that has emotion flickering in his eyes as he cups my face, thumb stroking over my cheek like I might break.

"Fuck, Angel. I lo—"

Ringo's eyes widen as he cuts himself off, the words hanging in the air.

Was he going to say what I thought he was?

"Let's just enjoy this while we can," he says instead, and my heart sinks again, a dull ache spreading through me.

Why is it so hard for people to love me?

"How long do I have you?" my voice cracks as I ask, and I have to clear my throat, my eyes dropping to his chest as I fight to hold back the flood building inside me.

"Just for a few days, Angel. The faster I end more of those fuckers, the faster I get back to you."

My gaze snaps back to his.

"More? You mean you've already..." I trail off, almost too scared to say the words because of how excited the prospect is to me.

That's not right. I shouldn't be excited for people to die.

Ringo nods. "Two," he offers simply.

"Who?"

A frown creases his brow. "You sure you want to know?"

"Yes," I say quickly, pushing myself up on the bed to look down at him. "Please. I need to know."

"Tim and Michael," he sighs, his gaze locked onto mine like he's trying to read me.

Out of all of them, those two were the least horrible, and even they did some pretty bad stuff to me. Even so, I'm glad that's two less rapists I have to worry about.

"How?" I dare to ask, and this time Ringo sits up, too.

"You don't need to know that."

"Yeah I do," I protest, staring him dead in the eyes. "I want to know, dammit."

My small outburst has a smirk tugging at his lips, making him look sexy and sinister enough to almost distract me from the conversation.

Almost.

"Fine, Angel," he rasps, weaving his fingers with mine. "I'll tell you, but I'm not going into detail. You can have the CliffsNotes version."

"Fine. Whatever." I wave him off, and he chuckles, shaking his head at my eagerness.

"We had Tim for about four weeks. Beat him daily. Inflicted some torture. Cut him up good until he broke. Then he told us everything."

Four weeks?

Torture?

And…

For a moment, I can't breathe.

"*Everything*?" I squeak.

"Everything." He nods.

My cheeks heat with familiar humiliation, my mind flashing back to some of the vile things those arseholes did to me.

I never considered that Ringo would find out the whole truth. I kind of assumed that once they were dead, I'd be the only one left to remember.

"Hey." Ringo reaches for me, dragging me onto his lap. "Don't think about that part."

I can't look at him, and I know that with a simple demand he could make me. It is, after all, the way I've been unknowingly conditioned. But Ringo doesn't force that on me. He allows me this grace.

"Who is *us*?" I whisper after a long moment, my gaze darting back to his. "You said he told *us* everything."

"Me, JD, Murf, Trunk and Stocky," he answers quickly, not holding back any secrets.

"They all know what those arseholes did to me?"

"Yes, and they want their blood as much as I do," he growls, anger flashing across his expression.

"How about Smitty? Does he know?"

Ringo shakes his head. "No. He's given me free rein on this one, as long as I keep up with club business."

Club business.

It's hard for me to comprehend what they class as business.

"How is that going?" I'm not even sure if he'll elaborate, but I'm curious, and want to know what he does with his time aside from hunting down my attackers.

"Good actually. Moving out of the city was a smart move. We do small daily runs in the Timber Valley area, coordinated with the Marx crew, although it's not exactly sanctioned by Ewan Marx."

I frown at his words, not entirely sure what all of that means. Ringo obviously notices, so with another chuckle and shifting me closer on his lap, he elaborates.

"Timber Valley is Griffin and Devon's region, so they can do what they like, but I have a feeling if Ewan found out they were letting us take a major slice of the trade in the area, he wouldn't be too happy."

"What trade?"

At my question, Ringo shakes his head.

"You don't need to know."

Frowning, I cross my arms over my chest.

"I have a right to know what my husband does for work," I snap. "What trade?"

"Hmmm. I do like the sound of you calling me your husband." He leans closer trying to nip at my lips, but I arch away.

"Don't try and distract me with your sexy tongue, Cameron. What business are you trading in?"

A rumble sounds from the back of his throat, and his fingers dig into my thigh. Not painfully, but a warning. Still, he concedes.

"Drugs and guns, mostly. Some tobacco and vapes. Medical supplies sought after from this fucking pandemic."

"What about the sex trade or trafficking? Do the Southern Sadists trade in that?"

"Fuck no, Angel. The only involvement in trafficking we have is killing the motherfuckers that run it."

A smile kicks up my lips, Ringo's words a reminder that while his club are outlaws, they are the better of the evils.

"Do you have any more questions, Angel?" He smirks back, and I nod.

"Just one."

"And what's that?"

"When are you going to give me orgasm number three?"

He throws his head back as a laugh rips from his chest, and a moment later, he has me straddling him.

"Saddle up, Angel. Let's go for another ride."

I giggle at his playful smile, but the second his lips find mine, I'm lost once again.

Ringo makes good on his promise. I'm absolutely spent by the time he rips the tenth orgasm from me like he's conducting an exorcism. I don't even remember falling asleep.

It's the blare of his phone hours later that jolts me awake, just in time to hear him grumble a curse.

"Sorry, Angel. Let me grab that." He presses a quick kiss to my forehead before rolling over to snatch his phone off the bedside table.

"Speak."

I can't make out the words spoken, but the fact I can hear them like someone is yelling, and the way Ringo stiffens, has me instantly on alert.

"When?" Ringo barks, leaping up out of bed. "Fuck. Okay. I'm on my way."

Ending the call, he makes another putting it on speaker, tossing it on the bed as he quickly gets dressed.

"This better be a fucking emergency," JD snaps before Ringo barks.

"Get dressed. The new compound is under attack."

RINGO

Never in my fucking life have I pushed my hog so hard, but we make the trip in just over an hour, guns drawn as our bikes tear up the tree-lined driveway of the new compound in Fox Pines.

All we find is carnage.

Several of our freshly-built structures are ablaze, flames chewing through the timber like it's paper. A row of motorcycles simmers in coals, nothing but molten metal and smoke.

Apart from the light coming from the flames, it's near impossible to see a damn thing in the suffocating dark.

Bullets rip through the air from the treeline, giving us no choice but to ditch our rides and haul arse into the old barn.

"Here!" Smitty's familiar voice calls, and I look up just in time to see a sawn-off shotgun flying through the air towards me.

Catching the fucking thing, I check that it's loaded, feeling Celina at my back as she shoves extra rounds into my pockets.

"Fill me in," I bark, demanding an update as Celina moves to JD, stuffing his pockets the same way.

"Suicide trucker hit first. Took out the drug storage," Smitty snarls, inspecting more weapons as he hands them off. "Then came the fucking dirt bikes. Lit the place up good before taking cover in the fucking trees."

"And this has been going on for over an hour?" JD asks the same thing I'm wondering.

"Yeah, and our police contacts seem to be out of fucking reach."

"Shit," I mutter, a heavy knot forming in my gut. There's no way Jason Zimora would let this happen. Not unless he's been subdued… or worse. "Anyone called Griffin?"

"Of course we've called him," Smitty snaps, looking at me like I'm a fucking idiot. "He's unreachable too."

Fuck. This isn't just bad. This is completely fucked.

"How many are dead? Injured?" JD barks, and Smitty starts rattling off names.

"Among the dead is Kite. Roadie. Barts. Bowey and Zeus. No Doxies were killed but Darla and Nessy have been taken."

Fuck… Barts. Roadie… and my fucking mate… Bowey. I knew Kite and Zeus, but not as well as the others.

Someone will fucking pay for this!

"Where's the rest of my fucking team?" I snap, thankful Murf, Trunk and Stocky aren't on the list.

"Murf and Trunk are working their way through the pines, trying to flank them from behind." Smitty ushers us to the barn door, and I spare a quick glance at the Doxies huddled together, their cheeks stained with tears, some smeared with someone else's blood.

"And Stocky?" I growl, my patience wearing razor-thin.

"With Mex, Vender and Tups over by the row of shipping containers we haven't touched yet."

Nodding, JD and I pocket a few more guns off the hay bale, then slip back out the door.

We only make it a few steps before bullets spray past us again, and we both take off, sprinting for the shipping containers where some of the men are returning fire.

I dive for cover as the bullets get too close for fucking comfort, sliding across the grass and slamming into Mex behind the containers. Worried for my best mate, I snap my gaze in his direction just in time to see JD doing the same, skidding across the grass to take cover with us.

"Talk to me," I demand, pressing myself to the steel wall and peering around the corner.

"There's about ten of them," Mex barks. "They only shoot when they see movement or to return fire. Got no fucking clue what their MO is."

It's then that a loud voice cracks through the air.

My brows fucking hitch as Mex mirrors me, and we fall dead silent to listen.

"RINGO!"

"The fuck?" JD hisses, peeking around the corner. "How are they doing that?"

A high-pitched squeal makes us all flinch before it cuts out. It's that nasty feedback sound made when a mic gets too close to a speaker.

"Megaphone." Tups shrugs. "Has to be. I don't see how the hell they'd rig up fucking speakers out here."

I nod. It's the simplest explanation, and the most likely.

"RINGO!"

Hearing my name blare across the clearing again sends fucking chills down my spine.

"Why are they calling your name?" JD frowns, matching mine.

"That's what I'd like to fucking know," I snap, glancing back over to the barn, happy to see no movement outside it.

What the fuck is going on?

"They've been quiet 'til now. Nothing but bullets," Vender adds from where he's perched on a ladder, his rifle on top of the container.

"RINGO! IF YOU ARE HERE, PLEASE SHOW YOURSELF!"

"What the actual fuck is going on?" JD snaps, eyes practically bulging out of his skull.

"RINGO! WE WON'T HARM YOU! JUST SHOW YOURSELF!"

JD scoffs, not believing a word of whoever is speaking, and the dread curling in my gut tells me exactly what kind of trap this could be.

But I can't ignore it. If there's even the smallest chance I can shut this down… I have to try.

"What the fuck are you doing?" Stocky hisses, gripping my arm as I move to step out from the cover we're hiding behind.

"I have to put an end to this," I sneer, yanking my arm free.

"The fuck you do." JD's on me next, grabbing at my cut, trying to haul me back.

I spin and throw a punch at him, missing as he ducks, but using his distraction to break away and step clear of the container.

"I'm fucking here!" I bellow as loud as I can. "What do you want?!"

There's nothing but silence, and a chill runs up my spine as I sense too many fucking guns pointed directly at me. Then, a spotlight from the treeline flashes on, lighting me up like I'm on a fucking stage.

I stand there exposed. Waiting. Watching.

At any moment, they could open fire. There's no way I could get to cover in time. I'm a sitting duck. So what the fuck are they waiting for?

When nothing else happens, I hold for another beat, ready to step back and take cover when a second spotlight cuts through the dark. I stiffen, holding my fucking breath as I wait for something to happen, and then movement catches my eye.

A man staggers out into the clearing, limping slowly across the grass in my direction. I take a few steps closer, tracking the gun in his hand, his grip loose, muzzle aimed to the grass as he moves.

"What do you want?!" I shout, my voice echoing across the open space.

He doesn't answer. He doesn't flinch or look up from the ground as he staggers. He just keeps coming.

Glancing back, I see JD has stepped out from behind the shelter, with Mex at his side. Stocky and Vender remain hidden, their guns trained on the man approaching.

"Is that…" JD frowns, leaning forward to squint at the figure getting closer.

When I do the same, I find a hint of familiarity in the approaching man as he lifts his head.

Fuck.

It's Cookie.

Not thinking twice, I stride straight for our missing prospect, relieved he's still breathing, but with a thousand fucking questions bouncing through my head.

Where the hell has he been?

Why did he bail the second the cops showed up at the Western while we were stuck dealing with the warehouses?

Does he know Morris died that day?

"Cookie," I bark, now just a few metres away, which is when he stops, and slowly raises his gun, aiming it straight at me.

I freeze, taking in his face, the tears leaking from his red eyes, and the fading bruises marring his skin.

Fuck. He's in bad shape. The round belly he used to carry is gone, like he hasn't eaten properly in weeks.

"I'm sorry, man," he chokes out, voice cracking. "I had no choice."

"No choice about what?" I snap, knowing Vender has his scope trained on Cookie's head, and he won't hesitate to pull the trigger if needed.

"I didn't want to do it." Cookie sobs, choking on his own words. "They had my sister, man. I had to let them through the gates."

"You talking about the cops?" I curl my fucking lip. "Allen?"

Cookie nods, but then shakes his head. "Not just them. The pigs came with backup."

"Who?" I snarl, fists clenched, jaw tight, about ready to head-butt this fucker.

Cookie moves to glance over his shoulder, but thinks better of it, his bloodshot eyes snapping back to mine.

"Satan's Rebels."

Fuck.

Leo Marx was right. Our rival club is involved, deeper than we fucking knew.

"What about Morris? Were you the one who killed him and stuffed him in Casey's trunk?"

"Yes," Cookie splutters, his face contouring in agony. "Fu-uuck… his fucking face man. When he realised what I'd done. That I'd betrayed him." Cookie presses his hand, along with the clip of the gun, to his temples, crumbling under the weight of his betrayal.

"You could've come to us. We could've tried to save your sister. We still can."

"No." He shakes his head, his arms trembling with pain and fury. "It's too fucking late. The Satans raped her for days… and killed her this morning." His voice breaks. "She's fucking gone, man. Fucking *gone*."

Cookie buckles in half, a wailing scream tearing out of him.

A loud shot cracks through the air, and a bullet tears up the dirt at Cookie's feet.

He jumps in fright, before spinning to face the treeline.

"Okay! Fucking give me a second!" he yells, his voice ragged, soaked in despair.

I glance towards the thick pines, not able to see a damn thing through the glare of the spotlights, before Cookie turns back to face me.

"I don't wanna do this." Cookie chokes out. "I'm so fucking sorry."

"Do what?" I ask, a chill slicing down my spine as dread pools thick in my gut.

"I have a message for you… from Ian Allen."

"What the fuck is it?" I growl, squeezing the gun in my hand, itching to unleash hell.

"This… me." He swirls his free hand through the air. "I'm nothing more than a diversion."

I stop fucking breathing, as I watch an eerie calmness settle over Cookie's face.

"While you're here dealing with me…" he deadpans. "Allen is taking your woman."

The words slam into me like a freight train, rage exploding in my chest, my heart hammering against my ribs… but before I can move… before I can say a single fucking word, Cookie lifts the gun, presses it to his temple, and pulls the trigger.

31

ABBEY

Another storm is rolling in, leaving me with an eerie feeling as I sit beneath the Jacaranda tree in the darkness of the early morning.

Ringo left over an hour ago. I've felt nothing but dread since. That familiar feeling has crept back in, but this time, it's settled deep, like it has no intention of going anywhere.

Everyone is still asleep. The call came in around 1am, so everyone here was out cold. Except for Stoner, who I know is stationed at the front gate.

Mule, my constant shadow, must have taken the night off with Ringo's arrival earlier, which is fair. There was no need for him to remain on my watch with my husband here.

But he's gone now, and for the first time in weeks, as I sit at Hope's gravestone, I am truly alone.

The entire sky lights up, illuminating my surroundings with a blinding flash of lightning… and I stiffen, the air in my lungs getting trapped.

Surely my eyes are playing tricks on me, because I could have sworn, at the last second, I caught sight of the silhouette of a man up on the ridge.

Thunder cracks loud overhead, making the hairs on my arms stand on end. As my heartrate kicks up, thrashing wildly in my chest, I stand from the ground, my paranoid eyes darting around me.

There's no one there, Abbey. Stop conjuring up stuff that isn't real.

Another flash, this one delayed, sending forks of lightning streaking across the sky, but I barely register it.

A gasp lodges in my throat, my eyes locking onto not one, but six or seven moving silhouettes up on the ridge… heading straight for me.

I nearly slip as I stumble backwards, heavy drops of rain splashing against my cheeks as I spin and run.

My legs won't move fast enough as I charge uphill towards the house. My run is a desperate mess, a frantic mix of leaps and waddles, as I try to put distance between me and the men closing in.

"Help!" I scream, the barn and house coming into view as I reach the top of the hill. "*Help!*"

By the time I scurry over the rise, Brody and Tucker come crashing out of the barn, guns raised, their eyes scanning as they assess the situation.

"Men!" I yell, pointing over my shoulder. "*There are men coming!*"

Gunfire explodes through the air, but not from the ridge. It's coming from the direction of the front gate.

"Get her inside!" Tucker bellows over another clap of thunder, and I practically dive into Brody's arms, never more grateful to see him.

"Lock it down!" The yell blasts from the mouth of the driveway, and I gasp as Stoner comes sprinting from the treeline, turning mid-run to fire shots back into the dark.

Time, as I know it, slows.

Every gunshot is a heartbeat.

Every pop sparks a flash in the dark treeline.

Every step Stoner takes backwards looks like lead is weighing on his feet.

Then… he jerks, arms throwing wide as he flies backwards, his body slamming into the dirt with a loud thud.

"Abbey! Get in here!"

Time speeds up, my hearing returns tenfold, Alana's scream reaching me over the chaos.

Yanking on my arm, Brody drags me towards the steps of the house.

I don't even realise I'm crying until hot tears blur my vision, making it hard to see. I stumble up the steps, watching as Millie helps Jols load up with guns, like my new friend is planning on fighting.

"N-no. J-Jols. You can't go out there."

Hurrying to me, she presses her lips to my cheek. "This is what I'm trained for, Abbey. Now get inside and stay safe. It's gonna be okay."

Her calm confidence does nothing to make me feel better as Alana grabs my arm from Brody, before he follows Jols back out into the rain.

I don't even get the chance to protest before I'm dragged inside, the door slamming shut as Alana secures the lock.

My hands cradle my bump, trembling, as I stagger into the dark living room where Millie stands by the kitchen counter.

I frown, blinking past my tears at how *off* the kitchen looks right now.

The benchtop is pushed back, light glowing from where it had been, revealing a set of stairs leading down into a basement.

"Come on. We have to get you and Ma into the panic room," Alana rushes out as she drags me.

I stumble beside her, feeling like I've stepped straight into the twilight zone.

Is this real? Is all of this really happening?

"Come on, sweetheart. Let's get you safe," Doreen says with a warm smile, but it doesn't reach her eyes.

She's scared.

"The shutters!" Alana calls to Millie as I move deeper into the room, and a loud burst of gunfire just outside the house freezes us all.

Millie is the first to move, dashing to a panel on the wall, frantically flicking a switch.

"Shit! The shutters aren't wor—" Millie's voice cuts off, snagging our attention to see her slowly lifting her hands as the barrel of a gun presses to her head.

"No. *Please*," Doreen cries, her voice cracking. "Don't hurt her."

Alana steps in front of her mum, arms outstretched like she can shield her.

My body shakes with violent tremors as I take in the scene. A beautiful family staring death in the eye, all because of me.

"Drop the gun." Jols' voice cuts through the air, vicious, steady, and laced with ice.

The man, with his face covered in a black ski mask, chuckles low, like this is nothing but a game. Millie is trembling under the press of his barrel, and Doreen's sobs are silent, but loud enough to hear.

Still, this man doesn't care. He's only here for one thing.

Me.

Time slows again, the man's eyes flicking to me before he spins suddenly, firing at Jols.

The crack is deafening inside, and I scream as Jols slams back into the wall, blood blooming out in an arc as it soaks through her white tee.

"No!" I scream, watching realisation shift over her face, the colour draining from it as she slides to the floor. "Jols!"

A trail of smeared blood is painted on the wall behind her, before she starts coughing up her crimson lifesource.

"No! Stop!" I beg, the man already taking aim back at Millie.

"Ms Delany, we don't want to hurt you." His gaze darts to me while keeping his weapon trained on Ringo's sister. "Just come with us, and this will all be over. No one else has to get hurt."

"Go fuck yourself!" Millie snaps on my behalf, and the man chuckles again before redirecting his gun.

Then he fires.

Millie screeches, crashing to the floor as the bullet tears through her leg. Her mum wails, trying to push past Alana, who's doing everything she can to hold her frail mother back.

"Fine!" I cry out. "I'll come with you. Just let them go downstairs, *please*," I beg, my voice cracking from the terror of it all.

"Whatever." The gunman shrugs, like him shooting people is no big deal.

I hurry to Millie. She's trying to be brave, biting back her sobs through gritted teeth, and I help her up.

Alana rushes forward, taking her sister from me, her eyes trained on the gunman, not trusting what he'll do next.

Glancing at the opening in the kitchen counter, I see Doreen's head disappear as she moves down the stairs, and Alana hurries after her to get Millie to safety.

"Come on then," the man barks, jerking his gun towards the front door, but I shake my head.

"Not yet. I need to know they are safe first. Then I'll come with you."

He rolls his eyes but gestures with a lazy swirl of his hand for me to hurry up, so I rush to the opening, peering down to see the three women who mean the world to Ringo stepping inside the small panic room.

Turning back, Alana's eyes lock with mine before she moves to shut the door.

"Come on," she whispers, waving me down, but the solid press of a gun to my temple stops me in place.

I swallow the huge lump in my throat, my lip wobbling as I try to compose myself to speak.

"Lans," I manage to call out.

"Yeah?"

"Tell Cam…" I swallow hard. "Tell Cam that I love him. That I'll never forget what he tried to do for me." This time my sob escapes as hot tears pool over once again. "And tell him that it's okay for him to move on. He deserves to find the sort of love he's given me."

Alana's rolling tears match mine as she nods, mouthing '*I love you*' before blowing me a kiss.

Reluctance has her hesitating a moment longer, but I give her a reassuring nod, and she slowly closes the door, locking them safely in.

"Do you mind?" I snap, shooting the man a glare over my shoulder, and he sighs, removing the barrel from my temple.

"Let's go," he barks with impatience, and I nod, my hand grazing over the benchtop where a sharp knife peeks out from a discarded tea towel.

The second it's in my hand, I scream and spin, raw and defiant, driving the knife deep into the man's chest. He howls, staggering back as gunfire erupts inside the house.

I don't wait another second, bolting for the stairs, forcing myself not to look at Jols' lifeless body on the floor.

More gun wielding figures burst into the house, and my heart jackhammers as I push harder, desperate to get away.

"Get her!" The man I stabbed roars, clutching his chest, blood blooming fast beneath his hand.

The newcomers take chase, their boots pounding behind me.

I clutch under my belly as I take the stairs, two at a time, desperate to get to Ringo's room where I know a gun is stashed under the mattress, and my phone is on the bedside table.

"You have nowhere to run!" a new male voice snarls, way too close, and I squeal as I feel his fingers brush my back as he lunges.

He slips, and I risk a glance back to see him tumbling into another man on the staircase. That man doesn't help him, just shoves him out of the way and keeps coming.

Hold on, little cabbage. Mummy will get us out of this somehow.

I nearly trip on the last step, but catch myself just in time, rushing forward to Ringo's door.

The moment I'm inside, I go to slam it but I meet strong resistance. A body. A hand. Someone is pushing through.

"Stop fucking fighting," the man snarls, pressing into the door from the other side.

"Never!" I scream, pushing against the door, somehow managing to get it closed and locked.

My heart is louder than the thunder and gunfire outside, so I take in deep steadying breaths as I charge down the passage, hoping to slow my pulse as I enter the suite.

Fists pound the door, before something else starts crashing into it, and I know it won't hold for long.

A loud crack claps through the air, and wood splinters from the gunshot. I squeal in fright, running as fast as I can, skidding around the corner into the bedroom before diving for the mattress.

Heavy feet pound through the suite, whimpers falling past my lips as I scramble to find the gun under the mattress, friction burns on my knees starting to throb as I kneel on the carpet.

The moment my fingers brush the metal I'm searching for, I cry out in relief.

Spinning to my butt, I raise the gun just in time to see one of the men lunging for me. I don't think. I just act, squeezing the trigger.

The kickback from the gun frightens me, and I lose my grip as the man crumbles to his knees, clutching his stomach.

"Bitch shot me!" he whines, glaring at me like I'm the bad one for trying to defend myself.

I blindly search for the gun, my hand patting over the carpet while my eyes lock onto the second masked man approaching.

"It's a pity they want you alive," he spits, his gun trained on me as another man barges into the room. "I'd happily kill you, right here."

"We don't have long. Let's get her out of here," the new masked man mutters, moving to the one I shot to help him stand.

"What the fuck do you think we are trying to do?" The one closing in on me snaps, but even though he's talking to his partners in crime, his eyes don't leave me.

Dammit. I need the gun.

Where is it?

In a last attempt to protect myself, I peel my gaze away from him and search for the gun.

It's only a few feet away, so I quickly move to grab it, but before I reach it, a strong fist slams into my jaw.

The hit is so hard, it rattles my brain, and for a moment, I fear I might black out from the pain.

I cry out, gagging, the impact completely messing with me, and before I know what's happening, the men are closing in.

"Hold her fucking arms." One of the men demands before two sets of feet move to either side of me.

Are there more men here now?

Shit. I can't make sense of anything. Everything seems darker. Noises seem further. And my head aches so bad.

Shit… Little cabbage… I'm sorry.

As I'm lifted by each arm, a figure steps into the room, a slow clap filling the space and a familiar vulgar laugh joins it.

"You put on quite a show, Ms Delaney." Ian Allen smiles, like he has a front row seat of my demise. "But your little disappearing act is over now. It's time to pay your dues."

I can't even find words to spit back as air seizes in my lungs. The mere sight of Officer Allen closing in takes me back to the day he threatened my sisters. Takes me back to the mouse I was only a couple of months ago.

Now, standing before me, he smiles, reaching out to snatch my chin as he leans in close. "I'm going to have fun with you."

I try to rear back, but it's no use, his grip, and that of his men at my sides has me stuck in place, and a moment later, I feel a sharp pinch in my arm.

"Wha—" My squeak is cut off when my gaze darts to my arm, a dead feeling rushing through it as the contents inside the syringe embedded in my skin gets pushed into my bloodstream.

No.

My gaze follows Ian Allen's hand as he withdraws the needle, and he smiles at me like we are old friends. "See you in your nightmares, Abigail."

Then, my room sways, turning fuzzy, right before everything goes black.

32

RINGO

The van tears over the bumps on the windy roads as I struggle to keep the fucking thing from veering over the edge of the steep incline.

"Everyone armed and ready?" JD calls to our team, as I speed up the road that leads to my home.

My fucking sanctuary.

The moment my front gate comes into view, dread so fucking heavy I feel like it could drown me flares in my gut. The strong metal bars of the custom made gate are bent and twisted, hanging loosely on its hinges like a fucking tornado swept through here.

I flatten my foot to the floor as I peel off the main road and up my gravel driveway, everyone inside the van white-knuckling whatever they can hold on to to stay upright as I drive like a fucking mad man.

And I am a fucking mad man. The moment Cookie's fucking brains were spraying the air, I was charging for a vehicle that could get me to my girl.

The moment we burst into the clearing, the flashing lights of an ambulance has me slamming on the brakes, throwing the fucking thing into park and leaping from the vehicle.

"Abbey!" I scream at the top of my lungs, my frantic gaze darting around to find a male body strewn on the grass in the clearing.

Trunk and Murf run in that direction while I charge around the ambulance to stare at the fucking destruction leading all the way into my house.

"Fuck." JD hisses next to me as we both find Tucker shot up like someone was using him for fucking target practise. "Brody," JD whispers, fear choking him up. "Brody! Jols!"

"In here!" Alana's voice echoes from inside, and we charge up the steps, bursting through the door where paramedics are working profusely, doing CPR on a body.

A female fucking body.

Air gets trapped in my lungs as we step closer to see our beautiful Jols, lifeless, laying in a pool of blood. Her blood.

"Fuck!" JD bellows, rushing forward. "No! Jols!" His strangled words tumble from him as he falls to his knees by her side, while the paramedics continue to pump her chest.

"Another ambulance is on its way," one paramedic tells him, but her eyes hold nothing but sympathy.

Fuck.

Jols is going to die.

Or maybe…. maybe she's already dead.

"Fuck!" I scream, fisting my hands in my hair, my gaze scanning over Alana and my ma huddled on the couch next to Millie who looks pale as fuck. "Someone tell me fucking something!"

I'm losing it. Fucking losing it.

"Brody got shot in the gut," Lans stands, but she doesn't approach me, "but the bullet went right through. I patched him up." Lans points to Brody who's sitting on the floor by the window, tears wetting his cheeks as he watches his brother fall apart over Jols.

"Mills got shot in the leg, but it's just a flesh wound," Alana rushes out, before pointing to our ma. "Ma and I are fine. Abbey made sure of it."

"What the fuck do you mean, Abbey made sure of it? Where the fuck is she?"

Lans and Millie share a look, and I expect Millie to start talking since she's usually the one to step in and take control, but it's Alana who continues.

"She made sure they wouldn't hurt us anymore… and made sure we were locked safely in the panic room."

With fury coiling through every muscle, I storm to my sister, and she shrinks back, falling into the couch as I jab a fucking finger at her.

"Explain. What do you mean, Abbey made sure they wouldn't hurt you? Where. The fuck. Is she?!"

Alana's lip starts wobbling, tears instantly bursting from her eyes as she starts muttering incoherently.

"Sarg." Murf cuts in, and I have a right fucking mind to shoot the fucker for interupting me, but I know he wouldn't unless it's something I need to know.

"What?" I snap.

"Stoner is dead on the lawn." The emotion is thick in Murf's throat, and he takes a moment to clear it as I drag my gaze from my sister to my club brother. "We also found Mule… up on the ridge with his throat slashed."

Tucker is dead.

Stoner is dead.

Mule is dead.

Jols… fuck Jols might be dead.

And Abbey… my Angel… Where the fuck is she?

Turning back to my sister, I make sure our eyes are locked before I speak.

"Lans, I swear to fucking God. Where the fuck is my wife?" I've never spoken to her with such cold malice before, but I'm done being fucking patient.

But, it does the trick. Finally, my sister breaks.

"She g-gave herself u-up. At least that's w-what she told them, but we h-heard her, Cam." Alana stands quickly, taking my hand. "She fought them. Stabbed one. Ran upstairs. I don't know what happened after that, but I couldn't find her or any sign of the men that did this. She was just… gone."

I thought I'd felt pain before. But nothing compares to this. Agony in its rawest form. Brutal. Tortuous. Crippling.

Buckling in half, my hands fisting in my hair as I drop my gun and scream.

"WHERE THE FUCK IS MY WIFE!?"

33

ABBEY

Ringo. He's my happy place. Everything about him makes me smile.

His smell. Those whiskey eyes that spark just a little brighter when they land on me. His lips, teasing and hungry, the way they nip over every inch of my skin. That tongue of his is wicked, and devouring, and can easily have me trembling from head to toe.

I love his hands, and the small calluses on his palms. His fingers, long, thick, and devastatingly skilled.

They're not usually this rough, but I guess he's feeling frantic. Feisty perhaps. Because he's kinda hurting me right now.

"Cam." I moan, trying to pry my eyes open as my body gets jostled.

Back and forth.

Back and forth.

Back and forth.

"Fuck yeah, you little cunt. Moan for me."

All the air leaves my lungs in a brutal rush.

My eyes spring open at the voice… A voice that is *not* Ringo's.

I stiffen like a board, a whimper escaping me, my horror turning my body taut. There's too much dry friction, painful and jarring, where Officer Allen drives into me.

"No. No. No," I whimper. "Stop. Please. Stop."

A cruel laugh slips from his lips, his heavy-lidded gaze fixed on my chest as he thrusts again and again, ignoring the way my body tries to force him out.

Oh shit… I'm naked. Completely… shamefully naked. My eyes track to the way my breasts jiggle with each violent thrust, but I hardly care about that.

Hell, as sick as it makes me, I don't even care that he's raping me. All I care about is how close he is to my unborn baby.

I try to move, but his grip is tight on my wrists, pinning them to the table above my head. My mind instantly goes back… back to the times his nephew and friends did this to me. Over and over.

No.

Not again.

I can't live through this again.

Not with my sweet baby inside me.

"STOP!" I scream. "Get out of me!"

"Like hell," he sneers, his face far too close, his breath foul, reeking of tobacco and rot. "I wanted to know what all the fuss was about." He leans back just enough to drop his spit on the place he disappears inside me. "Now I fucking know."

Rage bubbles inside me, thick and searing, and I start thrashing as best I can. Trying to shift my body away from his… but there's no escaping.

"Get off me!" I scream, hoping someone, anyone, can hear.

But no one comes. No one stops this.

Twisting my head to the side, I lash out with my teeth, the only weapon I have right now, and I bite down on his forearm.

He yells, the sound raw and furious, but I don't stop.

My teeth sink deeper as I scream, my voice loud and feral, and my mouth fills with the tang of blood. A chunk of flesh tears free, landing on my tongue, and I release his arm, gagging.

"You fucking bitch! You fucking bit me!"

His roar is deafening, right before his palm cracks across my cheek so hard, stars explode behind my eyes.

"Once this baby is out, I'm going to gut you like a fish!" he snarls, spittle spraying my face like venom.

Fuck him! If he thinks I'm going to make this easy, he's about to get a surprise.

I scream again, thrashing with everything I've got, wild and jostling.

His rhythm falters as he tries to piston into me, but I keep throwing him off, breaking tempo, nearly forcing him out a few times.

I keep screaming. I don't stop, his grip on my wrists now gone as he cradles his wound to his chest while he tries to complete his task.

I claw at his face, punching, grabbing, making sure nothing about this is enjoyable for him.

But then, a familiar voice cuts in, and I freeze, my eyes landing on Donny Allen.

"Get off her, Uncle Ian," he snickers, stepping into the unfamiliar room. "You've had long enough with her. Now it's my turn."

No... not again.

34

RINGO

Two days. Two fucking days, and nothing. No word about her. No word from my Angel.

I can't fucking think straight. I can't eat. Can't fucking shit. And I sure as fuck can't sleep.

I haven't stopped hunting for her for a goddamn minute.

Her parents' house has been abandoned. Completely cleared out like they fled in a fucking hurry. I've got no fucking idea where they are.

Lexi can't get a hold of Tahli on the app they use, and even Hush can't get a location. Not a fucking blip.

I've got everyone working on trying to find her. The Angel sisters. The Marx family. They're all helping.

Abbey's friends are just as frantic, and I'm pretty sure Lexi is just like me, and hasn't slept since she got the call about what happened.

This is all *my fucking fault.*

I should never have left her. What the fuck was I thinking? I should've fought Smitty's orders. Should've left him high and dry.

But fuck… it's not his fault.

It's mine.

All fucking mine.

Nothing good comes from splitting up. I've seen enough movies to know better.

Fuck.

Now I'm trying to rationalise this shit by comparing it to a fucking movie.

I need my head checked, for fucking sure.

But that, and literally everything else, can fucking wait. Because I'm not fucking stopping. Not until I've got my Angel safely in my arms again.

I won't stop for anything, or anyone.

The rumble of approaching motorcycles doesn't even claim my attention. My eyes and mind remain locked on the map pinned to the barn door at our new compound.

"Where are you, Angel?" I whisper, feeling more of the organ inside my chest breaking off and I wish for the impossible… wishing she could hear me.

FUCK!

Leaning closer, I draw a cross through the last known location of that fucked up cult-like church her family goes to, our search of it turning up jack shit.

They fled in a hurry too.

You can't tell me that's a fucking coincidence.

I stare at the map, absolutely stumped. Fucking lost.

Without more intel, it's like searching for a needle in a fucking haystack. She could be *anywhere*. Could be in another fucking state by now. Or worse, out of the country.

We might be thick in a pandemic, but that doesn't mean people aren't slipping across state borders or dodging coast guard in their fancy fucking boats.

"Sarg. There's someone here you need to see," Stocky mutters, stepping into the empty barn.

I grunt in response, right as Smitty comes barging in.

"Stop fucking crying, Wendy. Your tears won't work here."

I spin the second I hear Wendy's fucking name, finding Spud, our VP, dragging her by her elbow, his grip brutal before he shoves her hard.

She crashes to her knees between us. Trembling. Her eyes pleading as she peers up at me.

"What the fuck is this bitch doing back here?" I snap, about ready to throw down if anyone thinks I'm willing to let her slither back into this chapter.

"Come on, Celina. Get in here," Smitty snaps, waving Celina in.

She's hiding behind the door, looking like she'd rather be anywhere else.

"Tell Ringo. Don't leave a fucking thing out," Smitty growls, his eyes wild with rage.

Celina's tear filled eyes dart to Wendy, who glares at her through her own tears, and my fucking patience is about ready to snap.

Pulling out my gun, I flick the safety off with a click that fills the silence.

"Someone better start fucking talking."

"W-Wendy k-knows something about A-Abbey," Celina stammers, shaking as tears streak her cheeks, and Wendy spits in her direction.

"Snitches get stitches, Celina. What the fuck happened to the girl code?"

"The girl code?" Celina's brows shoot high. "What girl code, Wendy? Decent women hold each other up. They don't shoot them down. And they certainly don't play a part in another woman's kidnapping."

The moment Celina's words sink in, I've got a fistful of Wendy's hair in my grip, the barrel of my gun jammed under her jaw as I snarl in her face.

"Tell me where the fuck my wife is."

Wendy scoffs. "As if I'd do that. The moment I tell you *anything*, I'll be dead."

"Tell him, Wendy!" Celina cries. "You called me bragging about getting Abbey out of the way for good. Tell him what you know," Celina begs, but I catch the flash of acceptance in Wendy's eyes.

She knows she's a dead woman walking. She's just trying to stall.

I contemplate pulling the trigger, blowing her brains out and ending this shit show. But right now, she's the closest thing we've got to a lead.

"Prez." I look Smitty dead in the eye. "As Sergeant-at-Arms, I'm requesting permission to enact the maximum penalty."

"What?!" Wendy screeches. "No! I'm not a club member. You can't do that!"

Smitty glances from me to her, lifting a brow, unimpressed.

"Are you seriously telling me what I can and can't do in my fucking club, Wendy?"

"No... I—"

"Then shut the fuck up unless you're ready to talk," he snaps, his voice like ice before giving me his attention again. "You have my permission."

Nodding at my President, I shift my attention to the bitch on the floor.

"One last chance to speak up."

Her lips thin, like she is trying to seal the truth in with her sheer will.

Wrong fucking move.

In fact, I'm glad she's holding back. Punishing this bitch is well fucking overdue, and I'm going to enjoy every fucking second of it.

Turning to Murf and Stocky, I give them an order I can already tell they are eager to deliver.

"Gather everyone." I slip my gun away and crack my knuckles. "Strip her down and tie her to the pole out front. No one misses this."

35

ABBEY

I launch my spit straight into my mother's face, and I don't even care how undignified it is. I'm long past pretending to be a lady.

It was one thing to believe Officer Allen was after me for his idiot nephew and Daniel... but realising my own mother had a hand in sending men to Ringo's home to attack, makes me sick.

They *killed* people.

They would've killed Ringo's helpless mum if I hadn't tried to bargain with them.

And Jols...

I can't even let my mind go there.

Every time I picture her sliding down that wall... All the blood... I feel like I'm going to puke. I can't bear to think she's dead.

I just can't.

My mum gasps as my spit slaps against her cheek, her eyes disbelieving for a beat before her palm slices across my face.

Even though I knew it was coming, it doesn't make it sting any less.

"You ungrateful bitch! I stopped them from fucking you!"

I scoff. "Don't you mean *raping* me?"

She actually has the audacity to roll her eyes as she reaches for me, but I slap her hands away.

I don't want that bitch touching me.

"Don't act so entitled, Abigail." She curls her lip, her eyes filled with nothing but disgust as she takes me in. "You brought this on yourself."

I'm about to retaliate with a comeback when she lunges forward, grabbing for the t-shirt I'm wearing. The only thing they let me keep when they drugged me and kidnapped me.

It's also the only piece of Ringo I have left, besides the black band on my finger.

"Now you have what they want," she sneers, voice full of venom, "and all because you couldn't keep your legs closed in the first place. If you hadn't been such a *whore*, you could've married a decent man. Had children *without* the sin you've smeared on our family name... without the shame you've brought to our church."

I hate her! I hate her so much.

Not only is she blaming me for everything that's happened, but she won't even acknowledge that what Officer Allen did to me was rape when I first woke up in this hell hole. That what Donny spent the next day doing to me was rape. That the last four days I spent locked away with Daniel... well, for all she knew, was rape.

Daniel's behaviour was a surprise. He's been off his normal vile game.

He hasn't been interested in raping me or having any form of sex with me at all.

He just keeps asking if the baby is his. Telling me I don't understand, and that he needs to know… yet he won't tell me why.

"I can't help you if that kid isn't mine."

I don't know what the hell he meant by that, but since Daniel had such a massive hand at putting me in this nightmare, I spat in his face too. Because fuck him!

Of course, he retaliated by punching my thigh so hard I feared he broke bones.

Then, he told me I deserve everything I get.

"Put the dress on."

My mother's voice is jarring, snapping me out of my spiral of memories of the last few days since being stolen away from the only place that ever felt like home to me, even when Ringo wasn't there.

I glare at the white fabric draped over her arm, my stomach twisting.

"No."

"Yes!" She stomps her foot like a toddler throwing a tantrum, which is when Maggie, my traitor of a sister who's been watching silently in the corner, finally decides to speak.

"Mum, just drug her. She's never going to cooperate."

"How many times do I have to tell everyone? We *can't* drug her *now*. It's not good for the baby."

"Not good for the baby?" I laugh maniacally. "That didn't stop you when you first found out! And it didn't stop those fuckers when they kidnapped me the other day!" I scream and she has the nerve to shush me.

"Honestly, Abigail. You spent a few months in the company of ruffians and now you're speaking like them?"

I scoff. "You don't like my language, mother?" I lean closer, just to make sure she hears me properly. "The men you prefer I spend time with are rapist fuckers! Fuckers! Fuckers! Fuckers!" I'm shaking now, chest heaving, my voice full of manic rage. "I FUCKING HATE YOUR FUCKING GUTS, YOU FUCKING COW!"

The slap is loud, a sharp crack that rattles my brain as my head whips to the side. The second I taste blood, I start laughing.

It's ugly and unhinged, mustered from somewhere deep, and I embrace it as a flash of fear flickers over my mum's expression.

That's right, mother. Your daughter has fucking lost it.

Gathering the blood pooled in my mouth, I spit it on the beige carpet at my mother's feet.

"Don't be so vile." She curls her lip in disgust, stepping back from the bloody splat, like it might infect her.

God, I wish it would.

"You're so tough, aren't you, Mum?" I laugh again, the sound hollow and manic.

I'm pretty sure I'm losing my mind, so really, the laugh is fitting.

"You're nothing but their pawn. Don't you see what they are doing?" I hiss, flashing my blood coated teeth. "They've brainwashed you into playing along with their fucked up cult shit."

"Put the dress on!" she barks, completely ignoring the truth I just threw at her.

"*No.*"

I say it slowly. Clearly.

"If you won't put it on, then I'll get some of the men in the congregation to help you put it on, Abigail."

"I'm not wearing your shitty church clothes. You can go fuck yourself."

My mouth has never sounded more like a sailor's… and I've never felt more like me. I don't even know when that version of me disappeared. But she's back now, and she's done playing nice.

I know my situation is bad, but I'll be stuffed if I let them walk all over me any more. That version of me is dead.

In a huff, my mum storms out of the room, her brown skirt flaring around her as she goes.

With her now gone, I shift my glare to my sister.

"Where's Tahli?"

"Don't worry." Maggie waves me off. "They aren't interested in her, *yet*. Not until she becomes a *lady*." She air quotes the last part, and my heart sinks.

"Where is she, Mags?"

"She's with one of the church families. Probably doing crafts while learning about the Script of Symme." Maggie shrugs like it's no big deal, but it is. It's *huge*.

"Maggie, this church is a cult. It's not a real church." I take a few steps towards her, but she stands, balling her fists like she's ready to throw down.

"You'll say anything to get out of the mess *you* created," she snaps. "Be an adult, Abbey. Take responsibility for your actions."

"But Mags... this isn't normal. What they are doing to me..." I stare wide eyed at my sister, needing her to understand. "They've been *raping* me."

She scoffs. "It's just like you to spread your legs and moan like a whore but then cry rape when you get caught out. I hope you and that bastard child get exactly what's coming to you."

A sob lodges in my throat at her words. My little sister is totally lost to the brainwashing my mum and the church have done.

"No, Maggie. You, Mum, this church, and those rapists are the ones who'll get what's coming to *you*. Because it doesn't matter what happens to *me* or *my baby*." I let my grin slip free, watching her eyes flare with concern as I morph into someone she's never seen before. "We found a man. A *real* man. And he will burn this entire place to the ground and watch until every last fragment of your twisted little world turns to ash. And he'll do it all in *my* honour."

Maggie parts her lips to speak, but I shake my head, taking another step closer, and finally her fear shows as she tries to press herself back into the wall with nowhere to go.

"It won't matter if I'm alive or dead. He's coming. For all of you. And he won't stop until the evil inside you is wiped from this Earth."

My sister starts to tremble, but I don't falter.

She's done nothing to help me.

She's done *everything* to make sure I've suffered in the worst possible way.

I feel no sympathy for her. For them. For what's coming.

When the door creaks open again, the stare off with my sister severs, and my mum walks in. She's flanked by two men with eyes so familiar that my blood runs cold.

These men… they were the ones who stormed Ringo's home. Who shot Jols.

My gaze tracks to the one with a dressing peeking from under the collar of his shirt, and a slow, smug grin pulls at my lips.

"Oh shit. Are you the guy I stabbed?" I laugh, wanting them to think I'm unhinged, even though I'm freaking out inside.

"Unfortunately," he grunts, glaring daggers at me, while the other bites back his own smirk.

"Wanna know which one *I* was?"

My eyes narrow, because his smugness is nothing but cruel.

"Oh wait. Let me think…" I tap my finger to my chin in fake thought, before holding it up. "Oh, I know! You're the one who takes it up the arse from everyone else."

"Abigail!" My mum scolds in shock, and this time, the man I stabbed lets out a burst of laughter.

The one I'm taunting doesn't look impressed, his jaw so tight it looks like it might crack.

"I'm really looking forward to today," he snarls before lunging for me.

I don't even get the chance to run before both men are on me, wrangling me in place as my mother approaches with a pair of scissors.

"What are you doing?" I cry out, eyes trained on the huge shears.

"I have to get you out of that horrid t-shirt and into this dress," she answers calmly, like cutting my clothes off me is an everyday occurrence.

Desperate to stop this, I try to kick out, but then Maggie is on me, latching onto my legs, helping the men hold me still as my mum starts cutting through the fabric.

Ringo's t-shirt…

Even when I spit in her face, she doesn't stop. She doesn't even flinch when I snap my teeth at her like a rabid dog.

By the time she wrestles the ugly white dress in place, all the fight has drained from me, my eyes glued on the shredded remains of Ringo's shirt.

I'm in a daze as the men start leading me from the room, so it takes a moment for my brain to catch up with what my eyes see as we pass the mirror.

I choke on thin air, coughing hard as my lungs scramble for breath.

"What did you dress me in?" I twist, trying to find my mother over my shoulder, but the two thugs keep a firm grip on me, making it impossible.

"Don't be naive, Abigail." My mother sneers at my back. "You know this day has been coming. Running away won't change that."

This day?

This day!

A laugh bubbles up, breathless and deranged.

Because I finally realise what she's done.

She's dressed me in a wedding dress and still expects me to marry Daniel.

Today.

A manic laugh bursts from my lips.

"Ohhhh, this is going to be so good."

My unhinged behaviour has the men escorting me, turning their confused expressions my way.

They're probably trying to figure out if I'm right in the head.

If I've truly lost it.

Maybe I have.

Or maybe… I've just stopped giving a fuck.

Every moment they force me to do something is another moment my sanity slips away.

When I see a little country chapel up ahead on the path, I know I'm right, but I'm not prepared for how many men are inside when I'm dragged through the doors. Or the sight of my dad, waiting at the end of the aisle, tears streaking down his face.

"Please stop this," he begs, his voice cracking. "It has gone too far."

No one listens. Not a single one of them is here for me.

They are here for the show. Eager to see this twisted ceremony finally unfold.

Daniel stands just behind my dad at the altar, his face red with anger, probably wishing he never went along with his parents' madness in the first place.

As we get closer, my dad falls to his knees, hands clutched in front of him like he's praying. "Please. Put a stop to this. *Please.*"

I frown at my dad, wondering why he doesn't start swinging fists? Why doesn't he fight for me with more than words? Why isn't he the one that would burn the world down to protect me?

His voice. His words. Make me nothing but furious.

"Jesus, Dad, where are your balls?" I sneer as we pass him, curling my lip in disgust.

Instead of showing me he *does* have the balls I need him to have, he leaps up and runs from the chapel like a coward.

My mum settles in the front pew, smug and composed, Maggie sliding in beside her like the loyal little traitor she is.

The two idiots escorting me, drag me to the altar, placing me in front of Daniel. But they don't let go.

Daniel's gaze flicks to their hands, still clamped tight on my arms, before his eyes shift to meet mine.

"Is this everything you imagined?" I sneer, but he doesn't say anything.

The only reaction I get from him is the hard tick of his jaw.

"Thank you for joining us here today for the union of Abigail Eloise Delany," Minister Banes announces, and a laugh bubbles from my throat.

Frowning, Minister Banes glares at me, clearly rattled by my behaviour, but he clears his throat like it's going to reset the mood.

So, naturally, I laugh louder.

I throw my head back dramatically, giving them a good show, the anxious shifting on the pews from the men in attendance, fuelling my rebellion.

"Uhhh… is she right in the head?" someone in the congregation mutters, while thug one and thug two both shrug.

Stepping down off his righteous pedestal, Minister Banes stands before me, his eyes looking into mine like he's checking to see if I'm all there.

The thugs holding me in place, release their hold, stepping aside, and I continue to laugh, letting this cult leader see my crazy.

"What do you find so funny?" Banes asks stiffly, and I clutch my middle, drawing out the drama as I blow out a breath like I'm struggling to compose myself.

"I'm sorry," I say between fake gasps, waving my left hand in front of my face, wanting him to see the black wedding band on my finger. "I can't wear Daniel's ring."

Daniel mutters something under his breath, while Banes crosses his arms over his chest.

I don't think I've ever seen a man of God do that before. It's such a closed off gesture.

"Of course you can wear his ring," Banes says, voice clipped. "You *will* wear his ring."

Sighing dramatically, I roll my eyes and slap my hands lazily against my sides.

"Oh, my bad. I just thought since I'm already wearing a ring…"

I don't finish the sentence. Instead, I raise my hand and flash my black band in front of his face.

"That's easily fixed, Abigail." His eyes darken, sparing the ring a single glance. "Either you take it off, or we will."

I gasp, slapping a hand to my chest in mock horror.

"You would *never*." I feign terror before I start laughing again, the sound wicked and deranged.

Banes scoffs, before pointing to the thugs.

"Get it off her."

I keep laughing, even as one of the thugs wraps his arms around me from behind, pinning me in place, and the other starts trying to pry the ring from my finger.

"Hold still," he grits, his breath hot and angry as I squirm, trying to drag this out for as long as possible.

I don't know what they think the ring is for, given their reaction. Are they really that dumb?

Sure, the ring isn't traditional gold or white gold, so maybe they think it's something insignificant. I've got no clue how they'll react when they find out I'm already married, but I know in my gut it won't end well for me.

It takes the thug a few tries to drag the black band off my finger, and when he does, a stupid smile spreads across his face like he's just struck gold.

Idiot.

The thug behind me lets go, and I stumble forward on purpose, right into Minister Banes.

He reaches to steady me, which is when his eyes fall to my hand, pressed flat against his chest, I realise… this just worked in my favour.

"What's that?" Banes snatches my wrist, yanking my hand up to get a better look.

"What's what?" I blink at him, all innocent, fluttering my lashes.

His harsh eyes burning with rage meet mine, and my laugh returns.

"Is that a *tattoo*?" He curls his lip in disgust.

"What?!" my mum screeches, storming to my side, snatching my wrist from the minister to see for herself.

"Abigail! *How* could you get a tattoo? Now you look like *trash*!"

Yanking my hand back, I lean in close and hiss in her face like a snake.

She flinches back at the sound, before waving a dismissive hand, her eyes turning to the minister.

"It's fine. Laser will get it off."

Again, I laugh, louder this time, turning to face the sea of men watching this mess unfold.

"Whoops." I lift my hand, point to the ink on my finger. "I have another man's name on my body."

"Can we get on with this?" Daniel finally snaps, his tone clipped and full of barely concealed irritation.

Clearly he's not a fan of my little performance.

My mum nods like she's suddenly the one running this whole circus.

"Yes. Let's continue. Let's make this marriage official."

As she steps back towards the pew again, I sigh loudly, and shrug at Daniel.

"Sorry Danny." I use the name I know he hates. "This won't be legal."

"What?" He frowns, eyes narrowing as Banes steps back onto his precious altar.

"The marriage." I shrug casually. "It'll never be official."

"Stop talking nonsense, Abigail." My mum scoffs from her seat, rolling her eyes.

"Not nonsense." I shrug again, turning my eyes to the minister. "Just facts."

"What are you talking about?" Banes snaps, his patience now long gone. "We will do the service. Whether you agree or not, your signature will be on the papers, and we'll lodge it with the registry."

I smirk, because *this* is the best part.

"Really?" I tilt my head, giving a dramatic little pout. "Is it legal for a woman to be married to two men?"

The chapel falls deadly silent.

It's like every breath got sucked straight out of the room. I swear, you could hear a pin drop.

"You know damn well that's not legal," Banes growls through clenched teeth, his face turning red.

"You see. That's what I thought." I turn on my heel, casually strolling away. "I guess I can't marry Daniel, *or* anyone else for that matter."

I'm expecting one of the thugs to come after me, so when my mum's hand fists my hair, yanking me back, I'm helpless to hold back the high pitched squeal that launches from me.

"Stop talking garbage and trying to get out of this!" she hisses, her rage twisting into every syllable. "You *will* marry Daniel, and you *will* marry him today!"

She shoves me forward, right into Daniel's chest, his hands steadying me for a moment before he shoves me off him like I'm a contagious disease.

"I *can't* marry Daniel, Mother!" I yell, spinning back to face her and the rest of the stunned congregation. "I'm already married. I'm no longer Abbey Delany." I smile, smug as hell, ready to spill the best part. "I'm Abbey *Musgrove* now. But you can call me *Mrs Musgrove*, thanks." I blow her a kiss, slow and mocking.

Another deathly silence settles over the room.

"No," she whispers, her face turning red. "*NOOOOO!*"

"Yes, actually." I giggle, feeling rebellion surging through me like a drug.

"Someone check if this is true!" Banes bellows, before a couple of men hurry from the chapel.

"Don't let her fool you. She's just trying to delay the inevitable," my mum snaps, pacing as everyone in the congregation shifts uncomfortably.

"*Jeez*, Mum. You're beginning to sound desperate." I tilt my head, eyes narrowing at her. "Why does this marriage matter so much to you? Is it Daniel's money you are after? His trust fund that his mummy and daddy have been holding over him to keep him in line?"

I wag my brows at Daniel's dad, sitting stiffly in the front pew across the aisle from my sister, but it's the first time I've realised that Daniel's mum isn't here.

That… doesn't seem right.

Not that any of this is right, but if her son is getting married, shouldn't she be here?

Daniel's dad, Karl, looks away as his jaw twitches, his Adam's apple bobbing as he swallows thickly.

"Fucking hell, Abbey," Daniel mutters quietly, gripping my arm and dragging me back in place.

He leans in, his breath hot on my ear so only I can hear.

"You really have no fucking clue what this is all about, do you?" Bitterness laces his tone. "I *wish* this was as simple as fucking money. If it was, I would've paid someone off to make this whole fucking arranged marriage go away."

My stomach drops hard.

Yanking my arm from his grip, I stumble back, my heart beating out of control.

Once again, I feel unsteady. Out of the loop. Truly blind.

I always thought this was about money. That it started with a stupid bet. A competition with his mates.

He told me about the trust fund. That he wouldn't get access to it unless he did exactly what his parents said.

My mum has been obsessed with making this wedding happen, so laser focused on me walking down the aisle to Daniel.

I assumed it was about money. It had to be. An easy road to a more grand life. Her twisted version of salvation.

But if it's not for money… then what is it about?

Why have I been treated like this?

Why did my own mother sell me out?

Why did Maggie help them?

Why have I been raped, hunted, drugged, kidnapped, and stripped of everything by my own family?

Before the weight of the unknown can crush me, the doors fly open and one of the men that dashed out earlier strides in.

"It's true!"

All heads snap in the man's direction as he hurries down the aisle, holding up a piece of paper.

"I have a copy of the marriage certificate here." He's breathless as he glances at the sheet in his hand. "She married Cameron Musgrove on the twentieth of March."

Maggie gasps. Daniel curses. And his dad explodes from his seat, pure rage contorting his expression.

I laugh.

It's gleeful. Smug. And deliberate.

"Surprise fuckers." I giggle, giving my best impersonation of jazz hands, before a shriek, loud and piercing has me cringing and shooting an annoyed glare my mum's way.

The pure rage I witness on her face far outdoes any I've seen before, and for a moment, I feel victorious. Like I've won.

But then she charges for me like a bull, her wild eyes rabid, her fists balled at the ready.

"HOW COULD YOU!?"

Throwing up my hands, instinctively trying to protect my baby bump, I brace myself for the impact. But it never comes.

Instead, I'm quickly yanked behind Daniel, and I'm momentarily stunned as he wards off my mum's fists.

"Protect the baby!"

His yelled words punch the air right out of me, and I'm reminded of his obsession over the last few days, wanting to know if the baby is his.

I don't have time to analyse it right now. Not with my mum clawing to get to me, rage pouring off her in waves.

A wall of men I *hate* stand between her and me, now, keeping her from tearing me apart.

"You've ruined everything!" she screams. "You don't realise what you've done!"

"Well, shit, Mum!" I scream back before I can stop myself. "Maybe that's because you haven't told me anything!"

Standing on my tiptoes, I try to see past the wall of men, barely able to catch a glimpse of her face. "Why don't you *tell* me what I've done?"

"There has to be a ceremony." Minister Banes pushes through Daniel, Donny, Craig and the goons from earlier, silencing my mum's wails of protest as he grips her shoulders. "Priscilla, I'm sorry. Without a ceremony, you *know* what will happen."

"What will happen?" I shout, sick of not understanding what this is all about.

No one pays me any attention, their eyes trained on the minister and my mum.

"I'll marry him."

I stiffen at Maggie's voice, peering past the men to watch her step forward, her smile hopeful as she looks up at Daniel.

What the?

"I'll sacrifice myself for our family, Mum. Not like Abbey." Her last words come out as a snarl.

"No!" I shake my head, grabbing at Daniel, trying to pull him away from her. "You're too young to get married, Maggie! You don't want to marry him. He's a vile monster!"

"There's still the baby. I want to know if it's mine!" Donny sneers, his words making the entire room tense.

Banes slowly turns his stare to Donny, a deep crease forming between his brows.

"What do you mean?" Banes barks. "Daniel is the father."

Both Donny and Craig scoff, while behind them, Ian Allen rolls his eyes, and Karl Stone, Daniel's father, levels a death glare at his son.

Wait… does the minister *not* know?

"Look, Daniel is my mate and all." Donny steps forward, his eyes trained on the minister. "But that kid in her gut could be mine, Craig's, or Daniel's. Hell, there's at least three more guys she's been screwing too." He shrugs, like casually branding me a tramp is no big deal, and shit… I think I'm going to be sick. "I'm surprised Priscilla didn't fill you in on what her daughter has been up to."

All eyes snap to my mum, her mouth opening and closing like a fish before she manages to mutter something that makes sense.

"I didn't know any of this, Minister Banes. I swear."

That lying bitch!

I take a step back, stunned.

I don't understand what's happening. Why is Donny bringing this up? What does this have to do with the wedding? With my baby?

"Donny must be mistaken," Karl Stone cuts in, shoving past Donny to stand beside Daniel. "My son has done everything that's been asked of him. He deserves this."

Deserves what?

"She's pregnant out of wedlock," Ian Allen snaps, taking his nephew's side. "And there's a one in six chance Daniel *is* the father. It won't work unless you've got the right two bloodlines."

Right bloodlines? What the...

My hands are shaking so badly I have to wring them together, trying to calm the tremors.

"Exactly," Donny adds. "So even if you can use Maggie, since she's from Abbey's bloodline, she can't marry Daniel unless the baby is actually his."

Minister Banes narrows his eyes as he thinks.

"Well... since Abigail and Maggie *are* the same bloodline, it could still work. You're right about that." His voice is cold and calculating. "We just need to confirm who the baby's father is. Then the ceremony can still be performed."

What are they talking about? Why do they need bloodlines? What does this have to do with my baby?

My heart kicks into overdrive, pounding against my ribs like it's trying to escape my chest.

I take a shaky step back, my arms wrapping protectively around my bump, my thoughts spinning with what his words could mean.

Then, as if everyone else there knows what's happening, in unison, they all turn to look at me.

I freeze, tremors making me quiver, terror seeping into my veins like poison.

"No," I whisper, still not understanding, but I don't need to know anything more than they mean me and my baby harm.

"No..." I step backwards, and in unison they take a step towards me.

"NO!" I scream, the sound ripping from my throat, sharp and primal, and the moment they lunge for me, a deafening explosion shatters the air.

The walls tremble and the very ground we stand on lurches, and just like that, all hell breaks loose.

36

RINGO

Having the Marx family as allies has its fucking perks. And one of them is their private army led by Seth Riggs, who just happens to have a couple of explosive experts.

As the small building next to the chapel explodes, flames and debris flying in every direction, my men and I burst through the chapel doors, guns raised, ready to paint the walls red.

As we open fire on any motherfucker that stands between me and my wife, I shoot, reload, and fucking shoot again, picking off the congregation of armed men, one by one, filling them with lead before they can get a fucking shot off.

Then I hear it. My wife's scream.

It cuts through the air from the other end of the chapel, but with the sea of men between us, this small space suddenly feels too fucking big.

"Fuck you!" JD roars, fury ripping through his voice.

He's fuelled by what they did to Jols, and he starts blowing heads off without a second fucking thought as we move as a unit, deeper into the chapel.

"Three females spotted exiting the rear."

Riggs' voice hits my ear through the comms, always too fucking calm given the chaos around us.

"Don't shoot them!" I bark, knowing he can hear me, and he responds instantly.

"Copy that."

Ian Allen bursts through the sea of men, armed with a fucking fully automatic machine gun, and the moment he starts firing, we have no fucking choice but to dive for cover.

"Two males exiting the rear," Riggs announces in my ear, but when I shout, "shoot them," I get nothing but static.

"Fuck. Someone kill that fucker!" Smitty roars from somewhere behind me as Allen sprays bullets our way.

The doors burst open behind us, and I swear time fucking slows as Vender, the crazy fucker, strolls in with a fucking rocket launcher.

Everyone's eyes fucking widen at the sight, and a beat later, we all scramble for cover right before Vender unleashes hell.

The blast rips through the air like thunder, and rubble rains down on us in a cloud of dust.

I'm already moving, scrambling back out the chapel doors, my fucking heart nearly in my throat.

Abbey. I need to get to my Angel.

"Riggs. Can you hear me?" I bark into the comms, sticking my finger in my ear to nudge the earpiece, but still, I get nothing but static.

"Fuck. I think comms are down," JD pants, stumbling through the doors behind me. Smoke clings to him, blood smeared on his shirt, but his determined eyes are locked onto mine.

"We gotta find Abbey. She's the top priority." I tell him something he already knows, but he nods anyway.

I take off running, with JD on my heels, rounding the crumbling walls of the chapel, desperate to lay eyes on my wife.

A terrified scream echoes through the trees behind the chapel, and I fucking bolt that way, my gaze scanning wildly, my legs pumping fast.

"Abbey!" I shout, skidding to a stop, my chest heaving so hard I can barely hear over the thunder of my own pulse.

"Ringo!"

My Angel!

She can hear me.

Darting to my left, I chase the desperation in her voice, crashing through the shrubs and trees like a fucking freight train.

The sound of heavy feet pounding the forest floor up ahead, has me running faster, twigs snapping as angry male voices yell something I can't make out.

"Fuck. Someone's on her tail," JD barks beside me, keeping pace.

"Let's fucking end this," I snarl, eyes trained forward, my blood boiling, my muscles primed to inflict the worst kind of punishment.

"Over there!" JD points to my right, and I spot the flash of a white dress moving east with two males closing in.

Changing direction, I point and shoot blindly towards the men, losing sight of them a second later when they disappear down an incline.

I don't stop. I keep fucking running, pushing my thirty-three year old body to its fucking limit.

Another piercing scream rips from Abbey's lungs, only this time, it's laced with pain.

As I slide down the incline, I spot the men up ahead, standing over something.

"Fuck! I didn't mean to!" one of them shouts, and as I get closer, I can tell it's Daniel Stone, fisting his hair as he freaks out.

"Shut the fuck up! They'll hear us!" the other guy snarls, shoving Daniel aside.

In three more fucking strides, I'm already there, but my eyes shift from the men to something that stops my fucking heart...

My wife.

Curled in a ball on the leafy ground.

An agonising scream ripping from her lips.

No.

I step forward, momentarily stunned by the sight of crimson soaking through the white fabric of Abbey's dress.

"Fuck, man. I didn't mean to hurt her," Daniel stammers, stumbling backwards, his eyes locked on me as he tries to scurry away.

His idiot mate—who I recognise as Craig McRoe, Daniel's best mate... and one of Abbey's rapists—hasn't even noticed me standing right fucking beside him.

His attention is on my Abbey, his gaze unreadable and cold.

"Let's just get her back to Banes," Craig snaps. "He'll know what to do with her..." His words trail off as his gaze finds me right fucking there.

His lips part to speak, but I lift my gun, jam the barrel underneath his chin, and pull the trigger.

He doesn't even get a sound past his lying lips before his brains explode in a bloody shower, raining down over the shrubs and leaf covered ground. Then he crumbles like a sack of shit.

I don't even spare a glance at Daniel's retreating form as I drop to my knees beside Abbey.

"Angel," I breathe, brushing her hair off her face, only to find it twisted in agony.

"I fell," she gasps. "It hurts. The baby, Ringo. The baby!"

Fuck!

"You want me to go after Stone?" JD barks behind me, but I shake my head, my eyes scanning my wife, locking onto the blood pooling under her.

"No. Fuck," I snap my frantic gaze to my best mate. "Help. We need help!"

I'm fucking shaking, the sight of all that blood mixed with the smell of the dirt rips me back to the day I found Kylie… and my daughter dead by her side.

"I'll go get help. Watch your six," JD calls over his shoulder as he bolts back towards the chapel, leaving me alone in the trees with my haemorrhaging wife.

"Hold on, Angel. Help is coming." I force the words past the lump in my throat as I run my hands over her trembling form.

"It hurts so bad," she whimpers into the dirt. "Something's wrong."

Wrong is an understatement given the amount of blood seeping through her dress.

Fuck. This can't be happening.

Not again.

A guttural scream tears from Abbey's throat, echoing through the trees, startling a flock of birds into the air.

Then, she starts panting.

"No. No," she groans, slowly rolling onto her back as she clutches the swell of her bump. "It's too soon. I can't have my baby yet."

"What can I do?" I reach for her, but hesitate, not sure what to fucking do. If I should touch her.

Think.

Fucking think.

Abbey starts panting, blowing air in short bursts, curling in on herself.

Fuck! Is she having the baby now?

"Check," she cries, her caramel eyes wild. "I need you to check!"

"Check what?" My fucking eyes nearly bug out of my head, but I already know. I'm just freaking out too much to make sense of it.

Her trembling hands start dragging the blood soaked fabric of her dress up her thighs, and my fucking lungs seize up, like the oxygen around us has vanished.

"Oh my…" She heaves like she is bearing down before another scream rips from her lungs. "It's coming!"

More screams. Nothing but fear-laced agony echoing off the fucking trees, bouncing around us like the whole forest is in pain with her.

My heart is fucking hammering in my chest like it's ready to explode, agonising images from my past trying to slip into the present.

I don't know what to do.

What the fuck do I do?

As panic claws at me, I slap my own fucking face, trying to knock some sense into myself.

Get your fucking shit together.

She needs you.

She fucking needs you!

Scrambling across the dirt and twigs, I position myself between her bent, parted legs, bracing myself for something I've never had to see or do before.

Her big caramel eyes lock with mine, and fuck me, the fear in them is like a violent storm, twisting within her beautiful orbs.

"I'm going to take a look, Angel. Hang on for me."

My voice is fucking gritty, like I've swallowed half the dirt under us, but she must understand, because she nods frantically, her hands white-knuckling the fabric as she finishes dragging it up to her hips.

Fuck.

Blood.

There's so much fucking blood.

Her underwear is soaked through, and when I see her struggling to tug the drenched fabric down, I take over, gently pulling it down her legs and off her feet.

I'm not prepared…

I'm not fucking prepared for what I see.

Oh fuck.

How is her body even doing this?

"They are over there!" JD's voice calls from somewhere behind me, but it feels like his voice, along with Abbey's screams, are another world away.

This can't be happening.

No.

My beautiful Angel.

"Fuck, get out of the way!" a gruff voice shouts, before strong hands start dragging me back.

I start swinging fists, wild with rage at whoever would fucking dare to harm my Angel when she's already suffering so much, but I freeze the second I realise it's JD and Murf.

They hold me back, keeping me out of the way as two of the Marx security team drop to the ground and start working on my wife like they have a fucking clue what they are doing.

"Abbey, my name is Dylan, and this is Clive. We're trained medics," one says with a level of calm that has Abbey nodding.

"Help me!" she screams, clutching her stomach with another guttural cry.

"Fuck. I can see the head," Clive barks, already on the phone.

The head.

Did he just say he can see the head?

Shit, was that what I was looking at before? Her baby's head?

"No!" Abbey cries, her head snapping towards me where JD and Murf still hold me back. "Ringo! It's too early! I can't have my baby yet!"

Ripping free of my club brothers' grips, I stumble to my knees beside her, taking her cold trembling hand in mine, before she squeezes the fucking life out of it.

"I know it's too early, Angel. But it looks like your baby is coming…" I glance at Dylan between her legs, and he gives me a nod. "So he or she needs you to be strong, yeah?"

Even though she's crying and there's more terror on her face than I've ever seen, she nods, panting through what I can only assume is another contraction.

Fuck, I don't even know. This is all so fucking new to me.

Why didn't I read a book on this stuff?

Why didn't I prepare?

I thought I had more time.

I thought *we* had more fucking time!

"Get a van out here! We can't wait for the ambulance!" Clive snaps into the phone as Dylan's hands disappear between Abbey's legs.

"Abbey, your baby is coming fast," Dylan warns. "It looks small, so he or she is coming *right fucking now*."

"Cam," she whimpers, taking a shaky breath as her terrified gaze meets mine. "Make sure they save my baby. Promise me."

I nod, brushing her sweat soaked hair off her face, the strands clinging to her skin, as I swallow the fucking lump in my throat.

"Of course."

"N-no... you don't understand," she sobs, curling in on herself again as pain lashes her from the inside out. "*Make sure* they save my baby first. *Before me*."

I stiffen.

"What?" I fucking squeak so high pitched, I swear I must have lost my nuts.

Did I hear her right?

"*Promise me!*"

Her scream is excruciating, a sound made of agony and raw terror as she starts bearing down again.

"Okay!" I shout back, because I don't know what else to fucking say.

How the fuck am I supposed to mean that?

I can't lose her. Ever!

How can she ask me to choose her baby... over her?

37

ABBEY

H oly shit! I've never felt pain like this before.

So gripping.

So suffocating.

So bloody agonising.

I'm beyond terrified. This isn't how it was meant to happen.

Not on the dirty ground in a pine forest behind a chapel where I was about to be forced into a marriage I never wanted.

Not because hands shoved me so hard from behind, I couldn't even stop my fall and protect my baby.

Not going into labour at only thirty weeks with no actual nurse and doctors, just men, dressed in black, claiming to be medics, telling me my baby is coming now.

No… This can't be happening. Something is terribly wrong.

A scream rips from me as sharp, tearing pain slices through my pelvis. A crushing band tightens around it, so incredibly strong, that I'm forced to pant through it, even though I try to stop myself.

"Okay, Abbey. You need to start pushing. It won't take much to get this little one out."

What is he talking about?

There's a baby about to come out of my bloody vagina! What the hell does he know?!

I want to scream all the words in my head at this stranger, but my body has been possessed by something else, and it's doing whatever the hell it wants. Because even as I try to fight it, that overwhelming, uncontrollable urge to push, to bear down, rushes through me again, and I heave.

I swear, every single muscle inside me is contracting, forcing pressure down on my pelvis, trying to expel my little baby, far too fragile to leave the safety of my body.

Then, I tense... and the weirdest, most painful sensation I've ever experienced explodes between my legs.

"Ouch, *fuck!*" I scream, agony ripping from my throat as my eyes go so wide, I fear they're about to pop right out of my skull.

"That's it. Keep going," Dylan urges calmly, and my death grip on Ringo's hand tightens like I'm trying to break bone.

"What the fuck are you talking about?!" I snarl. "How would you like to squeeze this out of your dick?!"

Dylan, just smirks, completely unfazed by my rage, and Ringo leans in, pressing his lips to the back of my hand, trying to calm me.

"You're doing so good, Angel. You're so fucking strong." His voice holds familiar confidence, but when I look into his eyes, all I see is fear.

I bet he feels helpless right now, so I nod, wanting to reassure him that everything is okay, even though I know it isn't.

Another contraction crashes into me, my strangled scream rips free, just as uncontrollable as the overwhelming need to push.

"Here it comes!" Dylan yells as I push, my scream turning into one long continuous siren before Ringo joins me, his deep, guttural roar drowning out everything but him.

I need to focus on that. On him, because ohhhh shiiit….

White hot burning pain slices through my core, as a hard, round head scrapes my insides and settles between my legs.

I'm panting, breathing so fast I worry I might hyperventilate, but Ringo grounds me, pressing his forehead to mine.

"You're a fucking warrior, Angel."

"I'm a warrior," I whisper back, as hot tears spring from my eyes.

"One more push, Abbey." Dylan's voice cuts through our bubble, and we break apart to look at him. "It's time to meet your baby."

I nod, already feeling the next contraction building, so… I surrender.

I give myself over to the most natural urge I've ever felt, and I push.

It's fast, nowhere near as agonising as the others, just the strangest feeling of my baby quickly slipping from me.

Relief slams into me, and then… emptiness.

Dylan's hands move quickly between my legs, and Clive presses a towel down against my exposed skin, as the realisation of what just happened sinks in.

I just gave birth to my baby.

"Oh my God," I cry, trying, and failing, to sit up. "My baby."

"It's a little girl." Clive smiles, but even through my exhaustion, I don't miss the flicker of worry in his eyes.

Something is wrong.

"A girl?" I whisper, blinking past the haze closing in around me.

I'm so tired.

"It's a little girl," I repeat softly to Ringo, smiling up at him.

"Yeah, Angel. A girl." He quickly schools his worry, nodding down at me.

That's when I realise... my baby isn't crying.

Do babies even cry when they are born this early?

Glancing down my body at Dylan, I watch as his arms and hands move quickly, busy doing something, the panic creasing his brow unhidable.

"Why isn't she crying?" I try to sit up, but my arms aren't strong enough. My whole body feels heavy. "Is that normal? Is it because she came too early?"

My frantic gaze darts between all of them. Even to JD and Murf standing a few metres back behind Ringo.

No one answers me.

"Dylan?!" I cry, panic restricting my airways.

"Fucking answer her!" Ringo snarls, his voice deadly, and Dylan's worried gaze snaps to mine.

Shit.

His eyes don't hold reassurance.

They hold sympathy.

"She's only just breathing," Dylan says softly. "We need to keep her warm."

"Give her to me," I slur, barely able to lift my hands up to reach for her.

I never knew giving birth would make me this tired. But then again, I didn't get much time to educate myself on what to expect, other than some online research. But nothing could have prepared me for what just happened. Maybe feeling like this is normal.

"Ringo," I whisper, dropping my hands to the leafy ground at my sides. "Tear open the front of my dress."

He nods, no hesitation, ripping the shitty white taffeta apart before the cool air hits my chest.

I don't even care that my boobs are out. I've just flashed the whole forest my hooha, so what's a pair of tits at this point?

The second Ringo parts the fabric, Dylan gently lays my little baby girl on my chest, and just like that, all the world, every single thing in it, falls away.

It's just me and her. Here. Now.

She's so small, and a bit mucky, but I don't care, because I have my little girl in my arms, pressed to my chest, and she makes a small little noise.

"Oh Bobbi," I whimper, tears flooding my eyes so fast I can't blink them away to get a good look at this tiny little miracle resting on my skin.

Right over my heart.

"Bobby?" Ringo's voice cuts through my little bubble, and the world comes rushing back in.

I nod, as I look up to meet his eyes.

"Yes. Her name is Bobbi Cameron Musgrove. Bobbi with an i."

I wait a second, watching the man who fought for me from the moment he broke into my parents' home.

His brows hitch high.

The hardness that normally frames his eyes melts away, and for a second, he doesn't look like a biker or a soldier, or a savage.

He just looks like a boy, completely undone.

"You're naming your little girl after my dead brother?" Tears fill his eyes, and he takes in a shaky breath, clearing his throat, struggling with his raw emotions. "You're naming her after him… and me?"

A smile tugs at my lips as I nod again.

"I decided on the name a few weeks ago," I whisper. "I knew it would suit a boy or girl."

I frown, blinking at how slurred my words sound, and Ringo must notice too, his worried gaze shooting to Dylan and Clive, who are still positioned between my legs.

Shit. I kinda forgot they were there.

They're doing something. Pulling on something inside me, and now that I think about it… it kinda hurts, but also, I feel a little numb.

"Hey." Ringo's fingers gently lift my chin, guiding my gaze back to him. "Why did you name her after me and my brother?"

I hug little Bobbi closer, and she makes another little sound.

A fragile little whimper.

"I wanted to name my baby after the man who saved my best friend," I explain, my lids growing heavier as I shift my gaze between Ringo and my little girl. "So her first name is Bobbi."

"Bobbi with an i," Ringo confirms, smiling warmly at me.

"I also wanted to name her after the man who saved *me*." I blink slowly at him, my smile barely kicking up my lips as exhaustion blankets me. "So her middle name is Cameron."

"Shit… Angel," Ringo rasps, emotion thick in his voice, and he leans forward, pressing his lips to my forehead just as the sound of a car tearing through the trees, draws everyone's attention.

Well… everyone's but mine.

I can't even muster the energy to turn my head.

"Over here!" someone yells, before heavy footfalls rush from somewhere, and for a moment, I'm relieved.

We are going to be alright.

"Abbey?" Ringo's voice sounds unsure, right before his palm cups my cheek. "Angel, open your eyes."

I try to open them, but it's like they are taped shut. I can't make them part.

"What's happening!" Ringo demands, sounding frantic and ragged.

I wish I could open my eyes, because there's movement from both sides of me, and I want to see what's going on.

"We have to get them in the van, now," an unfamiliar voice cuts in.

"Dylan? What's wrong with her?!" Ringo snaps, ignoring whoever gave the order, his focus just on me.

I try so hard to open my eyes again, this time, I manage a fleeting glance.

Black-clad men blur past, rushing around like shadows in a panic.

"She's losing too much blood, man," Dylan snaps. "We need to get her to a hospital."

"Shit!" Clive's voice comes from right beside me. "The baby is turning blue!"

My eyes snap open.

All the hazy, the heaviness, the numbness vanishes in one blinding second of terror.

My eyes find Clive looming over me as he rolls Bobbi to her back on my chest, his hand flying in the air. "Hand me the bag!"

"Cam…" I manage to breathe out, my eyelids so heavy, I'm scared that if they close, they'll never open again.

"I'm here, beautiful." Ringo turns my head gently, and our eyes lock.

Ooof.

I hate seeing that look in his eyes.

Fear.

I don't want him to be scared.

"Remember…" My voice is just above a whisper, the energy to speak draining fast. "Save Bobbi… Her life is… more important than mine."

"Don't speak like that," Ringo pleads, cupping my face, his touch trembling even as he tries to stay strong.

Gosh… he really is the most beautiful monster I've ever seen.

"Everything I've done…"

I force the words out, needing him to hear this.

"Was to protect her." My words slur, and that's when I see it… tears, glistening in Ringo's whiskey eyes.

"Give her my blood… or organs… or anything it… takes," I whisper, my voice cracking.

My own tears spill over, tracking down into my hair, soaking the dirt beneath me.

"Please… raise her… as your own."

"Angel, stop. Please. *Stop talking like that,*" he begs, pressing his forehead to mine.

I feel my little girl being lifted off my chest. I don't know if she's alive, but someone is yelling to keep feeding her oxygen.

"You're going to be fine," Ringo says, trying to reassure me, or maybe, he's just trying to reassure himself.

His lips press to mine in a chaste, wet, salty kiss that tastes of goodbye.

"Angel, please…" he pleads before I feel him shift next to me on the ground. "Someone tell her!" he bellows, begging for backup. "She's going to be fine!"

I don't hear anyone answer. There are too many voices now, all deep manly voices, and I know, with them, my little girl will be safe.

"Cam…" I breathe, my lids fluttering closed, now too heavy to keep open.

"Angel…" he breathes over my lips, his nearness filling my heart with one last beat of warmth.

"I love you… But I need you to… let… me… go…"

Ummm… what just happened?
Are you ready to find out?

Continue to the next instalment:

BEAUTIFULLY SHATTERED
SECRETS AND SCARS BOOK 3
https://geni.us/secretsandscars3

Want to know what Ringo and the Southern Sadists did to Wendy?

Get your bonus copy of
Wendy's Punishment now.

Secrets & Scars Book 2 Bonus Scene
WENDY'S PUNISHMENT
https://BookHip.com/NNNQDCW

By downloading a copy of Wendy's Punishment, you will be signing up to Sarah JD's Darker Shades of Romance Newsletter. *(Please note, if you are already signed up to Sarah's newsletter, you can still access the bonus scene by completing the same process)*

READ MORE BY SARAH JD

Sarah JD's Books

https://sarahjdauthor.com/books

STALK SARAH

Want to join the conversation about your fav characters?
Join my Facebook Readers Group
SARAH'S VICIOUS KITTENS

JOIN HERE!
https://www.facebook.com/groups/
sarahjaneduncanreadersgroup

For more information on books & book signing
events please visit:
https://sarahjdauthor.com

***

STALK SARAH HERE:

SCAN
ME
STALK ME

Sarah JD, also known as Sarah Jane Duncan, is an Australian dark romance author living her best life with her high school sweetheart, Mr Duncan.

Sarah can be found in her writing room plotting out her next smut filled romance, packed with angst, violence, and themes so dark you should probably question why you love it so much.

Sarah enjoys torturing her characters. There's nothing easy about their stories. They are hard, gritty, and painfully heartbreaking at times. But what doesn't kill us makes us stronger, right? And when you throw in a swoon worthy guy, or an alphahole you just want to slap, but also fall to your knees and obey, it's the recipe for a rollercoaster ride.

So buckle up. Read the warnings. And let yourself get lost in the dark stories Sarah creates.